KINGS OF
THE COMPLETE DAR

Robert Ryan

Copyright © 2020 Robert J. Ryan
All Rights Reserved. The right of Robert J. Ryan to be
identified as the author of this work has been asserted.
All of the characters in this book are fictitious and any
resemblance to actual persons, living or dead, is coincidental.

Cover design by Amalia Chitulescu

ISBN: 9798634412627
(print edition)

Trotting Fox Press

Contents

THE PALE SWORDSMAN — 5

1. The Runes of Life and Death — 6
2. That Sort of Man — 22
3. The River Crossing — 30
4. Sword or Knife? — 41
5. By Sword and Magic — 50
6. The Touch of Magic — 58
7. Deep and Dark — 67
8. Eye of the Eagle — 74
9. A Long Night — 87
10. The Noblest of Tasks — 96
11. The Helm of the Duthenor — 103
12. There Must be Blood — 114
13. A Hero of Old — 120
14. Will You Surrender? — 128
15. A Man of Secrets — 142
16. Least Expected — 146
17. The Pale Swordsman — 155
18. Sleeping Magic — 160
19. The Mists of Prophecy — 170
20. Promises to Keep — 178
21. It Comes — 190
22. The God-king — 194
23. I do a Man's Work — 200
24. Fortune Favors the Bold — 208
25. The Blood of Heroes — 215
26. Old Mother — 227

Epilogue — 234
Appendix A: The Runes of Life and Death — 238
Appendix B: Encyclopedic Glossary — 248

THE CRIMSON LORD — 261

1. A Magician of Power — 262
2. The Blood of a Hero — 270

3. Battle and Victory!	276
4. The Trickster	285
5. A Place of Ill Omen	293
6. Sorcery	300
7. Bones and Metal	309
8. The Power of the Gods	316
9. Calm Before the Storm	326
10. To the Death	333
11. Word Spreads Like Fire	343
12. The Wise Man Reads the Future	352
13. The Runes of Life and Death	355
14. You Need Swear No Oath	367
15. Dark Dreams	378
16. Char-harash	384
17. Patience	392
18. If I Don't, Who Will?	401
19. The Breath of the Dragon	409
20. Blade and Hilt	413
21. Duels are for the Reckless	418
22. Battle and Blood	425
23. Gormengil	432
24. Two Battles	440
25. The Prophecy of the Witch	446
Epilogue	462
Appendix: Encyclopedic Glossary	465
THE DARK GOD	476
1. The Broken Sword	477
2. Will You Serve the Land?	482
3. The Tomb	487
4. Homecoming	491
5. A Time of Change	495
6. The Witch	500
7. All the World is Yours	507
8. Is it True?	515
9. A New Banner	525

10. Like Whey from Curds	529
11. He Would be a King	536
12. The Old Masters	541
13. Nothing is Destined	549
14. Only by Chance	555
15. Not my Heritage	560
16. A Long Night	564
17. Ambush	571
18. The Enemy	583
19. Five Tribes	591
20. There Goes a Good Man	599
21. The Golden God	604
22. Let Them March to Us	608
23. I Will Not Kneel	613
24. First Blood is Spilled	620
25. Worthy of That Axe	624
26. Like A Torch	638
27. The Hunter Becomes the Hunted	643
28. Advance!	651
29. Free of Ambition	657
Epilogue	664
Appendix: Encyclopedic Glossary	668
Sample: Prologue for The Seventh Knight	682

THE PALE SWORDSMAN

BOOK ONE OF THE DARK GOD RISES TRILOGY

Robert Ryan

Copyright © 2018 Robert J. Ryan
All Rights Reserved. The right of Robert J. Ryan to be identified as the author of this work has been asserted. All of the characters in this book are fictitious and any resemblance to actual persons, living or dead, is coincidental.

Trotting Fox Press

1. The Runes of Life and Death

Horta chanted, and there was magic in his words. He felt it buoy them with life. Yet such magic was dangerous. None knew that better than he, but he was dangerous also, and he gathered his power about him.

The sound of his voice was harsh. But the language he spoke, the tongue of his people who once contended to rule the world but were now scattered, was a harsh speech. He thought it fitting, for they were a callous people. The *Kar-ahn-hetep*, the Children of the Thousand Stars they called themselves. A pretty name for a race whose ancestors' swords dripped blood.

Horta raised his chanting to a higher pitch. His people were as nothing now, no more than a tattered race haunting a petty kingdom in the forgotten south, but he would raise them up as once they had been. He would make them great again, and all the blood his ancestors spilled would be but as a drop compared to what was to come.

He chanted, the power of his magic one with the words. His disciples, his *Arnhaten*, chanted with him. And the hidden roof of the cave mouthed their words back at them hollowly like the voices of their long-forgotten ancestors. And well might it be so, for the magic he invoked summoned the dead.

The stale air of the cave grew ice-cold, and the fire of the burning torches set against the walls gutted erratically. An acrid odor rose, though from smoke or some otherworldly origin Horta did not know. Nor did he care.

The magic was everything to him, and with a final surge of determination he loosed the last words of the spell.

He ceased to chant, and the Arnhaten fell silent with him. The magic surrounded him, drew on his strength and gave form to his purpose. He sat still, eyes open but gazing at the sandy floor of the cave before him. What he had summoned was not visible, but he felt its presence.

There was a whisper of sound behind him that should not be, and he turned to look. One of the Arnhaten groaned softly and slumped to the ground. It was Asaba, the weakest of them all. He had fainted, or perhaps his heart had stilled. No matter.

Horta shook the small pouch that hung from his slim cloth belt ten times. It was the ritual, and it existed for good purpose. But though he fulfilled it dutifully, still impatience gripped him.

Slowly, carefully, he dipped his right hand into the pouch and felt the dry bones gathered there. Finger bones. The bones of dead men, magicians all. One, that of his own master, who having taught all he was able Horta had slain. These were the *Kar-karmun*, the Runes of Life and Death.

His fingers slid through the rasping bones, and he was careful to grasp only some of them. To hold and cast all at once presaged ill-fortune of the highest order. He would not permit that, though the spirits of the dead that surrounded him, the possessors of the bones in life, anxiously awaited such an accident and he felt their ill-will like a cold exhalation on the back of his neck.

He drew forth the bones, and with a quick but sure jerk of his hand cast them onto the sandy floor before him.

The Runes of Life and Death rolled and scattered over the ground, then stilled. The future he sought to foretell was now laid bare and revealed by the agency of the summoned spirits. And though they wished his death, or worse, the force of his magic constrained them to obey.

A sense of uncertainty settled over him. Four bones had fallen, and the runes were never wrong for he possessed true power, but he saw things that he had not expected. Strange things.

He must study the casting carefully. But the presence of the dead was unsettling. It seemed to him as though they looked over his shoulder with anticipation. This was distracting, and he needed them no more, so he chanted again, this time only a few short words of command.

The spirits were released, their work done, and the power that summoned them now forced them away. One of the torches flared and then snuffed out as they resisted, and Horta felt their hatred rage in the shadowy cave. It was of no concern, for they must obey. Momentarily, the air seethed and roiled about him with invisible forces, and then they were gone.

Away in the distance the cave mouth moaned as a rush of air was expelled from the earth. And then silence fell, deep and profound. Horta turned his mind once more to the runes and studied them.

Small beads of sweat broke out on his forehead. He wiped them away with the back of his hand. Behind him, he heard Asaba groan. The man had fainted rather than died. A pity, for now a way must be found to kill him. He was too weak to learn more of the mysteries. Yet he knew some, and that was his death sentence. A little knowledge was more dangerous than mastery, and returning him to Kar-fallon in shame would see him killed anyway. His family would arrange that, for his failure would taint them.

A frown creased Horta's brow, and he realized he was prevaricating. He turned his mind to the runes and their meaning. Destiny would be what it would be, and he would accept it.

He read the runes from top to bottom and left to right. The first was *Hotep*, and it showed the Change aspect of the rune in ascendancy. Cut into the bone and then filled with blood that dried within the symbol, the stark lines showed dully. Better if it had landed on its reverse aspect, Quiescence.

Horta considered the rune's meaning. It was true that, as the lore of the Kar-karmun taught, it was the nature of the world that things existed in a state of flux. The wise man looked for opportunities that arose from turmoil, and so he must do. But that this rune landed above the others signaled a time of great change, and that was disconcerting.

He turned his attention to the next rune. It had landed a little lower and to the right. This fingerbone was older and yellowed, but the symbol cut into it remained clear: *Orok-hai*. It was The Hanged Man – or The Fugitive. In this case the rune had landed showing the fugitive aspect. But this was difficult to interpret. Did it signify that he himself would have to flee? Or the king he served? Or that the man he knew was returning to the realm from exile had finally arrived? He took it for the last, because it was against the threat of this man's coming that he had cast the runes.

Next, he looked at the third rune. This was *Fallon-adir*, usually interpreted as Soaring Eagle and Roosting Sparrow. It had fallen upon the sparrow aspect, and this was a clear warning.

It was universally acknowledged that eagles were birds of nobility, creatures of majesty that wheeled in the sky and rode waves of warm air with grace. Meanwhile, the sparrow chattered raucously in shrubbery. Yet, in truth, eagles were opportunistic feeders that hunted or scavenged carrion as circumstances dictated. The one was no nobler than the other, and the warning here was to beware false assumptions. He, and the king he served, were sure of their power and secure in their unchallenged strength. But circumstances could change. The threat of the man who was coming was real, and must be acknowledged as a danger.

He turned his attention to the last rune. *Karmun.* This disturbed him most. Its aspects were Death and Life, yet the bone had fallen on its side and showed neither clearly. The lore of the Kar-karmun dictated that this indicated uncertainty. But *whose* fate was uncertain?

Horta stilled his mind. His wishes, hopes and plans were irrelevant. He must not allow them to color his interpretation of the runes. The truth, the destiny revealed, was all. And much as he disliked it, the clearest reading was that uncertainty applied to all parties involved. Destiny had not yet been set. Brand, the man who was coming, could live or die. So too the king, and most importantly himself.

It was a shock to him that it might be so, but his own death would not matter so long as he had achieved his great purpose before it occurred. It was for this that he lived, and he must let nothing interfere with his fulfilling of it. The runes indicated that fate was uncertain. So be it. Yet he now had the advantage of foreknowledge, which his opponent did not, and he would ensure that uncertainty turned to certainty, that his own possible death turned into his enemy's.

His mind made up, he quickly gathered the runes and returned them to the pouch. They had served their purpose, and now he would accomplish his. Nothing would stop him.

Horta stood, and the Arnhaten rose with him. It was time to leave the cave and enter the world again. Much needed doing, and many plans required putting in place.

"What did the runes reveal, master?"

Horta turned his gaze to the Arnhaten who spoke. According to the lore, it was within the man's right. Nor should he be told a lie, no matter that Horta wished to keep things secret until he had resolved the uncertainties. The man, along with the others, had taken part in the sacred ceremony.

"This is what the Kar-karmun revealed," Horta answered. "Change comes, and the man we are cautious of is he who will bring it. We are warned to be wary of false assumptions, which I take to mean the man is a greater threat than expected." He paused, and the other man's eyes narrowed. He knew there would be more. "And death shall walk among us, though if it be our own, the king's or the man who comes is yet to be decided."

"But *someone* shall perish?"

"It is so," Horta replied. "But forewarned, we shall ensure it is our enemy."

Horta led them out of the cave now. It was not his way to answer questions. He had told them all they needed to know. Too much perhaps, for he heard the whispering of their fear in the dark passages as they trailed after him.

He did not judge them too harshly though. He himself felt the shadow of doubt upon him. This person that came was known to them by rumor of his deeds. Brand. Rightful heir to the realm, and a dangerous man. The runes were not needed to tell him that. And Brand came for just cause. King Unferth had killed Brand's parents and sent assassins to hunt him all through his childhood. Unferth ruled now from the high seat in which Brand should sit.

Horta sighed. He did not blame the man for coming, and in another time and place he would have ignored him. But for the moment, Unferth was necessary to further, even if unwittingly, the great task of Horta's life. Therefore Brand must die.

They neared the cave mouth. It would be best to see what Unferth did first. That was regrettable, for the man was small and petty and incapable of understanding the great game that was afoot. No doubt, he would try to kill Brand, as he had always tried. But if he underestimated him and did not take the proper steps, then it was time to act himself. And that meant magic. The thought of it sent a shiver up his spine. Magic was to be feared, and yet he loved the sense of danger it brought. But it came with risks that could not be ignored. The game was finely balanced however, and the one thing he needed most was time. But it was the very thing that was running out, and every step Brand took toward Unferth cut it shorter. The man *must* die.

He walked from the cave, and felt the lush green grass beneath his sandals. Below lay the Duthgar, the land of the Duthenor tribesmen whose king he now served. Immediately, the chill breeze of this northern land cut through him. It was spring, approaching summer, yet it was colder than the bitterest winter in his homeland. The simple linen *shenti* he wore, what these northern barbarians called a kilt, was not warm enough. He and the Arnhaten had been forced to wear a portion of bearskin over their normally bare shoulders. This was barbarous beyond description, but it *did* keep the cold at bay.

How he hated this land, so cold and damp and chilly. But the inhabitants loved the greenness of it. It seemed unnatural to him, for he remembered the beauty of the arid wastes of his home and the struggling tufts of grass and the vultures circling in an azure sky devoid of cloud. He remembered them, and yearned for them. But his loss was nothing against the great task he had set himself.

He strode down the hill, determined. The Arnhaten followed behind. They passed through crude farmland, fenced by hedges and scattered with fields of green grass grazed by fat sheep and sleek cattle, lustrous-coated and beautiful even after winter. But neither would survive in his homeland under the hammering sun and the moisture-sucking air. The people though, they were tough. They would adapt to such an environment. But that was not their fate. Destiny promised a different future for them: one they would eventually embrace. Or they would die.

The hall of Unferth was not far away. They came soon to a track and then a road which passed through a hamlet. The buildings still amazed Horta, for he was used to stone and mudbrick constructions. These were village huts, often of wicker and round in shape. Others were small cottages built of sawn timber.

The youths playing in the dirt ran when they saw the procession come. Horta had never been good with children, but it distressed him every time to see this. The adults noticed him too, but they went about their tasks as though he and the Arnhaten were not there. This was of no concern. They did not like him, nor he them. But it did not matter. He had cultivated Unferth's trust, and that was all he needed for his purposes.

It did not take long to reach the hall. They climbed a hill toward it, for it was set at the highest point of the land round about except for the hills that Horta had just descended.

The road came to an end. Smaller tracks veered away to right and left toward stables and storehouses. Ahead, where the road led, commenced a flight of broad stairs segmented by wider platforms where people could rest. At least this was built of stone, and well-crafted too.

Horta climbed the stairs, his disciples behind him as was proper. He was old, very old indeed, though he did not look it. He spurned the resting platforms, though it irritated him that his left knee began to ache with the strain imposed upon it. It had been injured of old and rheumatism had set in. He put the pain from his mind and walked faster.

In a short while he reached the top. A platform was set here, broad and wide. To each side stone benches were placed, and hall guards sat there, the naked steel of their drawn blades resting across their thighs. These men were warriors, and they were not positioned here for show. They would kill intruders swiftly, for Unferth was a man of many enemies.

The hall guards stood. They came to him, one man at their front.

"Are you bidden to this hall, master Horta?"

Horta looked up into his eyes, cold and blue. There was no friendliness there, but despite the drawn sword the man carried, and the swords of his men behind him, there was fear.

"I am bidden."

A moment the doorward gazed at him, weighing him up and assessing him. He wished to refuse entry, but that would cause his own death. Either by his lord or Horta himself, and he knew it.

"I shall tell the king of your coming, and he will bid you enter. No doubt."

The man turned and entered the hall. His men remained at guard, a wall of cold steel and colder eyes.

Horta waited patiently. Their enmity meant nothing, and he told himself that the wise man rose above insult and animosity. He thought of his great task, so long in the making, so close now to fruition. Patience here was but a small thing.

The doorward returned. "The king bids you welcome. You may enter, and one of your … assistants also."

This was not unexpected. It was a slight, one of many, but Unferth knew no better. None in this backward land understood the customs of his people and that a magician kept his Arnhaten about him. It was not kings alone who needed protective guards. Quickly, he gestured to a man in his retinue and that disciple stepped forward. Together, they followed the doorward toward the hall entrance.

The hall was large, larger by far than any other buildings in the district. The broad gables were decorated, and the long sloping roof steep to shed snow. The doorward opened the great doors, huge constructions of oak slabs bound by black iron.

They entered the dim hall. Light came from wooden louvers high in the timber-paneled ceiling, and from a fire that burned in a long pit in the middle of the floor. The scent of smoke lay heavy in the air, and the aroma of food and mead from the previous night lingered.

The doorward led the way. Down the long aisle they passed, massive timber pillars carved with the strange legends of the Duthenor upheld the high roof. The fire warmed the room, casting flickering shadows into the recesses where mead benches were set and beyond them private rooms.

On the walls woven cloths hung, bright in the shadows, and the footsteps of the three men on the timbered floor echoed loudly. Here and there men sat, warriors all, their eyes grim in the shadows, their long-bladed swords by their sides and their war-scarred hands close to the hilts.

Horta gave them no heed, but he felt their eyes on his back as he passed. After some while they approached the high seat where Unferth, King of the Duthenor, sat. A king he styled himself, but rather was he a chieftain of a barbarous and wild people, quick to anger and quick to laugh, dressed in trousers and tunics and wearing boots. They had clothes, and habits, and a temperament that Horta did not like nor understand. But he knew well enough, despite all the strangeness, what motivated

Unferth. Greed and fear. Like all men, whatever their origin and customs, he was easy to manipulate.

"Hail, Unferth, king of the Duthenor," the doorward proclaimed. "I bring Horta, guest of the realm, into your presence."

Horta gave a bow, but his eyes never left Unferth, sitting high and proud upon his carved seat of black walnut. The doorward left, his footsteps hastening back to the entrance. He had no wish to stay.

"Welcome, Horta," the king greeted him. "Do you bring news?"

"Indeed sire." He looked about at several others seated near the king. These were his close advisors, men from his own neighboring tribe rather than the Duthenor. The king trusted them, but Horta did not.

Unferth noticed his concern. "You may speak freely in front of these men. Hold nothing back."

"Very well. You asked me yesterday to consult the Karkarmun." His gaze flickered to the king's advisors, many of whom would not be familiar with the term. "The Runes of Life and Death," he added for their benefit.

"And have you done so?"

Horta detected eagerness in Unferth's voice, though the king tried to hide it.

"I have. The divination was difficult, and the results not easy to interpret. Yet this much is clear. Brand returns to these lands, as our information already suggested. He is a dangerous man, and he brings change with him. Not only change, but the runes revealed the mark of death also."

Unferth leaned forward. He was close to fifty, yet still a man in his prime and the sword belted at his side and the chainmail he wore were not for decoration. But always there was the shadow of fear in his eyes, and it fanned to life now.

"*Whose* death?" the king asked.

Horta did not hold back. The truth would serve him best here. "It could be yours, sire. Or mine. Or Brand's. That he comes is certain, and that also with him he brings great danger. But the consequences of his coming? Fate yet hangs in the balance. But forewarned of danger, we can turn it aside."

Unferth sat back in the high seat. The black walnut was one with the dim shadows of the hall, but the swirling, intricate designs upon it of gold inlay gleamed brightly.

"He cannot come unobserved," the king stated.

"Sire," said one of his counselors. "The crossing of the river is guarded night and day, as you have ordered. He cannot return, nor has yet attempted to do so."

The king nodded slowly, but Horta sensed his doubt and attempted to spark it to life. "Perhaps. But our enemy is a canny man. At the very least, he will not come openly."

"There are men at the crossing who know him by sight," the king countered. "One is on duty at all times."

Horta nodded. "So I have heard, sire. And your precautions have been wise. Yet the last time these men saw him he was a youth. Will they recognize him now?"

"They had better," Unferth said. "No man changes that much."

Horta capitalized on the slight doubt in those words. "They should, but they may not. Nor is the crossing you speak of the only way to enter the realm."

"The Great River lies between Brand and us," another of the counselors said. "It's called great for a reason. It's wide and deep and cold. The currents are strong also, and only a fool would seek to swim it, with or without a horse."

"That is true," Horta replied. "Yet swimming is not the only way. As I have heard the tale, he escaped this realm long ago by crossing the river when it was frozen."

Unferth shook his head. "That was in winter, and far to the north. Besides, against that possibility, or the chance of boat, I have set men to patrol the river border all the way north into the mountains from which it issues. He will not come that way, and if he does he will be marked and killed."

Horta gave a slight bow. "Even so, I suggest you send more men to guard against his coming. Even, though this would be inconvenient, I advise closing the river crossing to trade temporarily."

The king pursed his lips and thought on that. But Horta knew before Unferth answered what decision he would make. Too much tax was raised from incoming merchants, and the king loved gold. He needed it to maintain the loyalty of his men.

"I think that unnecessary," the king announced at length, and his counselors vigorously nodded their agreement. "Brand is a dangerous man, and I accept that he will try to enter the realm. And also that he has proven difficult to kill in the past. But is he a god to defy all the measures I have set in place against him? No, he is not. When he comes, one way or another, his threat will be eliminated. Permanently."

Horta disguised his chagrin. It would serve no purpose to press the matter futilely. "As you wish, sire. I am but a humble servant."

The king smiled. "You speak humbly enough, yet there is enormous pride in you, Horta. I like that. And you have served me well. I have learned that your runes are worth listening to, and your counsels also, but you are wrong to fear Brand." He paused. "Nevertheless, I will send an extra ten men to the river crossing. He shall not pass, and live."

Horta bowed again. "I live to serve, sire."

"I do not think so. You are a secretive man, as well as prideful. Your goal, whatever it is, remains your guiding force in life. I do not hold that against you, but see that it does not cross my purposes."

"Of course, sire."

"You may go now." The king gestured to one of his men who handed Horta a pouch. It rattled with the dull clink of gold coins.

"Thank you, sire." Horta took the pouch and turned to walk back through the long hall, his assistant one step behind him.

He had not gone far when the king's voice halted him. "It seems to me that you wish Brand dead as much as I do, magician. Why should that be?"

Horta went perfectly still for a heartbeat, the blood in his veins turning chill as the air of this land he hated. And then he slowly turned, his face a mask. He must reveal nothing.

"I serve you sire, as I have these last several years. I think only of your interests, and Brand's death best fulfils that purpose."

Unferth laughed, and then stroked his uncouth beard, black and silver. Horta was disgusted. Why did so many of these northern barbarians not shave? But the king, for all his vulgar ways, was not stupid. He fixed him with his pale eyes.

"I do not think so. And yet you have served me well. Best that you do not falter now."

It was a threat. Veiled, but still a threat, and Horta felt anger rise within him.

"I shall not falter, sire. I serve, and I give myself to that service, in life and in death."

The king waved him on, and Horta turned and kept walking. He allowed himself the hint of a smile. He had not said *what* he served.

As he walked, the smile faded. Still the men in this hall gazed at him with their pale eyes, full of enmity. They mistrusted him. And that thought nearly made him smile again. Unferth saw much, too much perhaps. But at the same time he did not see enough. The men in this hall, as with many of the men who held power throughout the realm, were not Duthenor tribesmen. They were from a neighboring tribe, Unferth's tribe. They were his hold of power on this land, subduing the Duthenor. But the Duthenor were like dry grass waiting to be fired. They could rise at any time. And the king's own men … they did not like him. Under the right circumstances they could turn on him too. Unferth saw the first danger, but was oblivious to the second. The wolf dreamed only of the fatted sheep, not the tearing fangs of other wolves.

He went on, the scuff of his sandaled feet loud in the dim hall. The bag of gold he placed within one of the pouches that hung from his cloth belt. Gold? It was an insult. Did Unferth think he was a dog whose loyalty could be purchased with throwaway scraps? Time was when he dined off gold platters and drank from gem-encrusted goblets. Servants tended his every need and dark-haired women with bright smiles massaged oil into his skin and eased away the day's care. He had wanted for nothing, and those days would come again. He must just bide his time a little longer.

He and his assistant exited the hall, and the Arnhaten waiting gathered to him, following him down the stairs. They all sensed his mood, but the assistant he had taken with him knew the cause and spoke when they were out of earshot of Unferth's guards.

"What now, master?"

Horta came to a stop and took a deep breath before he spoke. "Now, we ensure the death of Brand. He is a threat. The king cannot see past his hatred, cannot see his enemy as anything but an exiled man. The precautions he has put in place should work. But they may not. Brand is greater, more dangerous and touched by a higher purpose than the king dares admit to himself. Therefore, I will take my own steps."

"Magic?" his disciple whispered.

"Indeed. Magic of the darkest kind. Brand will *not* survive it."

2. That Sort of Man

Brand endured the lash of the whip in silence. Seven times it streaked across the skin of his back. Seven times he gritted his teeth and rode a wave of pain that tore his flesh, churned his stomach and set fire to the marrow in his bones. And seven times he swore vengeance. Silently.

The head guard of the merchant caravan enjoyed whipping the junior guards. Brand was not junior to him in any way, shape or form. Yet just now, in this time and place, he was. Fate had willed it so, and Brand knew he must endure. But not for much longer.

He felt hands upon him then, deft hands undoing the rope that tied his arms around a tree. Brand had allowed himself to be bound, had accepted this punishment for a misdemeanor. It was necessary to his purposes. But he would not forget. Not ever. And the man who whipped him, who decided his punishment and enjoyed meting it out so much, he was marked for death.

The tight-bound rope fell from his arms and Brand staggered away from the tree. His legs were weak, and light-headedness threatened to see him fall to the ground. He fought it off, and those same hands that unbound him now gripped his shoulder. They held him steady and helped keep him upright. There was kindness in those hands, and he would not forget that either.

The world seemed to swim before his vision for some moments, and then he realized that the hands belonged to several men. He saw their faces now, concern in their expression and the glint of anger also. Not at him, but at the head guard. Yet they were careful that only he saw it, and not the head guard himself.

The pain began to recede, and Brand felt the sting of splashed vinegar flare it to life once more. Yet there was honey in the mixture, and this took some of the edge off the sharpness. This too he endured, for it was the standard preventative of infection, and he could not afford to succumb to sickness. Too much needed doing, and too many people depended upon him.

A moment later the guards began to ease his tunic back on, and he raised his arms to help them. The movement sent new spasms of pain through his body. He gritted his teeth once more, desperate for the agony to cease. It would pass, as all things passed, and he strove for a sense of serenity amid the turmoil that wracked his mind and body.

He did not quite attain the mental state that he sought. But he needed no help to stand, and he kept his hand away from the hilt of the sword belted at his side. Now was not the time, and if he could not rise above the urge to kill, he would never fulfil the purpose that he was needed for. Yet still, a cold gleam of hatred burned in his eyes as he slowly turned and faced the head guard.

The man stood a dozen paces back. The whip was still in his hand, the cord trailing along the ground before him, a satisfied smile on his face. Yet that smile faded as Brand stared at him.

Laigern stared back. The smile was gone, and his massive frame seemed taut and ready to explode into action. His muscles rippled and flexed as he began to fidget with the whip. He sensed the threat in Brand, the unspoken menace sparking through the air between them.

"Do you want more, boy? Turn around and get back to your duties."

Brand held his ground. "I did not know that looking you in the eye was also a misdemeanor."

"It *is* when you look at me like that."

The two men glared at each other, and tension filled the air.

"Enough!" called another man. This was the merchant. "You take offence too easily, Laigern. You just whipped the man. Have done with it."

The head guard turned to where the merchant sat in the driver's seat of one of the wagons, seemingly impatient to get underway again.

"You need guards," Laigern said. "Any time you feel like interfering with *my* men, and how I discipline them, just let me know. There are other caravans and other merchants."

The merchant shook his head. He was an old man, thin and scrawny, his hair and beard silvery white. But his eyes were shrewd and bright.

"You're the best, Laigern. I know that. Your caravans never get attacked by outlaws, but trouble will find you one day, mark my words."

Laigern grinned at him. "I eat trouble for breakfast, old man." His gaze flickered back to Brand. "Don't get any ideas, boy. If you think to try something against me, you'll get a sword in your belly. Do we understand each other?"

"Perfectly," Brand answered. He understood also that the reason Laigern's caravans were never attacked was because he bribed the outlaws and fed them information about other merchants, their whereabouts, schedules and the goods they carried. He was a robber as much as the outlaws.

Laigern turned away, coiling the whip and stowing it back in the saddlebag of his horse that was tethered nearby. Brand only took his eyes off the man when he heard footsteps approach him from the side.

Tinwellen walked up to him, all curves and dark hair and deep-brown eyes that swallowed a man whole. How the merchant had fathered a daughter like her, Brand did not know.

"You're a fool, city boy," she said while she shook her head. But the words were not meant unkindly. "There are no town guards here, no king's rule. If he were to kill you, there would be no one to stop him. Best let him be and forget about it."

Brand knew her words came out of concern for him. It was all she would say openly, but he had felt her eyes on him for days now. Her father had seen it also, but said nothing.

"Would *you* forget about it?" he asked quietly.

For a moment her eyes flashed, and he glimpsed her fiery side. "I would if someone as smart as me gave me the same good advice. At least until I was in a position to do something else."

"Ah, well, now that *is* good advice. I shall bide my time."

Brand guessed well enough that any man who raised a hand against her would wish he had not. Especially when one of her many daggers slipped across his throat. She would not be one to delay retribution a moment longer than necessary.

He decided to shift the conversation. "Why does your father put up with him?"

She frowned. "I don't know. Sometimes I think he's scared that Laigern would rob him if he were dismissed. He's a bad man. You're not the first one that he's whipped, nor will you be the last."

"Don't bet on that."

She held his gaze, and there was worry in her eyes. "Don't take him on. He'll kill you."

"Perhaps."

She ran a hand through her hair. "I can't make up my mind about you. You seem so smart. You seem like you've been far more than a caravan guard in your time, but you can be stupid too. Very stupid."

Brand did not answer that. There was nothing he could say at the moment.

She dropped her hand. "Come to my wagon when we stop tonight," she said, "and I'll rub oil and special herbs into your back to ease the pain."

Without waiting for an answer, she left him then, all dark hair once more and a purposeful stride. She had fire in her, that one, and he liked her. But she would be trouble too.

The caravan would not stop just because of the whipping of one man, and Brand had used whatever time had been allotted to him to recover. He must ride now, and more depended on it than the merchant's schedule.

He went to his horse, a sleek roan mare that had drawn the eyes of all the guards when he joined the caravan days ago and signed on. Gingerly, he mounted.

One of the twenty guards drew close to him, his own mount nearly as fine. He was older than most of the group, his bushy moustache silver, and Brand had sensed his experience and skill at this business from the first day.

"You should have cried out," the rider murmured. "Laigern has you marked now. You challenge him, and in his mind he must break you. That's how he thinks. He'll be looking for an excuse to whip you again."

Brand shrugged, and regretted it. Pain flared in his back once more. "You're right. But he doesn't need much of an excuse. He didn't have one just now."

The older man looked at him knowingly. "You're right. Dismounting to help up an old man who had tripped and fallen on the road as the caravan passed isn't much of a misdemeanor. But Laigern is like that. He has his rules, and the old man could have been a ruse to distract us while an attack was launched by outlaws."

"Maybe so," Brand said. "But what others were there? The old man's wife and grandchildren? And there was no cover for an ambush."

The older man let out a sigh, but did not reply.

"You're right," Brand continued. "His rules may be stupid, but I should have known better than to break them."

"They *are* stupid, but it's best not to talk that way. You're new with us, and he likes to make sure that new starters understand right from the beginning who is in charge."

Brand wondered if the man had cause to remember his own introduction to Laigern, but he did not ask about it. They fell silent. Around them, all the other guards had now mounted, their expressions grim. They looked neither at him nor at Laigern, and Brand realized they sensed trouble brewing. He sensed also that they wanted no part of it, for Laigern was feared.

The lead wagon gave a sudden lurch, and then began to roll forward. The merchant sat high in the driver's seat, looking straight ahead and ignoring all around him. He did not like what was happening either, but Brand knew he had given him as much time as he could to recover. More than Laigern would have wished.

Another four wagons followed the first, packed tightly with valuable goods. Around them the twenty guards nudged their mounts into a walk, Brand likewise, and the caravan began to move forward once more. They were heading toward the Duthgar, the land of the Duthenor. It was a wild land, populated by wild tribesmen.

City boy, Tinwellen had called him, but she did not know the truth, nor any of the others. He had traveled further than she had, further than her father, and though he had come from the city and acted as such, he was born in the Duthgar. And he was returning home. But trouble would come of that, and a whipping was the least of it.

Ahead, leading them all, rode Laigern. He sat his horse like a king on his throne, but he turned from time to time, and his dark eyes, sullen with menace, found Brand on each occasion. Brand stared back. And trouble would come of that, too.

The caravan had started in the great city of Cardoroth. That was where he had signed on. They did not know who he was nor his history, and that was the way he wanted it. Laigern had looked him over gruffly and accepted his word that he was good with a sword. He had been forced to, for he was short of recruits. Word of his fondness for the whip had obviously reached the ears of many.

The merchant had gazed at him shrewdly, seeing through some of his guise, seeing that despite appearances he was more than he seemed, even a man of wealth and influence. That old man said little, but saw much. Still, he did not guess the truth. Had he done so Brand would have seen shock in his eyes. What he saw instead was curiosity, and a mind that gnawed away at mysteries. That was dangerous too, for the old man might eventually work out who he was.

The great city of Cardoroth was not his true home, if he even had one anymore. It was a haven for him though, a place of exile that he had come to love. But all things ended, and as they did something new began.

He was returning home now, the land where he had grown up, and yet where he had been pursued as a boy by assassins and hunted from place to place and farm to farm. Only now, coming home, he was a greater swordsman than he had been, a better strategist. He was older, wiser, more confidant. And, though none in this caravan knew it, he possessed the use of magic. These were not small things, and they would stand him in good stead. Yet his enemies were powerful, and still they would seek his death. And coming back to the Duthgar, where their power was greatest, placed the advantage with them.

Dusk came and the wagons drew to a stop. Camp was set, horses fed and rubbed down, fires lit and meals cooked over the embers. Night fell, the stars sprang into the sky and music from pipe and drums and voice filled the darkness. Brand liked it all. There were worse fates in life than traveling with a merchant, seeing new ground every day and camping at leisure under the stars. But it would not be his fate, not for long.

By dawn the caravan was rolling again. Not long after, the river came into view. Not just any river, but the Careth Nien, the great river that divided the continent of Alithoras. Trees lined its winding path, hiding much of it, but here and there the glint of silver and wide stretches of water showed. And soon the crossing came into sight. It was here that the caravan must pass, and here that the first great danger lay. Brand looked ahead with determination.

3. The River Crossing

They came to the crossing before mid-morning. Nothing special marked the place, except a small group of cottages. Why this place had been chosen, Brand did not know. It was the same as any other stretch of the river. Yet even so, his instincts flared to life. There was danger here.

The crossings were not a ford or a shallows of any kind. Perhaps the two banks were closer together, but they were still hundreds of feet apart. Between lay the river, beautiful but deadly for man or horse that attempted to swim it.

Men came out of the cottages. Laigern and the merchant went off to speak to them. They would negotiate the fee for the crossing, and while they did so Brand studied how it would be achieved.

His eyes were drawn first to the barge. It lay anchored in the river. It was a boat, of sorts, but very wide and flat in order to carry the livestock and wagons over the water. Large as it was though, there would need to be two trips to get all of this caravan across.

At least the barge was on this side of the river at the moment. That would speed things up. Also, the men that had come out of the cottages were men from Cardoroth. The danger, if danger there was, would come from the other side. There would be Duthenor there, but how many and who Brand did not know.

Would his enemies be waiting for him? It was possible. The crossing would certainly be guarded and there would be men with his description there, even men who had once known him. That was the greatest danger of all. He had taken precautions against the first, but against the second there was little he could do.

He removed his hand from his sword hilt when he realized he was touching it. It was a sign of nerves, and nothing would give him away swifter than that.

The merchant soon returned with Laigern. The old man muttered something about being overcharged, and Brand smiled. Merchants always thought anytime they had to pay something it was too much. But they each charged as much as they could for the goods they carried themselves.

Laigern called most of the guards forward. Brand was not one of them. These, and the first three wagons moved forward and were loaded on the barge. Eventually, it began to move across the river. It would be a long wait here with the last two wagons.

Brand looked about. He saw that his friend had been left behind too. The older man approached, his expression slightly amused and his mustache almost twitching.

"It seems that we are both out of favor," he said.

"You spent too long talking to me, it seems. I'm sorry about that."

The older man laughed. "To be sure, that wouldn't have helped. But Laigern and I have never seen eye to eye. A pox upon him and his type."

"Likely enough," Brand replied, "he sells information to outlaws about caravan movements. But I've a feeling his day is done."

The older man looked at him thoughtfully. "You see things quickly, especially for a man that's new to this guard business. It's almost like you've done it before. But if you had, I'd know you. I've been at this a long time."

Brand said nothing, but the older man looked at him not unkindly. "We all have our secrets, I guess. And what you say about Laigern is probably true. There've been rumors for years. But this much I'll tell you for a fact. He's killed men. He's dangerous, and I've seen none better with sword, knife or fist. Stay clear of him. Let your anger go, and live. Push him too far, and he'll leave you lying by the side of the road for the crows to eat."

The older man did not wait for an answer this time. He had given his advice and now he wandered off to idle away the boring break they must endure before the barge returned.

Brand liked him, and he considered his advice. But it was hard to forgive or forget a man who had whipped you for no good reason. His back still felt raw, and he remembered the agony of the lash and the rising torrent of hatred that overwhelmed him. It had receded a little now, but not much.

Everyone seemed on edge, for the caravan and the guards had been split into two groups and should an attack by outlaws occur each group would be isolated and vulnerable. This only added to Brand's concerns. But he remained still, casually observing the river and trying to see what was happening on the other side without looking anxious. But it was too distant to tell much, other than that there were men there, and this he already knew.

Eventually, the barge returned. It was now the second group's turn to cross. The wagons rolled onto the barge first, and then the guards followed with their horses.

Brand led his roan mare over the landing. Her hooves clattered dully on the timber platform, and he saw flashes of the river between planks. Then they walked over the barge ramp and onto the boat itself. He kept to the rear of the wagons, not wishing to be seen any earlier than necessary when they made it to the other side.

"Cast off!" yelled the captain when all were ready.

"Casting off!" responded the crew.

The ropes holding the barge were untied and straightaway Brand felt the boat shift as the river current took hold of her.

Quickly now the crew worked, and they retrieved long poles and moved to the downstream edge of the barge. The poles speared into the water and found the river bed. The barge steadied. Then they withdrew the poles and began the arduous task of propelling the craft forward.

The current was slight at first, but then it grew stronger as the minutes passed and they ventured further out. The opposite shore remained distant. The current took hold of the barge, let her go and then gripped her again. Brand was glad that he had not attempted to swim, even with the horse. It may have been possible, but neither he nor the horse had the training for it. They would likely have died. He looked across to the far shore and wondered if he still might.

Not for nothing was this called the Careth Nien, the great river. It was wide and it took a long time to reach the shallows. But eventually they did, and the poles splashed through the water and hit the bottom quickly.

With a bump that thrilled through the deck beneath Brand's feet, and then a grinding noise, the barge came alongside the landing on the far bank.

"Tie her up, lads!" came the shouted command of the captain.

Some of the men ran to secure the boat, while the rest remained where they were, holding the barge steady in the water with their poles.

When the boat was securely tied, a ramp, this time at the front, was let down. The wagons rolled onto the landing and the guards followed them.

Across the timber landing they went. But soon there was ground beneath them once more.

Brand felt a strange sensation pass over him. This was home. He walked once more on the land in which he had been born. He felt pride and fear and love and hope all flow through him at once. He had returned from exile, had returned to right a great wrong done against his people, and the world would never be the same again.

This moment had been long in coming. He had so much to achieve. But it could end now, before it began, if he were recognized and killed. His great enemy would be sure to have the borders watched.

The wagons rolled forward to join the tail end of the first three. Soldiers were everywhere. And on this side of the river they were Duthenor warriors. No, he changed his mind. They were Callenor tribesmen, men of a neighboring land. Men who followed Unferth and who, by their strength of arms, had allowed him to usurp the chieftainship of the Duthenor and maintain it.

The soldiers moved among the wagons, checking their contents and assessing the value of all goods. This would be used to calculate the taxes Unferth charged. But at the same time the men searched the wagons carefully. This may have been for contraband, but he knew they were also looking for him. Better to hide in plain sight, he thought.

Even as he casually watched the men search, his stomach sank. Several tribesmen were also coming through, looking at the guards one by one. And Laigern was with them.

They came to him, and his stomach sank further. Among the Callenor soldiers was a Duthenor; one that he knew of old. Yet he had been but a child then, and had changed much and now spoke differently. Would the man recognize him? Perhaps. He had recognized the man.

Brand looked as casual as possible, merely checking the tightness of the girth strap of his mount when they approached. He made no attempt to hide his face and looked up when they neared.

The men paused and looked at him. He felt their eyes burn into him, and saw a frown appear on the face of the one he knew.

"And who are you?" the man asked, his eyes searching.

"Conmar," Brand answered, giving the same name he had given Laigern and the others.

The man did not take his eyes off him, and Brand tried his best to look bored.

After a moment the man turned to Laigern. "Is that so?"

The head guard grunted. "That's his name. Leastways the name he gave me. He signed on recently."

The man seemed to be interested by this. "Then he could be the one we're looking for."

Brand looked surprised. "Why would you be looking for me?"

"Where were you born?"

"In Cardoroth city. Midwinter night it was, and the howl of the wind was so loud my father said that—"

"He's not interested in the wind, idiot," Laigern interrupted him.

The other man's eyes were still on him, and the surrounding soldiers were growing uncertain. This was taking longer than it had with the other caravan guards, and he felt their eyes on him, weighing him up.

"An idiot, am I?" Brand said to Laigern. "Is that what I get for working day and night for a pittance. Is that—"

"Enough!" Laigern yelled.

Tension hung in the air between him and the head guard. Brand hoped it was enough. No man trying to hide would draw attention to himself in that manner. Yet still the Duthenor's eyes were on him.

"Pay no attention to this one," Laigern said. "I'll sort him out afterwards. He's a troublemaker his is, for sure. But I'll sort him out."

Brand felt the threat in those words, but the Duthenor warrior spoke again. "A troublemaker, is he?"

"Aye. The worst kind. I had to whip him yesterday."

The Duthenor looked at Brand once more, and then slowly shook his head as his eyes lost interest. "He's not the man we're looking for. That one wouldn't allow himself to be whipped."

They walked away, but Brand saw Laigern look back at him, his eyes smoldering pits of hatred. If he had known the truth, he would have turned Brand in quicker than blink and enjoyed the consequences. But he was blinded by his sense of superiority to the possibility that one of his junior guards was more than what he seemed. Brand was amused by the irony of that.

Not long after the caravan began to move again. The guards mounted and rode beside the wagons.

"Keep a sharp lookout!" Laigern ordered.

Brand knew why. They had now entered the Duthgar, the land of the Duthenor, but this was a wild region. It was a shadow land, ruled in name by the Duthenor king, but it seldom saw its supposed leader. Instead, it was a haven for outlaws. Most came from other Duthenor lands, but not a few from the kingdom of Cardoroth far to the east. Brand did as instructed, and kept his eyes open. But he did not look just for signs of outlaws, but also for friends; two in particular, and he would be glad to see them.

As they traveled, the land rose slightly away from the river. But they had not gone far when by chance Brand rode a little fast and passed some of the wagons. He drew level with the lead one, and felt the eyes of the old merchant fix on him. There was speculation in them, and more curiosity than had been there before. The old man knew that the soldiers at the crossing had been looking for a man. And he had guessed it was Brand.

Brand slipped back to his regular place as fast as he could without making it obvious. He should have known that the merchant would have figured things out. But he had guessed only half of it yet. That was half too much, and it was high time that Brand extricated himself from the situation. He did not think the merchant would say anything, but if Laigern got wind of things then anything was possible.

The ground rose more steeply, and the beaten track they followed shifted left and right always seeking the easiest incline. Wagons had been coming this way for years beyond count, and the best path had long been discovered.

About them rose a countryside of small hills and winding gulleys. Patches of forest ran across it, sometimes chocking the gulleys or covering the sides of a hill. At other times the land was bare, save for green grass. It was a haven for outlaws because at one and the same time it offered concealment and good lookout spots where the progress of a caravan could be watched and its guards assessed for their numbers, competence and routines.

In truth though, or at least so Brand believed, outlaw attacks were rare. There were too few bandits, and they seldom acted in unison. Also, the merchants always traveled with sufficient guards.

They moved higher into the hills. There were no farms here, though there were signs that farms once existed. It was not an area of the Duthgar that Brand was familiar with. But he knew there were settlements not too far away. Not of outlaws, but proper farms and villages. He was looking forward to talking to his own people again, and to seeing how they reacted to him. He had been away for many years.

He kept an eye out for his two friends as he rode. They would not have been troubled at the crossing, for though they were men coming from Cardoroth they bore no resemblance to him and would not have been bothered by the soldiers. Especially without him there.

But there was no sign of them. He had not expected to see them though. Not yet. But when the caravan stopped for the day he would leave it. Then he would head north into the hills. That was what they had arranged, and his friends would find him there. And though he could not see them now, he knew they were there somewhere, watching.

The track was dry and dusty. It was spring, and there had been rain, but the flow of traffic over the rutted lane was constant, and this kept it as it was. A cloud of dust rose up about the plodding hooves of the horses and the churning wagon wheels. Brand tried not to breathe it in, and thought as he rode.

He remembered the night his parents had been killed, murdered by Unferth and his men. It was long ago now, but the memory of that night and the days that followed haunted him. By chance, he had not been there and had escaped. He remembered the long years growing up, hidden by family after family who had been loyal to his parents. And why should they not have been? His parents were well loved, for they had ruled the Duthgar well and wisely.

His father was the chieftain, and Brand was the true heir. But he had escaped, and Unferth could not tolerate that. Brand's life must be a constant reminder that his rule was earned by spilling blood and treachery, and doubt would gnaw at him for fear that Brand might one day begin a rebellion and claim his own. For that reason

Unferth had sent the assassins after him. Over and over, again and again. But he had lived. He had endured. He had grown strong as a warrior, and later as a captain of men in Cardoroth's army. He had even risen to … but none of that mattered now. It was all dust on the wind. Those days were passed and new days had begun. At *last*, they had begun, and justice was coming after the long wait.

Despite all that had happened to him, it was some of his earliest training that would serve him best now. His father had taught him the warrior's ways, as well as strategy and diplomacy. After that, he had learned from some of the greatest fighters in the Duthgar. And he would need all the skills he had learned, of blade and mind both. He was about to start a fight, and he was badly outnumbered. At the beginning, it would be him and his two friends against the might of Unferth. But he had plans to change that disadvantage. But first, he must leave the caravan and deal with Laigern.

The day wore on. The caravan covered many miles, and the crossing of the Careth Nien was far behind. The sun set in the west, straight ahead of them, in a blaze of red and orange that streaked the sky and shot the scattered clouds through with crimson. Crimson like blood. And blood there would be, Brand knew. Soon.

His job would be to serve as a figurehead. He must get the people of the Duthgar to rally behind him. He must grow an army from nothing, and he must do so knowing that Unferth would be seeking to destroy him. No small task for one man alone with the aid of a few friends. But two friends was a beginning. If he could rally one person to the cause, he could rally fifty. And if fifty, a thousand. And if a thousand, an army. But Laigern was his obstacle now, and it was time to deal with him.

The caravan approached a small creek that ran down from the higher hills. Trees lined it, and it was a pleasant spot. But it was not where Brand would spend the night.

"Halt!" ordered Laigern. "Set camp!"

Brand nudged his horse toward the head guard. Laigern watched his approach, his eyes dark pits of hatred. He would be even more unhappy when he learned what Brand had to say. There would be trouble. Oh yes, Brand thought. There was big trouble coming. Laigern was that sort of man.

4. Sword or Knife?

Brand came to a halt before Laigern. The other guards were nearby, setting up a picket line for the horses. He did the polite thing and dismounted. He would talk to Laigern man to man, not from atop his horse. It occurred to him though that deep down he wanted to fight this man, to provoke him. And the head guard would not attack him while he was mounted.

"This is where we part ways," Brand said. He made no effort to speak quietly, and the other guards stopped what they were doing and watched. The merchant and Tinwellen were close by also.

Laigern smiled, but there was no humor in the big man's expression.

"No," was all he said though. Yet he said it with assurance.

"It's not your decision, Laigern. I'm leaving, and I'm leaving tonight. I'm just giving you the courtesy of notice instead of riding off into the night."

"You're not riding off anywhere, tonight or any other time. You'll do what I say, when I say it, for the rest of this trip. Or I'll whip you again."

Brand felt his temper slip. His back still hurt.

"You've whipped me once, and that will *never* happen again. Now, I'm going."

"If you make a move to mount that horse, I'll break your legs, boy. You signed on for the trip, and you're coming with us even if you have to crawl."

Brand looked Laigern in the eye. "Actually, I signed on for my daily fee. That was our agreement, and you know it."

"To hell with the agreement!" Laigern yelled. He was angry now, and his dark eyes shone with malice.

Brand stood his ground. More than that, he pushed it further.

"Pay me my day's wages, and be done with it."

Laigern shook his head like an angry bull. "No."

"Then I shall take it from you."

The head guard looked at him as though he were stunned by the idea, and then a slow smile spread over his face.

"You? A trifling man such as yourself, take something from me?"

"Yes."

Laigern's grin split his face, and it was not humor but an anticipation of inflicting pain. "Then what shall it be? Sword or knife?"

Brand felt his own hatred rise. This man had whipped him, and taunted him afterwards. He was a bad man, and the world would be better off without him. Yet should he be killed for that? The temptation was there, a strong pull, and it would be justified, to a degree. The man was asking for it. Yet for the very reason that it was a temptation, he must resist it. If he did not, would he not slip down the same slope that Laigern had? He had to do better than that, had to be a better man.

"Neither," he said at length. "We'll fight man to man, fist to fist. I have no wish to kill you, which I would with a blade."

Laigern chuckled. "You're sure of yourself, boy. I'll give you that. But nothing else." He removed his tunic, his great arms bulging. His upper body was thick and hairy, but corded with muscle.

Brand unbelted his sword and placed it on the ground. He was giving away an advantage here, for he was a better swordfighter than anything else, yet he did not regret it. He wanted to kill Laigern, and he must prove to himself that he was better than his baser instincts.

Suddenly Tinwellen was beside him, dark eyes flashing. He had not gone to her wagon last night, and she had avoided him since.

"Don't be a fool, city boy," she said.

"A man is no man who doesn't stand up for himself."

"That may be, but a live man is better than a dead man. At the least, he'll cripple you in some way. Just look at him, fool!"

Brand turned his gaze to Laigern. The man stood there, a picture of confidence. Brand was a large person himself, but the head guard stood six inches taller and weighed much more, most of it muscle. Scars showed on his arms and chest too, evidence that he was not all talk and bluff but had survived many dangerous fights.

With a shrug, Brand turned his gaze back to Tinwellen. "Thank you for caring, but this is something I must do. And besides, I'm going to win."

She looked at him, her expression incredulous, but whatever she had intended to say she never had the opportunity.

"Quit talking, boy." Laigern said. "There's no point in delaying this any longer."

Brand turned and walked toward him. He breathed deeply of the air and settled his nerves. He sought the mental state of the warrior. *Stillness in the storm*, his father had called it, though it had many names beside.

The world faded around him. There was only himself, and the huge man before him. Time seemed to slow, and his body moved with smoothness and ease. He was ready.

Laigern did not hesitate. He stepped in and jabbed with his left fist. It was a swift blow, and powerful despite the shortness of the movement. He was no common brawler rushing in and swinging wildly.

Brand shuffled back a pace. He moved with ease, sure of himself. But the big man moved faster than someone of his size had a right to.

Laigern followed with a right cross. Brand swayed to the side and let loose a right at the man's midriff. There was a satisfying thud as his fist struck flesh.

Brand moved away again, content to take his time. Laigern stepped after him, grinning. The blow he had taken had no effect on him. Brand was not really surprised. A well-muscled man, used to fighting, could take punch after punch to the body. The head, however, was another matter.

With a few quick steps Laigern bridged the gap between them. But he did not throw a punch. Instead he dropped and his leg swept out, trying to topple Brand.

Nimbly, Brand avoided the leg sweep. It had come as a surprise though, for its execution had been swift, and that was not easy.

They circled each other for a few moments. Brand saw an opening and jabbed with his left. The big man was swift, but the jab still took him square on the nose and blood began to flow.

Brand moved back. It was not his normal way of fighting, but his opponent was too big and too strong to take down swiftly. Patience must serve him here and not aggression. Laigern seemed unaffected. He ignored the blood and stepped after Brand.

The big man drew close once more and drove a left jab followed by a mighty right cross. Brand avoided them both and landed his own right to the man's body again before backing away.

None of Brand's blows seemed to hurt his opponent, but they would over time. Especially another one or two to the head. But if they were not hurting the big man yet, they were annoying him. He was hit and bleeding, but he had not touched his opponent. It made him look inferior, and that was the one thing Laigern could not tolerate. It burned his soul, and Brand knew it would. Fighting was a mental battle as well as a physical.

Laigern dropped his head and charged. Brand expected it, and his left jabbed out followed by a right that cracked into the other man's skull, opening up a cut and drawing blood above the eye. It did not stop him.

The breath was knocked from Brand as his opponent crowded him and an uppercut took him in the stomach. This was followed by a stomp towards Brand's foot, but despite the blow he received he was still nimble. He moved to the side, crashing an elbow into his enemy's midriff as he passed.

Laigern followed him, unleashing a succession of blows. Some took Brand in the head and body, but he avoided most of them. Just as well. The big man put power into his punches.

Brand feinted with his left. Laigern moved slightly to the side, straight into a hard right that sent him reeling backward. Brand moved in, sending a swift flurry of punches at the other man and then striking his neck with the blade of his hand.

The head guard had survived a hundred such fights though. He was bleeding and bruised, but not beaten.

A left cross struck Brand in the face, and he felt his enemy's fingers scratching and seeking his eyes. He dropped his head – directly into an uppercut that rocked him back and made his legs weak.

Brand stepped away and swayed. Laigern leapt in for the finishing punch, but Brand had also endured many such fights and the swaying was illusory. He seemed to stagger, then as he dropped low he sprang up again driving a massive blow under the other man's chin.

Laigern toppled and crashed into the ground. But then he rolled and was up on his feet again.

Brand cursed silently as the two circled each other with wariness. Would this man not just give up? But at least he was not smiling anymore, and his breaths came in great heaves of his chest. The longer this fight went, the more he would be disadvantaged.

As they circled, Brand had a vague impression of the watchers in the background. Tinwellen stood perfectly still, her face a picture of concern. Her father was beside her, frail and old but his eyes bright and alert. The guards watched carefully, aware that they witnessed a fight of two highly skilled protagonists.

Laigern charged again. This time he did not punch, but moved to sweep Brand within the grip of his great arms. If he did so, the fight was over, for Brand could not counter the other man's enormous strength and weight.

With a smooth motion, Brand retreated, but he hammered a left jab into his opponent's already bloody face. Yet Laigern kept coming, and one hand found an unrelenting grip on Brand's tunic. Brand fended the other one away, but it sought to grab him also.

A moment they stood thus, and then Laigern surged forward with his greater strength and smashed a headbutt into Brand's face. The world turned dark and pain shot through him. Dizzy, he began to fall, and he heard the cries of the watchers.

His legs buckled. Searing pain tore at his skull, and he felt Laigern loosen his grip. No doubt his boots would take up the attack when his opponent lay on the ground.

But letting Brand go had been a mistake. Expecting him to fall had been another. It was not the first great blow

Brand had taken to the head, and he rode the pain and weakness in his legs, and then surged back catching his enemy by surprise.

Brand caught him with a swift left jab, and followed it with a pounding range of combinations to Laigern's body and face. The big man reeled back, shocked and hurt. Not fast enough to counter the blows, they rained upon him in succession until his legs gave way and he fell to the ground himself. He tried to rise, but then slumped once more, beaten.

Silence fell, broken only by Brand's deep breathing. He felt blood ooze from the whip marks in his back, and the pain from them flared to life once more. He looked down on Laigern, and there was no pity in his gaze. The man had brought this on himself, yet still Brand was glad that he had not killed him.

He bent down, wary that his opponent might try something, and untied the money pouch from his belt. Then he stood, opened it, and removed the coin owed to him. Then he dropped the pouch beside Laigern.

"It would have been better to have just paid me," Brand said quietly. The big man groaned and tried to rise once more, but then slumped again.

A few of the guards came over and helped the fallen man. They did not like him, but these were good men and they did not like to see people suffer.

All the while Brand felt everyone's eyes on him. He had done what none of them had expected. Laigern had seemed invincible to them, and now they looked at the smaller man, the junior guard, who had beaten him.

The merchant studied him, his eyes glittering. He did not like Laigern any more than the others.

"Stay on," the old man asked him. "I'll make you head guard in Laigern's place. A man like you, with your talents, can rise high … very high indeed. Even to the top."

Brand grinned at him. The man may have worked out who he was, but if so, he was not saying it in front of the others, which was for the best.

"Thank you," Brand replied. "But being a guard, of any sort, is just not for me. I have other duties."

The old man raised his eyebrows. "Ah well, never mind. Thank you for your services here. You've been entertaining, to say the least."

Tinwellen came forward. "You're more than what you seem," she said. It was almost an accusation.

Brand shrugged. "I'm just a man passing through."

"What man, though? And passing through to where?"

The merchant glanced at her. "Leave it alone, daughter. All men are entitled to their secrets."

She looked as though she would argue, but then thought better of it. "As you wish, father."

She came to Brand then. "Best of luck, city boy. I don't know who you are, or what your task is, but we'll meet again. I have a feeling about that." She hugged him quickly, and then went to her wagon and disappeared inside.

Brand would miss her. But he saw no way that they would meet again. He turned to the merchant once more.

"May I offer a final bit of advice before I go?"

"Of course," the old man replied.

"Dismiss Laigern. But then change your schedule."

"Aye," the old man replied knowingly. "I think it was time I did just that. Best of luck to you."

"And to you," Brand said.

He mounted his horse. Dusk was falling, but there was still a little daylight left. The guards, quiet until now, cheered him and wished him well as he left. They were glad that he had beaten Laigern, and even happier that the man would be replaced.

He rode higher into the hills. The sun dropped below the horizon, but to the north two riders appeared and angled toward him.

5. By Sword and Magic

Horta was in the old woods, the woods sacred to the Duthenor. Their dark trunks marched away out of sight, their limbs creaked and scratched. The men he sought to avoid, the Duthenor themselves, came here but once a year. Now was not the time, and he and the Arnhaten would have the solitude they required for what now must be done.

That the woods were sacred meant nothing to Horta. Yet it was a strange place, and it gave him an eerie feeling. Especially now, at night, with the stars blocked out from above. That was not natural, not what he was used to. Even the snow was better than that, for the stars had shone on his people for millennia. By them they navigated, under their influence they cast auguries, by their light they hunted and feasted and sang their songs of power.

Even so, cut off from the nighttime sky, he still felt power about him. Not for nothing had the Duthenor designated this wood as sacred. There were places in the world where the magic of creation still ran strong, and this was one. Best of all, he had need of such power now and it would aid him in what he did.

A bonfire burned before him in a clearing. The Duthenor would not light flame in a place such as this, nor bear steel blades. Horta shook his head at their ignorance. Superstitious fools. They did not understand the true powers of the world, had no knowledge of the beings who ruled it, did not know their names nor their functions and even less upon whom to call in times of need.

But he did. He knew the lore. Bitter had been his life to gain it through long years of servitude. And many had been the enemies along that journey. He shifted position where he sat cross-legged on the grass, and he heard the Runes of Life and Death rattle in their pouch.

The bonfire had caught swiftly, nor would it last long. The timber used was pine, and though there were trunks in it, they would not burn till morning.

"It is time," Horta said to the Arnhaten.

They stood. Slowly they began to circle the fire, casting on green branches broken down from the sacred trees. The sap-filled needles smoked heavily, and soon the forest meadow lay under a pall of seething, roiling smoke.

Horta gestured, and his disciples started to chant. It was an old ritual, laden with memories of his homeland, and it reminded him that he missed it and of how much he hated his self-imposed exile in this cold, damp northern land.

They continued the slow procession around the bonfire. Each time Horta reached the northern end, he cast a pinch of special herbs onto the flames. The herbs were a mixture of hallucinogens, and he was careful not to use too much. But likewise, he must use enough. But this too was part of the ritual, handed down over the eons and tested. He followed the ceremony to perfection. There was little room for error, and none in what was yet to come.

He breathed in of the air, and he felt his mind steady. Nervousness left him, though in the back of his mind fear still lurked, even if it seemed a separate thing from him. So too his conscience. He was about to unleash terror and death into the world. Brand would be the focus of it. A part of him did not wish this, for the man was no personal enemy. He was merely in the wrong place at the wrong time, but this was a weakness he must overcome. Morals and regrets had no place in the great task that he must accomplish. He must rise above such frailties to serve a greater good.

Horta removed a single leaf of the *norhanu* herb from one of his pouches. This too was hallucinogenic, and he was wary of it. Yet it broke down the barriers of the mind and aided the release of a magician's powers. He slipped it into his mouth, tasting the bitterness of the waxy leaf but not chewing it. That would have too strong an effect too quickly. Moreover, it might kill him.

The night grew darker. The pall of smoke lessened as the fire burned. They cast no more green leaves upon it. Yet it was time now for the next part of the rite.

Horta stood still now at the northern end of the bonfire. The Arnhaten circled until they drew near him, and then they also stood still, gathering to each side of him. From another of his many pouches he gathered powder, and cast a small handful into the flames.

The fire roared to life. Red sparks shot up into the smoke-laden air, followed by trails of green. A stench wafted to him, but he did not hold his breath against it or falter. Now was not a time to waver or show weakness. Twice more he cast the powder, a little more each time.

Now, he began to chant, his words rising up with the smoke and heat-shimmer of the fire, up into the night and toward the hidden stars. The Arnhaten chanted with him, intoning the ancient words that he uttered as an echo.

Upon the gods he called, the old gods that ruled air earth and sky. The gods that existed before humankind and would endure beyond the fall of civilizations and the descent of man into oblivion once more.

Horta chanted, his voice resonant with power, not summoning a specific god, but beseeching their aid and asking that one would appear and hear his request.

And in the play of twining flames a form took shape. Vague it was, though it grew more distinct. It was manlike, but where a human head should have been was a flaring mane and the regal head of a lion, eyes sparking fire. And the eyes seemed human.

Horta recognized the god. It was Hathalor.

"Hail, great lord!" he exclaimed. "I beseech thee! O Master of the Hunt, Ruler of the Wastes, Voice of the Night. I beseech thee! If you are willing, lend me of your power."

The lion-headed god roared. Fire was his breath and thunder rumbled through the sacred woods.

"Hear me!" Horta continued. "Hear me, O Father of the Desert, Stalker in the Silence, King of the Hunt."

The god raised his arms toward the heavens. The trees leaned, the boughs bent to an otherworldly breeze, and the stars glittered in the now open patch of sky above.

"I beseech thee, Hathalor. Lend me of your power!"

Horta ceased to chant, and bowed his head, waiting.

"I hear you, Horta," answered the god. "Speak."

Horta did not waste time. Time was precious, and the god could grow bored at any time and leave.

"Great lord. A man comes. He is mortal, but he has power. He threatens all I strive to achieve. I beseech thee, crush him with the shadow of your thought. Let the dark eat his mind and the crawling worms devour his body."

The god looked at him, his gaze a window into other worlds.

"And why should I do this thing?"

Horta could not hold the gaze of the god, but he answered swift and truthfully.

"Because I serve the gods with loyalty and devotion. I would rebirth them into the world of men once more. Not just in white-walled Kar-fallon, but in Alithoras from shore to shore, atop all mountains, within all woods, across all lands and in the hearts of all people."

The god looked at him, the weight of his gaze as a mountain.

"The old gods you would rebirth into the world, as well as a new. Is that not so?"

"It is even as you say, great lord. The old gods I serve, as have my kind since the stars first arose, but the new god calls also. And the Kar-ahn-hetep shall once more conquer by sword and magic. And in conquering, the old gods and the new god shall walk among men together, for knowledge of them shall pass wherever sword slashes and the travails of battle pass."

The lion-headed god pinned him with his eyes that turned red and green like the fire in which his visage stood.

"You take much upon yourself, Horta."

"I am called to do so."

The god considered that. "It may be thus. Therefore, I will send hunters after this threat you fear, this man called Brand. But first they must feast on human flesh."

"It shall be so, great lord."

The fire died down, the image of the god flickered away and the Arnhaten gathered close around Horta, uncertain. Yet the hallucinogenic smoke they had inhaled dulled their sense of fear. He looked at them, glad of the old rituals. Nothing in them was done without purpose, and the old masters anticipated the will of the gods. Yet in this case, the smoke alone would not be enough.

He dipped into his pouch once more with strangely steady hands, and withdrew a norhanu leaf. This he passed to Asaba.

"Consume it," he said. "It will calm your nerves."

The Arnhaten took the leaf and sucked upon it. The disciples moved closer to the fire, but it was dying swiftly, dwindling to ash and embers. The night was old about them, and the sacred woods of the Duthenor alive with power.

But something else stalked the woods also. Wolves. Horta glimpsed their gray pelts and the glinting of their eyes.

He turned to Asaba. "I have a task for you."

The disciple replied, his voice slurred. "Yes … master. What shall I do?"

"Do you feel magic run through your veins?"

"I do, master," Asaba answered softly.

"Then swallow the leaf. It will enhance what you feel."

Asaba seemed to struggle to focus on him. "But is that not dangerous?"

Horta placed a hand on his shoulder. "It is dangerous to the weak, but you are strong, are you not? Do you not feel strength thrumming through your body?"

Asaba seemed confused, and he did not answer. Yet as Horta watched the man chewed and swallowed the leaf.

"Ah," the magician said. "Such power. With it you shall ride the night and destroy our enemy. You are the first and greatest of the Arnhaten."

No answer did Asaba give, but he sighed dreamily. And his eyes were now black.

In the woods, the wolves began to howl. Horta studied the darkness hemming them in, and when he returned his gaze to Asaba he sensed the magic surging within him, wild and unpredictable. The Arnhaten trembled, and he swayed rhythmically from side to side. White foam frothed at his mouth, but the man did not seem to notice.

"It will be soon now," Horta said. He took his hand from Asaba's shoulder and stepped away. "Stay clear of him," he instructed the others. "Be still. Watch, and learn. For the power of one of the old gods is loose in the world this night. Do not move, and you shall survive it."

The wolves came into the clearing on padded feet, their eyes alert and their long snouts sniffing. No one moved. All was still, except for the gentle swaying of Asaba. The wolves sniffed at him and growled.

Asaba slowly straightened. A dozen wolves circled him, drawing close. He raised his arms, and power flashed in his black eyes. Not for nothing had he been chosen to join the Arnhaten, but his courage was raised by the norhanu leaf. Without it he would have fled. Yet standing still or running, the result would have been the same. Horta watched dispassionately.

Several of the wolves leaped at him. Some tore at his legs, but one jumped high, its jaws snapping and gnawing at his throat.

Crimson blood sprayed. Asaba tried to scream, but his voice was torn away by the frenzy of the wolf. He staggered, clutching at his throat, and the rest of the wolves went for him, dragging him down into their scrabbling midst.

The wolves swarmed over the thrashing figure beneath them. The struggle soon ceased, and the wolves tore into the body, snarling at each other with reddened snouts. Bones cracked and blood spilled onto the ground, visible even in the dim light of the fire.

When the frenzy of feeding died down, the wolves began to howl. They had eaten of human flesh, but they had absorbed something more also. In their howls was something not quite wolf-like. There were words in their baying, something human, some form of communication amongst themselves. They were now more than wolves, for they had taken up some of the nature of the human they had devoured, and the touch of a god was upon them.

Horta looked at their eyes, and he saw that the amber they should have been had a tinge of blue. Like Asaba's had been. And they returned his gaze as though they knew who he was and what he had done. One of them, the leader no doubt, had the touch of the god more heavily upon him. His eyes were completely blue, and a fierce intelligence shone in them.

Then, as though each wolf caught the same scent of prey simultaneously, they turned as one and padded away into the woods, passing out of sight.

It was silent for some moments. No one looked at what was left of Asaba, but one of the Arnhaten eventually spoke.

"What did we just witness?" he asked.

"The power of a god," Horta replied. "And the beginning of a hunt that will end with the death of Brand."

6. The Touch of Magic

The two riders headed toward Brand, and he watched them carefully. It paid to be cautious in the wild.

They came closer, and he knew beyond doubt who they were. One was a short man, but he would stand tall beside any hero of the land, past or present. He was boisterous, swift to speak his mind and too fond of wine and gambling. Brand liked him anyway.

The other was taller, green-eyed and with pale, slightly freckled skin. He rode like a king, though there was hardly a drop of aristocratic blood in him. When he spoke, it was quietly. He rarely offered opinions, but when he did, Brand listened. He was a man to listen to, and he had served his land with the same courage as the other, could stand beside any hero of the ages.

And they were his friends. His sword brothers. No two men were ever more different, and no man had ever had better friends.

They pulled their horses up when they reached him, and they looked him over.

"I'd hate to see the other man," the first said.

"You'd hate to fight him too, Shorty. But he's not of concern any longer."

The second man raised an eyebrow. "You fought him hand to hand by the looks of it. Why? The sword is your best weapon."

"Yes, well, I didn't really want to kill him. Though he deserved it. And it's nice to see you too, Taingern."

The other man bowed his head slightly, but it did not stop him raising his other eyebrow.

"None of it matters now, my friends. What's done is done, and the future lies ahead of us."

"Right now," Shorty said, "the future holds a warm campfire and some hot food. At least, that's the one I'm looking forward to."

"Then let's start," Brand said. "This is as good a place to camp as we'll likely find before nightfall."

His two friends grew uneasy. "Not here," Taingern said.

"Definitely not here," Shorty agreed. "Not in the open. We've found a better place, not too far away. It's a small cave at the side of a low hill."

Brand's instincts suddenly flared to life. There was something out of place, here.

"What's wrong with camping in the open? Outlaws?"

"Let's talk as we ride," Taingern suggested. "It's growing dark quickly, and the cave is a little way off."

They nudged their mounts into a trot, and Brand followed them. These were men who knew what they were about, and if they wanted to camp in the cave then the cave it was.

Shorty let his mount fall in close beside Brand's. "We're just being careful. You warned us about the outlaws, though as yet we've seen no sign of them. But there are other things in this land. There are … wolves."

Brand was surprised. "There have always been wolves here. Same as back in Cardoroth. In neither place do they attack people."

Shorty grunted. "So I've always believed. But the wolves of the Duthgar are different, or else they've changed since last you were here. These ones might."

Brand was worried. These were not the sort of men who would be scared of wolves, either four or two legged. But neither of his friends seemed talkative, and he guessed that they were intent on getting to the cave. He would find out more when they reached it and had set up their camp for the night.

The three of them rode across the green grass of the hillsides as the light of the sun faded and night seeped over the land around them. The stars kindled in the sky and the air turned chilly. It was spring, but summer still seemed far away.

It was not long before they came to the cave. It was not a hidden entrance, but it was narrow and easily defendable by even one person. Brand approved of it as a place to hold against an enemy, and he wondered how different he would be if he had not been forced all his life to make such considerations. He could not guess, for that was all he had ever known.

The cave was more spacious inside. With difficulty, they led the horses in and tethered them to rocks on the back wall. After rubbing them down and giving them grain, they started a fire in the center of the floor. Shorty and Taingern had previously gathered dry timber for it. Rocks were positioned here in a circle, and they were blackened. This was a place used many times over the years, but most recently the occupants were likely to have been outlaws. This did not concern Brand overly, but his companion's reticence to speak of the wolves disturbed him.

When they had got the fire going to a point that they could separate away some embers and commence cooking a stew of meat and vegetables, Brand broached the subject as they sat around the warming flames.

"Tell me about the wolves," he asked.

There was silence for a moment, and his two companions exchanged glances. It was Shorty who answered though.

"You'll hear for yourself, soon enough. It started last night about this time. There was a great howling, but not from a pack together. They were all spread out, as though searching for something."

"And what else?" Brand prompted.

Taingern answered him this time. "They sounded like wolves, but not quite. If I did not know better, I would have said that it was men imitating wolves. There were words within the howls…"

"Outlaws, perhaps?"

"We don't think so," Shorty said. "We spoke with a wandering tinker also. He was scared out of his mind. Said that he'd seen a wolf with blue eyes, and that it spoke to him."

"What did it say?" Brand asked a little flippantly.

Shorty grunted. "Joke about it if you want, but you'll see."

"So you believed the tinker?"

"I believe *he* believed it."

Brand looked over at Taingern. "What do *you* say?"

"I wasn't there. The tinker was. And I have no reason to disbelieve him."

Brand thought about it. The news was disturbing to say the least. But he saw no direct threat, and Unferth possessed no magic nor was in league with a sorcerer. At least, he had never heard so.

"Well, this cave is a good place to camp. And if there's trouble, we're prepared for it."

The two men seemed relieved that he took the situation seriously.

"Speaking of trouble," Taingern said. "If it comes, you will want these."

He rose and went to the horses. When he returned, he held two objects out to Brand. One was a helm, the fabled Helm of the Duthenor that had long belonged to Brand's family. And the other a white oaken staff. These were objects of power, objects that he was known to carry and that the soldiers at the crossing would have been looking for. Shorty and Taingern had offered to take them across themselves, and they had gone separately. That way they had avoided recognition.

Brand took them. "Thank you. Had I been carrying these at the crossing, there would have been trouble. I was nearly recognized anyway."

Taingern fed the fire another dry branch. "Unferth is looking for you. He knows you're coming, and he's worried. There will be other men in other places too, and your return to the Duthgar will be noticed quickly."

Brand knew it was true. What he was going to attempt was risky, and he had none of the resources he had enjoyed in Cardoroth. But that was not his home. His exile there had served its purpose, more than its purpose. It had originally been just a place to live, free of assassination attempts, but it had become so much more. First a soldier, then a captain, then bodyguard to the king himself. Then regent for the crown prince until he came of age.

He could have made himself king, had he wanted to. King of a realm far, far greater than the Duthgar. Yet that was not what he wanted, nor would he have displaced the rightful heir. But he missed the resources at his command. With the army of Cardoroth, he could have swept through and deposed Unferth in just a few days. It was not Cardoroth's war though, and he was no longer regent. That part of his life was over, and he must start anew.

Shorty gave the stew a stir. The smell of it gave Brand hunger pangs. It had been a long while since lunch.

"What now?" Shorty asked. "As Taingern says, your coming will be marked soon."

It was true, and Brand knew it. "I can't remain hidden, and I can't achieve my aims by trying to hide. So, the best way forward is the opposite of hiding. I'll make my presence known quickly, spread word, and build an army."

Neither of his two friends seemed surprised. They would have given the question thought themselves, and probably arrived at the same answers.

"And how will you gather an army?" Shorty asked.

Brand placed the Helm of the Duthenor upon his head. To his people it served the function of a crown. Long ago it had been won by one of his ancestors through the performance of an act of high courage. The immortal Halathrin had given it to him, and it was crafted with their skill and their magic. It was worth more than all the gold in the Duthgar, but to the Duthenor it was a symbol, a talisman of everything that they were or yet could be.

"I'm the rightful chieftain, or king as Unferth now styles himself. And the Duthenor, I think, will rally to me. Slowly at first, and then swiftly as word spreads."

Taingern looked thoughtful. "It may well be as you say, but Unferth will not stand by idly while you gather an army."

"True. But the philosophy of a warrior is to turn your enemy's strengths into weaknesses. I'll send him a message, one that despite all the advantages he holds will cause him anxiety and increase the fear that's gnawed at him all these years. In this way, I may prompt him to act hastily, or do the opposite of what he should in a show of pride to prove that he's *not* anxious."

"A dangerous path to tread," Shorty said. "It may cause him to come against you with all he has and try to crush you before you even begin."

Brand shrugged. "That's possible too. All life is a risk, is it not? Nothing is certain."

They offered no answer to that, nor gave any advice. They knew the risks as well as he, and if they had a better plan, they would have suggested it. But good plans or bad, they would stick with him anyway. They were the best of friends, and danger was no deterrent to them.

The stew was ready, and Brand dished it out to them on wooden platters with a chunk of old bread each. He had rarely tasted anything better, but hunger was the cause of that rather than the food itself.

Shorty looked over at Brand while they ate. "You could have stayed in Cardoroth, had you wanted to. You may have stepped down as regent … but afterward you could have done anything. You have wealth, lands and business interests there. You could go back still, if you wanted to. Are you sure you want to go ahead with things here?"

"You mean why do I want to come to this backward and forsaken part of the world to risk my life?"

"That's what I just said," Shorty grinned at him.

"Because it's home. My heart is here, and it always was. And my people need me."

"All true," Shorty agreed. "But you left Arell behind as well."

Brand gazed into the fire. No matter what he did, he could not please everyone, least of all himself. He had no wish to be separated from Arell, and he felt a void in his life without her.

"She wasn't happy at my going, but she understood. More or less. She offered to come with me, you know. But the sick and injured of Cardoroth need her. Her fame as a healer continues to grow. Now, it's not just the ill who come to see her but other healers also, from all over Cardoroth. They want to learn from her. That's where she belongs, doing the work she's good at."

They fell silent as they finished their meal. The cave was getting darker as the fire died down, and the air was full of smoke. It hung heavy just below the roof, but there must have been cracks there that slowly let it out too. It was into that quiet that the first howling of a wolf came, and it sent shivers up Brand's spine.

The call was taken up by a second, and then a third. In moments the whole pack voiced their beastly yowling, yet they were spread out over the land and not in one place. Brand sensed that they hunted something, sought for some trail. But it was not game they were after. It was him. He knew it with certainty, just as he sensed the touch of magic also. There may have been words in the eerie sound as his friends had suggested. These were wolves, but magic infused them and gave them life and purpose. But it was magic of a kind that he had never felt before.

The three men looked at each other in silence. The howling faded away, and the silence after was alive with menace. Brand was glad to be in the cave, and he added more timber to the fire.

A long while they waited, but there was no further sound. The pack had moved their hunt elsewhere, for the moment.

"It will be a long night," Brand said.

His two friends nodded grimly in the flickering light of the fire, and they also added more wood to the hungry flames. There was enough to last through the night, though whether these wolves would be scared of fire was another matter.

They did not set a watch. But they slept on the other side of the fire, keeping it between themselves and the entrance. The horses would give alarm if they scented a wolf approach, and Brand trusted his instincts to wake him if something was wrong.

The night passed. The men slept. The fire died down, and the smoke in the cave swirled in slow eddies, gradually escaping through the cracks above.

When at last something woke Brand, it was dawn. There was light in the cave, but it was more from the slanting rays of the sun than the near-dead fire. And in the cave entrance a figure moved, but Brand could not see it clearly for the light of the new day streamed in around it.

Brand leaped to his feet, sword in hand. Taingern and Shorty, woken by the sudden movement and sound, did likewise a few moments later.

7. Deep and Dark

Brand felt the weight of his sword balanced smoothly in his hand, the instincts of a warrior lending his slightest motion deadly grace. Yet he remained near still, and his other talent, magic, surfaced. It told him that something of great power was before him, something as deadly dangerous as ever had lived in Alithoras.

It was no wolf though. The figure was that of a man. And a tall man at that. A sense of recognition began to infuse him, but he did not lower his sword.

"Hail, Brand of the Duthenor. Warrior that was. Regent that was. Lòhren to be. Greetings, and well met."

Brand knew that voice. He lowered his sword, but did not sheath it. He still could not see the figure clearly. But the man sensed his uncertainty. Slowly, so as not to cause fear, he moved into the cave.

He was a tall man, white-robed and silver-haired. He was old as the hills, yet his face had a perfect complexion. His eyes missed nothing, seeing right through whatever they saw, weighing and assessing, finding the measure of every man and every situation in a glance. Yet they were eyes that had seen terrible tragedies, and sorrow and compassion lay behind them.

Brand let out a long breath and sheathed his sword. "Hail, Aranloth. The days have been long since last we met."

It was a formal greeting, but Aranloth was not just any man. He was greater than kings, more powerful than armies, deadly as an enemy but the greatest of friends to those in need.

Aranloth grinned at him. "It's good to see you."

"And you, too. Much has happened since we spoke last, but it seems that you're well informed of events."

The old man walked further into the cave. "I hear much. The land tells me what I need to know. Sooner or later, one way or another."

Shorty and Taingern sheathed their swords as well. The old man turned to them. "I should have expected as much. You two are never far from Brand. Or he is never far from you. And just as well. Trouble has a way of finding you all."

They shook his hand, and Brand did as well. His grip was strong as steel sheathed in silk.

"Speaking of finding things, how did you find *us*?" Brand asked.

"Ah, well, that's interesting. I didn't find you. I wasn't looking for you and this is a chance meeting, although there are some who don't believe in chance. I was just passing through, and I sensed the wolves. I knew they were hunting something, and I put them off the trail."

Shorty and Taingern exchanged a look. "We thought it strange that we only heard them howl once last night."

Aranloth looked thoughtful. "There's much about this whole thing that's strange, the wolves especially. They're more than wolves, and the shadow of dark magic is upon them. That was what raised my curiosity. Who were they hunting? For if the hunters were so unusual, so too must be the quarry."

"Well," Brand said, "no one has ever accused me of being normal, so the wolves are after me." He had felt that last night, and nothing had happened to change his mind.

"No, you've never quite been normal. Not since the day we first met," Aranloth said. "You draw trouble to you like no man I've ever seen. And the trouble of the wolves is not over. I put them off the trail, but that won't last long. You must be wary of them, for they'll find you soon."

Brand knew it was so, but he was not looking forward to it. He trusted in his skill as a warrior, and the sword he carried. He trusted less in the magic he possessed, but he might need it against the wolves. He retrieved the oaken staff he had long carried, and handed it to Aranloth.

"This is yours," he said, "and I thank you for the lending of it."

Aranloth looked at him keenly. "You have the magic. The staff is an aid to that. But it's more. It's a symbol of being a lòhren, a wizard as we're known here in the Duthgar. Do you seek to escape that fate, to be seen just as a warrior? Is that why you offer me my staff back?"

Aranloth always knew. Those eyes of his missed nothing, and his sharp mind even less. In truth, some of what he said was correct. Brand had no wish to be a lòhren. Yet he had accepted it was so, whether he wished for it or not. But he would be lying to himself if he did not admit that a part of him, now coming home to the Duthgar, did not want to reclaim his old life.

"I offer it back simply because it's yours. And I understand better what it is, and what it represents, better than I did when you first lent it to me. A staff is earned by a lòhren, given to him at a time of need by the land itself. That's how the magic works. And this staff isn't mine."

Aranloth reached out, and slowly he took the staff. Brand saw relief on his face, for it truly *was* the lòhren's, linked to him by magic. But he saw worry also.

"I don't doubt that you're a lòhren," Aranloth said. "Yet I find it strange that you've not found your own staff yet. One way or another, and each of us in a different way, a lòhren discovers his staff. The land itself sees to that, the land which we serve and protect."

"Maybe it will not be so with me," Brand said.

"It is *always* so. Yet, perhaps, it will be different for you. Time will tell."

Aranloth gripped the staff and ran his hands over it. "Truly, it's good to have this back. I've had it a *very* long time. It may even be that while you carried this, you could not find your own true staff. Perhaps. The ways of the future are often unseen, and even when we plan them out ahead with precision, thinking to leave nothing to chance, yet still things turn out quite differently than we expect."

The lòhren's sharp eyes fixed him for a moment, and Brand knew there was a warning in his words. But then he seemed uncertain, which was not like him at all. He gave a slight shrug, as if to himself, and then spoke again.

"It may be, in this case, that your duties as heir to the chieftainship of this land and as a lòhren are one. For while a chieftain or a king must first think of his own people, a lòhren must think of *all* the land. The two concerns rarely match. Yet, just now, in this time and place, they may for you."

Brand did not quite like that. The words signified that there was more going on than what he had thought. It tied in with the wolves. Magic was at play, and forces that he did not yet know or understand.

"What do you think is happening?" he asked Aranloth.

The lòhren pursed his lips. Another sign of uncertainty that he rarely showed.

"I don't know. But I have seen things, heard words in the wind and seen messages in the starry sky. The earth murmurs of it in the quiet of the night, and birds of the field call it out in flight. It is there, and yet not there. Call it intuition, if you like. Perhaps even imagination. But I have listened to the land for years beyond count, and know its ways. Something stirs."

Brand knew it was more than imagination. He had felt it with the wolves. There was a power abroad of which he knew nothing, except that it existed.

"What do you think it is?"

Aranloth leaned on his staff. "Trouble. That's what it is. And it's old, old and patient and wise in the ways of evil. Men will serve it, wittingly or unwittingly. Sorcery is at its heart, deep and dark. A power is waking, or being woken, that has long slumbered. Almost I recognize it, but not quite. It has the feel of something that long ago I knew, but it cannot be that."

"I'll watch for it," Brand said.

The lòhren straightened. "It watches for *you*. That much is certain. Who sent the wolves? And why? When you discover that you'll have found the power that stirs to life in the Duthgar, or whoever seeks to wake it. And whoever, or whatever, aids Unferth. For in this the enemy who you know, and the one which is hidden, are working together for a common purpose."

Brand felt a shiver work its way up his spine. That was all he needed. Two enemies when he thought to confront only one.

The lòhren seemed to sense his thoughts. "Worse, I'm not able to stay and help. I'm needed in the south of the land … I would stay if I could, but it cannot be. And I must hasten away even now."

"I know, Aranloth. There's a dark shadow over all Alithoras, and evil stirs to life everywhere. I wish you luck."

"And luck to you also."

Aranloth studied him a moment, his eyes keen and sharp. "Be wary Brand, just now you ride the breath of the dragon."

It was a term that Brand had not heard before, and his confusion must have shown on his face.

"Forgive me!" Aranloth said. "I forget sometimes. That's an old, old saying. It means though that you ride the winds of fate."

Brand did not much believe in destiny or fate, but he knew the power of being in the right place at the right time. He felt that he was *meant* to return to the Duthgar just now.

"I know what you mean. There's a sense of fittingness to what's happening. But fate, if there's such a thing, is a two-edged sword."

"Indeed it is. When the dragon's breath falters, and it never lasts forever, you could end up in serious trouble."

They clasped hands, and Brand sensed the good wishes of the lòhren wash over him almost like a blessing. He truly would stay if he could, for he held grave fears for the Duthgar. The wolves had disturbed him more than he had said aloud.

"Take care, old man," Brand said.

Aranloth grinned at him. "You too, boy. And if you do, you might just live to be my age."

He glanced at Shorty and Taingern. "Be careful lads. The Duthgar isn't like Cardoroth, but it's just as dangerous. More so now, for something is coming after Brand. And if you're with him, that means it'll be coming after you too."

Shorty grinned. "We're an army of three. We'll teach it to fear us instead."

"Let it be so! And farewell!"

The lòhren glanced once more at Brand. "Remember, you begin a battle now against Unferth. But there's another player to this game, greater and more dangerous. Beware of him." Then he turned and left.

Brand was sorry to see him go. He was not just a lòhren, but the *leader* of the lòhrens. But what would be would be. And whoever this other player was would be revealed. In time.

8. Eye of the Eagle

The morning passed swiftly, and Brand and his companions made good time. The hilly country did not hinder them greatly. Each slope they climbed had as its opposite a downhill incline. What they lost on the first, they mostly made up on the second.

It was a wild land, and beautiful to Brand's eye. But he was born in the Duthgar. Taingern and Shorty looked around them, thinking the hills unfit for all but sheep. It was certainly true that it was good sheep country, as was most of the Duthgar, but the soil was more fertile than it looked. When cultivated, it produced good crops, and there was water to be found, sweet and good to drink for those who dug wells.

There was evidence of farming about them too. Here and there were patches of land that once had been ploughed. Remnants of small orchards survived. Now and then, there was even an old cottage to be seen, though long abandoned.

"Why did the people leave here?" Taingern asked.

Brand sighed. "There was war. The Duthenor have many rivals, for there are quite a few tribes covering this region of Alithoras, shifting back and forth with the ebb and flow of food, famine and politics. We are all closely related, but we fight amongst ourselves. Some hundred years before I was born the Duthenor were attacked. We held the Duthgar, but it cost many lives. There are other regions such as this, where the people left were too few to farm it. They died out. And the Duthgar was only beginning to recover when Unferth usurped the chieftainship. He was chieftain of a neighboring tribe. So far as I know, he remains so. Perhaps that's why he styles himself as king now."

Shorty was in the lead, and he slowed. "It looks like here at least is one village that didn't die out."

Brand drew level with him and looked downslope toward the cluster of buildings that lay in the middle of a shallow valley. "It's small, even for a Duthenor village." He looked closer, and frowned. "But the patches of cultivation are full of weeds. They've not been ploughed since well before winter. And there are no fires from any of the chimneys."

They rode down, warily. They did not draw their swords, but each of them was ready to unsheathe their blades at a moment's notice. Brand led them, and the other two fanned out some distance behind and to either side in a staggered manner. It was standard practice when going into a dangerous situation. If there were an archer or ambush, it would make it harder to kill them all at once.

Brand studied the village as they drew close. It had the feel of something abandoned, and he did not sense any danger. Yet something had caused the villagers to leave. Or killed them. It was not a place to take chances.

They came to the main street. It was dusty, and no weeds as yet grew in it. But the thatched houses seemed untended, and here and there were signs of fire.

Brand drew to a halt. Before one such house lay the remains of several men. They had been picked over by scavengers and the bones spread out. But there were swords too. Rusted now and pitted by weather, but that they had been drawn and used Brand did not doubt.

"Outlaws?" Taingern asked.

"Perhaps," Brand answered. "Certainly there was fighting. But whatever the cause of it, no one buried the bodies."

Shorty grunted. "Outlaws would not trouble to bury their victims."

"That may be so," Brand agreed. "Yet word would have spread, one way or another. I would expect Unferth to send soldiers to hunt the outlaws, and whether they found them or not, they would still have buried the dead."

He nudged his roan onward. There would be no one here, else the bodies would long since have been buried, and whatever danger there was had passed. He felt a sense of shock creep over him though. The Duthenor were called barbarians, but whatever crime had been committed here had gone unpunished, and that was not the Duthenor way at all.

They left the village and moved up the slope opposite. They did not look back or speak. There was nothing to be said. But leaving the village behind did not reduce Brand's unease. Had the Duthgar changed in his absence? Were the Duthenor not the people he had grown up believing they were?

The path they followed was a track, of sorts. There were signs that wagons and horses had used it, though rarely. And none recently. It led them through some timbered country, and they moved warily, watching all about them with a sense of being scrutinized back. But they neither saw nor heard another person.

Somewhat later the countryside opened up again. The trees grew sparse and the land leveled.

"There's a farm ahead," Shorty observed.

Brand had not seen it. He had been deep in thought. But looking up he noticed it straightaway, and saw also that it had the same abandoned look to it as the village. Yet there were a handful of sheep in a paddock behind the large homestead.

"There's a well there, close to the path. We might as well water the horses."

They moved along the path, well-used here for this farm had evidently once been quite large and a central gathering place for smaller farms nearby. There was a barn behind a stand of trees and stone-walled enclosures behind that separating off fields for cultivation and livestock.

Brand dismounted first. He hauled up the bucket, and tasted the water. It was cool and good to drink. The others stayed mounted, alert to the surroundings. The three of them rarely spoke of such things, but they were all careful men who thought alike and did these things by second nature. With many other men, Brand would need to give a command for a watch to be kept. Not so with them, and that was the way he liked it.

There was a wooden trough near the well, and this Brand filled again and again with the bucket. He had just brought another one to the surface when he heard a quiet warning from Taingern. He let the bucket go, and drew his sword from its sheath in one swift movement.

A man had come from the barn, and a sword was in his hand. Brand moved away from the well in case he needed room to move. Then he studied the figure as it approached. It was not a man, but a boy of perhaps fifteen summers, though large for his age.

"Be off with you!" the boy commanded. "I'll not have your type here, and if you come back again you'll end up with an arrow in your guts. That's more warning than you deserve."

Brand did not lower his sword, boy or no boy. "A strange greeting for travelers," he said. "It's been some while since last I came to the Duthgar, but it seems hospitality is not what it was."

For the first time, the boy showed signs of doubt. "It's customary for travelers to ask permission first." While he spoke his gaze flickered over the three horses and the accoutrements of the men. They were better quality than any he had ever likely seen, and a long moment his glance rested on Brand's sword.

"I apologize," Brand said, giving a slight bow but not lowering his sword nor taking his eyes off the boy. "You are correct, and we should have gone to the homestead first. Only we've passed through the village and saw that it was … empty. And we thought the same of this farm. No harm was intended."

The boy studied him, his uncertainty growing. "Then you're not outlaws?"

"Indeed not," Brand said. "Just travelers, passing through."

A few more moments the boy scrutinized them, and then he sheathed his sword. "I'm sorry then, please go ahead and use the water. You're the first people, other than outlaws, that I've seen in months. I thought you were more of them, but their kind don't apologize. Or have horses like those."

Once more the boy looked at Brand's sword, and Brand slid it back in its scabbard. At the same time, he saw Shorty and Taingern surreptitiously sheath the daggers they had drawn, ready for throwing. He was not sure if the boy noticed that. Otherwise, he had handled himself remarkably well for someone of his age.

"What's been happening around here?" Brand asked.

The boy looked grim. "There's not much to say. The outlaws rode through and killed everyone in the village. The outlying farmers thought they would be safe – farmers don't have much worth stealing – but we were wrong." He paused and gathered himself, showing little of the emotion he held in check. "They destroyed every farm in the district, so far as I can tell, including this one. I was out hunting, and when I returned … it was all over. I buried my family and I've been getting by since."

Brand looked at him, taking in his gaunt frame and threadbare clothes. He was surviving, but only just. Yet that alone was impressive. It was no easy thing to deal with such a trauma, and then go on living. Especially by yourself.

"Didn't Unferth send soldiers? Surely word must have reached other districts."

The boy spat. "Someone somewhere around here must have escaped. Unferth knows, but he does nothing. A pox upon him."

Brand felt a slow anger creep through him. Unferth was a murderer and usurper, yet still he had a duty of care as leader of the Duthenor. And he had done nothing.

The boy kicked the ground with a worn-out boot. "I'm Sighern," he said. He held out his hand and Brand took it. They shook the warrior's way, wrist to wrist.

Brand indicated his companions. "The short one is best known as Shorty. The freckled one is Taingern."

The boy shook their hands one at a time. "Taingern? That's not a Duthenor name."

"No. We're from Cardoroth. At least we two are. Our illustrious leader over there," he pointed to Brand, "is from hereabouts though."

The boy looked them over again, assessing them. "I'm sorry I took you for outlaws. You have the eye of the eagle about you, but there's a kindness to you as well."

"The eye of the eagle?" Shorty said.

"The look of a warrior," Brand said. "It's a saying around these parts."

Brand gestured to the water trough, and his two friends dismounted and watered the horses. They also filled the water bags.

"What now?" Sighern asked.

"Now we ride away. We have places to be and things to achieve."

The boy looked at him, nodding slowly. "You never said what your name was."

Brand had a feeling that question would come. The boy was not only courageous but swift of thought. And he had looked with interest at Brand's sword. He would not have seen its like before, but he would have heard stories about blades of that kind. And who they belonged to.

"I'm Brand."

Sighern eyed him again, but there was little surprise there.

"You really are, aren't you?"

"I am. Brand, son of Drunn and Brunhal, and the rightful chieftain of the Duthenor."

Sighern looked at him long and hard. "If you're Brand, who I have never seen, but of whom I have heard stories, that sword you carry will be your father's and your father's father's deep into the history and legend of our people. Let me see it again."

Shorty laughed. "I like the boy! He doesn't have much trust for strangers, and that's a good quality."

Brand lifted the sheath of his bade slightly for the boy to see. It was an ordinary scabbard such as any warrior would have. But the sword it hid was another matter. He drew the blade slowly, and the music of the steel sliding free was the hiss a warrior loved.

The blade came free, and it glittered in the sun. Halathrin wrought it was, with all the skill the immortals had acquired over long, long years of life. The blade was silver, shimmering with pattern-welding, the light shifting and swirling along its length, the edge so sharp as to nick other blades yet never blunt itself. The steel strong as an ancient oak tree, yet pliable as a whip, but for all its flexibility able to withstand the mightiest blow of any enemy.

Sighern looked at it keenly, noting its every aspect and feature. This was a sword that tales told of, that everyone in the Duthgar had heard a hundred times. And the boy knew it. Brand saw it in his eyes when he looked up from the blade.

"And the ring?" the boy asked.

Brand slid the blade back into its sheath. Then he lifted up his right hand. A ring glittered there, and a design upon it of stars gleamed. It was the twin constellation of Halathgar. "This," Brand said, "I obtained in Cardoroth in service to a great queen. It is a treasure beyond compare. But this also I hold dear, dearer even, for it is as old as the sword and has passed through the same hands, was worn by my ancestors each in their turn."

He lifted up his left hand then. Upon the index finger was a smaller ring, less well-crafted but still beautiful. It was cunningly designed so that the band of gold looked like a coiled snake that ate its own tail. Yet where head and tail met a sapphire gemstone glimmered like a winter's sky. He had hidden it in his boot at the river crossing; otherwise it would have identified him even more surely than the sword.

Brand lowered his hand. Sighern looked him in the eye, and then did something Brand had not expected.

The boy knelt on one knee, but he did not drop his gaze. And he voiced the oath of loyalty that had come down through the ages and was remembered in story and legend.

"Lord. My sword is your sword. My heart is your heart. As the great dark descends, we shall light a blaze of glory against it."

Brand could not quite believe a farm boy knew the loyalty oath, but the Duthenor were a surprising people who loved their history.

"Rise, Sighern," Brand said.

The boy stood, his gaze unwavering, and he surprised Brand again. "Take me with you."

Brand knew he should have guessed what was coming before the boy spoke. But he had not, and though he liked him he could not let him come. His two friends came up beside him, listening intently.

"You know who I am, and what therefore must come of that since I've returned to the Duthgar. Everywhere I ride now, danger will be with me. Unferth *must* stop me, and he will try his best. Everyone with me is in as great a danger. You're safer here."

Sighern shrugged. "That much I know already. But though I'm surviving here, there's no future. I'd rather take the risks with you."

Brand was impressed, but he just could not risk the boy's life. "There is another danger too. There are wolves hunting me. There's sorcery about them, and though I cannot be sure who sent them, I know they come for me, and that they will not give up. They, or whoever sent them, may be more dangerous than Unferth."

There was a look of recognition on Sighern's face. "I have heard the wolves. They passed close by last night, or some of them did. They did not sound like any I've ever heard before, and I don't doubt they hunt you. It's rumored that Unferth has a magician in his service. He must have sent them. But still, I would go with you if you will allow it. I can fight as well as a man, and I'm good with a bow. I can track, ride and swim. I'll not be a burden to you."

Brand understood what they boy wanted, and that he was willing to take risks. But he could not allow it. He spoke slowly, and reluctantly.

"I understand everything that you say. And I know you would not be a burden. But … but," he could not get the words out. When they came, they were not the one's he intended. "Very well. You may come, and may fate have mercy upon me."

The boy looked at him with excitement. "Do you mean it? Really?"

Brand did not hesitate this time. "I mean it. Quickly now, go and get whatever you would bring with you."

Sighern turned and raced away. Brand and his companions stood in silence a moment, watching him run to the homestead. Then Brand felt the gazes of his two friends turn to him.

"I like the lad," Shorty said. "He has courage. Great courage. But he's only a boy. What on earth are you thinking?"

Brand had no answer. He could have said that he had a hunch the boy would prove useful. But it would mostly be a lie.

"I just don't know. I was going to say no, but what came out was yes. I can say no more than that."

His two friends seemed puzzled, but they said nothing. Brand was puzzled too. And yet now that the decision had been made, there was a sense of rightness to it.

"It starts with one," he said. "Perhaps it always does."

"But the nation is still to come," Shorty replied.

"One such as that boy," Brand went on, "has the heart of an army all by himself."

Shorty sighed. "But not the swords."

"No, not the swords. But they will come too."

Sighern came out of the homestead. One moment he turned back and looked at it, then his gaze swept over the farm. And then he was jogging toward them, his sword dangling at his side and a hessian sack in his hands. No doubt it contained a few treasured items, a change of clothes and some food.

Brand and the others mounted. "Stash your things in the saddle bag, and then you can get up behind me," Brand said when the boy reached them.

Sighern did as asked and then climbed up awkwardly behind Brand. "You'll not regret this. I promise."

"Perhaps not. But you might yet. I wasn't lying about the dangers we face."

"I know. But better them than staying here."

Brand nudged the roan forward and his two friends did likewise. They were on the road again, and soon they followed it up slope and toward the crest of the next hill. When they reached it, Brand felt the boy turn for one last look at his home. And then they slipped down the other side and the farm was out of sight.

They moved through the countryside, and it felt strange to Brand. There were more farms, but there was no sign of people. Sighern seemed to be the only survivor of the outlaw raids. But there must have been others too, if not many.

Passing another homestead, Brand turned his head to speak to the boy. "Did Unferth truly do nothing?"

"Nothing at all," Sighern said. "And the raids were carried out over a few weeks. There was time for him to act, had he chosen. The rumor was that he sent the raiders himself. It's said that he's short of coin, and certainly taxes have been going up."

Brand let it go. There was nothing he could do now to help the people of this district. All he could do was work to ensure others did not suffer the same fate.

They crested yet another hill, and the farming lands were behind them once more. Ahead, the countryside was ungrazed by livestock. It was uncleared also, and the track continued through a patchwork of woods and scrubby hillsides. The sun was lowering, and midafternoon lay dozily upon the land. But a sound rose far behind them that sent chills up their spines and destroyed any thought of rest. Wolves. Howling wolves.

Brand drew his mount to a stop and looked behind him, but there was nothing to see.

"Some have our fresh scent," Taingern said calmly. "And they gather the pack to them."

Brand thought he was right. He looked back at Sighern. "I'm not familiar with this part of the Duthgar. How far is it to the nearest lord's hall?"

"Not far," the boy said. "A day's ride from here."

Brand refrained from cursing. "That's going to be further than you think, with the wolves behind us. This may be your last chance, Sighern. You can leave now if you want. The wolves are after me and will follow where I ride."

The boy shook his head. "No. I'm coming with you."

Brand grinned at him. "Then it will be a ride such as you won't ever forget. And let us hope there are good men at the hall."

"There are," Sighern answered. "It's Galdring's hall, but it's small with few men."

Brand thought he recognized the name. "Is he the son of Baldring?"

"That's him."

"Then let us hope the son is as loyal as the father was."

Brand waited for no answer. He nudged his mount into a canter with the others and they began to ride. It was not as swift as he would like, but they had to preserve the horses. They would be riding through the whole night.

Behind them, once more, the howling pierced the quiet afternoon. This time it appeared to be split up, with the chase fanning out to left and right behind them. No sound came from ahead, but that did not mean there were not wolves there also. Wolves were known to herd their prey into a trap, and these wolves were smarter than most. Brand was sure of that.

"Can the horses run all night?" Sighern called out from behind him.

"They're fine animals, but they'll need to be rested at times too. We shall see."

9. A Long Night

Brand led the way as the small group of riders cantered through the night. It was difficult going, for the dark created dangers. A horse could kill itself, and its rider, by placing a hoof in an unseen hollow. Yet the track remained clear and free of obstacles, so far as Brand could tell, and the risk was necessary.

The wolves continued their hunt. Fanned out behind the riders they gave vent to their eerie howls from time to time, and each time it seemed a little closer.

"They grow more eager!" Taingern called as they rode.

Brand sensed it also. The wolves had their scent, and knew their quarry was on the run. This caused them to chase harder, and excitement was in their howls that bordered on frenzy. Something other than hunger drove them, and Brand knew what it was. Sorcery. It explained something else too. Wolves on the hunt did not howl. These wolves were different. They were sure of bringing their quarry to bay, and the purpose of the howling was to instill fear.

The track took them into higher ground. Behind, the land was wrapped in the shadows of night, and the patches of woodland were darker still. And those patches grew increasingly thick. It was a long way from civilization, from help of any kind.

Despite the gathering pursuit, Brand took good care of the horses. Every hour he signaled the riders to dismount and lead the animals by foot. Then they were rested briefly. He knew the wolves took no such rest, yet the horses might need speed at the end. A horse could outrun a wolf, but not for long. But at the end of the pursuit that could mean the difference between life and death.

They rode in this fashion until the middle of the night had come and gone. Ever the wolves gained on them, until at last the howling seemed just behind and grew in such frenzy that Brand feared the wolves might have even sighted them.

"Ride!" he called, and finally he led the others into a gallop. The horses needed little urging. Fear was on them now, and this lent them strength and speed even after their many hours of cantering. But it could not last.

They rushed through the night. The sound of the hooves of the horses was as thunder in Brand's ears and the wind of their passage whipped at him. On they went, and the wolves came after them.

It was a race, and the prize was life. The muscle, bones and will of the horses was pitted against that of the wolves. The horses strained, sweat foaming at their sides, and the wolves fell away. But already the horses began to tire, and Brand's most of all for two riders weighed it down.

"How far away is the hall?" Brand asked.

Sighern thought for a moment. "It's hard to tell in the dark, and I've been this way only twice. But it's at least an hour away, probably more."

Brand looked around. There was no lightening of the sky in the east yet. Dawn was still some way off, and he did not think that light would hinder the wolves. It would make them easier to fight, though.

"We'll not get to the hall in time," Brand called to the others. "Look for a good place to make a stand."

They rode on, the flanks of the horses white with sweat and their pace slowing. All about them was forest. It was dark and grim and filled with fear. The wolves had not given up the chase. They would never give up, for sorcery drove them. He sensed frustration in their occasional howls, and though they had fallen back it was not by far. Even now they were gaining ground as the horses slowed.

"There!" cried Shorty.

Brand saw straightaway the spot his friend had meant. He had been looking to the left where the forest had grown thick, but to the right there was a steep bank, almost a cliff. The ground before it was clear of trees, and the wall of dirt and rock rose at least fifteen feet high. The wolves could not come at them from that side. It was the best defense they would find.

They drew the straining horses in and dismounted. Swiftly they drove in their picket stakes and tied the horses up. If the men were killed, the horses would die also, there would be no escape from the wolves. But Brand did not intend to die. Not if he could help it.

"Keep watch," Brand told the boy. "Yell if you see anything."

He did not wait for an answer but signaled Shorty and Taingern to him. "We need wood for a fire."

They ran across the track and into the forest on the other side. There they quickly gathered some fallen branches and old pine cones lying on the ground. The wolves were close now, the howling filling the night all around them.

They ran back. Sighern had realized what they were doing and drawn a flint from his few possessions. Even as they dropped the branches and cones into a pile on the ground he was kneeling and striking sparks. His hands trembled, and he tried again and again but at last one of the cones caught fire and a curl of smoke rose in the air, fueled by a tiny flame that grew and then, slowly, began to spread.

The cone began to blaze, and they each grabbed other cones and held them to the first. When they caught, they spread them through the pile of branches. The fire took, growing rapidly.

In its flickering light they drew their blades. It was none too soon.

"There!" yelled Taingern. The others looked where he pointed. Along the track they had just ridden themselves, some gray shadows loped toward them. The wolves drew up and stopped before they came into the light of the fire.

"Over there too!" Sighern said. There were wolves now in the timber across the path where they had gathered their firewood.

"Well, Sighern," Brand said. "Do you regret coming with us now?"

Before the boy could answer some of the wolves on the track leaped forward. They crossed the ground swiftly, all bristling fur, snarling lips and white fangs. The men stood in front of the shying horses, and Brand stepped before Sighern. They faced the left, toward the wolves, but these wheeled away as the ones in the forest leaped in to attack instead. It had been a distraction, and Brand realized these wolves were intelligent. Unnaturally so.

Yet the men were not caught by surprise. Shorty guarded their left flank, Taingern the right. And Brand held the middle. The main attack came against him.

The blade of his forefathers swept in shining arcs through the night. Blood spurted. Wolves yelped in pain. Animals fell dead. To either side Shorty and Taingern fended off attacks. But again and again the wolves came for Brand. They crawled and bit and scrambled over each other to reach him. And died.

Yet one slipped through, leaping high for his neck while his blade swept low. The creature smashed into him, knocking him back. Even as he fell he twisted so that his neck avoided snapping jaws. Then he crashed into the ground.

The wolves swarmed over him, but even as they snarled in fury, Sighern loosed a battle cry. "For the Duthgar!" he yelled, and his sword cut and chopped.

The boy now stood before Brand, protecting him from death. Yet he was not skilled with the sword and the wolves gathered to him. One clamped its jaws to his left leg, and another, though its neck streamed blood from a previous blow, bit down at his sword arm.

But Brand was up again, his glittering sword in his right hand and a burning branch in his left. This he thrust into the face of the wolf that hung on Sighern's arm. Taingern impaled the animal attacking the boy's leg.

Swift as the attack began, it ended. The wolves loped back into the rim of firelight, and there they padded in agitation. Some whined with pain. Others barked and yelped. And one, blue-eyed and calm, stood motionless in their midst.

"They will come again," Shorty warned.

Brand summoned his magic. It came to life within him, woke from the dormancy of his everyday life. He sent out faint tendrils toward the wolves.

He sensed some of the dark sorcery that went into their making. He became connected to them, and merged his mind into the magic that gave them purpose. It was a strange feeling to him, for this was a power beyond his experience. It did not have the feel of anything that he knew.

And then he sensed another presence. His enemy was connected to the wolves also. He who had made them of dark sorcery and horror was within their minds, was looking out through their eyes.

Brand softly withdrew. It would be best, if they were able, to fight these creatures with swords alone. He did not want to reveal his own power just yet. It would give his enemy a measure of him. Better to keep that a surprise for when it was needed later.

The wolves rushed in to attack once more. Snarling filled the night and gray shapes hurtled through the dark. Swift steel met them.

With the wolves came a wave of hatred, for the magic that made them drove them on against blades, against the certainty of death. The creatures knew what swords could do, knew the skill of the men who wielded them, and they came on anyway, unable to stop themselves. Brand felt sorry for them even as his sword rose and fell.

The bodies of the dead animals piled up. Ever the blue-eyed wolf was in the thick of the attack, but ever it evaded the fate of its packmates. Yet like a wave that spent itself against a rocky shore, the attack lost force and dwindled.

But this only drove the remaining wolves into a greater frenzy. One leaped high and crashed into Brand. He staggered back, then surged forward flinging the snarling animal back into the pack. He felt blood wet his shoulder and a slow throb began.

Sighern now fought to his right, unwilling to be protected, and though unskilled his sword swept among the pack with speed and strength. But one of the wolves slipped through his defenses and tore at his hip with wicked fangs. The boy fell, but Brand turned and his sword flashed, the Halathrin steel hewing the head from the beast in a single cut.

The boy struggled up. Taingern killed another that leaped for him while Sighern did not have his blade up. He swayed where he stood, blood coloring the right side of his trousers.

But even as the men stood, their swords weaving through the air ready to defend, they realized all the wolves were dead. All, bar one. Before them crouched the blue-eyed leader, snarling and growling, the lips of its muzzle pulled back horribly and blood welling from a sword slash to its chest.

Brand faced it. "Die, shadow spawn," he muttered. Then he stepped forward to attack.

But the wolf growled back at him, and there were words in its snarling voice.

"Die yourself!" And it rushed at him.

Brand was so taken by surprise that the wolf was able to crowd him, ducking under a weak sword blow and fixing its jaws to his leg. The leg gave way beneath him and he fell, exposing his throat. The wolf released the grip on his leg and pounced in for a killing snap of its jaws.

But Brand was swifter. His sword came up, tearing through fur and skin, and driven by the leaping weight of the creature, it slid through its belly, disemboweling it. Still it struggled to reach his neck, but Sighern kicked it away and Brand's sword flashed again, this time severing an artery in its neck.

The creature lay there, panting. Blood bubbled from its throat, and the pale eyes fixed on him until life faded out of them.

"Well done, lad," Brand said to Sighern.

The boy flashed him a grin, but Brand saw the blood on his trousers and knew he was wounded. They all were.

Brand set Taingern to watch in case there were more wolves, and while he did so the other two tended to each other's wounds, washing them first with water and then applying a salve and bandages. Then Shorty watched while Brand looked after a wound on Taingern's sword arm.

"A nasty fight," the freckled man said, indifferent to the pain the salve caused as Brand applied it to the jagged rent in his skin.

Brand worked quickly, one eye watching the shadows beyond the reach of the fire's light.

"They all are. But I fear there are worse fights to come."

After that they watched the dark for a little while, and Sighern moved back to pat the horses and calm them.

"The boy surely has guts," Shorty said quietly.

Brand nodded. Twice Sighern had helped him, and he may have died without that aid. It was a debt that he owed, but it puzzled him too. Few boys not yet full grown would willingly place themselves in such danger. Brand would not forget it. But where did such courage come from?

The forest was now silent about them. Nothing stirred. But Brand did not trust it. Perhaps all the wolves were dead, but what else may yet be sent against them?

The fire was dying down, but they dared not risk leaving the light nor the cover of the cliff face to gather more wood. Brand glanced at it, careful not to look directly into the flames and destroy his night vision. It would last until dawn. Just.

And dawn was not far off. They sat down and waited for it, but they did not sheathe their swords. No one was willing to risk sleep, even if they could so soon after an attack such as they had endured.

They spoke no more than a few hushed words now and then, and no one mentioned the blue-eyed wolf. But Brand thought about it. Sorcery had been invoked of the darkest kind, and he wondered what power his enemy had. Whoever it was must be someone of enormous skill. And also someone willing to do whatever it took to obtain their goals. It was a dangerous combination.

The forest lightened. Dawn came, and with it a growing sense of unease. The long night might be over, but a new day with new dangers was beginning.

They ate a cold breakfast of stale bread and cheese, unwilling to waste time cooking anything. All they wished was to leave their camp, where the bodies of the dead wolves lay nearby and the memory of a bad night was strong. And all the while Brand's sense of unease grew.

They removed the picket stakes and mounted. At last they were leaving, and they nudged the horses out onto the track. The sun was well up now, but even as they began to ride they stopped. A little way ahead of them a strange figure walked the dusty path directly toward them.

10. The Noblest of Tasks

Horta stirred from his trance, the shadow of death upon him.

He had broken the link with the last wolf, knowing even as it leaped that it must die. He had no wish to experience what that felt like. Not again. One of his master's had made him do so, repeatedly. It was supposed to inure him against the fear of dying. Perhaps it did, although that master certainly had fear in his eyes when at last Horta had learned all he could teach, and killed him.

The fire in the hearth popped, and a plume of smoke swirled upward. Horta felt the warmth of the flames, and eased back a little in his chair. He was alone in the small cottage set aside for him by the king. It was away from the village, surrounded by pastureland and sheep. The Arnhaten dwelt close to the king's hall, working in the village to support their keep. He did not miss them. The peacefulness of this place was near to the quiet of the desert wastes of his youth. Only the constant bleating of the sheep marred it.

Brand had surprised him. He had lived. So too his companions. It was worrisome, for the magic had been potent, and the wolves, though not powerful, were smart. Most of all, they were driven by the touch of the god. They attacked relentlessly, and that should have seen them overpower the men, no matter that all the pack died to accomplish it.

But the men were skilled. They fled when that was the best course of action, and fought when they had to. They did neither with fear, or anger or uncertainty. Each step they took was measured and spoke of confidence. They were men who had endured great dangers in the past, and learned from it. But this much he had known already.

He must learn more. He knew also that Brand possessed magic himself, though he had not been forced to summon it. What was it like? What powers did he have? This must be discovered. Brand intrigued him, and he must learn more of him. In that way he would ensure the next attack was successful.

He made a decision. Knowledge was the root of effective action, and he must discover more of his enemy. He withdrew a norhanu leaf from one of his pouches and reluctantly placed it under his tongue. The taste was bitter, but the effect was swift. Within minutes the color of the fire in the hearth changed, becoming red, and the air about him swirled and shimmered with shadowy shapes. This, he knew, was illusion. Yet it was but the first step to what he must do.

The air grew cold. He was unsure if this were the hated climate of the Duthgar or the effect of the leaf. Each time he took it the effects were different. He stoked the fire anyway, and then sat back again to wait.

The trance state crept upon him, yet a part of his mind remained lucid. This part he brought to the fore. Others would succumb to the drug, but long years of hard training gave him some control. He began to chant, no more than a mutter let loose in the smoke-hazed room, but it would be enough to invoke aid again.

He called upon the gods once more, yet this time he specifically spoke the name of one that would best suit his need: the falcon god of the flat deserts.

"O mighty Har-falach, hear me. I have need of thy aid. Hear me, and answer my humble call."

The room grew colder. The red flame in the hearth dimmed, and the bleating of the sheep faded from his mind.

A second time he called, but now he withdrew a tiny statuette from a pouch. It was made of a dull stone, highly polished and smooth to touch. It was an ancient thing, fashioned to resemble a man with angled wings and the head of a hawk.

"Hear me, O mighty one. Hear me, winged messenger of the gods. I call upon thee for aid."

The fire snuffed out. The room grew black as the tomb. Fear stabbed Horta's heart, for he felt a presence with him and thought he sensed the movement of air above.

"I beseech thee, Ruler of the Skies. Take my mind where I wish. Let me sit here, yet also walk in another place. Show me my enemies that I may know them. Lend my thought wings."

The room began to spin. Nausea gripped Horta, and a rushing filled his ears. Then it seemed to him that he fell from a great height. Blinding light stabbed like a thousand knives into his watering eyes. For some moments he was blinded, and then he began to see.

He stood upon an old track, dusty and surrounded by trees and hills. The sun was up, just barely, and its light lit the road but night lingered in the shadowy stands of trees to either side.

He knew where he was. He had seen this track through the eyes of the wolves, but of his enemy there was no sign. He walked forward to find them. They would not be far.

Ahead was the sound of hooves and the jingle of harness. Horta smiled. The enemy was coming to him. He came to a stop and waited with patience.

The riders saw him, hesitated and then walked forward toward him. Horta assessed them all in turn. The unknown boy with them was irrelevant. He was less than nothing and posed no threat. And yet Brand had allowed him to come. That must have some import. Brand saw something that he did not, and for that reason the boy must be assumed to be dangerous. He had a role to play in all this, if he lived to fulfil it.

Next, Horta's gaze fell on the short one. Here was a great warrior, and one swift to fight and slow to ask questions. Yet he was far more cunning than he looked, and inside him beat a heart that would drive him to deeds of loyalty beyond other men. He was dangerous.

Horta flicked his gaze to the tall one, pale skinned and freckled. He carried himself like a lord, yet somehow humility also exuded from him. He was a deadly warrior, yet would sooner study philosophy than ever draw a blade. He was at least as dangerous as the short one.

Finally, Horta turned his attention to his true enemy. Brand sat easily in the saddle. He was a man sure of himself, confident in his skills. His eyes were a pale blue, and though there was no sign of alarm in them, yet they gazed out at the world with an acuity that missed nothing, underestimated nothing, nor was daunted by anything. He was a man with no give to him. Had he a shovel and a reason to do so, he would move a mountain.

Horta shivered. This was a man of destiny, someone who worked the threads of fate himself rather than waited for them to be woven. There were few such as he, but it changed nothing. He must die, and that was an end to it.

Something else occurred to him then, some further insight. Brand was much like himself. He did what he did for duty, and nothing would stop him. Yet his heart was elsewhere. He did not wish to be who he was. Perhaps that could be used against him.

The riders drew up before him, and he sensed a little of Brand's magic. But not enough to determine its exact nature.

Horta gravely inclined his head. The riders did likewise, never taking their eyes off him.

"Greetings, friend," Brand said. "It's a lonely road, and a long one."

It was the customary greeting among the Duthenor for strangers meeting on the road. Horta nodded again, adjusted the portion of bearskin that he wore over his shoulders, and then sat cross-legged upon the dusty track.

"Greetings, and may your travels be swift and your night's rest long." It was the ritual response. The exchange was intended to declare that no hostility existed between strangers on the road.

"We have just eaten," the Short one said. "But we have a little food if you're hungry. Traveling by foot is hard going."

Brand gave a slight shake of his head. "This man came here by other means than his legs, and an image of a man needs no food."

Horta felt a cold stab of fear. Never before had anyone detected the difference between him and an image of the gods. It shocked him, but he would not show it.

"It is even as you say," he answered. "An image of light and air, no matter how real seeming, needs no sustenance."

A slight smile played over Brand's face, and Horta cursed himself for a fool. The man had not *known* he was an image, merely surmised it.

"What do you wish?" Brand asked. The man's blue eyes gazed at him casually, but Horta sensed that for all his seeming ease he could unleash turmoil with steel or magic in the blink of an eye. Here at least was a worthy adversary, and an intriguing one.

"What do I want? From you? Nothing but your death."

Brand's expression did not change There was no anger, or fear, or bluster. He merely answered.

"That is a gift I will not give."

"So I see," Horta replied. "The wolves were not enough. Yet the hawk plucks the rabbit from the field, and makes the gift his own."

"I am no rabbit."

Horta allowed himself a laugh. He *liked* this man. Nothing disturbed him. Nothing put him off balance. But there was no reason to show his admiration. It served no purpose.

"You mean nothing to me. Nor does this land. But I have a task, nearly achieved now, and your presence threatens it. Leave the Duthgar, and live. Stay, and die. The choice is yours."

Brand regarded him silently a moment, and then shook his head.

"No. It's my duty to return. It's my duty to free my people."

"Then you will die."

"Perhaps. Or maybe you will discover that this rabbit has claws."

Horta regarded Brand in turn. Then he stood, gracefully rising without the accustomed pain he would have normally felt in his left knee.

"So be it." He turned his gaze to the short one. "Thank you for your hospitality, even if not needed."

Brand's horse grew agitated, and he bent down to stroke its withers and whisper in its ear.

"What exactly is the task you mentioned?"

"Ah, I cannot say much. But it is the noblest of tasks, and it is a duty even as is yours. I shall not fail in it. The stars sing of it, and the earth calls for it. It is ordained."

Horta awaited no answer. He had learned little, but he would learn no more even if he talked for an hour. He willed it, and his image faded and his mind flew back to his body.

It was dark again, dark as the void, and his mind spun. Then he heard the distant bleating of sheep and felt the warmth of the fire in the hearth before him. He was back in the cottage.

He felt weak and nauseous. His glance fell to the small pallet bed within the room, and he wanted to rest. But he could not. His task was too important, Brand too great a threat. The wolves had not been enough, and he must act again and swiftly. More would be needed, and he knew now which god it would be best to call upon. From him, and that which he would send to kill, there would be no escape.

It was all a pity, for Horta truly liked Brand. But fate could not be turned aside. He sighed, then got up out of the chair, his limbs stiff from long sitting. He must gather the Arnhaten again. At once.

11. The Helm of the Duthenor

Brand led the small group of riders on through the morning. He rode silently, for he had met his true enemy at last and had much to consider. What occupied most of his attention was whether or not the man *was* his true enemy. He had a great duty to fulfil, which suggested that he served someone else. Perhaps.

It did not take long before they left the rugged hills and forests behind. Soon the track sloped downward, the forest thinned to isolated stands of trees and the land became cultivated.

They passed many farms now, and even several villages. Smoke rose from chimneys, sheep bleated on the hillsides and cattle roamed the lower slopes. There were people too. Shepherds, farmers in fields and tradesmen in the villages.

Brand felt at last like he had returned home. It was one thing to stand on the soil of the Duthgar, another to be among its people. And though they were wary of strangers, as was proper, they still gave a friendly greeting or wave. Not few of them looked long and hard at the horses too. They were fine mounts of a quality rarely seen in a land known for foot warriors rather than cavalry.

The Helm of the Duthenor was safely hidden away within a sack attached to Brand's saddlebag. It was in easy reach should a battle break out, though that was unlikely for the moment. More importantly he was not identified yet. Nothing would mark him more for who he was, except his ring and sword. The first was hard to see, and the blade of the second was sheathed. He was not ready to declare himself just yet, though he would do so when he reached the lord's hall, and that would be soon. But what reaction would he get when he did so?

The hall came into sight. It was small, for this was one of the most remote and thinly populated districts of the Duthgar. It showed signs of poor maintenance also, and the doorward when they came to the entrance was slovenly. Brand had heard that many of the true lords had been overthrown by the usurper, but this hall was not one of them if Galdring ruled it.

Despite his appearance, the doorward was polite enough, and he helped them hitch the horses. As they did so, Brand gave the hessian sack carrying the Helm of the Duthenor to Sighern, asking him to carry it for him.

When they were done with the horses, the doorward bid them state their names and business at the hall.

This was a moment Brand had long imagined, returning to the Duthgar and declaring himself. But it was anticlimactic when he did so.

"I'm Brand, and once I knew the father of the lord who rules here. The son should still recognize the name."

The doorward shrugged. "If you say so, but it's best not to displease him. He doesn't take kindly to being bothered for no purpose."

Brand raised an eyebrow. His name had not even been recognized, despite it only being used in the lineage of the chieftains of the Duthgar. No matter. The lord would know him, though what his reaction would be was hard to say. That he still ruled indicated he had not overtly opposed the usurper.

The doorward opened the building's great door and led them up the hall. Men seated at the mead benches to each side eyed the strangers carefully. It would be rare to see so many strangers, and neither Shorty nor Taingern had the look of Duthenor warriors about them. They were obviously foreigners, yet that they were warriors nonetheless would have been noted instantly.

They passed the firepit in the middle of the hall and walked up toward where the lord sat at a small table with some courtiers and guards. They were drinking and playing a game of stones.

The doorward came to a halt. Slowly he turned around, and Brand saw his eyes narrow and then widen. He had finally recognized the name.

"*What* did you say your name was?"

Brand gazed serenely back at him. "You heard it right the first time."

The man grew suddenly nervous. He looked surprised, scared and happy all at the same time. Then he masked his face so that it was expressionless and addressed Galdring.

"Hail, lord. I bring visitors to the hall who have business with you."

Galdring looked up with a bored expression on his face.

"What are their names?"

"Their leader is Brand."

The doorward said no more. Silence gradually fell over the hall, for if the doorward had not instantly recognized the name then many others did.

Galdring stood. He was not much older than Brand. His blond hair was long and tied back with a gold band, the sword strapped to his belt bejeweled at the hilt. And his eyes were piercing bright with authority. Once he would have impressed Brand, but he did not do so now. While he lived in luxury, outlaws plundered his district.

"That is a dangerous name to bear," Galdring said at last. "The more so if it is true."

"It's true, Galdring. But you overestimate the danger. What should the rightful heir to the chieftainship of the

Duthenor have to fear just for revealing his name in the Duthgar?"

Galdring was about to speak, but a black-haired man beside him placed a hand on his shoulder and silenced him. Brand understood at once where the true power in this hall lay.

The black-haired man took a step forward. "If you're who you say you are, you're a dead man. Perhaps you're a dead man anyway, just for claiming it. Either way, you're a fool."

Brand held his gaze. "I'm Brand, as I said. And I've returned to the Duthgar to bring justice. Unferth shall pay for his crimes. But I was talking to the lord of this hall, and not you. Not to the usurper's lackey, not to one who serves a traitorous cur."

They were hard words, and words that would lead to a fight. But Brand knew such a fight was inevitable. He knew also that the story of his coming to the hall, and the words spoken would spread like a raging grassfire throughout the Duthgar. He must appear strong and in control. Otherwise he would not gather an army.

The black-haired man drew his sword. "Kill him!" he ordered.

But Brand was expecting that, and a throwing knife came quick to hand from within a sheath at his belt. The black-haired man was the leader, and the first to die. With lightning speed Brand flung the knife. It arced through the air in a silver flash to strike the man's neck. Red blood spurted, but Brand was moving again before it hit.

He drew his sword, and even as its blade flashed he heard gasps. There was no other like it in the stories the Duthenor told, and the Halathrin-wrought blade confirmed his identity better than words. Two men moved at him from beside the now dead leader. The doorward drew his own blade, but he did not turn on

Brand. Rather he slew one of the two men. Brand leaped at the other, deflected a clumsy stab and hewed the man's head from his neck.

There was no further threat from in front of him. Brand spun and saw that Taingern and Shorty had killed a man each that had acted on the black-haired leader's instructions.

No one else moved. No doubt Unferth had more supporters in the hall, yet the unleashing of sudden death had shocked them to stillness. And their leader was taken from them.

Into the silence Galdring spoke. "You fool. You think you have won something here? You are already marked for death, but now all of us shall also pay that price. Unferth will kill every one of us."

Brand bent down and cleaned his bloodied blade on the trousers of the dead man before him. Then he sheathed it.

"You are wrong, Galdring. I can hear your heart quake from here with fear, and it speaks rather than your mind. I am Brand, and I have returned. Unferth shall die, and the Duthgar shall be free. This I swear, as the rightful chieftain of the Duthenor."

Brand spoke to the lord of the hall, but he knew all others would hear his words. They would be carried to Unferth and all over the Duthgar. It would unsettle the usurper and instill hope all over the land.

Galdring slumped back in his chair. For the first time, Brand noticed that a young woman was beside him, so like in appearance that she must be his sister. She was a shield-maiden, dressed in chainmail armor and with a sword at her side. But the blade would not have been as sharp as the glare she gave him.

The lord of the hall laughed bitterly. Then he turned to Brand once more. "All this, and yet there is no proof that you are even who you say you are."

"Of a time," Brand replied, "the word of a Duthenor warrior was taken as a matter of honor. This land has fallen, in more ways than one. Yet these tokens I will give. The first you have seen, which is the sword, and you know how I acquired it, even as a child from Unferth who stole it from my father. The second is this ring." He thrust up his hand so that the ring handed down through his line was visible. Galdring looked at it carefully, but said nothing. "And last, and greatest is this." He gestured to Sighern and the boy came forward bearing the hessian sack.

Brand took it, and let slip the cloth to reveal the shining Helm of the Duthenor. Then he placed it upon his head. It was battle accoutrement, yet to the Duthenor it was a crown.

Then he spoke, and his voice rang through the hall. "This is the helm of my ancestors, the Helm of the Duthenor. A thousand years ago it was stolen from us by Shurilgar, betrayer of nations. But I reclaimed it, at no small risk. I wear it now, and by these three tokens I proclaim myself, and I send warning to Unferth. His reign draws to a close. His past deeds will catch up with him. Justice, long delayed, is coming."

Brand stopped speaking. The hall was deathly silent. A long while Galdring gazed at him, and then slowly nodded.

"I believe you. And how you came to possess the Helm of the Duthenor, I cannot guess. Long it has been lost to us, but however you regained it must be a story of courage, I do not doubt. But even with sword, and ring and helm, even if you had the heart of your fathers of old, how do you expect to win back this land? Unferth has an army of thousands. How many swords do you bring?"

Brand grinned at him. "I have only my own sword, and the courage to wield it. That, and a handful of friends. But it is not I who shall win back this realm. It is the people, and they will gather to me. Have hope! The history of the Duthenor will be shaped anew, and the pride of old will return. Do not doubt it. Wait, watch and see. I shall set a fire before me that will overrun our enemies."

Brand took command. He turned to the others in the hall. "Go forth," he said. "And spread word of my return throughout the district. Let warriors, let those farmers with swords or spears or bows gather tomorrow morning. For tomorrow I march, and the first steps against Unferth will be taken, but not the last."

There was a cheer from the doorward, and many others took it up. The hall resounded with it, though not all cheered.

Brand turned to the doorward. "Where is the best place to meet?"

The man thought for a moment. "Things like this have always been done at the Green Howe."

Brand liked the idea. An ancient hero would be buried in the howe, and that would help fire the men's spirits.

"The Green Howe!" he called out to the hall. "I will leave from there on the second hour after dawn."

The cheering subsided and many men rushed from the hall. Some would be supporters of Unferth, and that was good. Brand *wanted* word to spread.

He took a chair at the table where Galdring sat, and did not ask permission. It was the other man's hall, but Brand did not like him and events had carried beyond the simple lordship of a district. Brand had proclaimed himself, and now the kingship was at stake.

Galdring gave orders to a few men that had stayed with him. They began to remove the bodies of the slain, and then the lord looked grimly at Brand.

"You have doomed us all. There are few warriors in this district. And against Unferth, they will fall as wheat before the scythe. And he will come against you, hard and fast."

Brand removed his helm and placed it on the table. "So I would expect."

The shield-maiden looked at him, and there was a cold fire in her eyes. "You're sure of yourself, aren't you? But I see no reason for it. Titles and tokens don't win battles."

"This is my sister, Haldring," the lord said. "She usually gets straight to the point."

"So I see. I like that."

The fire in her eyes grew colder. "What you *like* means nothing to me. It's what you can *do* that I'm interested in."

Shorty sat down at the table with Taingern. "Making friends again, Brand?"

"I try." Brand turned his attention back to Haldring. "You will see what I can do, if you come with me. Shorty and Taingern here are my generals." He gestured at his two friends. "I want you for my third."

She looked at him as though he were mad. "You know nothing of me, nor my abilities. I don't even like you. Why would you offer me such a role?"

"Because I know more than you think. You don't like me, you say? And yet moments ago when the fight broke out you had a knife to hand and you were ready to fling it. You could have killed me, but you stayed your hand. Not only that, I will have no man or woman about me who tells me what they think I want to hear for the sake of advancement. I want advisors who think of the land first and give counsel based on reality, not dreaming. In short, I want you."

She looked at him, stunned. "You saw the knife, even while other men were trying to kill you?"

"Of course. I see much, but not all. That's why I want your help. You know this land, while I only know what it once was and what it yet could be."

Haldring looked at him in silence a long while. "For someone with no army and little hope, you can be convincing. Very well, I'll come with you. Unferth had our father killed, so I would risk nearly anything to see him overthrown. I just hope you know what you're doing as much as you *sound* like you know what you're doing."

It was a good point, and Brand knew it. If he failed, life would be worse for the Duthenor. And if it were just Unferth that he had to worry about, he would not have doubts. But there was the magician to worry about too. Who was he? What did he want? What threat did Brand pose to him? About all this, Brand knew too little, and it was dangerous not to know. What he did know was this, though. The magician had great power. He was driven to fulfil his duty, whatever it was. And he was of a race of people that Brand had never met before. That made it even harder to guess his purposes.

Brand glanced at the Helm of the Duthenor. He had won it back from Shurilgar at great risk. But then the only stakes were his life and death. Now, the future of a nation rested on his skills. That helm was as heavy as any crown, and not by its weight in metal.

He made a choice, and it was driven by past experience. In politics and war, deception could gain much. But in matters of loyalty, honesty was the strongest bond.

He looked at Haldring. "This also I should tell you. I want you to come with me for all the reasons I said, but this is also part of my reasoning. You'll not like it, but you will appreciate the benefit of it."

She held his gaze, her blue eyes cold and remote, but this he was beginning to feel was a mask. She was a woman of passions, even if they were held tightly in check. And it was yet another marker that his choice of her as a general was good. A general, a warrior, must feel and believe in things. This drove them to fight. But they must also be able to distance themselves from everything when in battle. In battle, only the winning or losing mattered. Consequences were for afterwards.

"A shield-maiden will lend my army a certain mystique. It will give prominence to it in men's minds, give storytellers something to talk of and spark interest all over the land. I don't seek to *use* you for this purpose, otherwise I wouldn't admit this. But it is the truth of the matter nevertheless, and you should know it."

She looked by turns angry, surprised and finally thoughtful. "You're correct in what you say. So be it. But I *will* speak my mind when situations arise and not just be a figurehead."

Brand knew she meant it, and it was perhaps something he needed. Shorty and Taingern never hesitated to tell him if they thought he was doing something wrong, but they did not know this land as did she.

He looked at Galdring. Anger and frustration showed in his eyes, and Brand understood that. The lord had lost command of his own men, and now war was coming. He seemed beaten before it began. For all that he and his sister looked so similar, the one thing that was different was the fire in her eyes.

"I cannot command you to have hope," Brand said. "But have it anyway. Watch! And over the coming days you will see."

Galdring sighed. "Perhaps I've been under Unferth's yoke too long. It hasn't been easy. But I still think you've doomed us all." He paused, then spoke again. "You know, I met your parents once, when I was a child. You are your father's son. But you have your mother's gift of speech.

So even I shall try to have some hope, but I expect to die because of all this, and many others with me."

12. There Must be Blood

All day the Arnhaten prepared. They had to be gathered from the village first, then they had to collect dry timber for the bonfire. Finally, they ritually cleansed themselves by performing the sacred chants. And all the while Horta ran through in his mind what must be done. There could be no mistake in what was to come, for to err was to die.

What he attempted now was one of the grand rituals. It summoned not just a god, but one of the greater gods. He had done so before, at need. He did so now, because of necessity. To accomplish his task, there was no risk he would not take. Yet still, he felt his heart pound in his chest and the sweat on his brow was as ice against his skin. Only the slow sucking of a norhanu leaf eased the strain.

For this ceremony, he had need of a special assistant. Olbata aided him, running through with him the words of the ritual, helping him direct the others in what they did once more in the sacred grove of the Duthenor. Yet Olbata was unaware of one vital step in the ceremony, one part of the procedure that had vital significance. Had he known, he would have refused. Horta would not have blamed him, so that information he held back.

Dusk crept over the land. Shadows filled the already dark woods and a deep silence descended. Horta made a gesture, and Olbata lit the gathered timber. Some while it took to catch, but then swifter and swifter the bonfire caught until it roared to life and sent a plume of fiery sparks high into the night. But for all the flame, the darkness of the woods only pressed in closer.

Horta placed a fresh norhanu leaf under his tongue. It was dangerous, but necessary. And he had been sucking on the first for hours. Its potency had diminished.

He signaled Obata to join him, and he drew from one of his pouches a statuette of obsidian, black as the night around them. It was one of his great talismans, and it was in the shape of a man with a bat's head, teeth bared. This he gave to his disciple, telling him to hold it in his left hand and not to let go, no matter what occurred.

Horta moved to the southern end of the bonfire. His positioning influenced which gods may be called. So too the direction of circling, or whether there was circling or not. In this case, ancient tradition prescribed no circling, and he followed what had been handed down from the magicians of old.

The Arnhaten drew near him, and then they also stood still, gathering to each side of him. From one of his many pouches he took some powder, and this he cast in a single throw into the flames.

The fire roared and leaped. Red sparks plumed into the smoke-laden air, followed by trails of white and black. A sweet smell drifted to him, and he was careful not to breathe much of the scent in.

And then he commenced chanting, his words rising up into the darkness with the smoke and heat-shimmer of the fire, up into the fathomless night and toward the hidden stars. The Arnhaten chanted also, intoning the ancient words that he had taught them.

Upon a god he called, one of the old gods that ruled air, sky and earth. In this case, the god was of the earth. His voice rang with power, beseeching aid and asking for audience.

"I summon thee, O Shemfal, god of the underworld."

At the speaking of the god's name, the flickering flames of the bonfire parted as though they were a curtain. And even as a man looked through a window, Horta saw into another world. It was not clear, yet he discerned through the writhing smoke, not all of which rose from the bonfire, a great cave.

He did not wish to see, but he must, and his gaze was drawn despite his abhorrence. Within the cave towered a mighty throne of obsidian, polished to a sheen and glimmering with dark lights and myriad reflections. Upon it Shemfal sat, a vast figure of shadows and hidden power. His body was that of a mighty man, and the head was a bat's, and the sharp eyes within that animal head looked up through the window between worlds and pierced Horta's soul.

"Come to me, O Shemfal, Master of Death, and hear my plea," Horta whispered, his voice thickened by fear or the numbing of the norhanu leaf.

And Shemfal came. The shadows that were about him unfolded to become giant wings, leathery but supple. He swept into the air, leaving his throne and rising above his court. Other creatures there were beneath him. Some serpent-like, coiling, sliding, creeping within the shadows. Others walked as men, but were scaled and tusked. Horta saw beings from nightmare and myth, monsters of massive size and small creatures of fang, and sting and poison.

The air moved in waves, beaten by the vast wings of Shemfal. Sickly light from braziers of dull red flame flickered and died. And the god rose higher, higher, higher, his eyes unwaveringly fixed on Horta.

The god drew closer. The throne room and all within it were blocked by the vast wings. The bonfire roared to life, sparks streaming and scattering into the air. The Arnhaten fell to the ground like trees blown down by a storm, but Horta stood on quaking legs, sucking desperately at the norhanu leaf.

Into the world of men the god ascended, summoned from the underworld, and Horta felt the blast of those great wings beat upon him, heard the roar of wind flow through the sacred wood of the Duthenor. He glanced at where Obata lay sprawled on the ground, and relief washed over him when he saw the man still clutched the statuette in his hand.

Horta kneeled and closed his eyes. Like a man in prayer he spoke.

"O mighty Shemfal, Lord of the Grave, will you hear the pleading of your humble servant?"

Shemfal answered, and the voice of the god smote Horta's ears. He felt the words enter his brain, and make it thrum inside the casing of his skull.

"I hear you, mortal. Speak, and I shall pass judgement."

Horta told the god of his great task, of how he served the gods and of what manner of man Brand was. He told of how Brand threatened his plans.

And the god weighed his words, deciding on the worthy and the unworthy, contemplating life or death.

"You serve me well, Horta. I am not displeased. I shall send one of my own to destroy Brand. He shall be fit for the task, yet what you ask requires blood. That is the age-old pact."

"Mighty Shemfal, I offer Brand himself as the sacrifice. His blood is of an ancient line, and magic sings within it also."

"This I know, Horta. Even here echoes of Brand's deeds are muttered in the dark. He will attend me well, once in my realm and broken into servitude beneath my throne. And great is the one I shall send against him to ensure it comes to pass. Yet the chances of the world are ever uncertain. Should fate go awry, are you willing to pay the price and honor your debt?"

Horta bowed. He knew what the god meant. There must be blood one way or the other. But the blood would not be his own. He glanced at Olbata to ensure the man still held the statuette. Through this, the presence of the god in this world was invoked. If Brand were not killed, Olbata would serve as sacrifice in his stead.

"I accept the price, O lord."

The great wings of Shemfal beat once more, and the trees in the sacred wood bent against the blast. The god descended into the underworld whence he came, but a light glimmered as something rose in his place.

The force of the wind thrashed Horta's face onto the ground, but when it dissipated he lifted his head once more. Standing before him was the creature Shemfal had sent to kill Brand. Straightaway Horta sensed its power, greater than that of the wolves, and held in check by intelligence and an iron-like will. All this he read in the keen glance of its eyes, for it stood before him as a man.

Horta studied the assassin. Though he indeed looked like a man, there were differences. The skin, where it showed at face and hand, was pale as snow. And the eyes were a piercing blue, glittering like none he had seen before. The cheek bones were high, the ears delicate and slightly pointed. Trousers and tunic were of close-fitting leather, gleaming black. But over this he wore a chainmail shirt that glinted as though it were made of silver. On his back were strapped twin swords, the hilts of pale ivory and the little that showed of the blades black as obsidian.

The assassin was a warrior, yet Horta sensed magic also, but of a kind he did not understand. The warrior-assassin looked Horta up and down, and the magician felt the contempt of that deathly gaze. There was an arrogance about him that was immensely dislikeable, but Horta sensed it was born of experience. The man, if man it was, had defeated all his enemies in the past. And they would have been great, for he was a creature of the underworld where the one rule was survival.

Without speaking, the man turned on the balls of his feet and strode from the clearing. He moved with grace and purpose, his every motion that of a sublime warrior. Horta was glad to see him go. He had no wish to talk to him and potentially incur his wrath. Here was an enemy that even he would fear to have, and for the first time in a very long while he wondered if he had gone too far. But the man hunted Brand, and relief washed through him.

13. A Hero of Old

They spent the night in the hall, and for all that Brand loved sleeping beneath the stars, it was good to have a roof over his head for a change.

But they were up before dawn. Galdring did not join them, and for this Brand was glad. It did no good to have a lord in an army who at best only half believed in the cause. He knew it would be like that throughout the district too. Not all who were able to come would do so.

Haldring was there though, and for this he was glad. She would give him trouble at every step, but perhaps it would be of the kind he needed. He tended to reach too high, to expect too much. She would temper that, probably at every opportunity. She liked what had been done to her brother no less than Galdring himself.

It was Haldring who led them from the hall. A dozen men came with them. As many as that stayed behind. They readied their horses, but they did not ride. The Green Howe was not that far away she advised, and Brand had no wish to meet the beginnings of his army from atop a mount as though he were a king. Instead, he must be a general: in charge, but still one of them.

They walked south-west, continuing along the same trail they had yesterday. The sun was up now, roosters crowing from farms they passed and sheep and cattle watching them with mild curiosity.

There were trees here, and copses and woods mostly on the hilltops, but for the most part it was clear ground and farmed. It was a fertile land, the grass growing green and the animals healthy. It was still cool of a morning, for summer had not yet come, but it was approaching.

The track led slightly downward now, and they moved into a valley. It was less farmed here, and there were more trees. A creek ran through it, and it was mostly about this that farms had been established. But in the middle stood a large wood.

Haldring pointed. "In those trees is where the Green Howe stands."

Not long after, the trees were about them and the sound of men's voices, hushed by the morning and the nature of the event in which they were a part, drifted to them.

The trunks of the trees formed a wall, but one moment the track wound tightly between trunk and root and overhanging branch, and the next they were in a large glade. The grass was green and short. The murmur of the creek came from somewhere close, but hidden.

Within the center of the glade stood the Green Howe. It was a barrow, a burial mound for the final resting place of a lord of old. It stood some forty feet long and was at least half as wide. Its rounded slopes, smooth with green turf, rose to a domed summit as tall as two men.

And there were men around it, and they gathered now as they saw the newcomers arrive. These were Duthenor warriors. Most were pale haired, some brown haired as was Brand, yet others dark-eyed with raven-black hair. All wore chainmail. Some had helms. Here and there were spears and bows and long-handled axes, but most carried swords in the plain scabbards hanging from their belts.

"There aren't as many as I had thought," Sighern said quietly from beside Brand. He had been given his own horse at Brand's request.

His observation was correct. There were some three hundred of them, and many had the look of untested youths. But Brand smiled anyway. He had worried that there would be none.

"It is perhaps half of what the district could muster," Haldring said. She offered no comment on why that was so.

"Yesterday we were four," Brand said. "Now we are hundreds. It's all a matter of perspective."

"If we waited, more might yet join us," Haldring suggested.

"No. There is no time to wait. We must be swift and gather momentum." Brand handed his reins to Sighern and stepped a little way ahead of the others to meet the warriors.

They eyed him warily, as well they might. Many glances fell upon sword, ring and helm. They had *heard* the rightful chieftain had returned, but they wanted to see it for themselves.

"Warriors of the Duthenor!" he called. "You will have heard much. Most of it will have been rubbish. This I say to you now, as the truth. I am Brand. I have returned. When I went into exile, I was little more than a child, though one that had learned the ways of the world. But I return now as a man, tested in battle as a warrior. And also tested in battle as a leader of armies and a nation. I was victorious. I will be victorious again."

He fell silent. The Duthenor studied him. One man, perhaps in his fifties but still hale, stepped forward.

"We hear you, Brand. We recognize you. You are the rightful heir, and tales of your deeds in faraway Cardoroth are told even in this land. We are brave men, and true. Too long have we endured Unferth, and we shall follow you. But we worry also for our families. We are too few to challenge the enemy. We are hundreds, but he has thousands at his command. We fear, though this army may grow, that we will *always* be too few. And when

Unferth comes, he may not kill just us but ravage the land as well."

Brand studied him. "What's your name, warrior?"

The man spoke proudly. "I'm called Garamund. In my youth, I served your father."

"Then hear me, Garamund. I know you speak for all these warriors." He swept his arm out, gesturing at the gathered men. "Everything you say is true. I will not lie to you, even as my father did not lie to you. So this I say truly. Our first task is *not* to fight Unferth. That way lies disaster. That fight is for a later time. Now, our task is to bear a torch. We will hold it aloft, and it will be a beacon of hope. We shall sting Unferth, and then disappear. We shall sting him again, and vanish once more. All the while word of our deeds will spread. Our army will grow. When we are ready, then we shall strike him down."

As always, when people saw a plan they felt inclined to follow it. And in the plan, sketchy as it was, they saw hope because it acknowledged the difficulties and provided a solution. Brand knew by their expressions he had won them over. But with that winning came responsibility. Now he felt the weight of trying to make reality conform to the words he had spoken. It would not be easy.

"Where is the closest supporter of Unferth?" Brand asked. Now that he had them, he must get them moving before they had a chance to change their mind.

"That would be lord Gingrel," Garamund said. There were murmurs of agreement from the men, and Haldring gave a slight nod when he looked at her.

"And how far away is he?" Brand asked.

"He has a large hall," Garamund answered, "only half a day away."

"He's one of the usurper's own men, belonging to the Callenor, and he has many of that tribe with him," Haldring added.

"Aye, those pigs like to lord it over us." Garamund leaned forward and spat, accurately but not eloquently giving his opinion of Unferth's tribe that now occupied the Duthgar.

"Then it is to there that we shall march."

Brand had them now. He had given them a purpose, and through Garamund's actions emotion had been invoked; they hated the Callenor. Purpose and emotion served as the basis for any military effort. The two went hand in hand, and one without the other soon dwindled into failure. It was probably so for any human endeavor.

He drew his sword slowly, allowing men to see the Halathrin-wrought blade. Then he pointed it at the Green Howe.

"In there sleeps a hero of old. I know not his name, nor his battles, but they are finished now. I know this, though. He was Duthenor. The dark will take us all, in the end, even as it took him. But our battles are not yet finished. For a while we stand, as warriors, in the light. Our deeds yet need doing."

There was a roar from the men. They had been compared to a hero of old, and at the same time challenged to live up to his standards. Brand felt the surge of pride ripple through them, and for a moment he wondered if he were doing the right thing. Was he manipulating them for his own purposes, or speaking as he felt himself? Or perhaps both?

He lifted his sword straight up into the air, the pattern-welded blade shimmering. "We are few!" he called. "But we are like the point of the blade – the most dangerous part!"

There was another roar of approval, greater than the first.

"The edge of the blade is yet to come, but it will as our army grows. Then we shall swell until there is point, blade and hilt – until the sword is complete!"

The crowd yelled and cheered, but Brand was not done. "And when we are a complete sword, we will strike Unferth down!"

He swept the blade in a killing stroke, flourished it in the air a moment, and then sheathed it swiftly all in one smooth motion.

The men drew their own blades, yelling and cheering and lifting their weapons high. "Brand!" they began to chant. "Brand of the Duthenor!"

Brand pointed behind him. "These are my generals. I trust them with my life. Shorty, Taingern and Haldring. They will not fail me, and I shall not fail you!"

There was a deafening roar, and many eyes glanced at the generals. Not least of all at Haldring. She stood tall, her blonde hair spilling free as she removed her helm so that the men could see her.

"The time of words is done," Brand said more quietly. "Now is the time to march. Follow us, and believe that the journey we now take will be chanted by storytellers in times to come."

He led his horse forward, his generals with him, and the three hundred warriors fell into a tight group, marching behind.

They had not gone far when Taingern leaned in and spoke to him quietly.

"So, what's the plan?"

"It's simple," Brand answered. "Very simple."

Shorty, who was walking his horse on the other side, drew closer as well.

"Simple is always the best."

"So it is," Brand agreed. "In a nutshell, this is it. We need a win. It doesn't have to be a big one. It *can't* be a big one, yet. But that doesn't matter. A win is a win, and that will encourage others to join us. Momentum is everything."

Taingern seemed to expect this. "So far so good, but this lord we march on will have heard news of your coming by now. He'll be expecting us. Maybe even had time to summon warriors."

"Ah, that could be. But probably not. No doubt, he'll have begun to take steps. But he won't know for sure that I'm marching on him. There are other places I could go. And he'll not think that I'll march so soon. As was pointed out before, if I waited another day or two more people would join us. Most leaders would wait for those extra numbers."

"I see," Taingern replied. "Now all the better do I understand your reasoning for marching swiftly. Perhaps we will catch them by surprise."

They moved ahead at a good pace. Brand allowed little time for rests, stopping only once every hour for a short while. Surprise would be needed, and speed was the foundation on which that depended.

The track led out of the valley and toward a forest. By the afternoon they had moved within the trees and the track had become a road. Some little while later they ceased their march, and looked down through the cover of trees at the hall situated many hundreds of feet away. It lay below them, on a slight slope of green grass. There was a village too, but this had grown up near a stream further down slope. The hall itself stood in the open, and a path of the road branched off and headed to it.

Brand and his generals slipped through the trees that formed the eaves of the wood for a closer look. They saw signs of activity. Even as they watched two riders hastened toward the wall. They had come across country rather than by road. Otherwise, Brand's force would have detained them.

There were half a dozen guards at the hall entrance also. They looked alert.

"They've heard of our coming," Haldring said. "What do we do now?"

14. Will You Surrender?

Brand considered the situation. What to do was no easy question.

"They've heard of my return, but they're not ready yet. There are more warriors to come in, perhaps a lot more, I think."

"Probably," Haldring said. "So, will you attack then?"

Brand hesitated. "Some of the men down there will be Duthenor though, will they not?"

"Of course, but they'll be in the minority. They might even turn to our side."

"They'll need time for that. Just taken unawares by warriors attacking, they'll fight first."

"Maybe. But I see no way around it."

Brand knew he should attack. And he should do it swiftly. But it was not so easy as that.

"Duthenor killing Duthenor is no way to build an army. I must think not only of the battle at hand, but of what's to follow."

"But you *do* need a victory," Shorty said.

"I need a victory, but I must do it without killing Duthenor. I'll not do that unless I must. And here, just at the moment, I think we have the greater force. I'll give the Duthenor a chance to see what's happening and come to our side."

They seemed uncertain of this course, but he had made up his mind. He gave signals. The warriors formed a tight group, and then swiftly they walked from the forest and toward the hall. They blew no horns, nor did they draw any blades. Brand would not provoke the enemy into a fight, but rather he would give them an opportunity to surrender.

The opposition would hold tight in the hall, being outnumbered. And should other forces arrive, they would likely come from outlying areas in small groups and be outnumbered too. But it was not a situation that could last. The longer it went on, the worse it would be for Brand. But he was glad he had resisted the temptation to attack. There was that side to him that was violent, and could justify the violence as necessary. It was a side to all men, but it must be resisted. All the more so because he had authority over others. As he acted, so would they be influenced.

His warrior band strode forward. Ahead, the opposition saw them, hesitated and then moved inside the hall. There was yelling and shouting, and Brand had no doubt he would find the door to the hall closed and barred from the inside when he reached it.

So it proved. He set men to guard all sides of the hall so that they could not be taken by surprise nor anyone escape. And he set lookouts also, with an eye to any attack that might be launched from outside. The enemy would build out there somewhere in the surrounding countryside, but he guessed they would bide their time. It would take some while to find each other and join together. Only when there were enough of them, if their number reached that high at all, would they attack.

Brand himself hammered at the door three times. "Open!" he commanded. "I am Brand, rightful chieftain of the Duthgar. I would speak with the lord of this hall."

There was muffled talk from inside, and a few moments later a voice answered, calm and aloof.

"Unferth reigns as king in the Duthgar, and I do not know you or recognize any authority. But if you wish, you may come inside. You alone."

Brand smiled. He wondered how many steps he would take into that hall before a sword found his heart.

"I think not, Gingrel. But you will have men in there that know me. Duthenor men. Let some of them out so that they may see me."

"No." came the answer.

Brand expected that. "If you do not, then I will hold it against you when I come into my own and judge you. And I *will* come into my own, and when I judge you it will be harshly."

That would give him something to think about. He would not surrender, for then he would fear having to answer to Unferth. But he could not be certain that Unferth would prevail, so he would also be wary of what would happen if Brand gained control of the Duthgar.

The silence grew. There was muttering on the other side of the door, and then at length Gingrel gave an answer.

"Very well. Stand back, well back."

Brand gestured to those with him, and they walked well back from the door. Whatever conversation took place, he wanted to keep it private. But they drew their swords also, for Brand was not trusting. They could be attacked, but he did not think Gingrel had the nerve for that. If he attacked, he had nowhere to go but back in the hall. And that could be set to fire if he angered his opponents.

The door opened, and two men came out. They wore swords, but the blades remained sheathed. Men crowded behind the entrance they had come through, but there was no indication of bowmen.

Brand did not know the two men. They approached, slowly and cautiously, their gaze alert but not alarmed. They did not seem to distrust the warriors they faced, or Brand, and that indicated to him that they were Duthenor.

Very slowly, Brand drew his sword. "I am Brand. Rightful ruler of the Duthgar." He spoke softly, and he did not think those in the hall could hear what was said.

Their gaze had gone first to the Helm of the Duthenor that he wore. Then the naked steel of his Halathrin-wrought blade. When they had studied it a moment, he sheathed the weapon and showed them the chieftain's ring he wore.

They glanced at each other first, and then one spoke. "We know you, Brand. The tokens you bear are enough, but we know you also. We were young when we met, and it was but briefly. Our lord took us with him when he visited your father."

"Then you will tell Gingrel, and all else inside, that I am who I say?"

"We will. There is no doubt."

Brand spoke carefully. This was a delicate situation. "My return changes much. And I know a great deal has happened in my absence, but why do men of the Duthenor serve a foreign lord?"

The men looked uncomfortable. "Gingrel has supplied food for us, and our families. He need not have done so. Without that, we would have been reduced to poverty."

"I see. And I understand. I assume also that you, and the other Duthenor in the hall, have sworn oaths of loyalty to the new lord?"

"Yes," they answered simply.

Brand had learned something valuable. There were more Duthenor in the hall. Now was come the time to play on that, and open old wounds.

"And what happened to the old Duthenor lord?"

"He was murdered."

"By whom?"

"By the lord who now sits in the high chair," the first man answered. There was no emotion in his voice, which served to show to Brand that great emotion existed, otherwise it would not need to be so severely restrained.

"How many of you are there?"

There was hesitation here, for the men saw where this must lead. The second answered eventually, though.

"We are thirty, but they are seventy."

Brand hesitated himself, though it was deliberate. He would give them time to think on what had been said, for long suppressed emotions to bubble to the surface.

"Bring them out, and join me," he said at last.

The first man slowly shook his head. "We have sworn oaths to Gingrel."

"I see." Brand knew this would have been the case. "I guessed you had, and I would not ask you to break an oath. But that does not mean you are not needed, you and men like you throughout the Duthgar. Unferth's time of reckoning has come. And there is this too. What of the older oaths you would have sworn to your dead, and murdered lord? Which oath shall you keep, and which shall you not?"

The men did not look happy. "You put us in a hard place," the first said.

Brand had sympathy for them, and all like them across the land. There had been no exile for them. It had been a case of serve, or suffer.

"I know I do. I do not wish to, but fate has so decreed it. This is all I ask – think on what we have said."

The men returned inside after that. Brand waited until they were gone from view, and then he spoke to those who held the door.

"I have proven now that I am as I claim. Let Gingrel stand forth."

There was movement inside the shadows of the hall, and a voice answered him, though he could not see clearly who spoke.

"I can hear you from here, Brand."

"You know who I am, and this choice I give you. Surrender to my justice, or die."

Gingrel answered him. "I have done no wrong. Let me send a swift rider to Unferth, and I will ask him to come here. I am but a lord, not the ruler of the Duthgar. These matters are above me, and I must await his instructions."

Brand knew he would get nowhere here, not this way. Shorty also whispered in his ear. "The man is merely playing for time."

"There shall be no riders, no messages and no delays," Brand said loudly. "I give you until one hour after dawn tomorrow to surrender."

There was movement again, and the hall door was slammed shut. There would be no more talk.

Night came soon after, and Brand's men became restless. They knew as well as he that enemies could come upon them while they were in the open. It was a danger, but Brand did not think Gingrel's supporters would be here yet. His coming and march here had been swift, too swift for the enemy to properly mobilize. But that would change tomorrow. After that, they were increasingly likely to be attacked.

"What now?" Haldring asked.

"Now we wait," he replied.

"Have you considered attacking the hall?"

"I have, but we would lose men that way. The doors are narrow, and even if we broke them down one man could hold us off."

Haldring hesitated, and then spoke again. "We could burn them out."

Brand knew this suggestion would come up. It was a terrible thing to do, even to an enemy. But there was a history of it, though usually it was considered a crime in the Duthgar, no matter what prompted it.

"I'll not burn them out."

Haldring looked at him a long moment. "Do you have the guts to lead men into war? Not all decisions are easy."

He could not complain, because he had told her he wanted the truth from her. And it was a valid question. She knew as much as did he that he needed a victory, and that time was running out in which to obtain it.

"I have the guts," he said. "But I'll not kill Duthenor as well as the enemy. And besides, the night has only just begun. It will be long for us out here, but it will be long in there also. And the oaths the Duthenor swore to their old lord will grow restless."

She studied him a while longer, but said no more. She had suggested the burning, and it was her job to do so. But she pressed it no further for her heart was not in it either. He was glad of that.

Night fell. Fires were lit, scouts sent out and a perimeter of guards established. It was a dangerous situation. Nor could Brand rule out a sudden attack from within the hall either. It was not likely, but it must be guarded against.

The Duthenor he commanded were of good cheer. Finally, after years, action was being taken against the invaders. That good cheer would not last though. The long night would wear it down, and failure to secure a surrender tomorrow would erode it further.

Brand thought on what he would do if that occurred. He would not burn the hall, but he could attack it. The doors could be destroyed, yet both the one at front and the one at the rear were narrow. This was on purpose, and it ensured that even one man at each door could long hold off an attacking enemy. And all the while the threat increased that other hostile forces would arrive, group together, and attack.

He had another course of action. He could withdraw, and pursue one of the hostile forces that would soon gather. If he destroyed that, he would have his victory. But Gingrel would then be free, and able to attack.

Yet another option was to divide his forces. He could leave a large enough band here to hold Gingrel within the hall, and lead the rest to find and destroy what forces he could find in the district that supported Unferth. That was a dangerous tactic also, for he did not know how large those forces were and his own was not so large as to make dividing it an easy decision.

He had problems, and he knew it. But it would not help to worry over them all pointlessly. He would decide in the morning as he must, and the night would be long and could bring news or events to change his plans anyway.

They slept, but it was a restless sleep. Always there was the movement of sentries as they patrolled or changed shifts. At some point, the sky clouded and rain threatened. But it held off and remained dry. After a few hours, the clouds dissipated.

Brand woke, slumbered again and woke once more. All was hushed, and yet he sensed that something was happening. Had he heard a noise? He looked to the sentries, but from what he could see of their dim forms nothing had disturbed them.

It was some while yet until the dawn, but not that long. The eastern sky seemed a little paler, perhaps. And then there was a sudden noise from within the hall. Brand heard banging and raised voices.

Swiftly he rose and drew his sword. He had slept in his boots, as had the others. They were up quickly also, and Brand woke other warriors nearby.

There was more noise from within the hall, loud now and urgent, and the clash of steel on steel was a part of it. Suddenly, the door flew open and men struggled within it.

One fell, dead. Out staggered a Duthenor warrior, but there were others behind him. They held the door open against a force from within that sought to kill them.

"Attack!" Brand cried, and he led the way. The Duthenor inside had done what he hoped, but he knew also that they were outnumbered and would be killed swiftly unless help arrived.

Brand was the first in. There was light inside, and it showed turmoil within the hall. There was desperate fighting, mostly near the doors. There were several bodies on the floor, and the air was full of battle-cries and the clamor of sword against sword.

With a flick of his wrist Brand deflected a stabbing blow at his head and slew the man who had tried to kill him. He pressed forward into the fray, his sword flashing and his helm glittering. Men fell back before him and space opened to allow more Duthenor into the hall.

Somehow Sighern had found his way in, and his sword cut and slashed close to Brand's. He should have stayed without, and Brand knew he would not forgive himself if he were killed. But he could do nothing about it now.

A huge man with a red beard came at him, and Brand leaped forward killing him with a swift jab the other had never even seen coming. The clash of steel was deafening, and he saw Shorty and Taingern close by. Haldring was with them, her blonde hair spilling out behind her helm and her sword darting like a serpent's tongue, dealing out death wherever she strode.

The hall was become a charnel house, full of spilled entrails and the smell of blood and urine and smoke. More Duthenor entered the hall and pressed forward.

"Halt!" Brand cried. "Halt!"

He stood among them, Duthenor and Callenor alike. He was taller, and marked by a kingly sword and helm, but there was an authority in his voice that allies and enemies both heard.

"Halt!" he called yet again, and opponents who had been fighting stilled, eyeing each other warily. A hush descended with the stillness. Brand knew that at any moment turmoil could break forth again. It hovered in the air and a man just blinking at the wrong time could unleash it once more.

"There is no need for more death!" Brand called. "Stand back a pace. Everyone. Do it!"

Warriors all over the room shuffled. Some moved back more than others.

"There has been enough killing," Brand said more quietly. "Let it end now. Duthenor and Callenor alike are but following their leaders. Let Gingrel stand forth!"

A tall man approached from the back of the hall. He was thin, and dressed in princely clothes. His hair was red, grown long and tied back behind his head with a gold band. Rings glittered on his fingers. A prince he seemed in truth, living in wealth and luxury in his hall. Yet he had the look of eagles about him, and there was a cold light in his eyes, cold as the steel of the naked blade he held loosely in one hand.

"I am lord Gingrel," the man said.

Brand studied him momentarily. "Will you surrender?" he asked.

"No. I will not. You may be in my hall, and death may come, but we shall kill many of you before it does."

Brand was silent a long while. "Duthenor blood is precious to me," he said at length. "I will not spill it unless I must. And Callenor blood is precious also. We fight here as enemies, but of old did we not belong to one far greater tribe? Do we not sing the same songs and share many of the same heroes?"

No one answered him. He did not think they would. Gingrel continued to study him with those same cold eyes.

"Let there be an end to this," Brand said. "Let Gingrel and I alone fight. One of us will die, and that will be an end to it."

Gingrel seemed surprised. "You would duel with me?"

Even as Gingrel spoke Brand heard a hiss from Haldring and saw her give a slight shake of her head. It seemed that Gingrel had a reputation as a fighter. He certainly looked the part.

"This I swear," Brand said. "If I am killed, I command those who follow me to leave and return to their homes."

Gingrel grinned at him, and for the first time there was a light in his eyes. He was a man who loved to fight, and he saw a chance for victory in this.

"Will you tell your men to surrender, if you are killed, Gingrel?"

Gingrel moved slowly toward him. "I will not be killed, but yes. They will surrender."

"Then stand back, everyone. Sheathe your swords, and clear room for Gingrel and I to face each other."

The two men drew close. The fire pit in the middle of the hall was to Brand's left. Embers shimmered there, and he felt the heat off them even where he stood.

Gingrel moved like a viper, all smooth and effortless. He was a natural-born warrior, but so too was Brand. And Brand saw opportunity in this. What happened now would spread from district to district and cross and recross the Duthgar. If he won, and he intended to, it would help establish his credibility. Moreover, if he won in spectacular fashion…

Gingrel leaped forward, his blade cutting a shadowy arc in a backhanded strike. It streaked through the air, faster than thought. Time slowed. Brand watched the blade, allowed it to whisper death close to his head as he ducked just barely enough to avoid it. Before it had even passed over him he had begun to move forward himself, the blade of his forefathers sweeping out.

There was a sickening noise. Red blood spurted from severed arteries. Brand's blade took Gingrel in the neck between helm and chainmail coat. His body remained still, but the lord's head toppled away. It fell into the fire pit. Smoke rose as the long hair of the head caught fire. Skin sizzled. The body, still pumping blood, slowly fell backward.

It was over before it had begun. Brand lowered his sword, resting its point on the floor and leaning on it casually.

"Thus is justice done," he said solemnly. "As Gingrel fell, so too will Unferth."

The Callenor men looked at him, uncertainty and shock in their eyes. They knew their lord for a great warrior, but he was now defeated, and easily. And they were in a hall full of their enemies.

Brand spoke before they had a chance to decide what to do. "Callenor!" he called. "I am true to my word. I accept your surrender. Moreover, I promise you shall be allowed to keep your swords and walk freely from this hall. What say you?"

There was movement among them. One man stepped forward after a while, older and grizzled, his face showing a scar from a long-ago battle. His gaze fell momentarily down into the firepit, but he looked back up at Brand quickly.

"Truly? You will let us go free?"

Brand answered without hesitation. "I will let you go, with your swords. I will not ask oaths of loyalty from you. You may not give them, and if you did you may not keep them, for your alliance is to your old lord. It was *his* mistake to think an oath of convenience would bind forever. This only I ask of you. Swear that you shall leave the Duthgar, and never return here armed for war."

The old man looked at him hard. "And if we do not?"

Brand answered once more without hesitation. "Then you will die. And you will die for nothing. Think carefully."

The old man gazed at Brand, his expression unreadable. "We shall so swear it."

Each man then came before Brand, and he swore the oath as Brand had asked. And then they followed the old man out the door of the hall and disappeared into the new day that was beginning.

The Duthenor held the hall, and Brand had given the men the victory they needed. And the story of his growing army and quest to unseat Unferth had been enhanced. But Shorty was not so certain.

"Can the men you just let go be trusted? I fear, despite their oaths, that we might end up fighting them anyway. Only next time they'll be with Unferth."

He did not say it in front of the Duthenor, but spoke quietly to Brand while the men were clearing the hall of dead bodies.

"It could be," Brand agreed. "But I don't think so. They seemed good men to me, it was the lord they followed who was bad. And besides, the story will spread among the Callenor. Better to face men in battle who know they can surrender than those who know they must fight to the death. Because then they will, with everything they have."

Brand gave orders then. He had the treasury of the hall brought to him. This was in a locked box, and it was no great treasure. But there were gold coins and rings and precious stones. It would help him keep the men on side, and it would pay for supplies also.

He also ordered whatever food could be found to be gathered up as well. Haldring raised an eyebrow at this. She understood what it meant, but did not say anything.

A little while later they left the hall and closed the door behind them. The Duthenor were gathered there now, and an extra twenty men they did not have before.

"See!" Brand said, addressing them all. "Our army grows and word spreads. It is a slow start, but sure. The usurper will come to fear us! This I promise, but for now we march again."

The men cheered and got ready to move. Sighern, standing near Brand seemed confused.

"Aren't we going to rest here first?"

"No, lad. We could all do with some, but we must move fast instead. We must *never* be where we are expected to be. Not while our force is small."

"The men are ready," Taingern said. "Where do we go next?"

"A good question," Brand answered. "But I don't know."

Shorty laughed. "A simple plan is good. No plan … not so much!"

Brand gathered the reins to his horse. "I'll have one when I need one," he said with a wink. "For now, the only plan is to get away from here. We've done what we came to do, but there could be other hostile forces anywhere. It's time to disappear."

15. A Man of Secrets

Unferth sat on the high chair, oblivious to the goings on in the hall around him. Brooding they called him, often. But they were fools. He was thoughtful, as a great leader of men must be. Few understood that. Of them all, perhaps only Horta.

The magician sat nearby, his disciple Olbata beside him. Strange names for a strange people, but they were useful, which was all that really mattered. And yet Horta always seemed to give him bad news. He had done so just now, and yet he always had a solution to any problem.

But why were there so many problems? Unferth shifted in his chair. Even the high seat seemed uncomfortable of late. He should be enjoying all his successes now, instead of worrying. It was the way of the wolf to fight toward leadership of the pack. This he had done, and he had succeeded. He ruled two lands now, side by side. The Callenor were his own, the Duthenor subjugated. He had become now a king instead of chieftain. And he could do more, yet. Surely things should be getting easier and not harder?

Horta would be a help with that. He *knew* things, not least of all the hearts of men. That he looked strange did not matter. That he dressed strange was irrelevant. He was a man who wore a skirt and a bearskin rug over his shoulder. But no one ever dared laugh at him.

Unferth cast his mind back to their first meeting. The foreigner had been dressed the same way on that very first day. He had felt the urge to laugh, but the cool, steady gaze of the other forestalled it. Here was a man of power, a man who could kill and who had used that skill often. And when he had proclaimed himself a magician, causing thunder to boom in the hall and mead in cups to turn to ice as proof, Unferth had believed him. More, he knew that together they could achieve much. And all the little man asked in return was permission to explore the Duthgar.

What the magician searched for, Unferth did not care. Treasure probably, for men had dwelt here long, long before the Duthenor came. But whatever treasures there were would long since have been found. But none of that was of import now. Now, that Brand had come back.

Of course, he only had Horta's word for that. Somehow, Brand had entered the realm despite the precautions set against him, and begun to build an army. Horta would not say how he knew, only that he had spies through the land and that the king's own messengers would confirm it very soon. Magic of some kind, Unferth guessed.

"*How* did Brand get across the river?" Unferth asked. "It was guarded!"

The magician gave an elegant shrug. All his movements were elegant, as though he were born of nobility. But looking at how he dressed, that was not possible.

"It doesn't matter. He's a man of skill and determination. He found a way, and he is here now, moving against you. That's what's important."

Unferth tried to restrain his irritation. "The man is a nuisance," he said. Quietly, he seethed, but it would not do to let his advisors see the effect Brand had on him. Horta looked at him silently though, as if he knew exactly what was going on. Unferth did not like it. The man knew too much, but kept too many secrets of his own.

"Brand has three hundred men," Unferth said. "He's hardly a threat, and yet I must take steps. For his effrontery, I will send a thousand against him."

Horta did not look happy, but he smoothed his face when he spoke.

"He has some three hundred and twenty now—"

"Another twenty men makes no difference!" Unferth stormed. He did not like being corrected.

Unferth bowed, unruffled. "The twenty men are nothing," he said. "Their only relevance is that Brand is gathering more followers. What will his band number in a day, or a week?"

"Who is to say it will not diminish? That's just as likely."

"Perhaps." Unferth somehow made the word sound as though it were a denial. "Whatever the size of his band, it will take four or five days for him to reach us. Much could happen in that time. His army could multiply. Or he could die. The latter is preferable."

He said the last words drily, and Unferth caught a hint that he had already taken steps. A strange look passed over his face too, before it was smoothed over once more. Always, he was a man of secrets.

But Brand must be stopped now, before he gained momentum. He turned to his advisors. "Muster two thousand warriors. Choose our best general, and send them against Brand. He'll not survive that."

His advisors stood to leave, but Unferth was not finished. A new thought occurred to him, and he liked it.

"And make sure the word spreads to each of those two thousand men. There shall be a reward. I will give five gold pieces – no, I will give *fifty* gold pieces to the man who hacks Brand's head from his body and brings me the Helm of the Duthenor."

They looked surprised, but there were various murmurs of "Yes, my lord."

Unferth sat back, and he felt good. Two thousand men and fifty gold pieces were extravagant. But to see Band killed? For that, he would do anything.

16. Least Expected

Brand led his band of men back up to the path. Then he turned southward once more. The path was now a road, and better known to residents of the Duthgar as the High Way. And high it was, for it wound its way over the plateau of a range that divided the Duthgar in two.

They marched swiftly. Ahead of them, scouts were sent out to determine if the enemy were ahead. Likewise, men ranged behind them to see if they were followed. So far, the men had found nothing. It was a stroke of luck, but it was founded on Brand's speed, and he knew it.

Haldring led her horse a little behind him, and he knew she did not like walking. But she also recognized his thinking: the men followed leaders better who walked when they walked and endured what they endured. He beckoned her forward.

"What lies ahead," he asked.

"More halls, just as the last one that we left. All the way to where the king sits in his own."

"Yes, I know that. I've traveled this road before. But my memory is better of what's further south. I mean, what halls are close by?"

"There is a hall coming up on the left, and not long after another on the right."

"And whom do they favor?"

"They are both ruled by Callenor lords."

"And the next hall after them?"

"That is ruled by a Duthenor. Though there will be Callenor there also."

Brand considered that. What should he do next? He now had a force probably as great as any lord of a single hall could muster. At least in this part of the Duthgar. Further south they were more prosperous and larger. But he need not worry about that yet.

"Are these halls close to the road?"

"Aye, both of them."

"Good. Spread the word back among the men. We're approaching enemies, and they should be ready for battle. But we intend to pass by the next two halls unless accosted. We go to the third instead."

Haldring hesitated. "But are we going by the road? If so, the enemy will see us."

"Good," Brand said. "I want them to."

She fell back then to pass on the decision.

"I see you have a plan now," Shorty said.

"The beginnings of one," Brand answered.

It was not much of a plan, and he did not like calling it such. It was really no more than they had been doing. The unexpected. But that was perhaps the greatest military strategy of all.

They passed the halls. No one was visible, the fields around them being empty. It was a slightly eerie feeling, but there was no sense of danger. Word had reached the enemy of their coming. That was to be expected traveling along the main road. The scouts had seen no one, but the purpose of scouting was to identify if the enemy laid in wait somewhere, not to find one or two men in the wilderness that may be watching them.

At regular intervals along the road were chest-high cairns that served as markers. Each one measured five miles progress. Brand counted them off, knowing they marched swift and hard. Twenty-five miles in a day was a fine effort, and they had achieved that.

He stopped as daylight faded, allowing the men a rest, campfires to be lit and a meal. But he told them the day was not over yet.

Night fell. The fires blazed and then died down. But Brand let them burn on as embers as he gathered the men and led them off the road and down into a valley. The hall he sought was not far away, and he decamped in a grove of trees and lit no further fires. With luck, any enemy following would stop well before they reached the fires on the road for fear of scouts. They would not attack themselves, for it was foolish to attack at the end of such a long march except in extremity or with superior numbers. And that he was sure they did not have. Not yet, but Unferth would send warriors when he learned what was happening.

By dawn, Brand had marched to the third hall. But there he found a pleasant surprise. Word of his coming had spread this far already, and the lord of the hall, an old man, slight and frail yet with fire in his eyes, had expelled the Callenor who lived there. He had done this in the expectation that Brand would raise an army, though he knew nothing specific of events yet.

It was pleasing, and Brand thanked him. The lord surprised him again then by bowing deep. "My hall is your hall," he said. "More importantly, my men are your men. And you will need them, for the task you face is great."

"But the more I meet like you," Brand replied, "the easier it becomes."

The warriors camped outside and the lord took Brand and his generals into the hall to break their fast. It was not a large hall, but when they left they had a hundred new warriors with them. It would have been more, but at Brand's insistence the lord retained a large enough force to protect himself.

A cheer went through the army as the new men joined it.

"So far so good," Shorty said to Brand as they surveyed the growing force. "Now what?"

"Now, we backtrack."

"I thought as much. The enemy behind is more dangerous than the enemy ahead."

Brand grinned at him, but never answered. One of the new warriors approached, a younger man, tall and blue-eyed, with a red tinge to his blond hair.

Brand recognized him. "Caraval?"

The younger man bowed. "Yes, sire."

"There need be no sire or the like for me, Caraval. Not from you or your family."

The young man grinned. "Then you remember me?"

"Remember you? Of course! How could I forget that time we stole apples from farmer Thurgil's only tree? And he set his dogs after us even though you said his son had the dogs with him at a neighbors?"

Caraval grinned. "I lied, just so you would do it with me. But the apples were sweet, as I remember."

"Ah, that they were. The sweetest apples for miles all around."

"It's still there, you know."

"Really? It was an old tree even then."

"The apples are even sweeter."

Brand narrowed his eyes. "Are you trying to get me into trouble again? I bet the dogs are still there too."

The younger man laughed. "The tree and the dogs are still there. Thurgil too, but he'd set no dogs on you now."

"I'm not so sure of that! But I tell you what, when this is all over we'll go and see."

"Really?"

"Truly. But we'll call at the farmhouse first and ask permission this time."

The younger man grinned, and then his face grew serious.

"Are we going to win, Brand?"

"I got us away from the dogs that time, didn't I? And I'll outsmart Unferth now. Just watch me!"

Caraval grinned again. "You always did have a trick or two up your sleeves. Unferth better watch out."

A horn blew and the band was ready to march. Fresh supplies had been given to the men of food and equipment. Brand shook the younger man's hand and he went back to his place among the warriors. Brand gave a gesture, and the force began to march behind him.

"An old friend?" Taingern asked.

"An old friend, and a good one without a doubt. After Unferth … killed my parents I was hidden in house after house, district after district. Sometimes I only spent a night or a week in one place. Other times, months. I must have been with Caraval's family for near on six months, and I liked it there. But ever I had to move before the assassins learned of my presence. It protected me, but it protected the families also. So yes, he was a good friend during that time, and I know others like him all through the land. They were all good, strong country folk. And loyal."

Brand led them into the woods, and not back onto the road. He knew better now where he was, for these lands were familiar. But still he sent out scouts ahead and had them watch the backtrail behind.

They traveled swiftly, for though their number was growing they were still a small force. And though they moved through the woods there was a forest trail to follow, and Brand led them at a grueling pace along its length.

Toward nightfall, they had approached the last hall that they had earlier bypassed. There was no sign of a special watch, and it was a small hall anyway. Though the men were tired, this was a time where surprise counted above all.

Brand attacked. His men swarmed from the woods and converged on the hall. They took the doors swiftly, and crowded the occupants of the hall into the building's center.

Three of the enemy had been slain, Callenor warriors who drew their swords and tried to hold the door. Everyone else fell back in confusion, including the lord. They had not expected Brand to come back once he had gone past them, nor had they anticipated the speed at which he had done so or the direction from which he came.

Swords were drawn. Battle was near to breaking out. Only Brand standing there, slowly sheathing his blade gave the two sides pause.

"Let the lord come forth!" Brand commanded.

The lord came. He was an older man, gray haired and with a white beard streaked with darker hairs. He bowed, slightly, and kept his hands away from the hilt of the sword he wore. But he was not as old as he had at first looked. The beard gave him that appearance, yet no doubt he was still able to fight as a warrior, and Brand noted the way he stood, at ease but ready to act.

"I am your humble servant," the man said. "There need be no further killings."

Brand did not trust him. "You will swear allegiance?"

"I swear it, my lord. I am loyal."

Brand still did not trust him. He was not the true lord of this hall, at least according to the traditions of the Duthenor. The previous lord had died without children, and Unferth had given this man the lordship. But the chieftain of the Duthenor had never had that power. In such cases, the people of the district met and chose their own lord.

"Very well. This is what you will do then. First, you will expel any Callenor warriors from the hall. Let them go freely, if they will, with their blades but under an oath to do no harm in the Duthgar. And then your men will move on the next hall back down the road. This is ruled by a Callenor lord. You will take the hall, and expel the Callenor there, including the lord. You will have this done in my name, but the hall must not be fired."

The man bowed. "It shall be even as you say."

Brand still did not trust him. "And as a sign of your goodwill and loyalty, you shall order all this done, and your warriors to march tonight, but you yourself will come with my army."

The man hesitated at that point. He looked as though he were about to argue, but when he spoke he showed no sign of it.

"It shall be as you say, my lord."

Brand watched and listened as the man gave the orders to his most senior advisors. They did not seem pleased, but Brand detected no attempt to circumvent his instructions.

He had been using the stick so far, now it was time for a sweetener.

"If all is carried out as desired," Brand promised, "then you shall retain the lordship of this hall, and your heirs after you."

The lord nodded grimly. He had been forced to take sides when he would have preferred to have remained neutral and then claimed loyalty all along to him, or to Unferth, whichever one triumphed in the battles ahead. Brand did not like that, nor did he see it as a crime. But now the lord understood well enough that his future was linked to Brand. Unferth would not forgive him for supporting the enemy, even if he had done so under duress.

The warriors of the lord left, unhappy and yet also under the same compulsion as their lord. Even as his success was now tied to Brand's, so too was theirs to their lord's. If they did not carry out their orders, and their lord was deposed, a *new* lord, coming to power under either Unferth or Brand, would have little use for them. He would pick his own advisors and battle leaders.

Brand and his army watched the band of warriors depart into the night. It was good to see others march while they rested for once.

"Nicely done," Haldring said. "You rounded them all up and herded them like sheep."

"But?" Brand said. He could see by her expression that there was more.

"But you now have a sheep in your herd, one at least, that will turn into a wolf and bite you if he can."

Brand glanced over at the lord, standing by himself and watching the dark where his men had vanished.

"You're right. Keep an eye on him, but at least while we're winning I think he'll be true to his word." Brand looked at his own men, tired but happy. They were due not just a rest but a celebration of their successes. He grinned. "And since that lord will never be my friend, we may as well stretch things further. Leave his treasury intact, but crack open his larders and distribute his mead to the men. It's time they enjoyed things a little. But tell them we march at dawn tomorrow."

Haldring seemed amused as she went to carry out those instructions. And why not? So far, things were going well. Brand felt confidence creep up and over him, but he pushed it down. So far, things had gone well enough. But there was a lot yet to do, and there was the magician to worry about as well as military strategies.

Shorty broke his line of thought. "What now?" he asked. "The army is growing and morale is good. Back to the road and our next victory?"

"No," Brand said quietly. He did not wish anyone to hear. "Tomorrow will be a forced march. We go to a place that we must, but not one the men will like. It'll be unexpected to them, and therefore to Unferth."

17. The Pale Swordsman

It was a bright morning with a clear sky. A soft breeze blew, and it was neither cold nor hot. It was perfect weather to walk the farm and check the hazel-branch fencing. It was a job Dernthrad enjoyed. But not today.

He had come to a section where an ancient hedgerow served as a fence between his and a neighbor's land. He liked the hedgerow, though of late his sheep always seemed to find a way through to his neighbor's property. And his neighbor was never in a hurry to herd them back or try to fix his side of the hedge. There were signs today that sheep had got through again, and he had forced his own way through until he was peering out onto the field beyond.

His neighbor's cottage was not that far away. Smoke rose lazily from the chimney, but of the neighbor himself there was no sign. Dernthrad felt his temper rise. The man was lazy, never working his land properly and always complaining about how hard it was to earn a living. But curiosity drove Dernthrad's temper away.

A man was walking across the field, and toward his neighbor's barn. He was a man such as Dernthrad had never seen before. He moved with grace, as though each step were part of a dance, but he also moved with a sense of unhurried speed. He crossed the land like a fox, or a wolf, intent on his own business. And there was something of the predator about him.

The man was dressed in black, but silver chainmail glinted against it. And over his back was strapped two swords, the hilts sticking up and within easy reach. He was no farmer, that was for sure. But nor was he a warrior, at least not a Duthenor warrior. They dressed differently from that, and never had he seen one with two swords. Nor had he seen one with skin like this either – pale as new-fallen snow.

The warrior went into the barn. Dernthrad watched, uneasy. He should do something, but what? This man was up to no good, but he *was* a warrior.

He still had not made up his mind by the time the man emerged from the barn. He sat atop young Starfire, a mare that showed promise in the district for racing. With a kick, the warrior sent the horse into a gallop and they raced across the paddock toward where Dernthrad watched.

The path of the rider would take him close, and the farmer knew at last what he must do. He thought little of his neighbor, but he could not allow horse theft to go unchallenged. He forced himself through the rest of the hedge, tumbled into the grass on the other side and then rolled swiftly to his feet.

Thunder sounded in his ears as the black mare, the white star on her head blazing, raced toward him. He could see the rider clearly now. Fear stabbed at him. This was no man. The eyes burned like blue fire, the ears were pointed, and he moved in the saddle as though he were a part of the horse. This was an elf out of legend, though the tales did not describe them as so pale-skinned.

The eyes of the elf caught and held him. There was death there, cold and unmerciful. With a nudge, the rider angled the horse straight at him. In one swift motion he drew also one of his swords. Dernthrad caught the sheen of black steel. The blade swept at him.

Like a fool he had been standing there, like a fool caught by elf magic, but with a wild curse he dived to the side. The wind of the dark blade passed by his head. The thunder of the horse's gallop rolled by.

Dernthrad came to his feet, expecting now to die. But the rider did not even look back at him. Deftly, the black sword was sheathed, the rider bent low in the saddle once more, and the horse leaped a hazel-branch fence and raced away into a wood.

Starfire was gone. The rider was gone, but the fear of death remained. The cold eyes of the elf haunted him. All the more so for tales told that the elves were good people. But that had been a creature from the pit.

It had not been a good night. The hunters, empty handed, tired from a long night and irritable, made their way back home along the High Way. The sound of hooves came to them, louder and louder of a galloping horse.

They moved to the side petulantly. Around a bend came the rider, his black mount sheened by sweat that foamed its flanks, its great lungs straining for breath. If ever a rider was going to kill a horse, it was this man.

But the yells forming in their throats died. It was no man. It was a creature of nightmare, an elf out of story, a fiend from the pit. The elf looked at them, if elf it was, and the flash of his eyes burned with hatred and contempt. And then he was gone, vanishing around another bend and the thunder of his passage dwindling away like a storm that did not strike. But if a storm missed one village, it hit another.

"That thing, whatever it was," said one of the men, "had murder on its mind."

"It was an elf," said another of the hunters.

"No, not an elf. They're good folk."

"But it's ears. Did you not see them? It was an elf."

"No," said yet another. "It was a devil, and I pity the poor soul that it's chasing. Devils are summoned to kill men."

"How do you know it was chasing someone?"

"Why else would it ride like that?"

The men hurried on. The cooking pot might be light tonight, but at least they would sit around it. Alive. They knew that they had never come so close to death as just then.

The boy had climbed the old oak tree, as he often did. It was quiet in the branches, and he had a view of the land around, and especially of the road that ran past below. It was a good view, and a comfortable branch on which he sat, if a branch could be called such a thing. But it was better than his chores which he had finished. Now he had some time to think, some time to himself away from his brothers and sisters.

He thought of Brand, and the stories he had heard. He thought of the coming of a new king, and what it would mean for the land. Brand was of the old blood, descended from heroes of legend. And it seemed that the old stories were coming true. Rumor spread from farm to farm. Tales were told, hopes voiced. He was only a boy, and no one paid him any mind. So he listened and learned.

Luck had been with him too. He had been here in the tree when Brand and his men had come through. He had seen the great man, the silver helm of kings gleaming on his head, the way the men he led looked at him. He had seen it, and he would remember it all his life.

But now he saw something else from his high vantage. And suddenly he wanted to climb down the tree and run, but he would never be fast enough. A rider was coming through, but not like one he had ever seen before. It was a black rider, but his armor glittered silver like Brand's helm. The horse was black, and yet silver also, for the foam of sweat all over it glistened.

He felt sorry for the horse. It staggered and lurched, yet still the rider urged it ahead. Two swords were strapped to the warrior's back, and he drew one and used it as a whip to spur the horse on. There was blood on its flank where this had been done before.

The boy *hated* the rider. If he were old enough, he would stop him. The thunder of hooves and the harsh breathing of the horse came up to him. The rider passed beneath, all black and silver and pale skin. It was no man, but some kind of monster.

It too was from the old stories, whatever it was. Legends now roamed the Duthgar, and the boy realized something else. He did not know how he knew, but the certainty of it fixed itself in his mind. It was no coincidence. That monster, that creature of evil, was after Brand.

The rider passed. All noise died away. But the boy stayed in the tree. He was scared.

18. Sleeping Magic

Brand led the army forward. He knew this part of the Duthgar, but not as well as he liked, or needed. As they marched, he sent Haldring back among the warriors to find one who knew it well. That would be needed if he was going to do what he had in mind.

He led them through the low ways that he knew, following old trails into dark woods and avoiding farms and villages. Most of all, he avoided the High Way. He had been seen there, had traveled it, and could expect forces that supported Unferth to be looking for him along its length.

The march was quick, but they could not match the pace they had set previously. The terrain did not allow for it, and the men needed more rest. Some were still paying for last night's celebrations, but for most a rest was needed anyway. He stopped regularly, and he allowed a longer break than he had previously.

It was at one such break that Haldring returned to the front with a man.

"This is Hruidgar," she said. "He's a hunter."

Brand shook the man's hand. "I'm looking for a guide," he said. "How well do you know these parts?"

The man had a strong grip, a farmer's grip. But farmers made the best hunters. They knew the land like few others ever did, and they had patience.

"I've hunted, fished and herded cattle and sheep all over this part of the Duthgar. Ain't no one knows it all, but I know it better than most."

"And do you know where we'll end up if we keep heading as we are?"

"I was wondering about that. There's nothing in these parts but wild lands and trees. Good for hunting, but there are few folks about. I figured you wanted to lay low for a while, but you'll need to turn west and climb up to the High Way if you're looking to get far from here."

Brand kept his voice down, not wanting others to hear yet.

"But if we don't? If we keep heading south as we are?"

Hruidgar gave him a long look, as if seeing him for the first time.

"Aye, well, I guess from the question you know the answer as well as me. That way lies the swamp."

"The swamp indeed. And have you been there, Hruidgar?"

The hunter looked at him, his brown eyes darker than his tanned skin, and Brand guessed he had hunted in many places including some that he should not have. Some lords liked to set aside forests for their own use alone, but Hruidgar struck him as a man who would take such a thing as a personal challenge. Brand began to like him.

"I heard the stories as a youngster. It's a bad, bad place. But I took that as a dare. So yes, I've been there. I had to see if the stories were true."

Brand had heard the stories too. A beast-man was said to roam there, strong as ten men and evil as a cold-hearted snake. Men had seen his dark shape at dusk, haunting black-watered tarns and climbing the fells that rose above the swamp. Grinder, he was called. According to legend, he liked to lay hidden in water and lurch up to catch unwary men. He carried no weapon and killed them with his bare hands, and then ate them. So legend said.

The hunter studied him. "Aye. You've heard the stories. I see it in your eyes."

"I've heard them. And other things beside. The swamp is a bad place, of that I don't doubt."

"You don't know the half of it. I saw him once. *Him*. You know who I mean. He right proper put the wind up me, and I ain't been back since. What do you think of that?"

Brand did not answer straightaway. A hunter this man might be, but he was testing him. And Brand did not blame him. He did not like to follow a stupid man either.

"The old stories became a story for a reason in the first place," he answered at length. "I have no wish to go into the swamp, but necessity compels me." He gestured with his hand to take in the men resting all around. "I have an army here, of sorts. But in truth it's only the beginning of one. If Unferth catches us at the wrong place at the wrong time, he'll crush us. My job is to see that doesn't happen. The swamp will help me do that, because I'll disappear and then reappear, at a time and place of my choosing. Unferth will be looking for me in all the wrong places."

The hunter grinned. "Unferth is one that needs setting to rights. He's low as a snake's belly that one. Alright, I'll lead you through, if I can. It's a strange place, and I may not rightly know the way out again. We'll see. But even with an army it could be dangerous. You might disappear from folks out here looking for you, but there's lots of things in the swamp, and there's no hiding from *them*."

Brand took his hand and shook it. "You're the man I need. What I do is a risk, but so is staying out here."

Brand called an end to the rest after that. They went on, and now Hruidgar led them. The man took his time, studying the trail ahead and casting his gaze from ground to trees and back again. He even seemed to sniff the air at times, but Brand let him do as he would. There was no point in seeking expertise if you did not pay attention to it when you got it. And though Brand was no great hunter or tracker, he recognized that this man was. He just hoped he was good enough.

Grinder was one danger in the swamp, but he had heard of others. And as if that was not enough, he knew that generals had led armies into swamps in other lands than the Duthgar and never been seen again. Shifting waters, pathless mazes, land that was not land and sickness were only some of the problems a general faced in such a place.

The track they followed dropped down steeply into a valley. Thick scrub grew about them, and the path had dwindled and nearly died. This strung the warriors out in a long line, which was something Brand did not like. It made them vulnerable to attack, but less and less he feared Unferth's men. More and more he worried about the swamp. Already the smell of it was in the air.

He sent Haldring back along the line to tell the men where they were headed. He used her to deal with the Duthenor more than Taingern and Shorty. She was one of them while the others were not. He must grow the trust between the army and those two slowly. But they knew that as well as he, and he often saw them at breaks mingling with the Duthenor and talking, establishing a bond and getting to know one another.

There was a creek nearby. Brand heard it, but he could not see it. It would no doubt run at the bottom of the valley, which meant they were close to that themselves.

Their progress slowed. Some of this was the narrow track, but some was the reluctance of the men. Many would have heard of the swamp ahead, and those who had not would soon hear tales from others. He had given Haldring specific things to say. It would not be pleasant … have courage … walk warily … and think of the enemies we are leaving behind. He hoped that would be enough, and he knew the Duthenor were doughty men.

But if they balked at this he would be in serious trouble. His enemies would be gathering behind him. And if he had to turn back his leadership would suffer irreparable harm.

On the other hand, if they followed him through the swamp and came out the other side, they would be bonded to him and to each other all the more strongly.

Haldring returned. "How did they take it?" Brand asked.

"Not well."

"But they are coming?"

She looked at him coolly. "Have you been gone from the Duthgar so long that you forget what the Duthenor are like? You lead, and they will follow. Loyalty drives them, and pride. Wherever you walk, whatever danger you face, they will too."

They continued on. Brand would have felt relief, except for the fact they were going to the swamp. But he knew he was right to do so. It would give him an advantage over his enemies, and he needed that given they far outnumbered him. And it would help build the reputation of his growing army too. One of their generals was a shield-maiden. They came, stung their enemies and vanished into thin air. They had walked through the legendary swamp … all things to build their aura so that allies were more likely to join them, and their enemies to fear them. It was not swords, nor spears nor the clash of arms that won battles. It was the hearts of the warriors who fought them.

The army trod on. Hruidgar led them, slower and slower. The hunter seemed to have eyes everywhere, for he saw each bird that flew in the dim light of the tree canopy, watched every step he took to find a trail where the path they followed had disappeared. Only it had not. It might have been years since a man had walked this way, but the hunter found the path they took. Brand would not have seen it, yet once he strayed a little to the side of where the hunter led and noticed that branches scratched his face and the ground was uneven and grown over by tufted grass and twisted tree roots.

He had long since decided the hunter knew what he was doing, and there was no point in having scouts ahead. They would probably get lost, or killed. He had sent them to the rear where there was a far greater need for them. They were to discover if the army were being followed, and to kill any of the enemy that did so.

The noise of running water grew louder. It was more of a roar now, and Brand realized it was not the river. More aptly, it was still the river but it had become a waterfall.

The ground dropped suddenly. They clambered down, and to their right the trees thinned. There was a rocky outcrop there, and slightly above them but to the side the river disgorged into the air, flashing, turning and twisting in threads of silver. Foam flew from the rushing streams. The roar was louder, and the spray of water misted the air with swirling vapor. Through this, rainbows arced to the ground far below.

The hunter had no eyes for the waterfall. He kept his gaze mostly on the trail now, for it was rocky and slick with water. Carefully, he descended. Brand followed, leading his horse. The army came after.

It seemed an eerie place to Brand. It was like no other land that he had journeyed through, within or without the Duthgar. The trees changed, turning from the oak woods that they had been passing through into stands of black alder, old and weary looking with arched crowns and crooked branches. The trunks were dark gray and fissured, and here and there catkins still hung.

Down they went, deeper into the swamp, and the trail eventually leveled out. There was water everywhere, but land too. The rocks had given way to spongy soil. Mosquitoes swarmed around them, insects chirped and frogs croaked. Yet there were no birds that Brand could see, and for all the noise the land itself seemed quiet and brooding.

And well might it be. For in a place such as this the old magic was strong. Brand sensed it, a dormant thing, slumbering away through the eons. But there was power here, and he had no wish to wake it. Yet even as he thought that, he sensed that not all the powers of this land were asleep.

He realized with astonishment that the stretch of land that they now walked over was not land at all. It was a pathway of corrugated logs, like a bridge over water. Only they were set in mud, covered by slime and slowly decaying like everything else around them. Someone had laid this track. But who? And when? He looked up and saw Hruidgar looking back at him, a gleam in his dark eyes. It was almost like a question, or a challenge. *Did he still want to come this way?*

Brand stepped forward. One hand held the reins of his roan mare, the other was close to his sword hilt. But he went forward, and the hunter turned and stepped carefully ahead also. His hand was near his sword hilt too. If he knew who had built the path, he was not saying.

The hunter led them deeper into the swamp. The army trailed behind, each warrior following in the footsteps of the one before, the whole mass of them, one after another, stepping where Hruidgar had trod.

About them, the alders grew thickly, then thinned, and then grew thickly once more. Sheets of water lay to left and right, sometimes with clumps of swamp grass and weeds and lilies growing through. At other times the water seemed deep as though it were a lake. At yet other times there was ground, seemingly dry and above water level. The hunter led them over this at whiles, but not always. If some land was safe while other land was not, Hruidgar did not explain.

They were deep in the swamp. Brand felt like an intruder into a world in which he did not belong. There was a plop in the water beside him, and then a ripple over the hitherto still surface. Something large, very large indeed, had moved. He saw a glimpse of a creature, shadowy and vast as it turned and twisted in the depths, and then it was gone. Or at least he hoped so.

They climbed a little now. The land became rocky, but lined with moss and slime. Footing was treacherous. The swamp had become small ponds, covered in green algae. Through this maze they walked. But Hruidgar rarely seemed to hesitate. He seemed relieved though to be away from the deeper expanses of water. Or what dwelled within them.

The ground changed. It was dryer, and there was grass here. Brand knew, however, they had not begun to leave the swamp yet. It was too soon. The ponds were fewer. They had in fact become tarns, stone rimmed and dark watered. The hunter kept as far from them as was possible, but ever he found a way forward.

It was hard to tell time in the swamp, for the growth of trees was mostly thick and the sky was obscured. But it was clearer here on the rocky ground, and Brand realized the day was nearly over. Soon, they must find a place to gather together and camp. He whispered as much to the hunter, and the man nodded.

"I know a place," he said. "A good place, if such exists around here." He trod on, and Brand wondered if the army would find its way out of the swamp if something happened to the hunter. But so far, for all the eeriness of the place, he had sensed no great danger. But that meant only that for the most part the creatures that could bring it slept, not that they did not exist.

The hunter led the army to a rocky slope. It was not quite a hill, for there was no such thing within this swamp, but it was as close as they would get.

"Do not drink any water." Hruidgar warned.

It seemed good advice to Brand. They had supplies enough of food and water to last them until out of the swamp, and that would do. There would not be any fires either. There was no such thing as dry wood here.

Brand supervised the establishment of a camp. He was glad at least that all the warriors could be brought together in one place, and at a distance from any water. The rocky slope offered little concealment for anything to stalk them too. Another benefit. Yet he set a watch of roving guards as an outer ring to the camp as well as a closer ring of stationary sentries. This was no place to take any chances. Who knew what was out there? But if anything was drawn to them in the night, the many watchful eyes of the guards should give it pause.

It was a cold dinner. And the men spoke only in hushed tones. Brand walked among them, sharing a word here and a joke there. He was getting to know them. Shorty, Taingern and Haldring did likewise.

The dark grew deep. The night became old, and everyone settled down to sleep as best they could on the hard surface. They slept with their boots on, because it was the sort of place a warrior always wanted to be ready to stand and fight. But the boots also kept the mosquitoes at bay. Against this nuisance the men also wrapped a spare cloak, tunic or cloth of some sort around their faces.

Between the hard surface and the insects, sleep did not come easy. And when it did, they were woken often enough by strange grunts and moans and shrill cries that came from all around. The swamp at night was alive with animals, with hunters and prey and prey that could defend itself. Screams tore the air at whiles, the last breath of some creature that defended itself less well than it needed to. Death was all about them, and the old magic stirred. It was stronger in the dark.

19. The Mists of Prophecy

Brand spent most of the night dozing but never quite asleep. Nearby, other men snored softly. Haldring tossed and turned. And the hunter lay still. He was awake though, and at times Brand thought he saw his dark eyes gleam as they gazed out toward whatever cry had last signaled the final misfortune of some animal.

Dawn finally came, and the army trudged on. The men were scared. A night in this swamp was more than they had bargained for, and in some ways it was worse than a battle. They were trained for that, but they had no idea how to deal with a place where the land itself seemed an enemy.

The rocky ground gave swiftly away to wetlands once more. Again, there was a patch of felled logs that formed a corrugated bridge over stretches of black mud. They were slippery, but they felt secure beneath Brand's boots. He wondered how old the timber was. In places such as this, submerged in water or covered by mud, wood did not rot for decades. Even centuries. He had heard once that timber and even human bodies could be preserved for thousands of years. That was a possibility too. Whatever the case, he did not believe the Duthenor had ever laid this trail. But someone had, and he guessed it was long, long ago.

The hunter raised his arm and pointed. Away in the distance, steam rising from it in a slow-drifting cloud, lay a tarn.

"That," whispered the hunter, "is the home of old Grinder." He smiled then, his sun-browned face a flash of teeth and a glint of dark eyes, and then he led them on once more.

They avoided the place. There was no sign of the legendary creature though, but Brand sensed a presence, alert, brooding and watchful. Even a monster was wary of an army, and as Brand sensed him the thing probably sensed Brand. Sleeping dogs were happy to let other sleeping dogs lie. There was nothing to fight over, no need to stir up trouble.

The hunter came to an alder tree. It was an ancient thing, leaning over and its trunk heavily fissured. Its bark had been scored in places by an axe. Or claws.

"This is as far as I have ever been," Hruidgar told Brand. "But I learned from the old man who showed me the ways of this place that when he was young he found a way out not far ahead. He went that way only once though, and never dared return."

They pressed on. Brand was no longer sure if there was a trail, but the hunter seemed confident of where he walked. Soon, a wailing noise drifted to them, a sound full of the woe of the world. The hunter nodded to himself as though he expected that, and he walked on, his hand gripped tight to his sword hilt.

The alder trees grew thickly here, as though they formed a fence, even, perhaps, had been planted as a barrier. And from the branches hung human heads. Some were mere skulls, but others were fresh and the smell of rotting flesh hung in the air.

Brand moved ahead of the hunter and investigated. He walked slowly, his gaze taking in the scene but also searching out any sign of a trap or ambush.

A slight breeze picked up. All there ever was in the swamp. One of the heads moved, and it moaned. The sound was horrifying, and behind him Brand heard swords being drawn and also the sound of retching. He stayed still, his gaze fixed on the head.

The lips did not move, yet the moaning continued. The head swayed in the breeze, and then its movement lessened as the breeze died down. The air became still again, and the moaning faded to silence.

Brand reached out. Gently he touched the head, sought its mouth with his fingers and withdrew a length of pipe. It was made of a reed, and there were holes in it. The back end was narrowed, perhaps bent by steam to catch the wind and whistle. Tooled leather, with holes in it, slid back and forth over the holes as the head swung in the air. It was a flute and the source of the noise.

He examined the head now, dismantling it. The hair was woven of animal hair, probably from a goat. It was glued to a skull constructed of various animals. Skin and nose and ears were made from thin leather, now rotting.

Brand turned to the men. "These are not real. They are fake, and the noise of the moaning is caused by this."

He threw the flute to Shorty. The little man caught it deftly, shrugged, put his lips carefully to its end and blew. The flute moaned, and he danced a little jig. The men nearby laughed nervously.

"Pass it back through the army," Brand said. "Let everyone see the fakery. While we march."

He gestured for the hunter to lead them forward again. Hruidgar muttered to himself. Had he known what they would find here?

They pressed ahead, finding a gap between the trees. What Shorty had done was no surprise to Brand. He had thrown it to him for a reason. Shorty always had a sense of humor, and that was precisely what the army had needed just then. Laughter banished fear.

But the question hovered in Brand's mind; why had he thrown the flute to Shorty? Had he just known it was the thing to do? Was it his instinct as a leader of men, especially warriors? Or was it what Aranloth had called riding the dragon's breath? How much of his life, of moments just like that, had been blind luck or the operation of some hidden force, some sort of destiny or fate?

The feel of the land subtly changed. Brand sensed the creature known as Grinder out there somewhere, perhaps close enough to watch them. But there was something else too, something older and stronger.

To their right the land dipped into a series of murky lakes, one at the back very large. A gray heron flew overhead, gracefully lumbering, its head turning to the side in midflight as though it were deciding where to land and then thinking better of it. The bird disappeared behind a stand of trees ahead.

To their left the land rose higher into some craggy slopes, strewn with tumbled rock and overgrown with moss and tufted grasses. Ahead, through the stand of trees, was a kind of meadow. There seemed to be good, solid ground there. Green grass grew upon it, and a cottage stood in its center. Smoke rose in a lazy column from a rickety chimney that looked as though it were about to fall into a pile of bricks on the ground.

"The witch!" hissed Hruidgar.

Brand had not seen her at first, but as she stepped out of the cottage and walked toward them he studied her. His magic flared to life, ready. She had power, and she looked as though she had the confidence to use it. An old woman she seemed, an ancient crone. Her hair was lank and bedraggled. Teeth were missing. Warts tufted the skin of her face, and her eyes were rheumy. But they fixed him with a stare that belied her outward appearance. Old she was, but strong.

She came up to him, and Brand bowed, not taking his gaze off her.

"Good morning, lady," he said.

She closed one eye and studied him. "A lòhren is it? Yes and no I'd say. You have the look about you. But not quite."

"A leader of men, at the moment. My name is Brand, and I seek out Unferth."

Sometimes it was best to be direct. She would know who he was and what he intended. And she would know he intended no harm to her. He had made that clear by declaring Unferth his enemy.

She peered at him through her other eye. "Yes, well. I know that. What do you take me for? A stupid old hag?"

"No, lady. You choose to look like one just now, but you could look any way you want."

She looked at him for the first time with both eyes, her bushy eyebrows raised. "Yes indeed. And don't forget it." She laughed then, a cackle suited to her appearance. "In truth," she said, "I *am* old. Very old. But I like you anyway, despite your youth. Doesn't mean I won't kill you though, if it suits my purposes. I'm a bad, bad person."

Brand grinned at her. "I like you too. And likewise."

She regarded him then a moment, and she seemed amused. "You have style, boy. I like it. Because of that I'll tell you something." She dropped her voice to a hoarse whisper that half the army could hear. "You're being followed."

Brand nodded slowly. "I have sensed something. Perhaps it is the … creature that lives in the swamp?"

The old woman grinned at him, her blackened teeth showing.

"No. Not him. Someone else. *Something* else, summoned from the pit. Something new, and that intrigues me."

She reached out quickly and took his right hand between her own two. Her touch was cold, the feel of her skin like tattered leather. Brand did not flinch. He had a feeling what would come next.

The witch closed her eyes and muttered incomprehensibly to herself. Then her eyes flashed open and they fixed him with a milky stare. Her irises had changed color, and he knew she saw nothing of this world but the world of the future.

"I shall prophesy for you, boy. I have the talent, if you have the courage."

"A man makes his own fate, so tell me the future if you will. If I don't like it, I shall change it to suit me better."

She cackled. "The confidence of youth! Well then, let me see." There was a pause, and then she spoke again. Her voice was different now, less breathy, younger, sure of purpose.

"Ah, yes, the mists pass and I see. You shall succeed in your quest. But you shall fail also. Yes, yes. That is the way of it. And what you want … you shall never have. Oh, but I have seen that so often before. And … this one is new. Who you are is not who you were meant to be."

"Are you done, lady?"

She gave him an irritated look. "Hush, child. There is more. I see a darkness, old as the hills. It sleeps, but it wakens. Your sword shall be broken, but the land will make it new again. I see … I see. Nay, the mists return and obscure it all."

She dropped his hand, and Brand felt for the first time that it was cold as ice. When she had withdrawn her touch, she had withdrawn her magic.

"Aye boy, the mists are cold."

"So it would seem. Thank you for your foretelling."

She looked up at him, her gaze suddenly fierce. "Don't patronize me, child. I'm older and stronger than I look.

And I have the true talent. You think my prophesy is vague and uncertain? You think it made up charlatanry? Well, you will see!"

Her mood shifted again, and she cackled. Brand wondered how sane she was, but looking into her eyes he also wondered how much of all this was an act. Perhaps she really did have the talent. Perhaps she had learned more than she said.

"This has been interesting, lady. But we must march on now. Yet there are dangers in this swamp. Are you safe from the creature who lives here? Will you be safe from that which follows me?"

She pursed her lips, the skin of her mouth wrinkled and fissured. "Ha! I'm safe from the first, safer than all others. As for the second. Well, aye, I am safe from him too. We are much alike. We will walk warily around each other. *You* are what he hunts."

Brand hesitated. "I don't think you're quite as bad as you pretend. Will you help us?"

She grinned at him. "Oh, you overestimate me. I'm a bad, bad person. I've done things that would shrivel your soul. Oh yes, yes I have. You're safe from me, today. But I'll not help you. Nor will I help that which hunts you. I care for nothing outside of this swamp, and you will both be gone soon enough to leave me in peace once more. I offer no help, nor will you ever see me again. I have given of my gift, and that is enough. From time to time I feel the need to do so. If a bird has wings, does it not wish to fly?"

"Then, lady, we shall be on our way. Fare you well."

She did not answer, but she cackled as she turned and walked back toward her cottage. Brand signaled the army forward, and they crossed the meadow in silence. On the far side was another wall of alder trees, and they pressed through it.

They were back in the wetlands, and most were happy for it. Better the swamp than the abode of a witch, yet she had offered them no harm.

The day drew on. At whiles they glimpsed higher ground through gaps in the trees. Again, there was a path of sorts, but probably only one the hunter could find. And though he said he had never been this far before, he seemed to lead them true enough.

By dusk, they reached a strange land of tree ferns and rocky soil. They were higher now, and Brand sensed the swamp stir to life below. He felt also the presence of that which followed him. It was vague, and he could detect little of it. The witch's senses were keener than his own, and he was grateful for the warning.

They came out of the stand of tree ferns, and there was solid ground all around them. It was neither rock nor swampland, but the earthy smell of soil made rich by eons of leaf fall. It was a forest, mostly of oaks, and they had passed through the swamp without harm. It was one danger survived, but Brand felt there were other obstacles ahead, drawing close swiftly, and deadlier yet. He would not sleep soundly again until his task was accomplished.

20. Promises to Keep

The army moved through the growing dark, happy to put distance behind them and the swamp. They were tired, weary to the bone as few of them had ever been before, but they plodded on regardless.

Brand led them now, the hunter moving back into the ranks after a handshake and quiet word of thanks for his work. They climbed gradually uphill, and this meant toward the High Way. But Brand had no intention of traveling that way yet. When they had gone far enough from the swamp, he veered left. There, amid a stand of oaks with a small stream nearby, he finally set a camp.

The men nearly collapsed, but he had walked every step they had, and he knew exactly how tired they were. It was nothing that a warm meal and a good night's rest would not fix, but they had gained much in return. Unferth did not know where he was, and he could move with relative ease. His force was small and quick, and could strike unexpectedly.

It occurred to him that he could attack Unferth himself. His force was not great, but he could pass over the land in secret. He knew the ways. If so, he could strike at Unferth with total surprise. He could possibly kill him, for he would not have all his warriors to hand. But what then? He would be exposed, and he would not have sufficient numbers to hold the hall of his ancestors, the same hall that Unferth now ruled from, should Unferth's captains choose to move against him after their leader's death. And that, they might well do. No, something more was needed yet before he moved directly against the usurper.

The deeper into the Duthgar that he traveled, the better he remembered it. He knew these lands, for he had spent much time here. The districts around this area were the most loyal to his parents. He had hidden here in many farms, and the people who had concealed him had risked their lives to do so. Here, with luck, he could swell his force with warriors and not lift a blade to do so.

With such thoughts, Brand drifted slowly into a restless sleep. The fires burned low, and the army was still. But there were sentries moving about, double the normal amount, for he took the witch at her word: he was a hunted man. And the magician was no doubt behind it.

The next morning they decamped and moved out over a flattish land. This was rare for the Duthgar, which was mostly dominated by the rolling uplands through which the High Way ran, or the long slopes that flanked it.

All the Duthgar was farming country, but this was perhaps the best of it. And though some was pasture for sheep and cattle, most was cultivated fields. They trod a land where wheat and oats and barley were grown, where orchards stood in the sun and vegetables flourished in the deep soil watered by shallow wells.

The farms were smaller here, but more profitable. This showed in the farm houses, some of which were cottages but most double story houses. Some had barns as large as halls in other districts, while others made use of the lower story of the house as a barn in which to winter cattle. This helped provide warmth in the long, cold winters.

This was not country in which an army could easily hide. There were fewer trees and woods, and the farm houses were plentiful, which meant there were the eyes of many owners and farmhands to see them. So Brand made little attempt to hide here. Instead, he marched in the open, and the warriors sang as they marched. Old songs and good songs, stories of the Duthgar of long ago that made them proud of who they were.

There was a road, and Brand took it. Haldring had told him the Callenor did not like it here, and this matched his own experience growing up. The people hated them, and the Callenor in turn hated the flat land coming themselves from an even steeper and hillier country than the Duthgar. Instead of settling warriors here, Unferth taxed it heavily. It was a mistake, but one that Brand was glad of. It supplied the district with more reason to hate the usurper, and more freedom for its youth to join Brand's army.

He saw movement as he marched. Men raced away on horseback, people came out of the houses and watched. Farmhands in fields stopped what they were doing and peered at them. When the road took the army close to people, they clapped and cheered. Rumor flew on falcon wings in the Duthgar. They knew whose army this was, and what it was going to attempt. And they liked it. Not least did they like it when he drew his sword and raised it high. This brought the loudest cheers. Farmers they might be, but they came from a long line of warriors and there were swords and spears and shields in every house, and the youth of the district practiced with them. They were not seasoned fighters, but they were doughty men with passable skill.

Thus the morning passed. "It's a different land here," Taingern observed.

"It is," Brand agreed. "But also, my grandmother on my mother's side came from this district. There's a bond of blood between them and me. And it sings to them."

Taingern gave him a curious look, but Brand did not mind. He was in a curious mood. Almost fey, and he liked it. Danger was behind him as well as ahead. The future was uncertain. But this moment, this feeling he had right now, it was what it was to be alive. Or perhaps that was what Aranloth had called riding the dragon's breath. At any rate, the deeper he traveled into the Duthgar the more at home he felt.

Yet, suddenly cool of thought once more, he knew that in truth he could never come home. His feet might tread the same paths of his youth, his eyes see the same sights, but *he* was different.

The next few hours passed by, and it seemed like weeks. As the road came into settlements Brand greeted people, shook their hand and showed them his sword. At times, he wore the Helm of the Duthenor, but at others he lifted it free of his head and showed his face. The warriors he led continued to sing, and the countryfolk around often took up the song themselves. And wherever he passed, and to whomever he spoke, it always ended the same way. Brand told them he was here to overthrow the usurper, and he needed stout men, men willing to fight and risk their lives for freedom. If there were such men here, let them come with him.

And they came. At first in groups of two or three. Then in troops of twenty or thirty. And finally in their hundreds as word spread. They came now from before the army as well as behind it. There were older men, men who remembered Brand's father and grandfather when they sat in the high chair of the Duthenor. And there were younger men. Men who had no memory of Brand himself, but they knew who he was and what he stood for. And they trusted in him to rid them of Unferth.

Brand's mood changed. It was fey no longer, but cool and rational. These people depended on him. If he erred, they would die. That was responsibility enough to topple a mountain, for the weight of other people's hopes was heavier than the weight of stone.

But he went on. There was no turning back now. And the chances of the world were as great for fortune as misfortune. And he had skill besides. He had led armies to victory. He had outwitted enemies. He had command of magic. Neither he nor his army would be easy prey.

They camped that night outside a great village. Here, the army acquired food and supplies. Brand paid for it, for he brought gold with him, some his own and some from Lord Gingrel's treasury. This endeared him to the district all the more as many armies would simply requisition supplies without payment. And all through the night new recruits arrived.

The next morning saw them marching again, this time to not only cheers and song but the blowing of horns and the throwing of flowers. It was like a celebration, but Brand better understood the truth. Beyond doubt, some of the men with him would be slain in battle. Perhaps even himself. It was nothing to celebrate, and yet a man, nor a whole people, could go through life fearing death. Because if you did not go out to meet the great dark, it would creep into your house and sweep you into oblivion anyway. Celebration was as good a way to deal with truth as denial and fear. Perhaps even better.

While in view of the village, Brand rode his horse. The roan strutted proudly, and it was fitting that the people should see the rightful heir to the kingship with pomp and ceremony. But when he had passed beyond sight Brand dismounted and walked just as the soldiers did.

All the while he could see Haldring grow agitated. Finally she spoke.

"You might as well have written Unferth a letter and told him where you are. What use disappearing in the swamp only to announce your presence to the whole world soon after?"

Brand was not upset. This was why he had made her a general – to offer her opinions freely. And there was truth to what she said.

"I don't disagree with you. But Unferth has supporters everywhere. We've vanished from sight of those behind us. They may suspect we went into the swamp, but even so they'll not know where we're headed afterwards. And they'll not try to follow, I think."

She was not mollified. "And what of Unferth's supporters ahead of us?"

"A good question. In truth, I don't know the answer. I suspect Unferth will have already taken steps. And likely he'll have sent a force against me. But that force will be sent to my last known whereabouts. With luck, they'll have gone past us on the High Way. If not, then at least I have gathered a much greater force myself. Either way, I'm now in a position to force a battle if circumstances favor me, or to maneuver away if I so choose."

The army proceeded. They were coming now to a part of the district that Brand knew very well. He had lived here, and it was a strange feeling to be returning, stranger still that he had an army with him.

The flat land was giving way. It rose to hills in the east, thickly forested. He had hunted in those hills, and he had learned to fight there too. Many had been his teachers in the ways of the warrior, but one of the finest had been an old man who lived a secluded life as a hunter trading furs once a year. He had little money, and in truth was no great hunter. But he was a sword master of the highest skill and loved to pass on his knowledge.

There would be no chance to go visit him or see if he were even still alive. The road turned south west, and Brand followed it. But here also was a reminder of his past. These were farms that he knew. It was the fringe of the district, and the land was not as fertile as it had been, but it was still good land and there were good people here. The best. And these at least he might have a chance to see.

They came after a short while to the very farm that he had lived on. The cultivation at the front was now showing the new green shoots of a cereal crop. The soil was good there, and he remembered ploughing it, the smell of the fresh-broken earth filling his nostrils. He had cut hay there also, drying, turning and stacking it. A creek ran down the side boundary, and there he had caught his first fish. Near the cottage stood an orchard of pear trees. These he had pruned in winter and harvested later in the year. They were juicy and sweet.

But it was the cottage that drew his gaze. He had lived under that roof, eaten and laughed there, been protected from his enemies. For a while, it had been home. And the two people who had given him this stood there now before it, watching the army.

Brand signaled a stop. He told Haldring it was time for a break, and to Shorty and Taingern he suggested they have a drink at the farmer's well and see if they had any news. He had to be careful here, for he was hidden from farm to farm in his youth. The people who sheltered him had risked much, and he could do nothing here to reveal the identity of such a family. There could be spies in his army that would eventually report to Unferth.

When they were out of earshot, he told his two friends what was going on. They nodded, understanding.

They came to the well and drew water. From the cottage the two people walked out to meet them. They were older now, in their seventies at least. Harad had silver hair, and his beard was silver-white. Hromling was thin as a whip, her hair gray and her back slightly bent. They came over, hand in hand.

Brand felt a wave of emotion roll over him. These people had been parents to him, at risk of their own lives.

Yet he must be careful to give no sign of how he felt for fear they may be targeted by Unferth, and that hurt him.

There were tears in their eyes as they approached. "It's good to see you lad," Harad said.

"And you also. Both of you," Brand answered. "I wish I could hug you, but we must be careful. The army thinks I'm just having a drink."

"We understand," Hromling said. "Unferth has eyes everywhere. But welcome home anyway."

Harad glanced at Shorty and Taingern, and Brand knew what he was thinking.

"These are two friends of mine. I trust them with my life. They'll not say anything."

The old man seemed relieved. "You've done well, Brand. Most folks are lucky if they find one such friend all their lives."

"I've been lucky," Brand agreed. "All my life I've been lucky with the friends I've known."

Hromling wiped tears away from her eyes. Harad reached out and held her hand again, but he kept his gaze on Brand.

"Can you win?" he asked.

"I can win. I *will* win, for you and others like you through the Duthgar."

He saw belief in their eyes. They knew he would not have returned unless he could overthrow Unferth, but hearing it made that belief real. And saying it made it real to Brand as well. He *must* win, and he would. But it would come at a price.

For a while they talked. The two of them had heard rumors from time to time of his exploits. They were proud of him. They missed him. But talk returned to the battle ahead.

"When I had to leave here," Brand said, "I fled in a hurry. I left something behind. By chance, do you still have it?"

They knew what he meant. "We kept it," Hromling said. "We kept it hidden all these years."

"Fetch it for him," Harad said. "He'll need it now. And throw some bread in the bag as well. It will give him a reason to walk away from here with something in his hand."

Hromling hurried away. "Thank you for keeping it," Brand said. "Thank you for everything."

"It was our pleasure, lad. Don't worry about that. You just give Unferth what he deserves, and the world will be a better place."

Brand sensed the curiosity of his two friends, but there was no time to explain to them what Hromling carried as she returned. In her hands was a plain hessian sack. It seemed light in her grip, as though there was no more in it than a few loaves of bread. She gave it to him.

He thanked her, not with the hug that he wished to give, but with a handshake. But he had slipped a gold coin into his palm. He shook Harad's hand as well, and did the same with him.

They surreptitiously pocketed the coins. Two gold coins, as much as the farm would earn in a year, but he wished he could do more for them.

"When this is over, I'll return," he said.

They grinned at him. "We'll look forward to it. Then we can talk properly," Harad said.

"And I'll cook you roast mutton," Hromling offered. "It was always your favorite."

He left then, steeling himself so that his face showed no emotion as he went back to the army. To them it would seem he had passed the time of day with an old farming couple as he drank at their well.

The army moved off. Brand led them, his gaze to the front instead of his old home and people he loved. He hated it, but it was for a purpose and there was no sacrifice he would not make for the safety of people who had risked so much for him.

On they went, and Brand set a hard pace. His army was much bigger now, but secrecy and surprise were two of the greatest factors for military success. He may have lost it, but he did not think so.

By nightfall, he had veered back toward the High Way and established a camp. After the army had eaten, and he had carried out his customary walks, talking to sentries and soldiers, he returned to his usual place near the center of the camp. Sighern was there, tired and sleepy, sitting down near a dying fire.

Brand gestured to him to stand up and come over to where the horses were tethered.

"We haven't spoken much, lately," Brand said. "How are things with you?"

"I'm fine. I've been keeping my mouth closed and my ears open. And I've been watching how you lead the army."

"Really? And what have you learned?"

"Keep morale high. Keep your enemies guessing. Strike where you can win, and shun fights you might lose. All the while, gather your strength."

Brand was not sure what to say. The boy *had* been watching. He understood warfare, and politics for that matter, better than most men twice his age. He had a talent for it.

"Good! Keep watching. You just never know when such knowledge will come in handy. But in the meantime, I have a task for you. If you're willing."

"Anything," Sighern answered.

"You shouldn't be so quick to accept," Brand said with a smile. "It could be dangerous."

"Even so," Sighern said solemnly, "I'll do it."

Brand drew out the hessian sack from his saddlebag that Harad and Hromling had given him. He handed it to the boy.

"Don't be fooled by appearances. What's inside this simple sack could get you killed. Men have followed it and died. Unferth would murder you to destroy it. Do you still wish to carry out my task? If not, I'll understand. Just give me the bag back, and we'll speak no more of it."

The boy held the bag close to his chest. "I'm game, whatever it is."

Brand nodded slowly. Shorty was right – the boy had guts.

"Then you should know what it is that you carry. It's the banner of the chieftains of the Duthenor. My father, and his father before him owned it. It has seen war. Men have died beneath its shadow, died for what it represented. Say nothing to anyone, nothing at all. But cut yourself a staff when next we camp."

Sighern took it all in slowly. "And then what?"

"Then, if you wish it, you will be my banner bearer. Do you want to do that?"

"Yes!"

"Good!" Brand said. "Wait though to reveal it. Tell no one, show no one, until I give you the word."

"It shall be as you say," Sighern said. "Thank you, for I know this is an honor normally given to some trusted warrior who has proven his worth."

Brand clapped him on the shoulder. "And so it is. You've proven your worth to me when swords were flashing and death in the air. And in other ways too."

The boy stood taller. "Now what? Where does the army march?"

"We march to war, for I have promises to keep. And though you and I have fought together, the army speeds now to its first proper battle, but if we win, not our last."

Sighern seemed to think about that. He had a quick mind.

"It was safer when our army was smaller, was it not? Now, we'll have to fight and win just to keep the men fed?"

"Indeed so. It was safer when it was just you, me, Shorty and Taingern facing the wolves. What comes next will be worse."

21. It Comes

Harlach sat in the reed chair by her hearth. It felt cold, as it never did in the swamp, and she carelessly tossed another chunk of alder into the fire. It hissed and smoked as the flame took it, for there was more moisture in it than there should have been. It had not been properly cured yet.

She paid no heed to the smoke, ignored that it made her cough. She was always coughing. It was a symptom of living in the swamp. Once, she had lived elsewhere, but that was long ago.

She shifted uncomfortably in the chair. No use thinking about that now. Keep your mind on the present, woman, or the present will kill you.

Had she said that aloud, or only thought it? She was not sure. She spoke to herself often these days. Another symptom of living in the swamp, mostly by herself. And age, of course.

With age came a diminishment of power. Once she would have killed the creature that trod her swamp without pause. Now it came to kill her, and fear gnawed at her empty stomach. She had thought herself a match for it, even now, but the closer it came the more of its power she sensed. It might kill her, but then again, why should it? She would give the thing freely of the information she had. Brand was nothing to her, the fate of the Duthgar even less.

Think, woman. What does it want? The answer came to her quickly. It did not want information, as such. It knew as well as she that Brand had come through, and when. It was following him, and it was gaining on him. It did not need her for that. So, then, it wanted of her power. She had the gift of foresight. It wanted to know *who* Brand was, what he was capable of, what he would do. It did not take him lightly as an enemy, and it wanted to understand him before it struck. In that way, it would guarantee its success. As if the creature needed more advantage than it already had.

The swamp was silent, even though night had fallen. It was here, just outside. She sensed it, sensed its anticipation, and she cursed herself for a fool. It was going to kill her.

She stood, her back paining her as she did so. A knife lay on the table next to her, but that was useless. Her eyes scanned the room. For the first time she noticed what a hovel it was. It was no place for such as she to die.

Anger ran through her. She straightened. She had better weapons than steel with which to defend herself. Whatever devil this was, she would make it scream if she could.

At that moment, the door opened. The creature passed through the threshold, and she knew it for what it was. And fear quelled the rush of pride that moments before had enlivened her.

Tall he was, his every movement one of sublime grace. Black leather clad him, gleaming like polished coal. Armor he wore, chainmail brighter than silver. A helm was on his head, and he removed it, showing eyes that burned like blue fire and white hair, long but tied back with an obsidian ring. His cheekbones were high, his ears pointed and delicate. He was what the Duthenor called an elf, what many others called a Halathrin. But he was of a kind older and deadlier than others in Alithoras. He did not come from Alithoras at all, but from the pit itself.

"Speak, witch. And your death will be swift. Defy me, and you will endure torment beyond your imagination."

Harlach laughed. She was scared, but threats had no effect on her.

"Listen, boy. I was steeped in evil before you were spawned under a rock. Time was when you would be on your knees before me, begging to serve. Do not think to frighten me."

The elf looked at her, no sign of what he felt on his face.

"That time is gone, if ever it existed. Tell me what I want to know. Tell me of the warrior called Brand."

"Go to hell!" Harlach cried. She raised her hand. Fire spurted from it, a rush of crimson tongues.

But the elf was swifter. It ducked and rolled and came again to its feet. Its left hand knocked her arm aside, its right gripped her throat and squeezed. And its eyes bored into her own, probing her mind.

She felt its magic then. Her own rose in defense, but the elf swept it away. His eyes filled her vision, and she sensed her mind drawn into them, sensed him sifting through her thoughts and memories.

She resisted. He forced his will upon her. Pain tore at her brain, and she felt blood dribble from nose and ears. She could not stop him. His was the greater power, but hatred gave her strength, and the certain knowledge of her death added to it. If she could not prevail, then she would do something for Brand, some small thing that perhaps would give him a chance at life. Through him, she might yet have vengeance.

While the creature read her mind, she read his and saw how he would attack Brand, saw like pieces on a gameboard the greater strategy that was afoot, and who the true players were. She shuddered at the enormity of it.

She went limp, and though pain ripped through her, she allowed the elf to find all that he sought. All, save for one thing alone. This she concealed in her mind within a wall of flame. And when the creature probed it, seeking out what she hid, she turned that flame upon herself, burning out her mind and ending her life.

The last thing she sensed was the chagrin of the elf. He had failed to dig out that final secret, and he did not like it. He was one that could not abide being thwarted. Disappointment rushed through him also. He had been looking forward to tormenting her.

With a bloody smile on her lips, her spirit fled into the great dark.

22. The God-king

Horta did not like to ride. Riding was for peasants. Of old, when he had the need to travel from his estate he did so by sedan chair, the four litter-bearers mindful, for fear of death, to make the experience smooth.

Not so the horse. It jumbled him around like a sack of vegetables on its way to market. It was unfitting, as all of this land, its people and its ways were.

But despite his discomfort, the mount helped spare his arthritic knee and allowed him to cover a great deal of ground, and all the while his gaze never faltered. He looked around him wherever he went, studying the countryside, scrutinizing the ridges and cliff faces and the sides of hills. Always he looked for signs of digging or tunneling, or at least places where such things could be concealed.

And his heart quickened now, for the side of the hill that he approached was a little too steep, and recent rains had eroded soil that exposed rock beneath. The rock was smooth, unnaturally so.

He drew closer. Had his years of searching become fruitful at last? Too long he had wandered around, almost aimlessly, until he had come to an old storyteller west of the Duthgar who told him a tale of an ancient battle. Much was myth, much was a mixture of other stories and other battles far too recent, but some of the details, just enough, rang true. They told of a battle between that ancient race of tyrants called the Letharn, and their great enemies, the Star People. Could that be a twisted name for his own race, the Kar-ahn-hetep, the Children of the Thousand Stars?

He had thought so, and so it had proven. But the site of battle was in the place called the Duthgar, and there he must seek permission of its king to explore. The Duthenor did not let foreigners roam freely. So he had met Unferth, convinced him to allow him to wander the lands in return for his services. Unferth, fool that he was, did not know what a magician was capable of. But Horta had proved it to him, and worked his way into his confidences quickly.

It had not taken long to find the remnants of the battlefield after that. And he knew he was close then, knew his time was coming.

He studied the surface of the newly-exposed rock before him. It was smooth. Almost too smooth and too flat to be natural. His breath caught in his throat. Were there not faint chisel marks in the stone?

Quickly, he retrieved a shovel that was strapped to his saddlebag, and his hands trembled as he began to dig away more dirt.

Long he had looked, and long were the years since the great battle had been fought. More than ten thousand. Up from the south-west his people had come, warlike, their swords glittering in the sun, their armies marching as ranks of gods. Against the Letharn they struck, two mighty empires clashing in a war that spanned a continent. Blood had flowed. Rivers of it. Men fought men, sword clashed against sword, the spells of the magicians contended with the magic of the wizard-priests of the Letharn.

Sweat dripped from Horta's brow, but he felt a cold chill pass through him. He almost thought he had been called to this place, such was the certainty in his mind that he had discovered what he had long sought. And then there was a mark upon the stone. It was a rectangle, nothing within it and nothing without: but it was certainly carved by man and not nature.

His heart leapt. Reaching into dim memory, he drew forth long-forgotten words. It was a simple spell, primitive even. But it was known only to him and his kind. He uttered the words and passed his hand over the stone. And waited.

Of old, the kings of his people built mighty tombs. They were massive things, fortresses of stone, guarded by men, magic and traps. The dead kings rested in eternal peace, their bodies preserved so that they might keep their form in the afterlife. But the great king, the greatest to have ever lived, and the last of the Kar-ahn-hetep, he had no such tomb prepared for him. He was yet young when he set out in war against the Letharn. He was yet young though he led his warriors for ten years of war, surging against the enemy. And the enemy had fallen back. A thousand miles they withdrew, ceding land after land, country after country.

But what fate gave fortune stole back. The Letharn strengthened their positions, and held them. Then they began to creep forward, retaking lands they had lost. The great king could not abide this. West he went with one of his armies, and then north. He tried to catch his enemies by surprise, but was surprised in turn.

Battle followed, mighty and terrible. He who should have ruled the world was slain. But his loyal magicians saved his body from the enemy, and the army fought a fighting retreat. So the secret lore told.

Horta held his breath. The stone grew slowly darker under his impatient gaze, and then paled. The rectangle turned into a cartouche, what the ancients termed a *shenna*. Within it, the sign of the great king sparked as though the sun shone through the stone itself. Three stars, one ascendant over the other two, glittered momentarily and then blinked out.

He had found what he was looking for. No more was needed. He felt the weight of destiny on his shoulders, felt the call of his blood. It was for *this* that he was born. It was his life's work, nearly come to fulfillment, but not quite yet.

This was a tomb. Not the great tomb that should have existed for such a king, but a hiding place, a place to preserve his body from the enemy and from time itself.

The army had fled, pursued by the Letharn. The magicians took the body of the king, and by their arts of magic and the science of their lore, they preserved it. But death was upon them, for the enemy pursued relentlessly.

In the night, the magicians led a hundred men from the army. They excavated a tomb and hid it; a place safe from the enemy. There they laid the king to rest with what rites they could, and preserved a memory of their deed. So Horta had learned, for he was descended from one of those magicians.

Yet nearly all of the hundred men were killed. None could know the secret of the king's last resting place and live, for treasures were buried with him, and he himself was a treasure greater than them all. But even kings had enemies, *especially* kings, and these would seek to destroy him if they could, to deprive him of his enjoyment of the afterlife by maiming his earthly remains. But the secret story came down, even to Horta and others like him. They *all* searched, but *he* was the finder.

The magicians of ancient days were mighty. After the great battle, their empire crumbled around them and their arts fell into decline. Yet, in the peak of their powers, the magicians were supreme, and they could preserve the dead in a state very close to living. And the years would not have destroyed this.

Upon that knowledge, a prophecy was born. The king would be resurrected. The king would live again. The god-king, for such he was called, would return when the Kar-ahn-hetep were at their lowest ebb, and he would lead them to glory and conquest again. And now, the Letharn were no more. Who would oppose them as they swept across land after land, their swords red with blood and victory lighting their eyes?

Horta shuddered. What glory would be his if he made this come to pass? What rewards would the god-king bestow upon him? What power would he not command as the first lieutenant of a god, returned from death to rule the world?

And Horta knew he *could* bring this to pass. He knew the spells. He knew forbidden rites that even the ancients had shunned and feared. For he was mighty also, perhaps the greatest to have lived since those far off days of old. And he was of the house of the god-king, and blood called to blood. It mattered not that the laws of magic forbade what he intended. Prophecy was stronger than law.

But this he could not accomplish all at once. The god-king would be vulnerable after so long a sleep of death. He would need aid and succor until his strength grew. He would need an army to protect him, and to fulfill his will. It would not be fitting to wake him without servants.

Horta frantically worked with his shovel, piling dirt back over the stone. The time was not yet right to wake the god-king. First, he must summon an army loyal to his own house so that they might destroy any opposition. They must clear the way before the god-king came.

And Brand was a threat, and even Unferth. But the first would die soon, and the second would fall to unexpected war. The Duthgar would be ruled by the Children of the Thousand Stars. It would form the cradle for an ancient civilization to be born anew.

Horta hastily retied his shovel to the saddlebag and leaped upon his horse. He must send word back to his people, at least to his own sept. They would flock to his call. The Duthgar would fall, and the god-king would rise and have an army at his command. Small it would be at first, but it would grow. And the world would tremble.

23. I do a Man's Work

The time of skulking was over.

Brand veered west toward the High Way. The army followed, greater by far than it was before. Battle drew near, and lives would be lost. It was all on him, and that was pressure that made for poor decision making. So he did not think about it. At least, he distanced himself from it as best he could. Yet he must also keep it in his thoughts to some extent. Otherwise, he would forget that his choices had become life and death for other people.

It was a tight balance, the kind that a person needed in order to walk a narrow mountain trail with a vast drop into oblivion on the left, and a steep hill of snow to the right that could gather into a deadly avalanche. And all the while the trail beneath their boots was treacherous with ice.

The army passed through an empty land, and there seemed no sign of people, no indication of habitation. But the Duthgar was like that. It was a settled land, kept and cultivated, but still many parts were not. These were wild and remote areas, notwithstanding that at any time a farming district could begin nearby.

But he knew this land, remembered it well. Here there were rolling fields of grass and clusters of trees. Soon, when they neared the road, the farms would begin again.

He called a halt a mile or so short of where they started. The men settled for a rest, and Haldring approached him.

"It's soon, is it not, to stop for a break?"

"It is, but I need news. What's been happening? What has Unferth done and where is his force? He'll have sent one to defeat me, of that I'm sure."

"Really?" she countered. "How do you know that he hasn't drawn his forces to him and decided to wait for you to attack. That way his men would be better rested and closer to their supplies of food."

Brand did not think so at all, but he could not fault her argument. She might even be right.

"Taingern? Shorty? What do you think?"

Shorty gave a shrug. "What does it matter either way? Thinking about it won't change anything."

"What do you say, Taingern?"

"I think he'll try to hunt you down. He'll have sent an army, but where will it have gone? It's probably bypassed us already and traveled along the High Way further north, back where we came from."

"I hope so," Brand said. "But we know nothing for sure, and though knowing may not change anything, I'd rather know than not. So we're back where we began. It's time to get news. The army can wait here until I have it."

Brand looked around him, ready to pick someone to move forward into the farms and gather news. But Sighern had heard the conversation and stepped forward quickly.

"I'll go," he said.

Brand hesitated, uncertain.

Shorty clapped the boy on the shoulder. "You're game lad, but I think you're too young for this."

"I may be young, but I do a man's work. You can't deny that."

Shorty nodded slowly. "No, I'll not deny that. You do a man's work. You fight like one anyway. Better than many."

Brand felt everyone's gaze on him, the boy's most of all. Responsibility was heavy on him, and deaths would be on him soon as well when battle was joined. And he could not send a boy into danger, no matter how great his courage. The answer would have to be no, but what he said instead was yes, and it surprised him more than anyone else.

Sighern looked proud, and Brand did not have the heart to take it back, no matter that he did not understand what had just happened. Twice now this had occurred, and it worried him. Was this what it was to ride the dragon's breath? To have some sort of fate or destiny guide him, even force him, down a path that he did not understand? Or was it his own instinct surfacing and taking control?

But the decision was made now, and Brand accepted it. Quickly he explained to Sighern what was required, and then the boy was gone, walking off into the countryside with the gaze of the whole army upon him.

Haldring looked grim. "You've sent him into danger," she said. "He's too young for the task and many others would have been better suited."

Brand did not know what to say, so he just voiced his thoughts. "I think you're right. But there's *something* about him. He's everything a Duthenor should be, and more. He is, perhaps, even made for greatness. There's a destiny upon him."

Haldring did not look happy, but she said no more. Nor did Taingern and Shorty, but he felt their gazes upon him, burning with curiosity. Those two had seen this before, but he had no answers to give them.

Sighern walked at a fast pace. He was young, and this was an adventure of a type he had not believed possible just a short while ago. It gave him strength. That Brand believed in him was everything. He was a hero, and a man worthy to follow. And Sighern knew he would follow him anywhere, undertake any task asked of him.

He had a sword belted at his side. He knew how to use it. He had the trust of Brand, and the responsibility to do the right thing for the army. News was needed, and he would gather it. Who better than someone his age? He would not be taken for a warrior, and people would speak freely to him. An older man asking questions would draw suspicion, and the supporters of Unferth were everywhere. But a boy? They would not think him a scout for an army. He grinned to himself and pushed on. All was right with the world.

He soon passed a few farms, but they seemed small and there was no one in sight. It would be better to move up to the High Way where he could find out what was needed from those who would have heard or seen things first hand.

It did not take him that long to reach it. Straightaway he noticed that the grass of the road was trampled by the passage of many feet. It would take an army to cause so much damage. But how many men were there and which way had they gone?

He had no answer to the first question. He would have to talk to someone for that. But studying the tracks he soon realized they headed north, back were Brand had come from.

Sighern set off on the road following them. It might be that he had already discovered all that Brand needed. But he would be questioned when he returned and it would be better to be able to give numbers. How big was the army sent against them? Brand would want to know that. And also how long ago it had come through here. The tracks looked quite fresh to him, but again it would be better to get confirmation.

Ahead, a village came into view. It was quite small, little more than a gathering of huts. As Sighern approached, he thought of how best to go about his task. He could just ask anyone what he wanted to know, but the best people for him to speak to would be boys of his own age.

Just before the village, he saw a small creek running south-eastward. It was more a gulley than a creek, but it grew bigger as it went and other gulleys joined it. Further along, tall trees overshadowed its banks. If he lived here, that's where he would go to fish and hunt and while away the time. And if he were sheepherding, he would find a paddock close by. He bet the boys of this village would think the same way, and he turned his feet off the road and toward it.

He walked downhill, now following the little creek. There was a well-beaten path here. He came across women washing clothes, and he stayed clear of them. Further along, he heard the bleating of sheep. This was more promising, and sure enough there was a lad there his own age who stood up from where he had been sitting with his back to a boulder, his shepherd's crook in one hand and a curious look in his eyes.

"Who are you?" the boy asked, his tone neither hostile nor friendly. It was what Sighern expected.

"I'm not from around here." His own reply was neutral also. And he left the other wanting more. Obviously, he was not from around here, but he left the explanation hanging.

The other boy looked at him, and Sighern knew what he saw. A boy like himself, but one who carried a sword and traveled the Duthgar. Not old enough to be a warrior, and yet old enough for the other things.

The boy made up his mind, and stuck out his hand. "I'm Durnloth."

"Sighern."

"Ah, that's one of the old names."

Sighern let go his hand. "I was named after my grandfather. And he after his. It's a long tradition."

Durnloth heaved himself up to sit on the boulder. Sighern followed his lead. Sheep grazed placidly in a small paddock to their left and Durnloth eyed them momentarily before he spoke again.

"So, you don't look quite old enough to be a warrior. What are you doing here?"

"Maybe not quite yet. But soon. Mum and dad were killed by raiders. Since then, I've been wandering. I hear an army came through here. Maybe I'll join them."

Durnloth looked at him with sympathetic eyes, but he only spoke of the army. "I'd stay away from them. That was the king's army. He who should not be king, anyways. They went through fast, and cleaned out most of our food, without paying. Besides, they'll be fighting soon. You can bet on that."

Sighern answered cautiously. "I may not like them, but if they kept me around, even to run errands and messages it would be good for me. Three meals a day in the army, they say."

"If it's work you're after, some of the farmers around here might take you on. But you'd earn more in the army. And if you can use that," he indicated Sighern's sword, "they just might let you fight and pay you a full wage. Maybe."

"I can use it. When did the army come through?"

"Yesterday morning it was. Quite early, but they'd been marching a good while already. They sure were in a hurry, trying to catch Brand by surprise, we reckon."

"Do you think they will?"

"Hard to say," the boy answered. "All we hear are rumors, and one has barely spread before the next overruns it. No one knows where Brand is, or what he's doing. Only that his army is growing and he's coming for Unferth."

"Maybe I should join *his* army."

"Better him than Unferth. But Unferth pays better, I hear. Then again, a dead king pays no wages."

"Do you think Brand will win?"

"He's the true king. A hero in foreign lands, they say. He'll win, or he'll die. One or the other."

"How big was Unferth's army?"

"Two thousand men. So my dad tells me. They took his finest horse, and he was in a right temper about that. But he wasn't saying anything. Not until after they left. Then he swore the roof down, mum says."

Sighern was shocked. Two thousand men was more, much more than he expected. Brand would want to know that. Suddenly, he felt anxious. It was time to be gone from here, time to get back to the army.

He jumped off the boulder, and the other boy did likewise.

"I'd better hurry," Sighern said, "if I'm going to have any chance of finding either army."

They shook hands again. "Good luck," Durnloth offered. He seemed as though he meant it, but Sighern knew that Brand needed it more than him. He hurried away.

Brand sat with a small group of men, playing dice and getting to know them. His life would depend on them soon enough, and theirs on him. But he excused himself when he saw Sighern hurry out of the woods.

The boy emerged, walking quickly but with a telltale swagger to Brand's eye. Moreover, he held in his hand a fresh-cut pole for the banner he would carry.

Brand met him before he reached the camp. He was eager for news, and despite the boy's surprise information that an army of two thousand men had been sent to defeat them, Brand was pleased. The enemy had traveled past them, and that gave Brand several advantages despite being outnumbered. Above all, the enemy would now have to react to *him*. That was vital, if he could find ways to turn it to his advantage. And he would.

"You've done well," Brand told him after Sighern had finished his report. "Very well indeed."

News spread after that. Brand was happy for the size of the enemy to be discussed, for he did not believe in lying to his troops. With the news also went his confidence that they would win.

Dusk settled soon after. Brand told Sighern to keep the banner close. It would be unfolded soon, possibly even tomorrow. "Hold it proudly when the moment arrives lad, for the Duthgar is coming to a time of change. You, and those who follow the banner, will be a part of history."

"And against whom will we march?" Sighern asked. "The army that tries to find us, or Unferth himself?"

It was a good question. "I'll think on it overnight."

24. Fortune Favors the Bold

The next morning was an early start. And it would be both a long and hard day.

Brand took the army up toward the High Way. The men seemed eager. They were outnumbered, but they were confident nonetheless. They had outwitted the enemy repeatedly. But Brand himself was reserved. His tactics were successful so far, but when armies clashed people died and hopes burned away like smoke on the wind.

His three generals came to him. They all knew what approached was a pivotal decision.

"What's it to be, Brand?" Taingern asked gently. He understood better than the others what emotions would be running through someone's mind at a time like this. Brand knew his capacity for empathy was enormous.

"My heart yearns to turn south when we reach the road and strike at Unferth. He would be unprepared, believing the army he sent would have found and engaged me. And he is the real enemy, the one that must be defeated."

"But?" Shorty said.

"But Unferth has a magician in his service, one of great power. I'm wary of him. Therefore wisdom dictates that I turn north, defeat the army of two thousand sent against me with one of one thousand two hundred. This I believe I can do, and in the doing send a chill of fear through Unferth and his remaining forces. What would be disaster for him would be a resounding call to arms for others. The Duthenor would flock to me then by the thousands. And

I could confront Unferth, and his magician, with a much larger army."

"There's yet a third choice," Haldring said.

Brand sighed. "Yes, I could continue as I have been, and move by stealth, fight skirmishes and grow my army slowly. But though that seems the safest course of action, I believe it to be the most dangerous. At some point my enemies would pin me down, and I would have to react. But by attacking myself, either north or south, I have the initiative and an element of surprise. They are unprepared, and must react to *me*."

They approached the High Way, and the decision was upon him.

"What's it to be then?" Shorty asked.

Brand's mare trod the first steps onto the High Way. "It grates my heart, but Unferth will have to wait." He led the roan to the right. "North it is. And speed is important. I want to take the enemy by surprise. Spread the word that this shall be a quick march."

Down the High Way they moved. He saw the marks of passage of their enemy, and allowed himself a slight smile. By now they would have realized that he was not where they had thought. They would have heard rumor and gossip. They would imagine him lying in wait in every wood, hiding behind every ridge. They would fear that he had slipped away to wreak havoc elsewhere in the Duthgar. They would feel foolish, and frightened and angry. None of these things were good for morale.

The army moved quickly. Here and there men from tiny villages joined them. Should they win the upcoming battle, that trickle would turn to a flood as they moved back toward the richer and more populated lands closer to Unferth and the seat of power in the Duthgar.

Brand led the way, though there were scouts ahead and to the sides. He had the advantage of surprise, and he was not going to lose it. Speed was essential now, for already supporters of Unferth may have seen them and ridden ahead to take word to the enemy.

On the army hastened, and the road helped them. It was smooth, wide and well turfed. It was ancient too. According to legend, older by far than the Duthgar. He believed it. He had traveled the roads of the Letharn before. They built things well and built them to last. Few of the Duthenor would have heard of them, but he had traveled more widely than they. But why they had built it and to where had it led? Its other name, the older name from the Duthenor legends though not nearly as old as the road itself, was Pennling Path. That sounded like a Duthenor name, but he did not think it was.

Shorty leaned in toward him, keeping his voice low. "Are we still followed by … by whatever it is that follows us?"

"I can still feel it. Like an itch in my back. I don't know if it's any closer though. I can't tell much at all. The old woman had a better sense for it than I."

"Well, we'll be ready for it if it comes." Taingern, close on his other side, nodded grimly.

"Actually," Brand said. "I'm going to send you two ahead. I'll deal with whatever that thing is if it shows itself. We still have few horses, and none of the quality of yours."

He could see that they did not like that, but he had an army with him. He thought he would be safe. "I need you to talk to the scouts, to get ahead of them and scout yourselves. The enemy is out there, likely returning toward us by now. I want word of them as swiftly as may be."

They were reluctant, but they understood the need. They trotted off, wary now for what they did was dangerous. They worried for him, but he worried for them.

It turned out to be a good decision. Hours later they returned, the flanks of their horses frothed with sweat. They had ridden hard.

They drew their horses to a halt before Brand. "The enemy is ahead," Shorty said.

"How far?" Brand asked.

"Five miles at least," Taingern said. "And the lad's information was correct. We estimate their number at two thousand."

Brand remained dispassionate. A commander must be so at all times, and men were watching him. He must show neither excitement, surprise, anger or anything other than quiet confidence. He set the tone for the army, and he knew it.

Almost casually, he gave orders. The army encamped where it was, on the middle of the road. It was as good a place as any to force a battle, for the land was flattish in this spot with a slight advantage of slope. Any more advantage than that, and the enemy might not attack, and this Brand wanted them to do. The enemy was marching and caught by surprise. They would be tired and worried. His army would have the benefit of rest and a feeling of superiority despite their smaller numbers. They had outsmarted and outmaneuvered their opponents.

Brand studied the land, thinking. Well to the right, it dropped down a steep slope. The enemy would not veer out that way and come at him up the hill. Nor was there cover for any sort of strike force to secretly come up that way to try to create chaos while the main army approached from the front.

To the left, the ground dropped down into a tangled wood. This was some distance away. Again, he did not think the enemy would venture that way, but he sent scouts there to watch. Should the enemy come, they would be observed and have to attack uphill.

Haldring seemed to read his thoughts. "They'll come straight at us," she said. "With their greater numbers they'll try to push us back, disrupt our formation and then overrun us."

"Like a bull through a gate," Shorty added.

Brand thought they were right. He ordered his best troops forward, those with battle experience and those who were strongest. He would stand in their ranks, offering a target to the enemy and a rallying point to those less experienced in his own army. If they held against the first charge, the ranks of less experienced men behind them would gain in confidence.

And there was one more thing to do, and this he knew would raise morale. Timing was everything in war, and he had saved it for a moment such as this.

He glanced at Sighern. "It is time."

The boy knew what he meant. He retrieved the bag that held the banner. Slowly, reverently, he drew the cloth out and tied it by loops on its edge to the pole. Then he unfurled it and held it high above his head.

The cloth rolled back and a gust of wind stiffened it. Brand cried in a loud, clear voice so that all in the army could hear him.

"Behold! The banner of the chieftains of the Duthenor is with us. It is our banner of old. The same under which our fathers fought and their fathers before them. It has never seen defeat in battle!"

The wind gusted again, rippling the white cloth of the banner so that it shone bright in the afternoon light. Upon it, all in vivid red, was a dragon. Its four muscled legs, clawed and poised, seemingly walked as the cloth ruffled. It's long body and barbed tail undulated. Its head, held high and proud as it seemingly looked to the side, was royal as a king's and the eyes set in that head surveyed the field, two ovals of white gleaming to match the background.

"The Dragon of the Duthgar!" called some of the men, astonished, for it had not been seen since Brand's father was killed.

"The dragon! The dragon! The dragon!" men began to chant. They beat the sides of their swords against their shields also, raising a tumult that carried far. It was the music of war, the building up of fervor, the raising of the battle spirit of warriors. Brand felt it stir in him also, felt it fire his blood. But he knew also that it meant death for some, perhaps all. Whoever fell today would fall in his name. And he did not like it.

The men kept chanting. Sighern looked serious as he shifted the pole about so that the breeze best caught the banner. Haldring was looking at Brand, her gaze unreadable, but the fair skin of her cheeks was flushed and her eyes bright with emotion. Shorty and Taingern appeared normal. They had seen this type of thing before, and it was to them he spoke.

"Quickly," he said. "There are perhaps fifty warriors with horses here. Take them down into the forest. There will be paths there. Travel wide, and circle around the enemy. Come at them from their rear when they are engaged with us."

Shorty seemed surprised. "This is a … dangerous battle. Are you sure you want Taingern and me away from your side?"

By *dangerous* Brand knew he meant that they might well all die. "I'd always rather have you by my side, but there's need for this. Fifty is only a small force, but the skill each of you have with a blade is worth several men each, and your experience will be needed to judge when to intervene. Too early will achieve nothing, as will too late. Go swiftly, and go with good luck!"

He was sorry to see them go. They would be needed here too, but they could not be in two places at once.

"Was that wise?" Haldring asked. "We're already outnumbered, and if the enemy breaks through on the first attack, we're finished.

Brand did not disagree. "Fortune favors the bold, Haldring. And we'll need boldness to win here. Should we survive the first charge, they'll still come against us again and again and try to wear us down. We have the advantage of rest and morale. They have the advantage of numbers. I want one more thing on my side, and a well-timed attack to their rear will give it. The enemy will not have scouts behind them, so Shorty and Taingern will be able to loop around and approach from the rear unseen."

"You may be right," she said. "But fifty men here might make the difference between holding the line and defeat."

It was true, and he knew it. But he could not do both. Anyway, the decision was made.

Soon after the first scouts of the enemy were seen. The army would not be that far behind them. The day was wearing away, but before it was done battle would have been joined and a victor decided.

Haldring echoed his thoughts. "It will not be long now," she said quietly.

25. The Blood of Heroes

Brand watched as the enemy came into view. He was alert, but showed no sign of alarm. He may as well have been studying the sky for hints of tomorrow's weather as watching two thousand men march toward him, their swords eager for his blood. Thus the commander of an army must appear, or one man in a duel with another. Confidence was an act. Lack of fear in the face of danger was stupidity.

The enemy ran scouts before it. They were on the road, wary and watchful. They crossed the open farm lands and forest to the side. If they found sign of the passing of fifty horsemen earlier, Brand saw no indication of it. Taingern and Shorty were skilled warriors. They would have gone wide, beyond the range of footmen. That was one of the reasons why Brand sent cavalry, if fifty mounted men could be called such.

He was used to greater armies than these, to forces of tens of thousands and to ranks of spearmen and archers, but not to higher stakes. The outcome would alter the lives of an entire people. And just now, he knew that the success or failure of Taingern and Shorty would determine who won the day. They were the unpredictable in the battle to come. It was always so in any conflict. The masses did the job expected of them while the few who surprised often turned the tide. A skilled general waited for those moments and took advantage of them.

The enemy rumbled to a stop hundreds of paces away. This was a dangerous moment, because all depended on them coming forward. Brand did not want to delay battle.

That would give Unferth time to send more forces against him. He needed a victory now, clean and quick. If the enemy did not attack, he must attack it. This he would do, if he had to. But better they came to him, tired from marching and overconfident of their numbers.

Nothing happened. The moment was passing, and the longer they delayed the less likely they would attack.

"Why do they hesitate?" Haldring asked.

"I don't know, but if they do not come of their own volition, I will lure them."

"How?"

"Watch, and we shall see what sort of man commands the enemy."

Brand signaled for Sighern to come forward with him. He ordered also that his roan mare be brought forward and a horse for his banner bearer. This was done, and they trotted toward the enemy.

"Hold the flag high," he instructed Sighern. "Let them see it clearly."

As the two riders approached there was movement and commotion in the enemy ranks. These would be Callenor soldiers to a man, but they knew the banner of the chieftains of the Duthenor. It had flown in victories against them in days of old. And they knew also the stories of its origin. It was one thing to hear that Brand had returned, the rightful chieftain. It was another to see him in person, heralded by such a flag.

Two riders approached from the enemy. One would be its general, the other was his own banner bearer. This banner was white also, but upon it was the black talon of a raven: the mark of Unferth and a symbol the Callenor held as dear as the Duthenor did the dragon.

The two groups did not meet in the middle of the space between the armies. They merely came forward part way before their hosts to speak with their opponents, albeit over a distance that required shouting. This was good to Brand's mind, because he wanted his words heard by all the enemy and not just the general. This would help to influence them.

Brand knew the general. He had met him once, long ago as a child. He was one of Unferth's trusted retainers.

"Greetings, Ermenrik," Brand proclaimed. "Have you come forth to offer your surrender?"

The other man laughed. "I think not. I offer you the chance to surrender instead. You are outnumbered near two to one."

Brand grinned. "I am not a fool, general. There is no surrender for me. Unferth wants me dead. That is the simple truth. So, why do you hesitate to carry out his orders? Are you scared of the rightful ruler of the Duthgar? Could it be that since last we met, I have grown from a boy into a warrior and you have fallen into decrepitude? You don't look so young, anymore."

The other man did not laugh at that. He had been called a liar in front of his men. They knew as well as he that Unferth wanted Brand dead. And though they were the enemy, it was because Unferth was their lord rather than that they were bad men. They liked the truth, and justice, as much as the Duthenor.

"You are not the rightful lord, boy. The world turns and the chances of fate give as well as take. Unferth is king of the Duthgar, and I do his will. But this is my promise to you. If you surrender, I *will* take you to him. Mayhap he will show you mercy."

"Interesting words, Ermenrik. The words *chances of fate* mean different things to us. To you, that *chance* meant wealth and ease and a life of comfort. To me, it was the murder of my parents." Brand paused, allowing his words to have weight, and then he continued. "And tell me, Ermenrik, were you there that night? Were you one of the ones that killed a man and his wife? Murdered them? Is their blood on your hands?"

Ermenrik tightened his grip on the reins of his horse. "Enough!" he yelled. "I have not come here to bandy words with an exile and outlaw." He turned his horse and rode back toward his host, but Brand was not done.

"If you will not speak because my words cut, murderer, then how will you dare face me with blades of steel? You are a cur, a lapdog to a traitor unworthy of the men he rules. A king, he calls himself? He is no more than a pig in a muddy sty with a crown of filthy straw."

Ermenrik did not slow the pace of his horse or offer a reply. But his back stiffened and Brand knew his words had struck home. He looked across at Sighern, and saw the boy's eyes were wide. Then he turned his own mount and returned to the army.

Haldring met him. "Well," she said. "You know how to stir the pot when you want to. You've made him mad enough to attack us just by himself, I think."

Brand winked at her. "Words make sharper weapons than steel. Now, let's just hope he's not smart enough to wonder why I provoked him."

Brand dismounted and asked a warrior to lead his and Sighern's mount to the rear of the army. Then he turned to the front once more and studied the enemy.

There seemed to be a debate of some kind, for there were several figures gathered round Ermenrik, and there was much gesturing. But whatever the conversation entailed, orders were soon given. The men about Ermenrik dispersed, and the army began to move.

The Callenor came forward, a shrill horn blaring wildly, and the clamor of sword on shield came with them. Brand had achieved his aim. Now, he must hope that his tactics proved successful.

His own army was silent. The Duthenor did not bother to make noise or blow horns to scare the enemy. They trusted to their steel and the skill of their arms instead. And yet there was nervous tension within them that must be released.

The enemy ranks came close now, gathering into a trot as they came.

"The dragon!" cried Brand.

The Duthenor had been waiting for this. It was the battle cry that their ancestors had voiced, and they took it up.

"The dragon! The dragon! The dragon!"

Arrows were loosed from both armies. They flickered and slivered through the air. Brand gave a command, and the men raised their shields. The volley of arrows failed. Neither side had many bowmen.

Next, the long spears were thrown. This had less effect than the arrows. It was by sword and shield and the hearts of men that this battle would be won or lost.

Brand waited. He stood in the middle of the front rank. He was both a target for the enemy, and a rallying point for his own men. Of Ermenrik, he saw no sign.

The shield wall felt strong about him, and Brand breathed deep of the air. The noise of the trotting enemy was loud now, their cries fierce, the whites of their wide eyes gleaming.

The two forces came together in a roaring crash. Swords flashed. Shields resounded. Men cried and screamed and yelled. Like an ocean wave smashing onto the shore the enemy swarmed and crowded, seeking to move further, deeper.

The Duthenor were forced back a pace. Then two. Haldring, locked in close by his left side, killed a man with a sudden jab. Brand flicked his blade at just the right moment and tore open the throat of a burly warrior, his red beard bristling beneath his helm. Blood soaked it now.

The dead men fell. More died around them. Others took their place, coming forward through the ranks to fill the gap.

Slowly, the wave of enmity lessened. The Callenor came on, but the Duthenor held them back. The initial momentum had been diffused. This gave heart to the Duthenor but stole it from the enemy.

But the battle was far from done. The enemy had claimed no swift victory as they hoped, but their numbers were yet the greater.

The man to Brand's right fell, an axe forcing its way through his helm to bury itself in his skull. Brand cut the attacker's hand off as he tried to pull back the axe. The man wheeled away, screaming as he disappeared into his own ranks. He would not live unless a healer tended him swiftly.

A warrior pushed forward into the empty place in the line beside Brand, filling the gap. Behind, the shadow of the Dragon Banner fell over him. Sighern was where he was supposed to be, marking the place where Brand stood. And the enemy came against him, again and again. Callenor warriors almost seemed to fight among themselves to reach him, as though there were a prize for killing him. And well there might be. Unferth might have offered one. But this was for the good. The focus of the attack was on him, and where he stood. But this was the strongest part of the shield wall. If it held, and it was so far, the rest was safer.

A horn blew at the back of the enemy ranks. There was movement among the Callenor, and spearmen came forward. Ermenrik was trying something new.

Through the ranks they came, and men gave way to them. They reached the front, spears lowered, and thrust forward. The jabs were fast, and they could be delivered with more power than a sword thrust. Yet they were less agile.

"Forward one step!" Brand commanded. His call was taken up and repeated along the ranks of his men. They shuffled forward, and pressed the spearmen back.

But the spearmen were not done. The maneuver had taken them by surprise, for they required more room than swordsmen, and they were crammed. But they regrouped and pressed forward again, and this time it was the Duthenor line that buckled in several places.

A spear rammed at Brand's foot, and he lowered his shield to block it. At the same time another warrior drove his spear at Brand's face. He twisted, and the long blade smashed into the side of his head. The Helm of the Duthenor rang, and Brand stumbled and fell to the ground. In a frenzy, the enemy pressed forward to try to kill him.

Haldring threw herself down before him, her own body protecting his and her shield held before the both of them. And then Sighern leaped forward without a shield. In his left hand he still held the banner, but in his right he gripped a blade and it flashed and stabbed furiously.

A spearpoint gashed the boy's right side, but then Brand surged up again. Haldring rose with him. Together they reformed the line, allowing Sighern to move back.

Brand retaliated. He was upset at himself for his error, and angry that two people might have died to save him. He thrust his shield at the enemy, and the silver blade of his ancestors flashed and killed.

The Callenor stepped back before him, and Brand shouted. "Forward two steps! For the dragon!"

All along the line the shout went up, and the Duthenor tried to surge. In places the Callenor line rebuffed them, but in others it was pushed back two paces. And then, seeing their line fall back in many places, even those lengths of the Callenor line that had held their ground fell back to form one line again.

From behind him, Brand heard a message relayed by a warrior. "Brand! The enemy is sending a force to attack our left flank!"

Brand could not look back, but he raised the tip of his sword high to signal that he had heard. It was what he had feared, for the enemy's greater numbers allowed them to attempt it. But there was nothing he could do, not directly, and he knew the men on the left flank would form a shield wall and hold firm. As best they could.

He gambled, and shouted another order. "Forward march! The dragon attacks!"

All about him, up and down the line, the Duthenor and Callenor strove against each other. The spearmen were falling back, the tactic proving unsuccessful, and swordsmen replacing them. But if now the Duthenor could gain momentum and break the enemy, the attack on their left flank would falter. Yet it was a roll of the dice, and he knew it.

What would have happened, Brand did not know. But he knew he was right to place trust in Taingern and Shorty, for even as the Duthenor rallied to his call and tried to press forward, he sensed the battle shift.

There was turmoil in the enemy ranks. A commotion grew in the rear and spread. Above even the shout and din of battle he heard a swift thunder of hooves and knew that the fifty horsemen he had sent out had finally attacked. Their timing, or rather the judgement of the two men that led them, was perfect.

The thrill of battle surged through him. The chance of victory fed it. "Attack!" he roared. "Attack!"

And the Duthenor pressed forward. Their shields barged against the enemy's shields, their swords stabbed and their throats voiced their battle cry: *For the dragon! For the dragon! For the dragon!*

The Callenor were caught between two forces. They were tired, surprised and badly led. Panic ensued.

The Duthenor rolled forward, killing quickly. At the rear of the Callenor force, they tried to rally, for the initial thrust of the horsemen dissipated as they wheeled away and circled back to attack again. But now the panic from the front of their ranks caught them and their morale broke.

Some tried to flee the field, others to rally together. Some were slain fighting, others as they turned their backs to run. It became a rout and the blood of the Callenor flowed.

A group to the left managed to flee the field, but the bulk of the enemy were hammered between the separate Duthenor forces. Fully half their number were killed before they surrendered, throwing down their swords.

Brand gave swift orders. The Duthenor surrounded them, but stopped killing. Ermenrik appeared. He had not dropped his sword, as well might be expected. There could be no surrender for him. Only overdue justice, and he knew it. He harangued his warriors, urging them to fight, but they ignored him.

"Silence!" Brand yelled, and Ermenrik ceased, the sword still in his hand.

Brand strode toward him, his own bloody sword still in his hand. Others came with him. But when Brand spoke, he raised his voice so all the Callenor heard his words.

"Warriors of the Callenor! Your surrender is accepted. You will suffer no further hurt, but you will leave your swords on this field and return to your own lands. This you will swear, and then you will be free to go. Do any think these terms unjust and refuse them?"

There was silence. What Brand did was a risk, but at heart the Callenor were no different to the Duthenor. Honor mattered to them, and he believed they would be true to their word. Not only that, word would spread and the opposition he may face in future battles would more easily surrender and have less reason to fight.

Brand turned to Ermenrik. For this man, justice must take a different form. He was a murderer. But indecision wracked him. Should he kill him now, or put him on trial?

Ermenrik seemed calm, but without warning he leaped forward. Steel rang on steel as Brand deflected his blow. But then the enemy general swung wildly, and having failed to kill Brand he struck at Haldring who was close by. She blocked his strike, but staggered back under the weight of it. Again he struck, but she recovered and flicked her blade at his leg, opening an artery in his thigh. It was a killing blow, but as she moved back out of the way she stumbled over the body of a slain Callenor soldier behind her and Ermenrik's sword ripped into her throat between helm and chainmail.

It was Ermenrik's final move. Brand's sword half-severed his neck and Sighern smashed his blade against the general's helm. The man's head lolled to the side at an unnatural angle and he fell to the ground, one leg kicking.

Brand rushed to Haldring. Blood spurted from her neck, and she had fallen to the ground, her hands futilely trying to stem the pouring out of her lifeblood. One moment Brand looked, fear chilling his heat, and then he acted. Swiftly he grabbed the pole from Sighern and stripped away the Dragon Banner.

He must stop the flow of blood, or she was dead. He knelt by her side, pressing the white cloth into the wound. In moments it was bloody, and she looked up at him, the light fading from her blue eyes.

"Live!" he breathed.

She seemed about to speak, but then she gasped and died. His hands were covered in her blood. He bowed his head, tears running down his cheeks. He did not move, still pressing the cloth against her wound, but the blood had ceased to flow for her heart had stopped beating. But Shorty and Taingern were suddenly there, and gently they raised him up and eased the now bloody banner from his hands. It fell to the stained grass.

Brand's gaze dropped to Ermenrik's corpse, and he kicked it. The dead body moved, and then fell back, lifeless once more.

Rage infused Brand. Why did the good die while evil prospered under the sun? But kicking a dead man was no answer. Instead, he wept, and two armies watched him.

The sun hung low now on the horizon. Fittingly, it was a scarlet sunset, a ruin of scattered clouds colored as though by blood. But there was more blood on the grass of the Duthgar than blazed in the sky.

All around was death, and the smell of death, and the low rays of the sun, red through a growing pall of smoke, shot through everything with an eerie light.

Crows and hawks and ravens gathered. Animals that scavenged haunted the forest edges. But they would not feed off the dead. The smoke grew stronger, and the roar of fires louder. Brand had ordered timber collected and the bodies of the dead soldiers burnt on massive biers, one for the Callenor and one for the Duthenor. It could be done swiftly, and it would prevent the spread of disease.

The surrendered Callenor had left, marching west into the setting sun and toward their own lands. Brand and a few others stood now before Haldring's grave. She was the only one who had been buried, and a cairn of small rocks marked her resting place. Words had been spoken, memories shared, and her sword driven into the cairn as a sign that here rested a great warrior. It was the Duthenor way, and though over the years the sword would rust and time destroy it, while it lasted none would take or touch the blade.

There was a stir in the small group. "Who is that?" one of the warriors asked.

They turned and looked where he gestured behind them. From the south came a person, a lone figure shuffling toward them purposely along the road whence the Duthenor themselves had earlier come.

26. Old Mother

Brand watched the figure approach. If the remnants of a battlefield disturbed whoever it was, they gave no sign. Instead, they moved ahead purposefully, oblivious to all that was around them, one step after another straight toward him.

The breeze that had blown through the fighting died with the sunset. The air was still now, and heavy with acrid smoke. It drifted sluggishly over the ground like fog, obscuring the newcomer now and then until the person drew close.

The walker was aided by two walking sticks, one in each hand, crafted of some dark timber. These she used to help her, for Brand saw now that it was a woman, and she moved quickly despite whatever frailty required use of the sticks in the first place.

She drew close, and finally came to a stop. Brand sensed Sighern stir beside him. He no longer carried the banner. It had been reattached to the pole and set in the ground. It may not be clean anymore, but the blood of a hero was a better emblem than a dragon.

"It's the marsh witch," Sighern said, and he made to move forward to greet her.

Brand clamped a hand down on his shoulder, and kept him in place. Sighern seemed confused, but Brand was growing certain. He had already lost one that he liked today; he would not lose another.

He stepped forward a pace, and spoke. "Greetings, old mother. Did you change your mind and come to help?"

She shuffled a step closer on her walking sticks.

"Aye, lad. I did, but it seems I'm too late. The battle is fought and won."

"It's never too late," Brand answered. "Come to the light, and leave evil behind."

The old witch looked at him quizzically for a few moments, as though puzzling something through.

Brand, too, was making up his mind. The witch had the gift of prophecy, and she had said they would never meet again. Yet here she was, or one that looked like her but was not. One that had been hunting him.

They moved at the same time. Brand drew his sword, and it caught the red rays of the dying sun. The two walking sticks of the witch became swords, and her body shimmered and transformed.

She was the witch no more. The guise was gone, the strands of magic that formed it loosed. What stood before Brand was a Halathrin warrior.

He heard shouts of *elf* as the two blades flashed toward him, but he was already moving. Yet even so he barely avoided them. The elf warrior was fast, and Brand knew he would have been dead had he not been suspicious.

Their blades flickered and crashed together. There was recognition in the elf warrior's eyes: at first touch he knew Brand's sword had been wrought by his own kind, and it surprised him. Mortals possessed few such weapons. But it did not cause him to falter. His twin blades were in constant motion, testing, cutting, flicking and thrusting. He moved with sublime grace, but speed and power went with it.

Few could have stood against him. Or none. But Brand was no ordinary warrior. His skills had been honed in a crucible of necessity and danger that others would not have survived. But he *had* survived, and learned.

Brand swept his blade at the elf's neck, but at the last moment flicked his wrist and thrust. This threw off his opponent's deflection and nearly killed him. It would have killed anyone else, but the elf merely rocked back out of the way and drove in again, faster and deadlier than before.

Brand was pushed back. He gave ground grudgingly, and tried to find the warrior's state of mind: stillness in the storm. But it mostly eluded him. Too much had happened today, and there was a cold anger within him that would not give way.

The elf pushed him back further, and Brand swung to the side, being careful not to be predictable and retreat in the same direction all the time. He studied the elf as he blocked and parried and swayed. The creature *looked* like a Halathrin, but was not quite the same. Brand had met immortals before, and they never had such pale skin nor eyes that lusted after battle and blood as did this one. But they were possessed of magic that allowed them to assume guises.

What other magic did his attacker possess? Brand allowed himself to calm as he retreated. He still could not assume stillness in the storm, but he was closer. The cold fury that troubled him receded, and by just defending he allowed himself some opportunity to think. The elf would soon use whatever other skills he had. The longer this went on, the greater the danger to him. Even if he killed Brand as he wanted, how then would he escape an army?

The answer was clear. He would assume another guise in the turmoil and try to escape that way. But if then, why not sooner and during the battle?

Brand fixed his gaze on him, and he swerved once more as he retreated. This time he thrust forward with his blade even as his feet shuffled backward. Again, he nearly struck the elf, but his opponent recovered quickly. One of the black swords swept at Brand's neck while the other jabbed at his groin.

Stumbling, Brand fell back. The elf drove at him in a fury of blades, but Brand had feigned his imbalance. His own sword arced through the air in a beheading stroke, but the elf was no longer there. With blistering speed he ducked the blade, rolled away and came to his feet once more, black blades circling the air before him.

"A valiant attempt, mortal. But you are no match for my kind."

Brand grinned at him. "In my experience, warriors who start a conversation during a fight are frightened of losing. They need to try to talk themselves into the fact that they're better."

The elf did not answer, but the killing light in his eyes shone brighter and he darted forward, almost too fast to see. He moved as though he had no bones, only sinuous muscles that coiled and struck like a darting adder.

Their blades flashed and clanged again. Brand would rather have deflected than blocked, but his opponent was too good. He was forced off balance all the time, cramped in his movements and his own attacks mostly anticipated. He had never faced so skilled an opponent, and it was a battle he wondered if he would lose. Nor could he expect help. It was a one on one fight, and no one would dishonor him by changing that.

If he were to win, he must at least survive a while longer, but this was increasingly hard. His enemy was running out of time, for the army, though spellbound by the duel, was beginning to form a circle around the combatants. The elf had to win and escape soon, or he never would.

The elf drove him back, his cold eyes burning with battle lust, his every move smooth, graceful and deadly. In his hands, the two dark swords wove a spell of sharp-edged death, yet Brand held them off and launched a counter-attack. He was tired of retreating.

With swift movements of his own, if not quite so graceful, his pattern-welded blade arced silver fire through the gathering dusk, cutting, slashing and jabbing.

The elf reeled away, only to attack again, but Brand harnessed his anger and leaped to meet him. Hot sparks flew from the blades and cold metal shrieked. A moment they stood thus, almost uncaring of defense as they each strove to kill, and then the elf nimbly leaped back.

He stood there, his swords held loosely in his hands, barely seeming to draw breath while Brand panted. And then he grinned, his pale face white in the gathering dark, but a streak of red ran across his cheek where the tip of Brand's sword had marked him.

Brand knew what would come now. He had been waiting for it, though what form it would take and what would best combat it he did not know. He drew a deep breath and lifted the tip of his sword a little higher.

When it came, it still surprised him. The elf just stepped away from himself. There were two of him now, both black-clad, garbed in silver armor, pale eyes burning with battle lust. But each image held only one dark sword.

Which was real and which illusion? Brand was not quite sure, even though he had been watching closely. This he knew though: the elf would not wait.

Brand sent out a tendril of his own magic to the image on the right. It was the one that he thought may have been the elf himself. But he did not wait to be attacked by either. Instead, he dived to the right and rolled, moving first to take the initiative and coming to the side of the righthand image so that they could not both advance on him and attack at the same time.

He surged to his feet, his sword weaving before him. To the side, Shorty and Taingern advanced. It was no longer a one on one fight. But he doubted they would reach either image in time.

Swift as jagged lightning, both elves sprang for him, but the second was hindered by the first, and the tendril of Brand's own magic sensed the real from the illusory.

He darted to the side again, as though ignoring the closer illusion and moving to combat the second. But at the last moment he ducked a vicious strike from the closest image that would have beheaded him and stabbed his Halathrin blade up into its body.

Brand drove the blade with all his might, surging up from his bent legs, thrusting also with the strength of his arms and angling the point of the sword to reach beneath the ribs and pierce the heart.

He knew instantly that he had chosen the correct target. His blade struck no image but a real body. Even elvish chainmail parted when struck by the point of a Halathrin sword driven by the full might of a skilled warrior.

The sword sheared through armor and clothes, through flesh and blood. It drove up, higher and higher, lifting the elf off the ground. There he hung a moment, the fury in his eyes washed away by surprise. Blood fountained from his mouth, and he died.

Brand kicked the corpse off his blade. He swung to see the other image, but it drifted away even as he watched like a whisper of mist vanishing into the air.

He turned back to the dead elf. Pale skin shriveled. The eyes burned away. Its whole body, armor and swords as well, disintegrated and seeped into the very soil as though made of some dark water that soaked into a subterranean chamber of the earth, far, far beneath the sight or reach of men.

Brand stood there, leaning on his sword in great weariness. It had been an endless day, but he had survived, if changed and only just. The battle was won, but the war was yet to come, and the magician that sought his death was a power in the world not to be dismissed or forgotten. He would try to kill him again, and Brand knew now that freeing the Duthgar was but a secondary thing. Whatever power the magician served was of the Dark, and there lay a greater peril to the land than ever Unferth could dream to be.

Epilogue

Char-harash, Lord of the Ten Armies, Ruler of the Thousand Stars, Light of Kar-fallon and Emperor of the Kar-ahn-hetep dreamed.

And his dreams were of battle and dark magic.

From the north swept an army of Letharn. Rank after rank of infantry marched. From the east came an army also, this of cavalry and chariots. Before both forces advanced the wizard-priests of the Letharn. With them they summoned lightning that leaped from the sky at their gesture and tore the earth asunder. When they raised their hands, the solid ground heaved as though it were an angry sea.

Battle raged. Sword clashed against sword. Horses neighed and men screamed. Magicians opposed wizard-priests and the world spun in smoke and fire while the sky darkened and chaos reigned.

Out of the chaos drove a spear. Char-harash cried out in pain. It took him in the stomach and spilled his entrails into the trampled dust.

No. He *had* cried out in pain. And then came the great dark. He knew it for what it was. Death. The gateway to the realm of the gods. He embraced it, for he was a god himself.

He hesitated. No. It was not so. He fought it, for he was not yet a god. He fought to live, but pain engulfed him. He felt the spear drive deep toward his heart, felt it pull out again, heard his moan as death took him.

Yes. That was long ago. The great dark still surrounded him. Entombed. Chanted over by his magicians. He heard the echo of their ancient spells even now. Or was he still being interred?

No. Eons had passed. The stars had shifted in the sky. Or was his last breath still fresh upon his resin-embalmed lips?

The dark hid things from him. But not all. Slowly he began to wake, and he called one of his kind to him. Horta, a magician of his own line. He was a magician also. Charharash. The God-king.

And soon he would wake and tread the earth once again. Let his foes fear him.

He dreamed no more. Dreams were for men. He was to become a god, and he would not dream but rather send nightmares to his enemies.

Thus ends *The Pale Swordsman*. The Dark God Rises trilogy continues in book two, *The Crimson Lord*, where Brand must face the usurper, his army, and discover more of his true adversary.

Amazon lists millions of titles, and I'm glad you discovered this one. But if you'd like to know when I release a new book, instead of leaving it to chance, sign up for my newsletter. I'll send you an email on publication.

Yes please! – Go to www.homeofhighfantasy.com and sign up.

No thanks – I'll take my chances.

Dedication

There's a growing movement in fantasy literature. Its name is noblebright, and it's the opposite of grimdark.

Noblebright celebrates the virtues of heroism. It's an old-fashioned thing, as old as the first story ever told around a smoky campfire beneath ancient stars. It's storytelling that highlights courage and loyalty and hope for the spirit of humanity. It recognizes the dark, the dark in us all, and the dark in the villains of its stories. It recognizes death, and treachery and betrayal. But it dwells on none of these things.

I dedicate this book, such as it is, to that which is noblebright. And I thank the authors before me who held the torch high so that I could see the path: J.R.R. Tolkien, C.S. Lewis, Terry Brooks, David Eddings, Susan Cooper, Roger Taylor and many others. I salute you.

And, for a time, I too will hold the torch high.

Appendix A: The Runes of Life and Death

Halls of Lore. Chamber 7. Aisle 21. Item 426
General subject: Divination
Topic: The use of magic and talismans
Author: Careth Tar

In the south of Alithoras, west of the lands of Azanbulzibar and the barrow mounds of the Shadowed Wars, which the immortal Halathrin call Elù-haraken, dwell a strange people.

They name themselves Kar-ahn-hetep, which means "children of the thousand stars" in their ancient language. But the long ages since their days of glory, and the short memory and fast tongues of men have reduced this to "Kirsch." Yet the wise know their true name, and the remnant of their race that still survive cling to it – and also to their old ways of magic.

The land of the Kirsch was once fertile, but the eons have altered the climate. It has become arid. These people existed in the time of the Letharn, and well before them, and inhabited one of the few lands not overrun by that conquest-hungry race. The inhabitants were fierce fighters. They were also numerous. And the great distance from Letharn strongholds was an additional defensive advantage. But mostly, their survival and indeed aggression toward the Letharn sprung from this: the

Kirsch practiced arts of powerful magic unlike that possessed by others.

Briefly, this is the nature of their magic arts. It centers around a belief in the primordial powers that form and substance the universe. This is what we would term ùhrengai. From this primordial force, two alternate forces arose. Again, what we recognize as lòhrengai and elùgai. But after that their beliefs diverge.

We, as lòhrens, use the one power. Elùgroths use the other. The Kirsch, on the other hand, use both – but they do not believe they access it directly. Instead, they employ talismans to focus their thought. Also, and importantly, they believe that agencies intervene in this process on the magician's behalf. This is often thought to be the spirits of the dead and other forces of nature, call them gods if you will. All of these act as conduits between themselves and the primordial power.

An example of this is the practice of divination.

The chief means of foretelling among the Children is the casting of the Runes of Life and Death. These are bones. Sometimes animal in origin, sometimes (and preferably) human.

Human finger bones are favored for a specific reason. The more so if they are obtained from a person of power. Human bones, especially from a powerful person, increase the accuracy of the foretelling because the agency constrained to act on the magician's behalf is more puissant. Thus, the finger bones of dead magicians are highly sought after. This gives rise to graverobbing, and in turn elaborate means of disguising tombs to thwart exhumation. Also, it generates distrust among their society. Magicians hate (and fear) one another, always seeking to kill lesser rivals and protect themselves from greater.

The runes consist of ten bones. Each has two paired runes cut into them and colored by blood, two aspects of the same concept or force. By reading which opposite of a paired rune falls, and how the bones scatter in relation to each other, the future is told. Sometimes, a bone will not land squarely on one side or the other. This signifies doubt.

It is customary to shake the pouch that contains the runes ten times before use in order to prevent conscious tampering with the divination. It is also a tradition not to withdraw ten bones at once, this being considered to signal the highest ill-fortune should it occur by accident.

These are the ten runes and their double meanings, as translated from an ancient text.

Hotep: change – quiescence

It is the nature of the world that things change. Nothing is still. All things exist in a state of flux. The stars move in the sky. The wind blows across desert sands, shifting grains that once were boulders. Flowers bloom, and then in turn wither. This is change, and even the bones of the earth feel it. Yet there is that to humankind which is not material. It is of the spirit. And the spirit of man seeks quiescence. The wise know that true quiescence is the acceptance of change. The foolish seek always to grasp at starlight.

This then is the moral: when change is afoot, seek to be centered and accepting. Look for the opportunity that transformation will bring. If there is no apparent change, beware. Danger approaches!

Karmun: death – life

All things born of the earth return to dust. Only ideas are eternal. Yet an idea is nothing without a living mind to give it shape and purpose and voice. Death is not to be feared, nor embraced. It must be accepted. It, too, is an idea. In a living mind it can be fed by fear until it grows into a great, slavering beast that chases us without cessation. Or it can be accepted, its power used instead to nurture understanding of the beauty of transience.

This then is the moral: death is always close. Seek not to escape it, for in doing so you will run toward it. Rather, the wise accept it, and give themselves true life.

Harak: war – peace

War can exist without peace. But peace cannot endure without war, or the threat of war, because always there will be those that seek to steal, or enslave, or conquer. War also gives birth to invention. Yet too, it kills the young and the strong and those that one day may otherwise have achieved greatness. But this also is true. War brings vigor to the nation, training the strong in mind and body, giving them discipline and skill. Peace allows the weak to prosper. This in turn makes a society susceptible to those that would bring war. And yet, above all, it is in the heart of most people to seek peace. Yet the leaders of nations, though few in number, bring the many to battle.

This then is the moral: war and peace are two sides of the one coin. The wise prepare for war when peace reigns, as also they prepare for peace when war strides across the land. Only fools expect one state or the other to prevail without cessation.

Rasallher: mountain peak – valley

High atop the mountain, a man looks down and surveys the majesty of the world. "It is beautiful," he says. That same man, days before, looked at the mountain peak from the valley beneath its shadow. "How beautiful," he said. "What a creation of majesty!" The mountain and the valley are the same. The man is the same. Only his perspective has changed. It is no different with mountains than anything else. A man may invest his fortune only to lose it. But having lost it, he may say "such is life. I will rebuild my empire." Or he may take his own life. It is perspective only.

This then is the moral: in dealing with friends, family, warriors, rivals, other empires, put yourself in their shoes.

Discern their perspective. Understand them. Then you can better predict what they will do. And also, in this manner, you will learn of yourself.

Hassah: water – dust

Of dust, the earth is made. To dust, all life returns. Nothing is so barren as the dry sands of a desert, yet even in the arid waste life blooms. How so? The gift of water. When it rains life springs to action. A great race commences. Live. Breed. Send offspring into the world. Then comes again the time of sleep. Deep in the soil life burrows and protects itself. There, dormant, it waits through the long years of drought. Until the water comes again. Then once more the great race commences.

This then is the moral: even the witless seed and the dumb animal knows when to act and when non-action is required. The wise man follows nature's example. Act when it is propitious to do so. Hold back, wait, show patience when it is not. In this way, the wise turn the cycles of nature and the tides of human affairs to their advantage.

Durath-har: earth – air

Of the earth, life is born. It nurtures plants and animals, which in turn nourish man. Yet it is from the air that rain falls and through the sky that the sun shines. Without which no life can prosper and all the land would be barren as it is in a cave. And even as the earth is still, unmoving and unchanging, the air flits and drifts and grows hot and cold, ever transmuting. Yet what is earth by itself, or air on its own? Nothing. Nowhere places void of life.

This then is the moral: all forces on earth and heaven meet, and in that meeting opportunity is birthed. Rain gives rise to new growth. Heat withers grass and tree and shrub, but the desert flowers bloom where once the grass grew. Until the grass rises in its turn and smothers the land once more. Seek to anticipate the cycles of life and the hearts of men. When the cycle shifts, opportunity has already passed.

Orok-hai: the hanged man — the fugitive

Men are hanged in the empire for certain offences. Yet it is human nature to want to avoid penalties for crime. Some, though, on being caught will admit their guilt. Are these wise men or fools? Is it better to admit guilt and die with a satisfied conscience than to try to hide a crime? And what of the criminal who escapes, yet repents, and later does good in the world? Yet also there are those that are caught, admit their guilt, but remain unrepentant. The heart of a man is a dark place, a mystery greater than the thousand stars.

This then is the moral: in dealing with people expect that which is unexpected. The condemned may fight all the harder despite knowing they cannot win. Or the victorious tyrant may be magnanimous. But if you study them, learn how they have behaved in the past, and then you will better know how they will react in the future. Some men were born to be hanged.

El-haran: the wanderer – the farmer

In the heart of people is a desire to see new things. When the ibis gather and of a sudden flock north, do we not wish to go with them? The call of strange skies, the lure of the next hill, the next valley, the next wood or the taste of a new spring is strong. Such things sing to us and fill our hearts. Yet also something else takes root in our soul. The love of the land to which we are born. It is in our blood. We feel it in our feet as we tread the soil. It is in the familiar air we breathe, and being deprived of this land our spirit weakens even as a man falters that struggles to catch his breath.

This then is the moral: the hearts of people are divided. They will sometimes say one thing, yet do another. At one moment they are kind, at the next vexatious. A thief may do a noble deed, and an emperor steal from the poor. Such is the dichotomous nature of humanity. But people act under the influence of their internal impulses or external stimuli. The wise man studies these internal and external rhythms in their associates and enemies. Therefore, they can better predict how a person will react under what forces.

Fallon-adir: soaring eagle – roosting sparrow

It is a fact universally known to mankind that eagles soar in the sky, wheeling, circling, riding the waves of air with nobility. But the sparrow is a creature that chatters away in shrubbery. It is plain. It is the least beautiful of birds. It gathers in flocks for it is timid and there is safety in numbers. Therefore, the eagle is admired and the sparrow a pest. Yet, is it not also true that the eagle is an opportunistic feeder that hunts or scavenges carrion as circumstances dictate? Is this then more noble than a sparrow? Is the eagle to be admired more because of its size? Is the sparrow lesser because it congregates as a community?

This then is the moral: all creatures and things have their place under the sun. Beware of false assumptions, unearned grandeur, reputations and the prideful opinion of others. Watch, learn, study and draw conclusions based on fact and untainted opinion. Test your discoveries against reality. This is the path to wisdom.

Urhash-hassar: multiplicity – nadir

Life teems in soil, air and water. Yet catastrophe comes in its turn through flood, drought, earthquake and sickness. Disaster razes life and destroys worlds. Yet from calamity new life rises, different, stronger. What then is the normal state of affairs of humanity? Is it multiplicity? Shall we spread over the earth, leveling forests, drying swamps, harvesting river and sea until the teeming waters are emptied and the tread of our boots tramps all the world? Or shall we in turn succumb, our bones and flesh nourishing the soil for new life? In days of old it is rumored civilizations existed before us. The tales tell that they were stricken down. And well may we wonder if they in their turn heard rumors of those that went before.

This then is the moral: it is foolish to believe in gain without loss and endless growth. It is not the way of nature. Yet also it is foolish to believe in defeat and oblivion. The wise man hopes for one and strives to prevent the other. The sage accepts all fates, and thereby rises above them. That person can smile in the face of nadir and feel the sadness of multiplicity – yet is chained by neither.

Appendix B: Encyclopedic Glossary

Note: the glossary of each book in this series is individualized for that book alone. Additionally, there is often historical material provided in its entries for people, artifacts and events that are not included in the main text.

Many races dwell in Alithoras. All have their own language, and though sometimes related to one another the changes sparked by migration, isolation and various influences often render these tongues unintelligible to each other.

The ascendancy of Halathrin culture, combined with their widespread efforts to secure and maintain allies against elug incursions, has made their language the primary means of communication between diverse peoples.

For instance, a merchant of Cardoroth addressing a Duthenor warrior would speak Halathrin, or a simplified version of it, even though their native speeches stem from the same ancestral language.

This glossary contains a range of names and terms. Many are of Halathrin origin, and their meaning is provided. The remainder derive from native tongues and are obscure, so meanings are only given intermittently.

Often, Duthenor names and Halathrin elements are combined. This is especially so for the aristocracy. Few other tribes of men had such long-term friendship with the immortal Halathrin as the Duthenor, and though in this relationship they lost some of their natural culture, they gained nobility and knowledge in return.

List of abbreviations:

Cam. Camar

Comb. Combined

Cor. Corrupted form

Duth. Duthenor

Hal. Halathrin

Kir. Kirsch

Prn. Pronounced

Alithoras: *Hal.* "Silver land." The Halathrin name for the continent they settled after leaving their own homeland. Refers to the extensive river and lake systems they found and their wonder at the beauty of the land.

Anast Dennath: *Hal.* "Stone mountains." Mountain range in northern Alithoras. Source of the river known as the Careth Nien that forms a natural barrier between the lands of the Camar people and the Duthenor and related tribes.

Aranloth: *Hal.* "Noble might." A lòhren of ancient heritage and friend to Brand.

Arell: A famed healer in Cardoroth. Companion of Brand.

Arnhaten: *Kir.* "Disciples." Servants of a magician. One magician usually has many disciples, but only some of these are referred to as "inner door." Inner door disciples receive a full transmission of the master's knowledge. The remainder do not, but they continue to strive to earn the favor of their master. Until they do, they are dispensable.

Asaba: *Kir.* "White stone – marble." A disciple of Horta, but not of inner door status.

Azanbulzibar: A fabled city in the far south of Alithoras.

Baldring: *Duth.* "Fierce blade." Once a lord of the Duthenor. Father of Galdring.

Black Talon: The sign of Unferth's house. Appears on his banner and is his personal emblem. Legend claims the founder of the house in ancient days had the power to transform into a raven. Disguised in this form, and trusted as a magical being, he gave misinformation and ill-advice to the enemies of his people.

Brand: *Duth.* "Torch." An exiled Duthenor tribesman and adventurer. Appointed by the former king of Cardoroth to serve as regent for Prince Gilcarist. By birth, he is the rightful chieftain of the Duthenor people. However, Unferth the usurper overthrew his father, killing both him and his wife. Brand, only a youth at the time, swore an oath of vengeance. That oath has long slept, but it is not forgotten, either by Brand or the usurper.

Breath of the dragon: An ancient saying of Letharn origin. They believed the magic of dragons was the preeminent magic in the world because dragons were creatures able to travel through time. Dragon's breath is known to mean fire, the destructive face of their nature. But the Letharn also believed dragons could breathe mist. This was the healing face of their nature. And the mist-breath of a dragon was held to be able to change destinies and bring good luck. To "ride the dragon's breath" meant that for a period a person was a focal point of time and destiny.

Brunhal: *Duth.* "Hallowed woman." Former chieftainess of the Duthenor. Wife to Drunn, former chieftain of the Duthenor. Mother to Brand. According to Duthenor custom, a chieftain and chieftainess co-ruled.

Callenor: *Duth.* One of several tribes closely related to the Duthenor. This one inhabits lands immediately west of the Duthgar.

Camar: *Cam. Prn.* Kay-mar. A race of interrelated tribes that migrated in two main stages. The first brought them to the vicinity of Halathar, homeland of the immortal Halathrin; in the second, they separated and established cities along a broad stretch of eastern Alithoras. Related to the Duthenor, though far more distantly than the Callenor.

Caraval: *Hal. Comb. Duth.* "Red hawk." A childhood companion of Brand.

Cardoroth: *Cor. Hal. Comb. Cam.* A Camar city, often called Red Cardoroth. Some say this alludes to the red granite commonly used in the construction of its buildings, others that it refers to a prophecy of destruction.

Careth Nien: *Hal. Prn.* Kareth ny-en. "Great river." Largest river in Alithoras. Has its source in the mountains of Anast Dennath and runs southeast across the land before emptying into the sea. It was over this river (which sometimes freezes along its northern stretches) that the Camar and other tribes migrated into the eastern lands. Much later, Brand came to the city of Cardoroth by one of these ancient migratory routes.

Char-harash: *Kir.* "He who destroys by flame." Most exalted of the emperors of the Kirsch, and a magician of great power.

Conmar: *Cam.* An alias of Brand.

Dernthrad: *Duth.* "Head shield – a helm." A farmer of the Duthgar.

Dragon of the Duthgar: The banner of the chieftains of the Duthenor. Legend holds that an ancient forefather of the line slew a dragon and ate its heart. Dragons are seen by the Duthenor as creatures of ultimate evil, but the consuming of their heart is reputed to pass on wisdom and magic.

Drunn: *Duth.* "Man of secrets." Former chieftain of the Duthenor. Husband to Brunhal and father to Brand.

Durnloth: *Duth. Comb. Hal.* "Earth might." Young sheep herder of the Duthgar.

Duthenor: *Duth. Prn.* Dooth-en-or. "The people." A single tribe (or less commonly a group of closely related tribes melded into a larger people at times of war or disaster) who generally live a rustic and peaceful lifestyle. They are breeders of cattle and herders of sheep.

However, when need demands they are bold warriors – men and women alike. Currently ruled by a usurper who murdered Brand's parents. Brand has sworn an oath to overthrow the tyrant and avenge his parents.

Duthgar: *Duth.* "People spear." The name is taken to mean "the land of the warriors who wield spears."

Elùgai: *Hal. Prn.* Eloo-guy. "Shadowed force." The sorcery of an elùgroth.

Elù-haraken: *Hal.* "The shadowed wars." Long ago battles in a time that is become myth to the Duthenor and Camar tribes.

Elùgroth: *Hal. Prn.* Eloo-groth. "Shadowed horror." A sorcerer. They often take names in the Halathrin tongue in mockery of the lòhren practice to do so.

Ermenrik: *Duth.* "Tallest tree in the forest." Trusted servant of Unferth.

Galdring: *Duth.* "Bright blade." A lord of the Duthenor. Son of Baldring.

Garamund: *Duth.* "Spears of the earth – trees." An old warrior of the Duthenor.

Gingrel: *Duth.* "Yellow river – a river mined for gold." A Callenor vassal to Unferth. Given lordship of a hall by the usurper.

God-king: See Char-harash.

Grinder: A man-like creature of Duthenor legend that haunts fells and fens. Said to be born of a lightning strike in swamp water, but there are other tales of his origin. He hates men, and hunts those who stray into his shadow-haunted lands. Reported to shun weapons, but to kill by the enormous strength of his arms alone.

Halathar: *Hal.* "Dwelling place of the people of Halath." The forest realm of the immortal Halathrin.

Halathgar: *Hal.* "Bright star." Actually a constellation of two stars. Also called the Lost Huntress.

Halathrin: *Hal.* "People of Halath." A race named after an honored lord who led an exodus of his people to the land of Alithoras in pursuit of justice, having sworn to defeat a great evil. They are human, though of fairer form, greater skill and higher culture than ordinary men. They possess a unity of body, mind and spirit that enables insight and endurance beyond the native races of Alithoras. Said to be immortal, but killed in great numbers during their conflicts in ancient times with the evil they sought to destroy. Those conflicts are collectively known as the Shadowed Wars.

Haldring: *Duth.* "White blade – a sword that flashes in the sun." Sister of Galdring. A shield-maiden.

Harad: *Duth.* "Warrior." An old farmer, and husband of Hromling.

Har-falach: *Kir.* "Ruler/heavenly/mystical falcon." One of the lesser gods of the Kar-ahn-hetep. Often depicted as a man with wings and the head of a hawk.

Harlach: Etymology unknown, but not considered to be of Duthenor origin. An ancient witch of Duthenor and Camar folklore whose life has spanned hundreds, perhaps thousands, of years. Reclusive, often wicked and according to some legends the mother of a monster that roams the night hunting and killing men.

Hathalor: *Kir.* "Tresses of the sun – a lion's mane." One of the lesser gods of the Kar-ahn-hetep. Often depicted as a man with a lion's head.

High Way: An ancient road longer than the Duthgar, but well preserved in that land. Probably of Letharn origin and used to speed troops to battle.

Horta: *Kir.* "Speech of the acacia tree." It is believed among the Kar-ahn-hetep that the acacia tree possesses magical properties that aid discourse between the realms of men and gods. Horta is a name that recurs among families noted for producing elite magicians.

Howe: A large mound of turfed earth, usually covering a stone structure, that serves as a tomb.

Hromling: *Duth.* "Frost foam – snow." An old farmwife, spouse of Harad.

Hruidgar: *Duth.* "Ashwood spear." A Duthenor hunter.

Immortals: See Halathrin.

Kar-ahn-hetep: *Kir.* "The children of the thousand stars." A race of people that vied for supremacy in ancient times with the Letharn. Their power was ultimately broken, their empire destroyed. But a residual population survived and defied outright annihilation by their conquerors. They believe their empire will one day rise again to rule the world. The kar-ahn element of their name means the "thousand stars" but also "the lights that never die."

Kar-fallon: *Kir.* "Death city." A great city of the Kar-ahn-hetep that served as their principal religious focus. Their magician-priests conducted the great rites of their nation in its sacred temples.

Kar-karmun: *Kir.* "Death-life – the runes of life and death." A means of divination that distills the wisdom and worldview of the Kar-ahn-hetep civilization.

Kirsch: See Kar-ahn-hetep.

Laigern: *Cam.* "Storm-tossed sea." Head guard of a merchant caravan.

Letharn: *Hal.* "Stone raisers. Builders." A race of people that in antiquity conquered most of Alithoras. Now, only faint traces of their civilization endure.

Light of Kar-fallon: See Char-harash.

Lòhren: *Hal. Prn.* Ler-ren. "Knowledge giver – a counselor." Other terms used by various nations include wizard, druid and sage.

Lòhrengai: *Hal. Prn.* Ler-ren-guy. "Lòhren force." Enchantment, spell or use of mystic power. A manipulation and transformation of the natural energy inherent in all things. Each use takes something from the user. Likewise, some part of the transformed energy infuses them. Lòhrens use it sparingly, elùgroths indiscriminately.

Lord of the Ten Armies: See Char-harash.

Magic: Mystic power. See lòhrengai and elùgai.

Norhanu: *Kir.* "Serrated blade." A psychoactive herb.

Olbata: *Kir.* "Silence of the desert at night." An inner door disciple of Horta.

Pennling Path: Etymology obscure. Pennling was an ancient hero of the Duthenor. Some say he built the road in the Duthgar known as the High Way. This is not true, but one legend holds that he traveled all its length in one night on a milk-white steed to confront an attacking army by himself. It is said that his ghost may yet be seen racing along the road on his steed when the full moon hangs above the Duthgar.

Ruler of the Thousand Stars: See Char-harash.

Runes of Life and Death: See Kar-karmun.

Shadowed wars: See Elù-haraken.

Shemfal: *Kir.* "Cool shadows gliding over the hot waste – dusk." One of the greater gods of the Kar-ahn-hetep. Often depicted as a mighty man, bat winged and headed. Ruler of the underworld. Given a wound in battle with other gods that does not heal and causes him to limp.

Shenna: *Kir.* "Royal rectangle." A kind of cartouche.

Shenti: A type of kilt worn by the Kar-ahn-hetep.

Shorty: A former Durlindrath (chief bodyguard of the king of Cardoroth). Friend to Brand. His proper name is Lornach.

Shurilgar: *Hal.* "Midnight star." An elùgroth. One of the most puissant sorcerers of antiquity. Known to legend as the Betrayer of Nations.

Sighern: *Duth.* "Battle leader." A youth of the Duthgar.

Sorcerer: See Elùgroth.

Sorcery: See elùgai.

Stillness in the Storm: A mental state sought by many warriors. It is a sense of the mind being detached from the body. If achieved, it frees the warrior from emotions such as fear and pain that hinder physical performance. The body, in its turn, moves and reacts by trained instinct alone allowing the skill of the warrior to flow unhindered to the surface. Those who have perfected the correct mental state feel as though they can slow down the passage of time during a fight. It is an illusion, yet one that offers a combat advantage.

Taingern: *Cam.* "Still sea," or "calm waters." A former Durlindrath (chief bodyguard of the king of Cardoroth). Friend to Brand.

Thurgil: *Duth.* "Storm of blades." A farmer of the Duthgar.

Tinwellen: *Cam.* "Sun of the earth – gold." Daughter of a prosperous merchant of Cardoroth.

Unferth: *Duth.* "Hiss of arrows." The name is sometimes interpreted to mean "whispered counsels that lead to war." Usurper of the chieftainship of the Duthenor. Rightful chieftain of the Callenor.

Ùhrengai: *Hal. Prn.* Er-ren-guy. "Original force." The primordial force that existed before substance or time.

Wizard: See lòhren.

Wizard-priest: The priests of the Letharn, who possessed mighty powers of magic.

About the author

I'm a man born in the wrong era. My heart yearns for faraway places and even further afield times. Tolkien had me at the beginning of *The Hobbit* when he said, ". . . one morning long ago in the quiet of the world . . ."

Sometimes I imagine myself in a Viking mead-hall. The long winter night presses in, but the shimmering embers of a log in the hearth hold back both cold and dark. The chieftain calls for a story, and I take a sip from my drinking horn and stand up . . .

Or maybe the desert stars shine bright and clear, obscured occasionally by wisps of smoke from burning camel dung. A dry gust of wind marches sand grains across our lonely campsite, and the wayfarers about me stir restlessly. I sip cool water and begin to speak.

I'm a storyteller. A man to paint a picture by the slow music of words. I like to bring faraway places and times to life, to make hearts yearn for something they can never have, unless for a passing moment.

THE CRIMSON LORD
BOOK TWO OF THE DARK GOD RISES TRILOGY

Robert Ryan

Copyright © 2019 Robert J. Ryan
All Rights Reserved. The right of Robert J. Ryan to be identified as the author of this work has been asserted. All of the characters in this book are fictitious and any resemblance to actual persons, living or dead, is coincidental.

Trotting Fox Press

1. A Magician of Power

Unferth sat still, a mask over his features. A king should at least *look* as though events moved at his control, but he worried that even the guise of orderly rule had slipped away from him.

Frustration made him want to smash his hand against the table. But he could not, for it would only prove that he was angry and therefore *not* in perfect control. This fed the anger that burned inside him even more. And that anger was red hot, raging and desperate to be unleashed.

But deeper inside, in his innermost thoughts that he shared with no one, was something colder than ice. It was the thing that troubled him most. Fear.

It was an ever-present whisper. It was the voice of doubt. It was the rasp of steel blades drawn in a nightmare from which he could not wake. Fear. It sent a chill through him that nothing ever warmed. And unlike the fear of most men that was formless and vague, his had a specific name. Brand.

Brand haunted him. Even as a child, having escaped the killing of his parents, Brand had been like a sore that would not heal. If only he had been there that night, if only he had died as he was supposed to, the world would be a better place. Unferth knew it, knew that the sun would have shone upon him and he would have ruled both the Callenor and the Duthenor in a noontide of glory.

But Brand was a shadow upon him, and the shadow lengthened year by year. And now came this. A final insult like a crack that could widen and destroy the life he had worked so hard for. Why did other men have it so easy while he must he fight tooth and claw like an animal for what was his?

His fury boiled over. Despite the look of calm he knew he should maintain, he smashed his hand against the table anyway. The sudden noise stilled everything about him. The hall became quiet, and his counselors turned surprised gazes upon him. Fools! They did not understand. They never would.

He spoke slowly, showing as much restraint as he could.

"Why do you all debate this? Horta has told you what happened. Brand defeated the force sent against him. Outnumbered, he found a way to grasp victory." That he must say those words humbled him, and the voice of doubt in his mind was more than a whisper now. "We'll not beat him by debating among ourselves. You can be sure that already he moves against us. What shall we do? *That* is the question we must answer, and swiftly. Otherwise, he'll be here in this hall with a sword to our necks. Do none of you understand that?"

"We understand the possibility of it," one of the men said. "But where is the proof of it?"

Unferth shook his head, dismayed. "Horta has told you it is so. What more do you need?"

"Horta has said that Brand won a victory. He has said the army we sent is defeated. He has said much, but I will believe it better when word returns with one of our own men. As yet, we have heard nothing."

There it was. Unferth knew he was losing control, and he must act decisively to regain it. Not long ago, his very word was law. Now, though he knew Horta would be proved right in what he claimed, the men awaited their own proof. The irony was that the military loss they yet did not believe was the thing that emboldened them.

Horta adjusted the bearskin serape that hung over his shoulders. If he was offended, he gave no sign. But he never did.

"Brand won a great victory," the magician assured them. "Of that, you can be certain. I would tell you how I know, but it would burn your souls to ash. Believe, and you have an opportunity to act quickly and turn adversity into triumph. Delay, and the kingdom will slip through your fingers."

"Easy for you to say," said another warrior at the table. "But why should we believe you?"

Unferth ground his teeth. He knew Horta's powers. He knew something of the magic the man possessed. Very likely, it *would* burn the souls of most men to ash.

A look passed between them. Horta's gaze said that magic was his province, and controlling the Callenor was Unferth's. The magician's disciple, Olbata, sat beside his master and stared at the men around the table, his eyes dark with hidden thoughts.

Once more Unferth slammed his hand down on the table, and this time he shouted with it.

"Fools!" He looked around, turning his cold gaze on the counselors. It was the gaze of a man who had killed, the gaze of a man who might yet hold the power of life and death over them. And their mood for defiance washed away, at least for the moment.

But he did not have a chance to speak. The fire in the pit at the center of the hall flickered and smoked. The air grew suddenly chill, and an acrid odor filled it.

Unferth looked at Horta, thinking he had begun to work magic. But there was dread in the other man's eyes. It was the first time he had ever seen Horta display fear. He had always thought the man possessed a heart of stone.

Horta stood and moved to the back of the room, drawing Unferth with him. Unferth did not resist.

All around the table men seemed confused. Some drew their swords. A sudden wind roared to life, and within it came another sound, regular and forceful like the beating of vast wings.

Unferth pressed his back against the wall. Even as he did so the wind died away and the great door to the hall crashed open with a booming clatter of oak planks and hinges. Timbers rattled, the hall itself shook, and within the opening a thing of huge shadows hulked. There it stood a moment, surveying those in the room. Its head swiveled, and Unferth thought that it sniffed at the air.

Horta, his own back to the wall, moved. Briefly Unferth glimpsed the man withdraw a leaf from one of his many pouches with trembling hands and slip it into his mouth. Then the man whispered in his ear. "Do not move nor speak, no matter what happens, and all will be well."

The mass of shadows in the doorway began to move. The intruder walked like a man, though it limped. Ten feet high it stood, at least, and as it came into the room the fire in the pit flared to life with a crackle of popping wood and colored smoke.

With the leaping flames came greater light, and Unferth saw the thing clearly. It had wings, vast and bulky that were furled behind it and still part-hidden by shadow. It had the form of a man, but its head was that of a bat.

"Shemfal," whispered Horta beside him. Unferth did not know who or what this creature was, but the name slipped into his mind like a dagger of fear.

On the creature came, striding like a king. Yet the limp marred his presence, and Unferth wondered what power walked the world that could give injury to such as this.

One of the warriors at the table screamed a battle-cry and leapt at the thing. His bright sword flashed through the air, but Shemfal, barely seeming to move, brushed the blade aside with his arm and then smote the man a hammer-like blow.

The warrior fell dead. Others had drawn their swords, but they milled about in fear and did not attack. They saw no way to defeat such a creature, and neither did Unferth. But he must trust in Horta. The magician had said all would be well.

Shemfal came to a stop. His dark eyes, round and burning with a fierce gaze beneath pointed ears, turned to Horta.

"The price must be paid, mortal."

"Indeed, great lord."

Horta said no more, but his glance turned to Olbata. So also the gaze of Shemfal.

The massive wings of the creature unfurled slightly, and he pointed with a bony hand, black talons dripping from the ends of his fingers like curved daggers.

"You are mine, mortal. Come hither."

Olbata trembled. He swung to Horta, his mouth working several times before words were voiced.

"Why? Did I not serve you well?"

Horta turned a cool gaze upon him. "Yes, you did. Yet also, you knew the risks. Knowledge does not come without cost. You are unlucky to pay the price, for it was no fault of your own. But the risk was always there. Do not dishonor yourself by trying to fight your fate. It is written now."

"It is written in my blood!"

Horta did not answer, merely looking at his pupil as though at an ant beneath his feet.

Unferth admired him in that moment. He was so calm, so assured of the rightness of his actions. Whatever lay behind this, no one understood fully but Horta. And yet Unferth guessed that this creature had been summoned from the pit and constrained to perform an errand. Now, it sought payment for the deed done. Such was the way of demons, which this thing must surely be.

Olbata swung back to the creature and swiftly began to chant. He raised his hand, a tiny statuette in his fingers, and this he held high as some sort of talisman.

Shemfal laughed. His wings beat and he darted forward, one hand snaking out to grab his victim by the throat.

Olbata screamed, but the sound was muffled. With another beat of wings Shemfal hovered in the air a moment, and then he glided toward the fire pit.

The flames roared once more as though in greeting. The demon descended, Olbata thrashing as tongues of fire licked his flesh. And then the fire pit was no more. In its place opened a fissure in the earth, and down in its depths Unferth glimpsed a mighty cavern, lit by flickering flames and wreathed in shadows. A dark throne rose in the center, and all manner of wicked things moved and writhed about it.

Fire flared once more, and Olbata's screams died away in a puff of greasy smoke. When that cleared, the vision of the underworld was gone and the fire pit burned as it always had. Silence filled the hall, but the beating of Unferth's heart thundered in his chest.

Here though was an opportunity to assert control again, and he took it. Despite his terror, he wore a guise of nonchalance.

He stepped forward with confidence and ease. Righting a chair that had been spilled when the men rose from the table and drew their swords, he sat down and leaned back comfortably.

"Our meeting is not yet over," he said. "Come, sit down. We must continue."

The men returned to the table. One by one, reluctantly, blades were sheathed.

"See," Unferth said. "Horta is a magician of power. If he tells us Brand beat the army we sent, it is so. Do not doubt it."

One of the warriors scraped his chair loudly as he sat. "If Horta is a magician of such power, how is it that Brand still lives?"

Unferth felt his frustration rise again. This time it was intensified by his terror at what had just happened, and he wanted to reach out and throttle the man questioning him. Was he not a king? Was it right that they contended with his every word?

Horta was the one who answered the man though, his voice smooth and measured.

"That will be remedied," the magician said. "Twice now I have tried to kill Brand, and he has survived. The man's life is charmed. But his luck must run out soon."

"How will you do it?" Unferth asked.

Horta shrugged. "I have … ways. Best that you do not know them, for they would only serve to give you nightmares."

Unferth believed him. He had no real desire to know the details. Almost, he could feel sorry for Brand.

The magician's gaze showed nothing, but there was a hint of amusement to the curl of his lips. He knew exactly what Unferth was thinking.

"This much I will say," Horta continued, now addressing all of the men at the table. "I will look after Brand, but whether I kill him or not there is yet his army to defeat. It will not disperse now, even at his death. That is a problem you must deal with."

It was sound advice, and Unferth knew it. The Duthenor were raised against him now, and everything he had striven for could be lost. He would not let that happen.

"Horta has summed up the situation well," he said. "We must defeat Brand's army, but how best shall we do that?"

The men seemed sullen, and most kept glancing at the fire pit. Horta excused himself and walked away. Unferth watched him go, knowing that he would gather his disciples and initiate some dreadful rite of magic. What its nature would be, Unferth did not even want to contemplate. But he had a feeling that the little magician took Brand's survival as a personal insult now. Brand, at least, would be one less problem soon.

"Well?" he said to the men. "How shall we defeat the enemy? Shall we march against them, or let them come here and spend themselves against our defenses?"

2. The Blood of a Hero

It was the morning after the battle. It was the dawn of a new day, after a great victory. And yet Brand found little joy in his triumph. Others had paid for it with their blood.

Haldring was especially on his mind as the army readied to march. He had instructed Sighern to hold the Dragon Banner of the Duthenor high, and it hung limply in the still air from the long staff it was attached to. Some had wanted to throw it away, soiled by Haldring's blood as it was, and make a new one. He would have none of that. The blood of a hero was a better emblem than a dragon.

But even in death he used her, as he had in life. At least, he could not help feeling so. He had not known what would happen, but he had guessed. And he had set the example himself. He had touched the cloth first thing in the morning, head bowed, and whispered an oath. *I will try to show the courage you did, and fight until my last breath even as you. Nothing shall stop me.*

Many had seen him. Some had heard his words. And when he had walked away, a line of soldiers followed his lead. They touched the cloth and said the words. It would bind them, fill them with purpose, and give morale to the army. Already word was spreading through the ranks. A legend was growing, and by the end of the day every soldier would have done the same thing, become part of the same group. In years to come, if they lived, they would tell their children and their grandchildren that they had sworn Haldring's oath.

Brand took the reins of his horse and looked ahead with steely eyes. How had he come to this? What cruel fate had shaped him so? He could not do anything, even grieve the death of a friend, without turning it into a means of manipulating soldiers and strengthening the army. And yet, if he did not, the army would be weaker and more likely to lose. Then, all those who had died, Haldring included, would have perished in vain. What he was doing was wrong, but it was also right, and he yearned for a simpler world. But he knew he would never have it.

"March!" he called.

Nearby, a man blew a horn and the army began to move. It would be no swift march, not today. Few were unscathed by yesterday's battle, one way or another. Including himself. And the army was smaller than it was. Behind them they left the dead. The wounded had already been moved to villages close to hand.

The sun rose to his left, for the army was heading south. He had a goal, but as yet no destination. That goal was the overthrow of Unferth. The man was at the heart of his woes, ever since childhood. He had murdered his parents. Who knew how many of the Duthenor had been killed at his hands? And last, though it was not murder, he was the ultimate cause of Haldring's death. For all those things he would pay.

Brand remained silent as the army progressed along the High Way. His thoughts kept him occupied, dark as they were. Even young Sighern, walking close by his side, recognized his mood and did not disturb it. Shorty and Taingern, leading their own horses on his other side, had long years ago learned when to leave him to himself.

A dark mood such as this came on him seldom, and anger and frustration less often still, but they had him now in a grip of iron.

The miles passed, and the rhythm of walking occupied his body but freed his mind. Walking was a good way to think, but it was calming too, and his mood gradually softened. He must put aside anger and vengeance. They were useless emotions. At least, they were not good in the long term. And that was how he must think. His every deed and action must be for the benefit and future of the army and the Duthgar. His purpose was to free them of Unferth, and that goal, and that goal alone, must guide his tactics. His personal feelings must be put aside.

He called the first halt of the day. The soldiers wasted no time sitting or lying down. They were wise now in the ways of war, and rested whenever opportunity arose.

Brand saw Taingern glance at him, assessing his mood. The man always read him well, and he must have sensed the change in his temper, for he spoke.

"We're making fair time," he said, "despite everyone's weariness."

"Fair time," Shorty echoed, "but to where? We're heading south, but does that mean we're striking for Unferth himself?"

Brand sat down, and the others joined him. Sighern did likewise, but he still gripped the staff that held up the banner.

"A good question," Brand answered. "Whatever we do next, our direction must be southward. But we still have a choice. Gather more men as we go, or seek to strike swiftly while the enemy is chagrined by their loss."

Taingern seemed relieved. "So you have not decided yet?"

"No."

"That's good. A hasty decision often leads to trouble."

"Wise words," Brand said with a grin, "but what you mean is that a decision based on emotion hinders sound judgement."

Taingern looked thoughtful. "No one would blame you for being emotional."

"Possibly not. But the Duthgar needs more from me than that. What I must decide now is how best to defeat Unferth."

Shorty grinned. "Strike out for him now, so that our army follows hot on the heels of the news of his loss. Catch him with his pants down, so to speak."

"Not quite the imagery I wanted," Brand laughed. "But your point is well made. And what of you, Taingern? What do you advise?"

Taingern stretched out on the ground and plucked a stem of grass, which he then rolled between his fingers.

"These are the two questions we need to consider. How many men can Unferth still muster? And how many more can you gather to you as you go? No doubt, the slower you travel the more you will get."

"I cannot be sure of exact numbers," Brand answered. "But likely enough, Unferth could muster another five thousand men."

"Fewer though, the quicker you strike for him and the less chance he has to prepare," Shorty suggested.

"Quite right," Brand agreed. "But our own army is now down to a little under a thousand men after yesterday's battle. If I march quickly, I may only have time to double that. I could end up facing Unferth with an army of two thousand, but even caught by surprise he might be able to match that."

"And if you march more slowly," Taingern said, "how many more men could you gather?"

Brand thought on that. "Another two thousand, I would think. That would give me an army of four thousand in total."

"It seems to me," Shorty said, "that the slower you go the more you will end up being outnumbered."

"So it could prove," Brand said. "But there's one other thing to consider."

Shorty grunted. "You're right. The magician."

"Exactly. What he's capable of in a battle, we don't know. But his magic is powerful, so we can be sure to expect something. And there's one more thing."

"What's that?"

"Horta may learn of our victory last night by sorcerous means. Unferth may have warning, and therefore a chance to prepare long before normal messages reach him."

Shorty kicked at the ground with his heel. "That puts a different light on things."

Brand remained calm. Even after such a great victory, all was still in doubt. His instincts were the same as Shorty's though. Move quickly and try to use speed itself as a weapon. But Unferth could at this very moment be thinking the same.

It was an interesting line of thought. Would Unferth come to him and attack? It was not really in the man's nature. He preferred to move in the shadows and manipulate things like a spider in his web. And yet, he had been poked. How would he react?

The more he considered it the more he formed a definite belief. Unferth would have word of the battle swiftly. Horta would see to that. When news reached the rest of them, support for Unferth would diminish. He would begin to lose control. He would worry that other uprisings among the Duthenor would occur, separate from what was happening here. How best to counterattack that? By moving swiftly himself and attacking. And he would do so with everything he had to try to crush the rebellion definitively.

"Gentlemen," Brand said. "I think we'll meet Unferth on the road, for he'll be coming to us."

"Likely enough," Taingern agreed. "And once more his forces will outnumber ours."

"Indeed. And he will think to have the advantage of surprise. But surprise works two ways."

Shorty grinned at him. "I like it when you have a plan. And I'm pretty sure I can see the glint of one in your eye right now. Am I right?"

3. Battle and Victory!

To march forward and fight, or to establish a fortified position were the choices Unferth gave his advisers. No one suggested any alternatives.

"Let Brand come," said several of the men. "We can excavate earth ramparts. No matter the size of his army, we'll have the advantage then."

"And what if he skirts our fortified position and takes the king's hall?" others argued. "Then the Duthenor will rise against us to a man and nothing will stop them."

Another group were all for defending the hall itself. "What need have we for ramparts? Our army will outnumber his. All we need is to hold our ground until he comes and then defeat him."

Few were the voices that argued in favor of marching forth to attack Brand. But to these Unferth paid most attention. It was the way he leaned himself. Too much was happening, and he had too little control of it. Setting out on a march would bring the men together, give him a greater position of authority as leader and help fortify his standing as a king. When Brand was beaten, there would be no dissent to his rule then. That was the one thing he must do above all others, and as quickly as possible.

His nephew had been the foremost proponent of this strategy. "Attack him!" Gormengil pressed. "Why should we suffer such as Brand to raise arms against us in our own realm? We have the advantage of surprise, thanks to Horta. Let us use that, and blot him and those who support him from the history of the Duthgar. Better that than to debate and whine and worry like a pack of half-witted dogs!"

Gormengil had not held back. It was his way, and he had enemies for it. But he had supporters too, and many of them. He was one to watch. Unferth had named him as heir, for he had no son of his own, but he intended to live a long while yet. But Gormengil knew no restraint when it came to ambition. What he said now was right, but he was to be trusted less for it. He always had secret motives.

"I have listened and considered and weighed all of your views," Unferth said. "This is my decision. Gather the army. We march to war, and we march at dawn tomorrow."

He turned to his personal servant. "Fetch my axe and armor. I ride to battle and victory!"

The man hurried off. He would retrieve the sacred battle apparel of the chieftains of the Callenor, what had never been worn in the lands of the Duthenor. Unferth had taken the rule without bloodshed, but there would be bloodshed now. The Duthgar would swim in a sea of red, and Brand would sink beneath the crimson tide.

Swiftly he gave orders and made plans. And the more he took charge the better the men obeyed him. It was a lesson learned, and he would not soon forget it. A leader must impose his will, and the more he did that the less dissention there would be.

As he slept that night though, the whisper of doubt returned to him. What if Brand won again, despite still having the smaller army? What if Horta failed once more to kill him by sorcery? And most of all, threaded through all his lesser fears was the greatest of them, the one that he did not just worry over but had seen begin, the loss of his authority over those he ruled. It was slipping away, and though he had drawn tight the reins of leadership once more, the dissention would return quickly at any setback.

It was a long night, and Unferth tossed and turned and drifted finally into a dark sleep. And he dreamed as he had never dreamed before. Here, in the shadow-world of his thought, he found his true self and the strength that was inside him.

A white-coated bull charged him, dark eyes blazing and head tilted down, his horns set to rip and impale. But with a deft touch of Unferth's hand the beast's anger was stayed. It shook its head and then wandered off, grazing the sparse grass nearby as though nothing had happened.

Unferth strode away. A hawk flashed through the air, all wings and speed and confidence. That was him now. Unferth the hawk, lord of the sky.

The ground beneath his boots was withered and dry. Dead grass crunched beneath his tread. The sun beat down, but even as he felt the oppression of it, he thought of a cooling breeze and one rose to caress his skin.

Ahead was a range of mountains, purple-blue in the heat haze. There he knew he would find good shade beneath stunted trees or in the lee of some cliff. He turned toward it.

In the way of dreams he found himself there straightaway, winding his way down a rocky slope. There were no trees, stunted or otherwise, and he felt a prickle of unease as though unseen eyes watched him. What land was this that he dreamed of? It was not like the green hills of his home.

The heat dissipated. Steep walls of stone now towered either side over his path, and he walked down a canyon that was silent, still and peaceful. It was daylight, though dim in the declivity, and the stars filled the daytime sky like a thousand beautiful lights.

Benevolence washed over him in waves, and all was right with the world. A clatter of hooves sounded ahead, and some sort of animal like a mountain sheep leapt nimbly away from a pool of water and disappeared into vague shadows on the canyon sides. Unferth moved toward the pool.

It was clear as glass, but on its dark surface he saw the reflection of his own face. It seemed to him that he was a king of old. Wisdom etched his features, but there was strength there too. The courage of the heroes of legend was in his glance, and upon his head sat a crown of stars.

He knelt and drank of the water, finding it sweet and intoxicating as wine. It refreshed him, cured his thirst and filled him with strength.

With a graceful movement he stood, and found that he was not alone. A young man, dressed in strange robes of a golden hue, sat cross-legged on the stone shelf beside the pool.

"Greetings," the man said. "I trust the water was pleasant?"

"Indeed."

The young man gestured, and Unferth knew it as an invitation to join him. He too sat cross-legged, opposite his companion.

"My name is Char-harash."

Unferth inclined his head. The man before him was highborn, probably royalty, that much was evident, but he himself was a king. He bowed to no one, though even seated he had the feeling that he should. He dismissed it.

Char-harash smiled, his face open and honest. "A king of your standing ever seeks wise counselors, does he not? And yet the voices of the multitude always clamor in your ears with petty concerns. Tell me that it is so?"

Unferth was pleased. Here was a man who understood his situation. "It is so."

The young man nodded sagely. "It is always thus. But you are special. To you, I offer my services. The wisdom of the ages is at your disposal, and I shall aid you in your troubles. This is what you wish, above all else, yes?"

Unferth bowed his head. "You read my mind."

The other man gazed calmly at him. "If I am to help you, you must say yes."

"Yes, my lord. I wish your help above all else."

Char-harash smiled. It was an easy smile, a smile to instill confidence. On another man, it would have seemed cruel. But on a lord such as Char-harash, it was fitting.

"Tell me of Brand."

"He is the rightful lord of the Duthenor," Unferth said. A vague feeling of unease overtook him once more, but the young man reached out and touched his hand.

"All is well. There shall only be the truth between us. That will be good, will it not?"

"Yes, my lord."

"What sort of man is Brand?"

"He is dangerous and hard to kill. His skill with a sword is said to be sublime. And he possesses magic too."

The younger man considered that. "But you could beat him, could you not?"

"Of course."

"What is his weakness?"

Unferth wanted to answer quickly, but this required thought. The water in the pool remained still and clear, and the gaze of the young man was intent.

"He has the weakness of all good men. Morals constrain him. If he cast them away, he could be truly great."

The young man did not seem best pleased at that answer. Unferth sensed he wanted to know more about Brand's personality, his style of leadership and the type of military strategies he employed. But Unferth knew none of those things.

Char-harash looked at him solemnly. "And how do you intend to beat Brand?"

"I will crush him by weight of numbers and surprise."

The young man considered that. "Yes, these are strong tools in the hand of a skilled warlord. Strong indeed, but the warlord who wields them must be the best." The young man looked at him intently once more. "Are you the best, Unferth?"

"I am. I was a chieftain, but I made myself a king. I united two tribes and I—"

"Who is second best to you?"

It was an easy question and Unferth answered quickly. "Gormengil, my lord."

"Tell me about him."

"The blood of chieftains is in his veins. He is young, ruthless and ambitious. He is quick to find trouble, but he can be subtle too, especially so for one of his age, though it's not normally his way. And he can fight also. He's a great warrior, greater than myself. Most people say he is the best fighter among the Callenor."

Char-harash remained quiet, listening carefully, and then he seemed to come to a decision. He raised his hand and Unferth stopped speaking.

"All will be well," the young lord said. "Rest easy and sleep now. Brand is a grave threat, but already steps have been taken against him and he is snared in a trap."

"But what shall I—"

"Hush," Char-harash commanded. "Sleep. All will be well."

The young lord reached out and brushed his fingers against Unferth's brow. A wave of contentment rolled over him. Sleepiness came with it and he felt his mind drift. The little canyon grew darker. The pool was lost from sight. Only Char-harash remained, a golden-clad lord standing tall and proud as a king of old. For the first time, Unferth saw that in his left hand was a wooden rod, pale white and gleaming with a sheen of sorcerous power. In his right was a sword, the edge wickedly sharp.

Char-harash leveled the wooden rod at him. "Sleep," he commanded. And Unferth slept.

The night wore on, and Unferth dreamed once more, but he did not meet again the golden-robed lord who promised to help him. When he woke, he felt better rested than he had in years. And calm too, considering that he marched to war.

He put the night's dreams from his mind. Reality called instead, for today would be a day of history, for he himself would ride to war and the armor and weapon of his great ancestor that founded the Callenor realm would once more inspire terror among their foes.

His manservant entered the room, bearing a tray of food. He did not speak, having long since learned to answer questions only. Unferth wished he had more like him: well trained, silent and obedient.

He quickly ate a meal of bread, thickly sliced ham and soft cheese. While he did so, the manservant waited nearby should he want something. But all Unferth wanted to do was ride. He dismissed him, finished eating and then looked at the armor. It was laid out on a chest before him, and it sent a thrill up his spine.

Reverently, he pulled the mail-shirt over his head, placed the gauntlets on his hand and the helm on his head. Then he took up the weapon of his forefathers. It felt good in his hand. Taking a deep breath, he flung open the door and strode down the length of the hall and outside.

Warriors gazed at him, and then bowed. There was fear in their eyes, or so he thought. If not, there should be. He knew he looked the part of a battle king. And soon the Duthenor would see him, and tremble at the folly of even thinking about rebellion.

He led a procession of his closest friends and best warriors down out of the hall and into the field beyond the village. Here his army was gathered, or at least the first part of it.

Over a thousand men waited. Others would swell the army in the next village and the next. But it was these men who saw him first, and their eyes were riveted to him. This was a sight most had not seen in their lifetime.

Unferth came to a standstill near where his mount was tethered. He stood before it so all could see him. The chain mail shirt he wore was of the finest steel, each ring wrought and linked by cunning skill beyond the reach of mortal blacksmiths. It was lighter than it should be, stronger than it seemed, invincible to blade or dart. The dwarves of the Anast Dennath mountains had made it, and spells were woven into the metal at both forging and joining. So at least the legends claimed. But what drew the eye was that each link was lacquered red, crimson as bright blood, and no amount of time nor strike by any enemy had ever tarnished it.

Upon his head rested a mighty helm. This also was fashioned by the dwarves, and spells were upon it too. Engraved into the same red-lacquered metal was a single rune: karak, which meant victory in their tongue. From the eye slit Unferth gazed out and saw his army. Pride and strength filled him.

He raised high now in a sudden thrust the weapon of his forefathers. It was made of the same metal as the rest, though lacquered black rather than red. The weight was somewhat less than it should be, for it was a double-bladed axe. Each half swept back like wings, but there was a stabbing spike in the center, slightly curved like a beak so that it could also hook and gouge. This was a weapon of legend to the Callenor, for it was made for their founding chieftain. And it was made in the image of the symbol he took as his own: a raven.

Unferth gave the axe a flourish, and then he slipped the haft through a leather thong on his horse's saddle and mounted.

The men began to chant. *The Crimson Lord! The Crimson Lord! The Crimson Lord!*

He liked it. Once more he felt confidence and invincibility flood through his veins. He would destroy Brand. And yet even as he thought of his enemy the whisper of doubt returned. He knew it would always be there. The only way to silence it would be to kill his opponent.

He kicked his horse forward and the army began to move with him, still chanting.

4. The Trickster

Horta was pleased. The place he had chosen was fitting for his purpose. And it would need to be, for the summoning of a god was no task to carry out unless all was in order.

Idly, he slipped a norhanu leaf into his mouth and sucked upon it. Too often he did so now, for useful as the herb was it also was a poison. But these were dangerous days. To survive them, he must take risks that otherwise he would not dare.

The hilltop was perfect. He hated this green land, swept often by wind and rain and trailing mists. But from here, he could see all around for miles. The air was sweet and pure, and it carried the scent of grass and herb and flower. Birds wheeled to and fro, and on a lower ridge he had glimpsed a herd of deer. Down below the halls and villages of men were so distant as to nearly not be there at all. That was good, very good indeed.

"Is all well, master?"

Horta did not turn to look. He did not like the Arnhaten to speak with him at times like this. Yet, now that Olbata was gone, he must look to another of his disciples for a chief helper.

After a while, he glanced at the other man. It was Tanata. He was a quiet person, secretive and sly. He had the makings of a magician, although he seemed very young for the dark arts that must be learned.

Horta sighed. "All is well, Tanata." He may as well begin to teach the lad what he knew.

"Then why do you look sad?"

Horta looked out once more at the view. "Because it is not easy to be a magician. Oh, to be sure, the spells and rituals are easy enough. Anyone can learn them and carry them out."

"Then what *is* hard?"

"Doing what must be done is hard, even when you know it must."

"It does not sound hard, master."

"And yet it is. Perhaps you need to be an old man to know that."

Tanata did not reply to that, and Horta shivered in the silence. He had a sense that one day, years from now, a young man would ask Tanata the same question. He wondered if his disciple would give a better answer.

Horta brushed the pensive mood from his mind. It was not like him, and it would only hinder what he had to do.

"See!" he said, rousing himself and sweeping out a long arm. "All about us is nature. The hand of man is distant. How will this help us in what we intend?"

Tanata did not answer straightaway. He considered the question, and Horta felt his mood lighten. Here was one who might have the temper to learn the mysteries.

"We seek to summon a god," Tanata answered at length. "And the gods are connected to the land, born from it even. There is power in the land. It lives, and its life will aid us."

Horta was surprised. It was a good answer. "And why avoid proximity to the works of men?"

"Because human life is fleeting. Human minds are filled with emotions that roil and seethe and disrupt the peace of nature. The land is the great power, and it is to this we must connect to perform our rites."

Horta turned his gaze full upon the young man. "And you? Do you feel the power of the land?"

Tanata gave a slight nod. "When I close my eyes, I feel it. When I am alone, I feel it."

"And now?"

"I feel nothing at the moment."

It was another good answer. Many others would have lied.

"Do not concern yourself with that. Your senses will strengthen over time. It is enough to know the theory. Practice will make your senses keener as the years pass. And you have many long years of study ahead of you."

The young man bowed, but remained silent and gave no foolish response. Horta was growing to like him.

He walked toward the flat patch of ground near the very top of the hill where the Arnhaten were gathered. What the boy had said about the land was true, but it was especially true just now. The god he intended to summon was Su-sarat. She was an old god, strongly connected to the land. She was the serpent god, the Trickster, and her symbol was the puff adder. The ancients had named her well, for she was tricksome as her namesake that flicked its tongue or tail to attract prey and then struck with killing venom. Tricksome indeed, but she was the one needed when other, and more direct, methods had failed.

He approached the spring that bubbled up water from the patch of ground he had chosen for the ceremony. There would be no fire here. The gods had their preferences, and Su-sarat would like the winding trail of water that turned and twisted its way down the hill. Serpentine it was, and more than many of the gods she had a greater affinity for the animalistic form she took.

"Gather round," Horta commanded the Arnhaten.

They came to him, but he saw doubtful looks on some of their faces. The fate of Olbata had bred discontent. So too had Brand's continuing survival. It eroded faith in the power of the gods. But they would see. A mortal might defy divinity for a time, but not for long.

"The sacred words of the summoning chant are the same," Horta told them. "But we will not stand or walk. Instead, we will sit in a line, a sinuous line like a snake. And I will be at its head, facing you."

He gestured and Tanata took the lead position of the line facing him. Some of the others did not like this. They knew it for a sign of favor, and much as they did not like how things had turned out lately, they still lusted after knowledge of the mysteries. Tanata would have to be careful, otherwise one of them might kill him if a secret opportunity arose. It had been the same for Olbata. They did not mourn his passing, only the manner of it. The same could have been done to them.

Slowly, he began to chant. His words were not the same as the Arnhaten. They joined him, voicing the sacred rite, but his words were the ones of greater power. His words were the ones lifted into the heavens and shot like an arrow from a bow toward a target. Yet the Arnhaten were the bow, for by their power they sped his arrow.

"Hear me, O Mistress of the Sands. Hear my call, Dancer in the Night. Thy servant needs you. Come to me, Queen of Secrets, I beseech thee!"

The water issuing from the spring frothed and bubbled, and it surged down the slope of the hill with a hiss of steam. A sulfurous odor wafted into the air, and the earth began to tremble. Even seated, the chanting Arnhaten swayed, the line of them like a serpent themselves.

Horta continued. Once begun, the Rite of Summoning must always be finished, else it was considered an insult to the god. He was not so foolish as to risk that.

He lifted his voice higher, his words rising and falling, turning and twisting through the air with the thrum of his own power. He knew what would happen next, for he once had been an Arnhaten and sat in a line as did these. He knew what would happen, and yet it shocked him still.

The column of disciples began to transform. An image lay over them, vague and faint, of a massive serpent. As the chanting continued, the image grew stronger, and soon it was an image no more.

Su-sarat lay before him, her dark serpentine body coiling and sliding over the grass. Yet her head was perfectly still, the slit-like orbs of her eyes fixed upon him and her pink tongue probing the air for his scent.

She raised herself, showing the bright yellow of her belly. From there she could strike, and that would be death, but Horta had long since schooled himself to such risks.

Slowly, he bowed his head. "O mighty Su-sarat, the earth is graced by your form. I am humbled by your beauty."

Thus had the words of greeting been handed down to him. It was not his place to dispute them, but rather to uphold custom.

The goddess towered above him, her head serpentine, and yet there was something human in it also.

"Why dost thou thus? You call upon me, yet only when my brothers have failed thee."

"O great one," Horta answered. "Brute force has not availed me, and so I call upon you, last but not least. Yours is the strength I need, for it is built on wisdom and understanding and knowledge of the frailties of men."

Su-sarat licked the air, and tension hung between them.

"Great goddess," Horta continued, cold sweat beading on the skin of his face. "You are a trickster, a mistress of deceit and a veiler of the truth. Yours is the power I need, for you can succeed where others have failed."

Her shadow fell over him. "Do you disparage my brothers?"

"Nay, Lady. I speak only the truth. The fault is mine, for I did not explain how dangerous my enemy is."

The sky seemed to dim, and he felt the cold breath of her mouth upon his face. Then followed the wet flick of her tongue against his fever-hot skin.

"I taste your fear."

Horta did not know what she meant. Fear of Brand? Fear of death? Fear of failing to carry out his great task? All could be true.

"O great one, I live to serve. If I have displeased you, strike me down. If you take mercy upon me, I beseech you, aid me in my task as only you can."

Silence fell. She made no answer. Sweat dripped from Horta's brow, but he dared not move to wipe it away.

"Tell me of Brand," Su-sarat commanded. "He intrigues me."

Horta tried not to show any relief. It was best when dealing with gods to be humble and yet confident. Flattery was wise, also.

"Brand is just a man. And yet, in some manner, he is touched by fate. He is a skilled warrior, and he possesses the use of magic. Without these things, and luck, he would not have defeated the emissaries of your brothers."

Su-sarat swayed in the air, at least her upper body and head. The rest of her coiled restlessly over the grass.

"And why is Brand, as you say, touched by fate?"

"I do not know, mistress. But that he is, I am sure."

"Perhaps you say this merely because he thwarts you?"

"The man *does* thwart me, and this happens so seldom that, truly, he must be touched by fate to do so."

"Ah, Horta. I remember you. I know you. I have watched your rise among magicians. You are too soft, and a streak of kindness runs through you. Yes, Brand is touched by fate. He has a destiny. Yet still, had you but tried hard enough, you could have killed him. You needed no aid from gods for this. Had you convinced Unferth to send a greater army your enemy would now be lying dead on a battlefield."

Horta felt a swell of pride. The goddess had noted him, and watched. Yet pride was an empty emotion, useless for the most part and dangerous beside.

"You are correct, for your wisdom is as great as your beauty. I had thought Unferth under my control, but that was prideful of me. He still rules the Duthgar, unwisely, and I did not assert my wishes upon him. Brand is just a man, though an accomplished one, and he should have died by sword long since. I am rebuked."

Su-sarat hissed, and the noise of it filled the air. Horta realized it was her laughter.

"Do not fear, Horta. You have failed in this, yet still do you serve the gods well. For this, and because Brand intrigues me, I will help you."

Horta bowed his head. "And the price, mistress?" It was a fool who never agreed on the price with a god first. Afterwards, it was too late.

"The usual price is blood, Horta."

So it was. And he would do what he must, but it was too soon to lose Tanata. He had been near invisible before, but after Olbata had had been taken, the man had proved to be everywhere at just the right time. It was no coincidence either that he had not drawn attention to himself until now. Olbata or one of the others may have killed him. He was patient as well as useful. The man could go far, if he lived.

Su-sarat moved above him, her yellow belly glistening before him. The movement sent her coils roiling, and the tip of her tale rattled like the puff adder of his faraway home.

"The usual price is blood," the goddess repeated. "A death for a death. And yet, truly, this Brand intrigues me greatly. I will not kill him, but have him for a slave instead. I would hear the words of flattery that you use, but voiced from his mouth. Would this displease you, Horta?"

It was not usual for one of the gods to talk thus to a man, even a great magician. But Su-sarat was capricious. She obeyed no rules save her own, followed no guide except her own cold heart. Horta wished Brand dead, and yet, bent to her will and in her service, he would be a threat no more.

"It would not displease me, O Mistress of the Sands. And for your service, what price do you set?" He had not forgotten, nor would ever fail to set the price before the bargain was made. The lore of magicians was clear on that point, and the story of the one magician who had failed to do so a matter of legend.

"This is my price, Horta." Her figure loomed over him, and then she bent her head forward until the cold breath of her mouth was upon his ear, and the whisper of her voice filled his mind.

5. A Place of Ill Omen

Brand looked solemn, but there was a glint in his eye. "I have a plan, but it won't be liked. Not one bit, but it *will* serve us well."

Taingern gave a faint shrug. "The worst plans are often liked best, and the best the least. Until the day of reckoning, at any rate."

Brand knew the truth of those words. Taingern, as ever, was philosophical. But he understood better than most the hearts of people. He would know also that once a disliked plan proved successful, everyone would claim to have supported it. Such was life.

"Well then," Shorty said. "What do you have in mind?"

"Unferth is likely to attack us, thinking that his best option. And it is. Therefore, we must do the opposite of what he expects."

"He expects us to march toward him, and a battle at some point, wherever our forces draw close."

"Exactly," Brand agreed. "So I'll deny him that."

Shorty scratched his head. "How? Will you try to play cat and mouse with him as you've done so far, building your army as you move into unexpected places?"

"I could try that, but the larger my army the harder that becomes. Sooner or later, he'll corner me and force a battle with superior numbers."

"Then how will you deny him what he wants?"

"All I need is a fortress. Men can gather to me there just as easily as on the road. My army can grow, and when the battle comes the advantage of his greater numbers will be lost attacking a fortified defense."

Sighern spoke for the first time. "But there *are* no fortified defenses in the Duthgar. We don't build fortresses."

Shorty glanced at him. "Brand has told me the same thing, more than once." He crossed his arms. "But if he says it, it must be true."

"I have said," Brand agreed, "that the Duthenor don't build fortresses, nor do we have skill at attacking or defending them. But that doesn't mean that no fortresses have ever been built in the Duthgar."

Sighern's face paled. "You can't be serious!"

"Deadly serious. It's the advantage we need. And if you're surprised, then Unferth likely will be too. He'll not even consider the possibility, I'll warrant."

"Out with it, Brand." Shorty asked. "What's the surprise?"

"The fortress I'm speaking of is called Pennling Palace. It's an ancient place, as old as the Duthgar and part of its legends, but probably older by far than that."

"If nothing else," Shorty said, "at least it has a fair-sounding name. I've been in many fortresses, but none so far would pass for a palace."

Sighern looked bleak. "Don't be fooled by the name. Although Pennling is a great hero, this place has a reputation of ill omen."

Brand glanced back at the army. They were growing restless, for the rest break had been longer than usual.

"Yes, it's a place of ill omen," Brand agreed. "And the men will not like it at all."

"Why does it have such a bad reputation?" Taingern asked.

"A good question," Brand replied. "But the answer will have to wait. It's time to march again, but first I must tell this decision to the men."

They stood up and walked the short distance to the front ranks. The army stood in response, thinking they were about to march again, but Brand addressed them instead.

"Men," he said loudly, though it was short of a yell. "I have made a decision, and I'll tell it to you now. I hide nothing from you, whether good or ill. And you will consider this ill, but I ask that you have trust in me. Have I not led you well so far? And likewise, this will work out for the best in the end."

Brand stopped speaking. He waited for his words to be passed back to the men furthest away.

"Where do we go now?" a man in the front row asked. "For that surely is the decision you reached."

"Where do we go?" Brand repeated. "Where else, but to the place we must. I believe Unferth will march to war himself. He'll outnumber us. Of this, we should have little fear. Already we have beaten a greater force, and we can do so again. But where I take you now, the place will lessen his advantage."

"And where's that?" It was Hruidgar who spoke, the huntsman who had led them through the swamp. There was a look in his eye too; he was a well-traveled man. Brand had the feeling he had guessed their destination.

"Pennling Palace," Brand answered. "That's the place for us."

The men reacted as he had thought. Many were the dark looks and the muttered curses and the boots kicked into the ground. They did not like it. Not one bit.

Hruidgar made the sign against evil. As he did so, Brand felt the gaze of Shorty and Taingern upon him. He had told him the men would not like it, but still they had not expected this.

"The swamp was bad enough," Hruidgar said. "Now you want to go into those ruins?"

"Old the fortress may be, but not ruined. Once, as a boy, I hid there from my enemies. I came to no harm. Surely everyone here has courage as great as that of a scared boy? And the walls of the place will serve us well. Unferth will lose his advantage attacking them."

"And did you see the dead men that haunt the place?" Hruidgar asked. "Are the legends true?"

There it was. The crux of the matter. It was almost like Hruidgar was the voice of the whole army, for they fell silent and awaited the answer to his question. But voice or no, it was a question only and not the stating of an intention to resist.

"I saw many strange things. Where there's smoke there's fire. The place is said to be haunted, and I believe it." He stood taller and spoke more proudly. "But I keep my fear for live men with sharp steel rather than dead men with grudges. And they will have no grudge against us, for despite the legends, it's never said that harm comes to anyone who travels by the fortress. Nor did harm come to me, as a boy, within it."

Hruidgar gave a shrug. "What you say is true. Men shun the place, and stories of its haunting are many, but no tale tells of any harm coming to someone. If you go there, I'll follow."

Brand gave a nod to acknowledge his words. He realized that the hunter was helping him, for he had voiced the fears of the soldiers, but then in agreeing to go himself he had deflated any opposition. It was a smart tactic, and once more Brand wondered about the man. He was far more than the simple hunter he seemed.

"We march!" Brand called, seizing the moment. "And if nothing else, soon you'll have walls about you to keep away the wind and a roof to protect you from the rain. He turned and walked to his horse, gathering the reins and leading the army off.

The men followed. He knew they would, for he had just led them to a great victory, but what Hruidgar had done helped. He would not forget, but one day soon he'd have to have a conversation with the hunter and find out more about him.

None of his companions said anything. Shorty and Taingern at least would have faith in his judgement. Sighern, despite his fear of the place, said nothing either. He was one who would go wherever Brand led, no matter his own feelings. It was one more responsibility on top of a long list of others, but Brand would do his best not to let him down.

The men followed behind, quiet and subdued. They had no wish to go where he intended, yet they marched at a good pace and did not let their doubts slow them. They were fine soldiers, learning to trust in their leader and work well together in a single unit. Had he the time, he could turn them into one of the best armies in all Alithoras. But what then? What would he do with them? It worried him that his mind even went to such places.

Throughout the day scouts reported to him. They were not being followed, nor was there any sign of enemies ahead. The battle they had won had given them freedom of movement, at least for a while. The High Way was theirs, and they moved quickly along it.

As the army marched, passing by villages and farming lands, new recruits joined them. Rumor of their victory went before the marching men. And rumor of their victory also brought its opposite: knowledge that Unferth could be defeated and overthrown. When the army came into view, it swelled people's hearts. Here were the soldiers who had fought back, who had outsmarted and outmaneuvered Unferth's army and given the usurper a bloody nose. Next would come the final battle, and they wanted to be a part of that, they wanted to do their bit as the men already in the army had done theirs.

So it went, mile by mile and village by village. Many who joined them were farmers, young men more used to tending sheep and cattle than fighting, but every man in the Duthgar trained as a child in the arts of the warrior and most had at least a sword and helm. Many had coats of mail armor also, and those who did not had vests of hardened leather.

The day passed. Another day followed, like the first, only now they were in a more populous part of the Duthgar and the number of recruits increased. Lords in halls also joined them, and Brand sent word ahead through his scouts that they needed food. This too, they increasingly were given as they progressed. And they would have need of it if Brand's tactics worked, for within Pennling Palace they would be under siege, and they would need supplies to last them some while. But it was not going to be a long siege. The Duthenor, neither attackers nor defenders, had the temperament for that.

The lords were useful with supplies. They had wealth, and this purchased many needful things. Their swords were welcome too, and they brought men with them, though most of these would have joined Brand's army anyway. Many a lord joined the army merely because without doing so they would be left in their own lands, bereft of warriors and prestige. Moreover, better than anything else, the lords spread the word of the army's coming and to whence it marched. They used riders for this, and word spread. Brand was done hiding. He did not care now if Unferth found him. He *wanted* his enemy to find him.

Late in the afternoon, the High Way climbed upward. A great forest of dark pines swathed the steep lands to left and right. Brand knew that forest, had hidden there also for a time. A dim and dreary place, yet he had liked it well enough once he had got used to it.

The road was steep now. There were no farms here, no people, no sign of habitation of any sort. The Duthenor came seldom here, and when they did they hastened along the road, wary of being forced to camp the night near Pennling Palace. And there, at last, it stood.

It was just as he remembered it. Like an outcrop of the stony ridge upon which it was built, ancient, crumbling in places, but not at the walls. The forest did not grow near it, though here and there some stunted trees made the attempt. It was a bulky thing, a hulking fortress, the stone of its making massive blocks that only a giant could move. So ran some of the legends, but Brand knew better. Men had built it, and they built it to keep at bay an attacking army.

Shorty let out a low whistle. "It sure isn't pretty, but whoever built it knew what they were about. Unferth will grind his teeth when he sees it."

"Aye," Taingern agreed. "But for the moment I'm less interested in Unferth and more in who built it. If it wasn't the Duthenor, then who are the dead men that are supposed to haunt it? And why?"

6. Sorcery

Brand had no answers to Taingern's questions. He did not know who had built the fortress, or why it might be haunted. But he had guesses that would serve for the moment. Soon enough, he would learn if his guesses were correct.

"It was probably built by the Letharn, that ancient race that once ruled much of Alithoras. Why? Who can say? It's a fortress though, and that means it had a military purpose. I was once told that the greatest enemy of the Letharn were a people known as the Kirsch. Legend says that their empire was far, far to the south. I would guess the fortress to be a defense against them."

Taingern kept his gaze on the structure ahead. "And what of the dead men said to haunt it?"

"That may be mere legend," Brand answered. "Or it may be true. I cannot say."

"But you have suspicions, yes?"

Taingern knew him well, too well it seemed sometimes. "Of course. If it's true, which remains to be seen, then there was sorcery involved. Whose, and to what purpose, I don't know."

"But to no good purpose," Taingern replied. It was not a question but rather a statement, and Brand agreed.

"No, there's evil behind it, that's for sure." He did not bother to pretend anymore that the fortress may not be haunted. He had seen neither ghost nor spirit when he was here as a boy, but he *had* felt unseen eyes on him and heard noises that could not be accounted for. And the long-dead remains of ancient warriors had been visible, and the relics of the final battle they had fought. No, he had not seen any ghosts, but he had not stayed there more than a day and a night. This time, he would be here longer, and the truth, whatever it was, would come out.

The army drew closer to the structure. A massive thing of gray stone it was, impenetrable and hopeless to attack. Yet once it had been, and the defenders had lost. That much he could read by the damage done to the defenses. He hoped that he and the Duthenor had more luck than those who last held the walls.

Behind, the army slowed. Every man looked on those same walls. They knew death had visited them in past ages, and they hoped to escape the fate, whatever it was, that caused the fortress to be haunted. They did not need the proofs that Brand wanted in order to believe with certainty, they believed as a matter of faith. The legends said it was haunted, and that was that. Yet even so, grim and fearful as they had become, they followed him, and he was proud to be their leader.

They came to a point where there were signs of an old road branching off from the High Way, and Brand took it. It led directly to the fortress. The path was covered by overgrown grass, and stumpy shrubbery dotted it. Yet it went straight as an arrow shot to the middle section of the wall that faced them.

The further they went, the more the true size of Pennling Palace was apparent. It was not huge in terms of the ground that it covered, but it had a *presence*. Brand had no other word for it. Massive stones were laid on massive stones. The walls ran straight and true despite their size, as though it had been mere child's play to construct them, and the proportions of towers and minarets to walls was beautifully crafted. At least to a military eye. Most of all, it was a construction that dominated. And that was no accident. But there were problems too, brought on by time and the effects of the last battle fought here.

"These will have to go," Brand said, sweeping out an arm to indicate the stunted trees that grew in patches close to the walls. "Not an ant should be able to find cover from arrow shot from above."

"I'll organize men to see to it," Taingern offered.

They came to a gate in the wall. A gate was always the weakest link in the defense, and so it had proved here in ages past. What remained of it was a thing of buckled metal bars, pitted by rust and covered in lichen. And yet the metal could not have been iron, otherwise Brand doubted it would have survived century after century in the open. No, it was a metal the making of which had likely not survived into the current age. For that reason, perhaps the gate could be salvaged.

He turned to Shorty. "You're in charge of the gate. Find whatever men in the army have experience with blacksmithing, and see what they can do with it." He did not have to say it was the first priority. Shorty knew that as well as he.

Brand led the army onward. At least the two towers that hulked to each side and allowed men to protect the gate appeared in good shape. From them, men could fire arrows, throw spears and drop stones or heated oil on an enemy.

The stonework around the gate, or where the gate would have stood if not broken, was a strange shape. Instead of square or rectangular, it was triangular. So too the gate itself, but that part of the twisted metal lay mostly beneath some rubble. He had seen such designs before. It was confirmation that the Letharn had built this place, for the triangle was a pattern they favored. The places where he had seen such workmanship before were all of a likeness to what he saw now. It was a strange design to his eyes, but it gave him comfort too. The Letharn built things to endure.

They passed along the dark tunnel that led through the wall. It was a creepy place, full of shadows and echoes. It was a killing ground, and slots within the walls allowed room for arrows to be fired and spears thrust. In the last battle, the defenses had served their purpose. Here and there were bits and pieces of rusted metal, likely to be all that was left of weapons and armor, the wooden shafts having rotted away eons ago. White bone glimmered in places too, dug up from beneath the rubble and dirt that lined the floor by scavengers.

Brand estimated the tunnel to be some thirty feet long when he emerged out the other end. That meant walls thirty feet thick, assuming they were the same all around the fortress. Let Unferth crack his head against that. It was a grim thought, but he liked it. Whatever frustrated his enemy was a thing of glory.

His grim humor was short-lived. Unferth would send men to their deaths here, but he would likely not fight himself. But time would tell on that point. If he did not though, he would have more and more trouble sending the men. They would dislike it, and morale would deteriorate swiftly.

He walked into a courtyard. This too was a killing ground, and many had died here. The remnants of ancient battle were still visible, but on a far vaster scale than in the tunnel.

"This will all need to be cleared," Shorty said.

It was a graveyard, of sorts, and Brand was mindful of that. "Yes, but ensure that whatever bones are found receive an honorable burial outside the walls."

It was not much, but it was the best he could do. He felt a kinship with the men who had died defending this place. He and his army would soon face the same.

He swung to Sighern. "For a while, this fortress is the heart of the Duthgar. Climb the stairs yonder," he pointed to one of the gate towers that would provide access to the battlement, "and secure the flag somewhere at the top. It will be visible to the countryside about and let new recruits know that Duthenor warriors occupy this place."

Sighern flashed him a grin and ran into the tower.

"The energy of youth," Shorty muttered. "The time will come when he'll wish that he conserved his strength."

"But it's good to see anyway," Taingern said. "He takes his role with the banner seriously, and well he might. Time enough in the days to come to learn the hardships of war."

Brand did not comment. His mind was busy, for it was his job to ensure that whatever hardships came were minimized. He could not stop them, but if he played his role well, he could lessen the tragedy to come.

He opened his senses to the courtyard and the ancient battle that had been fought here. In response, he felt the magic within him stir. It sent out tendrils, seeking, questing, discovering.

The battle was ancient, but this much he knew already. Death abounded, and the stone paving of the courtyard had run red with blood. This much he had already discerned. Yet there was betrayal too. He swung to the gate tunnel, and realized that it stank with treachery. This was good to know. The enemy had not overthrown the gate, but rather some small number of defenders had arranged ... had allowed ... the enemy to enter and destroy it. No. That was not it. Not enemy warriors. They would not have needed to bend and buckle the gate as Brand himself had seen just moments ago. No. If they were allowed in by treachery, the gate would not have been damaged.

Sorcery. That was it. Brand's magic flared to life. It felt the touch of ancient magic, both within the gate and from without that had been used to destroy it. It was not constructed of some strange metal, rather it had been infused with defensive magic. And the betrayers had allowed the sorcerer to work his spells unobstructed. After that, the tide of the battle had turned and death washed over the fortress in a mighty wave, unstoppable.

Brand swayed. This was a use of the magic that he had never attempted before, had not even known was possible. But the magic had a life of its own. Sometimes it prompted him, rose as though by instinct as it did now. Yet he had the disconcerting feeling of being in two places at once, and the world spun slowly around him, filled with shadows. He must learn whatever else he could quickly.

More than one type of magic had been used here. The one was unfamiliar, the other he had sensed in different places and times. It reminded him of Aranloth, and he knew then that this was not only a Letharn stronghold but one guarded by soldiers and a wizard of great power. There had been a battle here of enormous scope, and not just men against men and sword against sword but wizardry against sorcery. The memory of it lingered still, after all these years.

And there was more than memory. Somewhere, sorcery still lived. As his senses sharpened, he felt it all the more strongly. Black. Evil. A blight upon the Duthgar. He could not tell exactly where its origin was, but it was within the heart of the fortress, and down deep, deep in the earth.

He swayed again, and felt Taingern's hand on his shoulder, supporting him. The earth seemed to rush toward him, but his friend caught him and held him up.

"What is it?" Taingern hissed. He seemed to think they were under some sort of attack, for his sword was drawn in his other hand and his gaze darted to and fro, seeking some enemy but finding none.

Brand straightened. The magic faded away, and he felt strength return to his legs. But the memory of evil left a cold sensation in his very bones, and a dread chill settled into the pit of his stomach.

"All is well," he said. "At least with us."

Taingern looked uncertain, but sheathed his sword.

Shorty had drawn close too, a concerned look on his face. "Something just happened then. What was it?"

"First things first," Brand answered. He called over some of the lords and gave instructions.

"The foundations of all we need are here, but we must work hard to bring it all into the best shape possible. And we don't have much time."

He told them what he wanted done. Scouts must be sent out far and wide to discover what was happening in the Duthgar. The battlements were to be checked, cleared of rubble and manned. The trees before the walls were to be cleared, and they would report to Taingern on progress. The gate was to be looked at and seen if it would serve again. Shorty would supervise that. He also instructed that the fortress be explored, and that barracks for the men to sleep in and kitchens were to be found. Facilities for this would exist in the fortress. And water was to be located and checked. There would be wells here.

"In short," he said, "make this place fit to live in and defend, perhaps for weeks. But do it quickly. Unferth may be upon us in mere days."

The lords hastened away. Brand had given them much to do, and they knew he expected results. If they failed in their tasks, others would replace them as leaders.

"And what of us?" Taingern asked, meaning both himself and Shorty. "Someone needs to keep an eye on the lords. They've no experience of what it takes to secure a fortress."

Brand sighed. "No, but they'll manage for a little while by themselves. I gave them clear enough instructions."

"Then you want us for something else?"

"I do. Come with me. There's sorcery afoot in this fortress still, and I have to find its source. I may need your help when I do so."

"I see," Taingern said. "And this will be dangerous?"

"I don't know. But it may be. Something is terribly wrong."

Brand led them away then, but footsteps sounded loud behind them. Sighern was running to catch up with them.

"The banner is secured?" Brand asked.

"At the very top of the tower," the boy answered. "There was a metal loop there to hold a pole, and the flag is flying for all the countryside to see."

"Good!" Brand said. "That banner will serve us well. Soldiers will tell stories in years to come of how they fought beneath it. Best go now though and find a job to help with. Much needs doing, and little time is left, I fear."

"But where are you three going, by yourselves?"

It was plain that the boy had sensed their urgency, and Brand had no wish to lie to him.

"There remains sorcery of some sort still in the fortress. I must find it … and see what its purpose is. I don't want to lock myself into this place until I'm sure it's safe."

"Can I come with you?"

Brand looked at the boy long and hard. He was enthusiastic, but he was young and inexperienced. Whatever was ahead might prove beyond him.

"It could be dangerous. Very dangerous indeed. I just don't know."

Sighern did not hesitate. "No matter," he replied. "I'll take my chances, if you're willing. No one lives forever."

Brand looked at him even harder. The boy had enormous courage, and Brand admired that. But he was struck again by just how unusual he was. Where had a boy of his age acquired such bravery? And, for that matter, such a philosophical outlook on life?

But he had asked to go, and he knew it might be dangerous. It was not Brand's way to say no.

"Come along then. But keep your eyes open. And if something happens, run and get help."

Sighern nodded, but Brand had a feeling he would jump in with a blade drawn if there was trouble. He was not one to run away.

7. Bones and Metal

They moved through the fortress. Brand led them, allowing his senses to guide him. He did not invoke the magic again, but he did not need to. It was always a part of him, and some small element of it continually whispered in his mind and acted as a rudder to his instincts.

The fortress was dim, for there were many corridors and rooms and none had good windows. This was no accident. The passageways were killing grounds in their own right, just as had been the tunnel through the outer wall. Here, just as there, slits provided opportunity for defenders to shoot arrows or spear the enemy.

The floors were covered with the debris of long ages. The nests of rats and the signs of scavenges were everywhere. And well might they be, for the dead had once been everywhere too. The defenders had not surrendered even when the outer wall was breached, or had not been allowed to. The fighting continued throughout the fortress.

All that was left of those who once fought and died here were bits of metal that crumbled like dust when touched. And bones. The bones were everywhere, and they had endured better here than in the courtyard. Out there, it was open to the elements, while in here it was enclosed. Most parts of the inner fortress were roofed by stone tiles, and mostly they endured too, keeping sun, wind and rain out.

"It's like a tomb," Shorty muttered.

The words struck a chord with Brand, and his instincts flared. It was very much like a tomb, and the dead were everywhere. The deeper they went, the more he began to sense them. There was truth to the legends of the Duthgar, but he pushed on. He was deeper into the fortress now than he ever dared as a child. And that had been just as well. Could a ghost harm the living?

"What are we looking for, exactly?" Shorty whispered. "It all seems the same to me."

"This way," Brand answered vaguely. But he led them on confidently.

It all looked the same, yet it was not quite so. In places, the fighting had been fiercer and the sense of death stronger. It was a trail of sorts, for while the defenders retreated they had a destination in mind, one last bastion of hope, one final task to accomplish before they died.

At length, they came to the center of the fortress. This was a mighty dome, and above them the arched ceiling still gleamed with color and shifting lights from the many narrow windows in the walls. No doubt there were tiles on the ceiling forming decorative works of art, but the dimness and the grime of millennia obscured them.

But there was light enough to see the floor. Here men had died in the thousands, and the remnants of swords and spears and shields were everywhere. So too the bones of the dead. And even after all this time, there still remained in the air the faint scent of corruption.

Brand led them on, and every step was the desecration of a grave, but it could not be helped. To the center he led them, for here was a strange dais, triangular in shape, broken and half ruined, but not by time. The enemy had done this, and he saw why.

A trapdoor lay in the middle of what was left of the dais. The door itself lay discarded to the side, a thing of twisted metal and ruined wizardry. Once, it had been warded by enchantment, but sorcery had broken it. Had it been built to keep something locked beneath the dome? Or was its purpose to keep the enemy out?

There was only one way to find out. Brand peered into the hole the trapdoor once had covered. There were stairs there, and gently he stepped onto their surface and tested them with his weight. They were made of stone, and held.

He moved slowly, testing each step carefully as he went. The others followed him, and soon they reached an underground chamber with a level floor. There were torches set in the wall, held by metal brackets. He took several of these and handed them around. Whatever oil or tar had been used to make them seemed intact, and Shorty withdrew a small flint box and tried to make fire.

Several times he struck the steel striker against the stone. Sparks flew, and soon the fine and fibrous cloth he used for tinder caught. He breathed upon it, flaring it to life and held it against the torch that Taingern held toward him.

The torch did not catch. The cloth flickered out and Shorty flicked it away with a curse as it burnt down to his fingers. Three times he tried this and failed, but on the fourth the tar-like material at the head of the torch ignited with a splutter of smoke and sparks.

When the torch had caught properly, Taingern held it to the others until they too caught, and then they proceeded.

"What *is* this place?" Shorty asked.

"I don't know," Brand answered. "But the Letharn liked underground chambers, and there are places such as this all over Alithoras. Sometimes … the remnants of their magic guards them still."

"Is this one such place?"

Brand was not sure. "There are traces of wizardry and sorcery all about. I can smell it in the air. The sorcery is still alive, that much I can tell, but what form it takes I cannot say. I've felt nothing like it before. But no, I don't think there's any trap or guard left by the Letharn. From them, we're safe."

It was not reassuring. He was not certain what had happened, but just as the men of this fortress had been overwhelmed, so too had the magic, or the wizard, that defended it.

They moved along the path, the light of the torches flaring and subsiding by turns and filling the air with an acrid stench and greasy smoke. They were on a long corridor, and from it branched other tunnels. There were wooden doors in places, some still hanging from rusted hinges.

"I think this is a cellar," Taingern said.

Brand thought he was right. But the cellar was only a subterfuge. There was some other room beyond it, or below it. That much he knew, though he was not sure how.

He found nothing as he searched but more passageways and the remnants of ancient barrels. It was Sighern who called out, having made a discovery.

"Look at this," he said.

Brand looked, and he saw. It was the opening of a passage like any other in this place, but there were even more dead here than anywhere else. Hollow-eyed skulls gazed up at him. Rusted shards of swords and spear points littered the ground thickly. Arrow heads carpeted the ground like autumn leaves in a forest.

"You're right, Sighern." Brand said. "This corridor is different. The fighting was fiercer here than anywhere else, and that must be for a reason."

Carefully, he moved ahead. The others followed, and the flickering fire of the torches hissed and spluttered. If anything, the fighting had grown more intense as it carried down the corridor. But carry down it had, and it ended in a small room.

The battle had been at its worst here, and Brand could almost feel the terror of fighting in such a confined space. Arrows could not miss, nor spear thrusts nor the cut of blade. It was a bitter fight, without mercy or hope of escape. And the desperate shouting and screaming of their comrades would have filled their ears as they died.

At the back of the room was yet another trapdoor. Once, perhaps, it was secret, for the stonework of casing around it was well made, and perfectly level with the floor. But the door itself was a twisted sheet of thick metal that lay in a corner slowly turning to dust.

"The attackers fought hard to reach this spot," Shorty said. "As hard as any army ever has for anything."

Brand peered down into the blackness of the square opening. "And the defenders tried just as hard to keep them out. Why?"

There was a reason, even if he did not know what it was. And finding out could be dangerous, but they were close now to the answer.

Sighern gave a nonchalant shrug. "There's only one way to find out, isn't there? Let's go down and see."

The boy was right, but again Brand wondered about him. Did he never know fear? Had he been stupid, that was a possibility. But he was quick of thought and never needed to learn something twice. It was a rare man that was both smart and courageous, at least if he did not have to be. But Sighern had wanted to come, knowing the dangers. And now he wanted to push ahead.

Brand gave a shrug of his own. "Let's get this over with."

He eased himself down the opening, and as there had been last time there were stone steps here as well. He trusted these no better, and he took his time. But eventually he came to the bottom, perhaps six feet below the opening, and here he lifted his torch high to see better while he waited for the others to join him.

The walls were no longer built by the hand of man. Here, they were in a natural cave. But it was a narrow passageway still, else Brand would have worried about the weight of the fortress above.

He led them forward once more. The remnants of battle were still thick all about them, and it seemed the long-ago battle had continued to some other point.

They walked a good while, and Brand was sure now that they had passed beyond the perimeter of the fortress. And at that point the cave began to widen. He went ahead, more cautiously now, and drew his sword also. Wherever they were going, and whatever remained there after the battle, must be close now.

"The floor has begun to slope," Taingern said.

He was right. It was a light incline at first, but it grew steeper rapidly. Soon, they found a set of stairs carved into the natural stone of the floor. Brand moved down them.

The air grew colder as they moved deeper beneath the earth. Was this a secret escape route of some sort? Had the defenders fled the fortress?

The stairs ended. Ahead of them was a vast cavern, and the light of all the torches combined did not reach its extremities.

To the left were the still waters of an underground lake. The farther shore was not visible, nor was there the slightest movement or ripple disturbing the dark surface. And dark it was, black as midnight. Brand wondered if it were even water at all, but the light was strange and he could not tell. This much he knew, he would not touch it.

To the side of the lake ran a pebbly shore. It too, like everywhere else, showed the remnants of battle. The fighting had not ceased even here.

Brand paused. He felt the spirits of the dead all around him. Thousands of shadowy voices whispered in his ear. They were cries for help, he thought. The skin all up his spine tightened. Why were they here? What did they want?

"They are all about us," muttered Shorty.

The presence of the spirits was now so strong that no magic was needed to sense them, yet to Brand the invisible weight of their will was like a heavy fog that settled all over the vast chamber.

"The dead can offer us no harm," Sighern said with confidence.

Brand was not so sure, but he moved ahead anyway. Having come this far, he must go on and see this through to the end. But he did not like it. Did the spirits yet guard in death what they had guarded in life?

8. The Power of the Gods

Onward Brand led them. His boots crunched on the pebbly shore. At least, where there were pebbles. Most of the ground seemed to be bones, and they gleamed white in contrast to the black water of the lake. Brand wondered if this should even be so. Was it not the sun that bleached bones white? Underground, would they not be discolored? He dismissed such thoughts from his mind though. The whispering of the dead had grown more urgent.

They moved along the pebbly ribbon of shore. To the right, the cave wall rose high into darkness. To the left, the black water of the lake was silent as the void. All around them was a secretive darkness that pressed forward.

And then the shoreline curved to the left. The wall to the right receded. As they moved, a great space opened up around them, and a stele stood in the floor.

The stele was three-sided, and tall as a man. It was a marking stone such as the Letharn had used, and Brand knew there would be writing on it. But the light was not good, and he caught only glimpses of a strange script cut into the hard surface. He would not be able to read it even if he saw it well, anyway.

It did not matter. His eye was drawn elsewhere. If the battle had been fierce in the fortress, it was fiercer here. This was the place where the defenders made their final stand. Bones and rusted weapons lay everywhere. But that was not all. Over all were the marks of fire. Sorcerous fire. Brand could smell the stench of it, vile and evil.

The bones were scorched. The metal of blades and armor had melted into strange shapes before rust set in. Even the walls were blackened in long streaks. The battle of men against men had culminated here, but so too the one of wizard against sorcerer.

Brand moved with great care. Some element of the sorcery remained alive, and it was here in this place. A sense of dread filled him, but he eased forward, one cautious step after another.

The lake disappeared beneath a great arch of natural stone, and ahead a wall came into view. This was blackened and pitted also. Falls of rubble piled beneath it where sorcerous blasts had torn at the stone, shredding it to loose rocks and dust.

And against that wall was pinned a figure. Brand slowed, but did not stop. The others came with him, step for step, and what was before them gradually became clearer. The light from the smoking torches lit up what had remained in the dark for thousands of years while the world spun and the stars wheeled for countless nights in the open lands above.

The figure was that of a man. Unlike the dead that lay all around, scorched bone and mounds of dust, some sorcery or vestige of wizardry had slowed its decomposition. The man yet had arms and legs and a head that lolled to his chest. After all this time, the once-white robes he wore still hung from his body, though in filthy tatters from the withered frame. The marks of battle were upon him. Arrows pierced his flesh, the shafts dried and brittle with age, but intact. So too a spear that pierced his body, driven deep toward his heart. The gash of an axe opened up his shoulder, and the robe there was a mess of blood that had dried to black dust. Of the axe, there was no sign. One half of the man's face was burned and twisted by sorcerous fire. His left hand was blackened and burned to a stump.

This, Brand guessed, was the wizard. And he had died a terrible death. But the worst of it was that his staff had been taken from him. It too had been used to kill him, for it pierced him like a spear, tearing through the man's body and by the power of sorcery, boring into the stone beyond. Upon that length of wood the wizard hung, impaled.

Brand drew close. He saw now that the body hung not just by the staff. Four metal spikes had been driven through arms and legs to secure the wizard to the wall. Long-dried blood colored the robes at those points. This had been done while the man lived.

A shudder flowed through Brand, and he came to a stop before the body. What agony had this man endured? What person could have inflicted it upon him? It was obscene, and Brand felt a wave of nausea threaten to make him vomit, hardened though he was to battle and death.

And then, beyond comprehension, the body moved. Slowly, the head lifted from the chest and burned-out eyes, sockets of dried blood, gazed at him.

The wizard yet lived, and Brand understood the sorcery that had sickened him. It had caught this man on the cusp of death, and kept him there, kept him between worlds in eternal agony. It was the single greatest evocation of magic that he had ever seen, and the single worst act of humanity he had ever witnessed.

The mouth of the wizard moved, but the lips peeled and blistered. There was no sound, and yet Brand heard words in his mind. Not only did the wizard live, he retained some power of magic.

"Who … Are … You?"

Brand forced himself to remain still. "I am Brand, the rightful chieftain of this land. I now use your fortress as a defense against my enemies."

The wizard shuddered. It seemed that fresh blood oozed through his many wounds.

"The fortress. Has fallen. The enemy is within. No. No. That was … long ago."

Brand gritted his teeth, else he might vomit. "That was long ago. My enemies have not yet arrived."

"What then do you want?" The figure strained against his bonds, and the whisper of a moan came from his mouth. "Do you come to taunt me?"

Brand was appalled. He did not know why he did what he did, but he knelt on one knee.

"No, my lord. I don't know who you are or what you did, but no one deserves this. I will set you free, if I can. I swear it."

"Free?" The word was a whisper in his mind, but it was a scream of hope and anguish at the same time. "Free?"

"Yes, my lord."

There was silence for a moment. Brand sensed his companions behind him, restless and uncertain. Could they hear the wizard's voice? He thought so. And he understood as well that this man spoke a different language, but sending his thoughts mind to mind provided meaning.

"I am tired," the wizard said. "And I am bound. I cannot help you."

"I will do what is needed."

The wizard moaned again, a spasm of pain racking his body. "The staff is the key," his whispered thought came.

Brand did not hesitate. He reached out, albeit slowly, and traced a finger along the surface of the ancient timber that jutted through the other man's body.

Feelings of agony and despair washed over him, and a sense of roiling powers. Almost he snapped his hand away, but he forced himself to keep the contact.

There was magic in the staff, and it drew from the wizard himself. This part of what he felt reminded him of Aranloth, as well it might. Aranloth was of the same ancient Letharn race as this man, of the same order of wizards. There was great similarity there, but wizardry was only one of the powers that he sensed.

Sorcery he felt also, vile and terrible. And the two forces had been combined by the sorcerer himself after defeating the wizard. This he had achieved by the use of a third magic. The source of this power was all around them, for it originated in the land itself, and the lake nearby was a reservoir of it. There were places all of the earth where the natural forces were stronger, and this was one such. And the latent power of it was greater by far than any single person could hope to match.

But how to reverse the spell? Surely the wizard himself must have made the attempt? And yet it was the power of the sorcery, the binding of all these forces together that bound the wizard himself, both to life and to death, that held him transfixed between worlds as well as transfixed to the wall.

Brand understood. The spell worked in two ways. It had a magical aspect as well as a physical. By sorcery, the wizard had been impaled upon the staff, and the end of it driven into the stone. The key to unraveling the spell was to physically remove the staff, an act the wizard was not capable of. It was yet another form of torture, for the means of the wizard's release was a simple matter, and yet for all this time beyond him.

Gently, Brand gripped the staff. He hoped that he understood things correctly. With as great a care as he could, he began to pull.

The staff moved, but did not dislodge. And the wizard screamed. Whether the sound was in his mind or came from those blistered lips, Brand could not tell.

He pulled again, this time with all his might. He must end this now, but the staff did not come loose. The wizard shrieked in agony.

Again Brand tried, and this time the staff slid through the stone with a grinding motion. Faster it moved, and then the length of it came free.

Even as Brand held the staff and pulled it clear, it turned to dust in his hands. The spell unraveled all around him. Sorcery collapsed. Wizardry faltered and blew away like mist before a wind. And the enormous power of the land itself flowed back into the lake from whence it came.

A moment the body of the wizard remained where it was, pinned still by the metal spikes to the wall. Then, no longer caught by the spell, it fell to the floor as a heap of tattered cloth and ancient dust.

Brand stepped back, and the others with him. So died, at long last, a great man. Mighty he had been in life, and without knowing how he knew, Brand guessed the man was not only a wizard but also in command of this fortress and the men who defended it. They had been given no quarter, and fought to the end. They may or may not have been good men; he did not know. But they had courage, and he admired that.

"I have never seen the like," Taingern said softly.

"Nor I," Brand agreed. "And I want never to see it again. This was a deed of cruelty that defies belief."

"Then the dead are gone?" Sighern asked.

It was a good question, and it raised others that were important. That the wizard was transfixed between worlds, he could understand, but why did the spirits of the dead defenders haunt this place? They were not caught in the spell.

"We shall see," Brand replied.

They retraced their steps then, and the body of water, now on their right, had changed. No longer was it black, but rather it was silvery in the flickering light of the torches.

Brand paused. The water began to churn and bubble, and he heard the cries of the long-dead. A thousand, thousand faces he saw in the water, arms stretching forth, fingers grasping at the air. Mist rose from the lake surface, but it was pulled one way and then another by unseen forces.

The lake broke its bank, lapping up onto the pebbly shore. The light of the torches flickered wildly, and Brand sensed the desire of his companions to flee. But they held that desire in check, as did he.

Finally, one figure rose full up above the water. Tall he was, robed in white and a staff in his hands. Like a king he stood, and the glance of his eyes was stern as a statue of stone.

He glided over the water, his body unmoving but some force tugging at his robes, flapping the cloth crazily. It was the wizard, or at least the spirit of him, set free. But when he came to the margin of water and land, he ceased to move, and he fixed Brand with his kingly gaze.

"Brand of the Duthenor," he proclaimed. "You have freed me. It was a good deed, and better than you know."

Brand met the wizard's gaze. "How so, my lord?"

The spirit shook his head. "You know so little. Many things happened in my time, but things happen now also. Evil creeps through the world, and it may slither beside you without you knowing it. Even for one such as you, who rides upon the breath of the dragon, the task ahead will be hard. But these things I will tell you, for you will have need of them."

The wizard closed his eyes as though in thought. The spirits in the water all around him moved and flowed just beneath the surface. Then his eyes opened again.

"These things you should know. There is great power in the lake. Mother-earth is strong here, and the Letharn harnessed her power, sometimes not wisely, to defend our lands. I was one who did so. And at the end, I used that power least wisely of all, to enhance the strength of my warriors. It was not enough, but by that act I bound them to me in death. As I was trapped, so too were they. They who served me willingly with their lives in life, were bound unwillingly in death. You freed us all, and for that a debt is owed."

Brand thought about that. It made sense. And he saw how the sorcerer had grasped the opportunity to punish both the wizard and all who followed him at the same time.

"This also you should know," the wizard continued. "Great though my power was, the strength of the gods of the Kar-ahn-hetep was greater. They humbled me, who had not ever known defeat. Be wary of pride, therefore, lest you be humbled also. Be wary of he that is known as Horta, for he is successor to those who defeated me, and his cunning and his power is great. And he seeks to raise a new god of the south that shall scourge the land. He is your enemy."

The Kar-ahn-hetep Brand did not know, but Horta he had met. He would not underestimate him.

The wizard raised an arm, ethereal as mist, and he pointed straight at Brand. Otherworldly was the specter, but the command of his voice brooked no argument.

"Heed me well! This too I shall tell you, third but not least. You are hunted. The Trickster will deceive you, one of the gods of your enemies. Be wary of her most of all, for she does not come with armies nor might of arms nor the regalia of power. Yet her arts are the deadliest, and she can take any form, be anyone, find any way into your confidences. She will make you your own enemy, and there is none greater in life. Heed me well, Brand of the Duthenor."

This was unexpected. It was the last thing he needed, for already he had too much to contend with. But he knew good advice when he heard it.

"I hear you, and I take your advice." Brand bowed his head as he said the words.

The otherworldly wind that tore at the robes of the wizard intensified. "Three things I have told you," he said, lowering his arm. "One was that I owed you a debt. Call upon me in your need. And you *will* have need. Dead though I am, I am not without power, for a while at least. I will do as I can, though it will not be a great deed. This I owe you."

Brand had little desire for help from the dead. He did not think he would use that offer, for help such as that might be perilous, and he did not think he would ever have a need so great as to risk it. But still, it was nobly offered.

"Farewell, until that hour," the wizard said. His form began to fade, and he receded further back toward the center of the lake.

"What is your name?" Brand called. "I should know that much about you, at least."

As though from faraway the fading figure answered. "I was a wizard-priest, cousin to the emperor. Kurik, my name was in life."

The spirit descended into the water, and with a ripple that went out in a circle he disappeared from sight.

Brand sighed. A great evil had been redressed, yet still he remained uneasy. There was so much that he did not know, not least of all the intentions of Horta. What had the spirit said? That he seeks to raise a new god who will scourge the land? It was a troubling thought, and he realized he was playing a game for which he did not know the rules nor even the identity of the other players. He had returned to the Duthgar to right a wrong and bring justice. He had come back to topple Unferth from the rulership of the Duthenor that he had usurped. Instead, he now found himself fighting a war. And a war against gods. Truly, if there was such a thing as destiny, his was a twisted fate devised by a madman gripped in the vice of a fever-induced dream.

Brand laughed to himself, and his companions eyed him strangely.

9. Calm Before the Storm

Out over the battlements Brand gazed. It was midmorning. It was a clear day of blue sky and sunshine. It was a calm day, yet the men worked unstintingly and brought the fortress into shape, into the shape it must have, for a storm would soon break upon it.

Brand glanced up at the Dragon Banner of the Duthenor. A breeze stiffened it somewhat, and the rippling cloth made the feet of the dragon seem to move as though it walked.

The banner belonged to him, and had belonged to his line before him. It was the symbol of the Duthenor and the sign of his own house, but more precious to him was the blood that stained it. He looked away lest he cry.

Haldring was lost to him. She had died for his cause, and not victory nor fulfilment of justice would ever bring her back.

He missed her, and he wondered what she would make of what was happening now, and what advice she would give him. Probably, she would tell him that he was doing it all wrong. And he would listen to her, strive to justify to her every minute detail of what he did, and where he could not do so he would change his plan to her satisfaction.

But she was not here, and he would have to get by as best he could. Taingern and Shorty were skilled men, although they did not know the Duthgar as had she nor understand the Duthenor well either. He wondered if he did now himself. Too long he had been away, and much had changed. His home did not feel like home anymore.

It felt instead like a nightmare rising from the ashes of his dreams.

"You seem thoughtful," Sighern said.

Brand glanced at his companion, his sole companion for the moment as Shorty and Taingern were supervising the many tasks at hand to bring the fortress into fighting shape.

"Thoughtful perhaps," he answered. "Or maybe just reminiscing. Old men do that."

The boy raised an eyebrow. "You're not even middle-aged yet."

"No. But suddenly, I feel like it."

The boy gazed at him seriously. "You've been thinking of Haldring. You blame yourself for what happened, even though it was not your fault, and you know it. You know also that leading an army, at least one that fights, will result in death. And you worry now that you've not done all that you could to prevent more, but at the same time you know that soon these walls will run red with blood. You know these things, and you accept that as commander of an army you have responsibility for minimizing death, but no capacity to stop it, but still you will treat every death as though it were caused by you."

Brand returned the boy's gaze. He had to stop thinking of him as such. He had insight and wisdom beyond his years.

"And if you're right? What is the remedy for my problem?"

"There is no remedy. Not all the ills in life can be cured. Warriors will die … or live. You do what you must, and to the best of your skill. No man can do more. The harm that comes from your decisions, you'll learn to accept. You've done so in the past, and you'll do so in the days ahead. The Duthgar will have a glorious future, and that will be because of what you do now, mistakes and all."

Brand looked away and out over the battlement to the lands beyond. It seemed to him that sometimes Sighern was a stranger. Where had a boy acquired such wisdom, such depth of understanding? Not for the first time, Brand wondered about him.

"What you say might be right, but neither of us may live to see it."

Sighern shrugged. "There's truth to that. But I have a feeling that both of us will survive this. I don't doubt it, for a moment."

Brand fell silent again. He had much to think on, not least of which was whether or not he had missed any vital task that needed doing.

Out below, many men were working. They cut down the stunted trees that grew around the fortress. The work there was going well, and most of the trees were already gone, having been cut into smaller logs and hauled within the fortress to provide fuel for cooking fires.

The stumps of the trees were partially dug out and fires lit around them to catch the roots. They would smolder slowly for days yet, but when they burned out all that would be left was a clear killing field. From where he stood, Brand saw firsthand the advantage of that. Had he a bow, he could shoot a clean shot for a good way out beyond the fortress, and there was no hiding place or cover for the enemy. He wished he had more bowmen though, and ones better trained to the nuances of war rather than hunting. But he had what he had, and he would make the most of it.

Spearmen would also hurl javelins from up here, but their range was much less. Foragers had been sent into the woods around about to collect what timber they could turn into javelins. Ash was best, but other woods would suffice. And forges had been found and cleaned in the fortress too. The smiths would forge arrow and spear heads from whatever metal could be salvaged. In a stroke of luck, ancient bins of iron ore had also been found near the smithies, ready to be used in another age of the world and untouched since. How much the world must have changed since then. And how little.

Brand could not quite see the gate, though it was immediately below him. Shorty would be there, supervising repairs just as Taingern was away in the woods somewhere organizing the parties that were gathering timber.

Luck had favored them with the gate. It looked a mess, and yet with the forges repaired the smiths said they would be able to beat it into rough shape again, strengthen the weaker areas and repair the mechanism by which it was raised and lowered as a portcullis.

Barracks for the soldiers had been found and cleaned. Of these, there were far more than were required. The Letharn had garrisoned many more men here than he had at his disposal. At least, they had the space for them. That was a disquieting thought. Even with all those men, they had still been overrun. Sorcery had been involved there though, powerful and directed by an attacker without mercy. Yet, might that not happen now also? What might Horta be capable of?

He put those thoughts aside. He must be prepared for anything, but he could not guess in advance what it would be. Horta was beyond his control, and he must focus now only on what he had influence over.

The kitchens had been found, and some of those were being cleaned and repaired. An army fought best on a good ration, especially well-cooked food. It would be quite an improvement on the trail rations they had been eating so far, and so too the roofs over their heads and protection from the elements. All factors to raise morale. And yet the Duthenor had no experience of siege warfare, nor any liking of the idea. That might change though when the attack finally came and they saw firsthand the advantages of facing your enemy when they had to find a way through a barrage of missiles, and then scale a wall to get to you. Yes, the Duthenor would begin to like it very quickly then.

Lunch time drew near, and Shorty and Taingern reported on their progress. They ate a quick meal of fresh-baked bread, direct from the fortress ovens that had been fired. With this was some cheese and watered wine.

"The work goes well," Shorty said. "The men go at it hard, harder than most soldiers in Cardoroth."

Brand laughed. "That's because in Cardoroth they were professional soldiers. Most of the men here have to work for a living, and many of them are farmers. Few jobs are tougher than that, and the work breeds good warriors."

"True enough," Taingern agreed. "I've seen the Duthenor fight now, and though they may not quite have the technique and discipline of professional soldiers, they're not far behind. But whatever they do for a living, each of them is a warrior born in their hearts."

That was certainly true. Brand thought back to his days as a child. Every story he ever heard, every hero he ever looked up to, they were warriors all. The Duthenor were a warlike race. Necessity had forged them so.

Shorty sipped at his watered wine. No doubt he would have preferred beer, but there was little of that.

"All goes well, Brand. But are you sure you want to stay here? Soon there'll be no choice in the matter, but for now you still have freedom of movement."

"Are you worried?" Brand replied. "Do you think Unferth will pen us up here?"

"He might do. Once he comes, there'll be no escape, no alternative strategies. It will be defend the walls or die."

"True enough. And I don't much like not having other options, but the fortress will serve us well. Away from it, I think I'd begin to miss it very quickly."

"How will the Duthenor adapt to fighting behind a wall?" Shorty asked.

"They'll learn quickly." Brand was sure of that. "But perhaps we can speed things up. Appoint captains and talk to them day and night about what to expect. Let them practice mock battles on the ramparts, and teach them how to use long poles to dislodge ladders enemies used to scale the wall. Make sure there are axes to cut rope-thrown grappling hooks. Show them the uses of rocks and boiling oil, if we have enough of that."

"We don't," Shorty said. "Not oil anyway. The rest we can do."

"And I'll have the archers and spearmen practice their aim from the ramparts and learn their ranges and distances," Taingern offered.

"Best wait until my men have finished clearing the ground below," Shorty said with a wink.

Taingern seemed to consider it. "If you insist."

Brand was glad of their company. Banter was the warrior's way of dispelling tension. He needed that now, for it was in the calm before the storm that his nerves were always the worst. It was like that with most men. When the swordplay began, the heat of battle melted away nerves. At least, most of the time.

Sighern had been quiet, listening and watching as he always did, soaking up knowledge. He was a quiet young man, old for his age, and he showed less nerves than a seasoned warrior. But a strange look was on his face now.

Sighern had walked out to the very edge of the battlement, his hand up to his forehead to shade his eyes.

"What is it?" Brand asked.

Sighern pointed, and the others followed the direction of his arm.

Brand saw nothing at first, then faraway on a tree-clad slope he spotted a rider. Whoever it was, they came alone, and they rode swiftly. And they made a line as direct as slope and tree allowed straight for the fortress.

10. To the Death

Unferth was bored. A while since, he had set aside his double-bladed axe. He enjoyed the fear it inspired, but it was too heavy to drag around. He did not like his armor either, for it chafed and made movement harder than he was used to. He should have been proud to wear it. In his youth, he dreamed of doing so. But his youth was far away and long ago, his dreams only half realized, and the half that were so remained in jeopardy.

Most of all though, what annoyed him just now was the lack of a hall, a lack of cover from the night and the camp food that he would have cast in the cook's face had he dared serve it to him back at home.

Was he growing old? No, that was not the problem. He could still fight, perhaps better now than he ever had. He was still strong, but he had become used to the comforts of lordship. The problem was that traveling, he had nothing that he liked, not even a bard or storyteller to while away the smoke-ridden hours that each evening meal brought.

The army had been gathered though, the full army. Some five thousand men camped around him, ready and willing to do his bidding. That was a good feeling, and his authority was greater now that he wore the armor of his ancestors. The men revered it, and therefore must revere the man who wore it.

Unferth grunted to himself. Most men revered him, but not so his nephew. Gormengil was ever close by, even as he was now, sitting only a few feet away. And ever his dark eyes showed respect that was fitting for a servant when looking at his king, but there was a hint of judgement there. Not open, but Unferth saw it nonetheless.

His nephew was of the same line, had the same blood of chieftains in his veins. He was a prideful man, and full of the false confidence of youth. He thought he would be a better king. It was an absurdity, but a dangerous one.

Gormengil did not know, but his surreptitious meetings with Horta were not the secrets that he thought. There were eyes and ears everywhere among the Callenor, and they served the king alone.

Horta, he did not trust much, yet the man had served him well and loyally. So far, at least. Gormengil he trusted far less. He was heir to the kingdom, for Unferth had not taken a wife. But he was ambitious. Perhaps ambitious enough to attempt to speed up his inheritance. It was something that Unferth knew to watch for. All the great rulers had to be on guard against such as that.

It was not Horta's fault. He cultivated the younger man, threw him compliments and nuggets of wisdom. To Horta, it was nothing but a prudent backup plan. Unferth did not blame him for having one. The opposite, in fact. Had he not had one he would be showing incompetence, and that was a trait unwelcome in advisors. But Gormengil was another matter. He was of the same blood. The nobility of royalty ran through his veins, and he should be above such things.

Unferth stared into the fire. It was a large blaze, and it would burn through the night bringing warmth. That would be welcome, for he found the ground cold and uncomfortable to sleep on even though summer was drawing on. He had eaten, at least what passed for food at the moment. And he had been given news too. Bad news.

A hall away to the west somewhere had revolted. Some traitors were killed, but many had escaped. No doubt they would go to Brand. He had been warned that others might do the same, or perhaps had already done so and word had not reached him yet. Everywhere was betrayal, and annoyance only exacerbated his boredom.

A slow smile spread over his face. He was bored, and he held a grudge against Gormengil. That was one betrayal, even if it was only in thought yet and not in deed, that he might be able to do something about. With luck, he might remedy that situation and alleviate his boredom at the same time.

He clapped his hands together. "Entertainment! We need something to liven these dull hours."

One of the lords nearby kicked the dirt with his heels. "We have none, sire. There are no bards in the camp."

Unferth grinned at him. "Then we must make our own fun. And I've had my fill of words anyway. All I hear are reports and scouts coming in and the whining of the men. What we need is *action* instead."

"What would that be, my lord? Perhaps a wrestling match?"

Unferth seemed to consider the suggestion. "Yes, indeed. That was the sort of thing I meant. Only we need to make it more entertaining. We need something to liven our battle spirits for the days ahead."

They all looked at him blankly. "Swords!" he barked. "Let us have a duel of blades. That will get the blood flowing."

They did not seem overly happy at the suggestion. Not that they said anything, but he read it in their faces. They all looked down, hoping to remain inconspicuous. None of them wanted to be chosen for such a task.

Fools, Unferth thought. He was a king, but a magnanimous one. He would not order it.

"Two volunteers will be needed. Who shall it be?"

No one answered him, and he grew agitated. It was, perhaps, the mead he had drunk before eating. And after. But he was their king, and it was only proper for his wishes to be fulfilled.

"Well? Are there no men of courage here? Shall I send word to the common soldiers for two of them to come forth? Or are there lords among us who will do as their king wishes?"

Vorbald stood. He was a tall man, thickset and strong. He had a reputation as a fighter, and it was said that once he killed three outlaws that he was hunting. They had doubled back and found him without his retinue, but it was to their cost and not his.

Unferth clapped. "I salute you. At least there's one man here of courage, one man fit to sit in the company of a king."

The others remained silent. It was an insult, but they took it. Yet his words had found their mark, for they were targeted so.

Gormengil eventually stood, and he offered a stiff bow. "I too am of the blood of chieftains, and I fear no man nor any fight."

His gaze found that of Vorbald's, and the two men stared at each other, hard and flat. A moment Gormengil turned that gaze on him, and Unferth felt a shiver. The man was cold, cold as a blizzard and just as furious.

It was a look that Unferth did not like. "Let it be to the death then, if each of you are willing."

The two men faced each other again, gazes remaining hard and flat. Gormengil gave a sharp nod to signify he was willing, and Vorbald returned it, a gleam in his eye. Unferth thought the man was beginning to look forward to this. There had always been rivalry between the two.

All around, the group of lords stood and opened up a space for the combatants. They were silent as ghosts, and

Unferth was pleased. This was turning out better than expected. In addition to everything else, he had managed to find a way to cow them. Dissent was everywhere, if veiled for the moment, but a man who knew he could be fighting for his life at a moment's notice kept his mouth shut and his head down. It was good to know.

The two combatants donned their helms. They already wore chain mail shirts. At each of their sides was strapped their swords, and Unferth was eager to hear those blades clash. But Gormengil turned to him, his voice hollow-sounding as it issued from within the confines of his helm.

"What we do now, will give great *entertainment* for our king. But will not the king offer a great prize to whoever is victorious in return?"

Unferth did not like his tone. There was an edge of disrespect to it. More than an edge. But he could not refuse a prize.

"Very well. What shall it be?" He looked to the lords for a suitable answer, but it was Gormengil who replied, and swiftly.

"The axe of the Callenor."

Unferth's gaze fell to where he had left the axe lie on the ground.

"No! Not that!" he cried. "Never that. The axe belongs to the *chieftains* of the Callenor. It's mine by blood."

Gormengil gazed at him, his eyes dark pits within the shadow of his helm.

"I, too, am of the blood of chieftains. Have you forgotten? Or perhaps you think I'll shame my forefathers, carrying it?"

"I have not forgotten. All I have, all I build, will one day be yours. Unless I take a wife and sire an heir of my own. Even the axe will be yours, one day. But not today."

Vorbald laughed. "You get ahead of yourself, Gorm. Well ahead. You'll have to beat me to claim any prize, and that you will not do."

Vorbald turned to Unferth, but it seemed that he never quite took his gaze off Gormengil, and his hand rested lazily on the hilt of his sheathed sword.

"Sire. A few gold coins are prize enough for me. I have no ambition to be … a rich man. Or anything else."

"So be it," Unferth said. "But not just a few gold coins. As many as the winner can clasp in one hand from my coin chest."

Unferth moved back, and he gave a signal with his hand. The fight could begin.

The two combatants drew their blades. This would be no wild fight, full of bravado and rough swings. These men were skilled fighters, and neither was the kind to allow emotion to rule the battle. They would be cold and calculated, taking their time and testing each other carefully for weaknesses.

The two men inclined their heads, ever so slightly, and they settled into a fighting stance. Vorbald yelled, and he swung a mighty overhand strike at Gormengil. Unferth was amazed. He had misjudged the man, and he would die quickly for his folly.

The sword dropped, cleaving air, for Gormengil had already dodged aside, yet even as he moved away, his own blade was ready to drive forward.

Gormengil never got the chance. Vorbald twisted, quicker than anyone would have thought possible, and his downward stroke angled now straight for Gormengil's head.

Vorbald had planned this move out, taken a gamble as to which side his opponent would dodge, and prepared for the counterstroke even as the feint was in motion.

It was a dangerous move, but it had paid off. The sword struck Gormengil's helm, and the clang of metal rang through the night.

Gormengil staggered back, his knees buckling and it appeared that he might fall. Vorbald leapt after him, but even as he did so Gormengil sent a deadly riposte with the tip of his blade. Had Vorbald not worn chain mail, it might have disemboweled him, but the steel links of his armor deflected the blow. Even so, he reeled back in sudden pain. If he lived, tomorrow would see a massive bruise flower on his abdomen.

The two men circled each other. Unferth watched them, his gaze riveted. The two opponents were greatly skilled and evenly matched. He was not really sure who he wanted to win. Gormengil was a blood relative, but he was dangerous. More than ever, Unferth knew he wanted the throne. Vorbald, on the other hand, was nobody. Lords were common enough, and he could easily be replaced. Yet of the two, Unferth trusted him the more, and he was a capable leader of men. He would carry out orders, any orders, without question. And he was reliable. Such men were not so easily replaced as lords.

With a flash of swords the two men struck again. Steel rang on steel, and sparks sheared off the blades. This time no advantage was given or taken, and the combatants separated to think of their enemy, and their preferences and their habits in order to find a weakness.

Both men had them. Unferth saw that Gormengil leaned a little too far forward with each stroke, especially a thrusting movement. In this way he was slightly off balance and vulnerable to an attacker who had the skill to use that against him. This was a worse fault in a fist fight than with swords, though Vorbald might yet find a way to exploit the flaw.

Vorbald himself, though better balanced, was not as quick on his feet, and his footwork and the movement of his shoulder signaled in advance his intention to strike.

Gormengil attacked again, this time dropping low and slashing at his enemy's knees. It was a fruitless move. Vorbald, despite not being especially quick on his feet, easily shuffled back.

Vorbald's laugh came hollowly from his helm. "You can do better than that, Gorm. Or are you becoming too afraid to face me man to man? That's how dogs attack, going for the legs."

Gormengil gave no reply, nor was there a change to his smooth movements as he circled the other man. There would not be any sign of anger from him. Gormengil was coldblooded, and all the more so in a fight. He was ice itself, and no taunting would get under his skin. But he would remember, and if he had the victory, Vorbald would regret the insult.

The men circled each other, blades weaving slowly before them, eyes fixed on their enemy. It was like a dance, for every move was full of grace built on years of hard work and practice.

Gormengil skipped forward, his blade lunging. Vorbald skipped back, keeping the same distance between them.

"You speak of dogs," Gormengil said quietly. "You should know. You run away like one."

Vorbald did not like it. But he kept his mouth shut and offered no taunt himself.

Unferth felt sweat trickle down his back. There was tension in the air, for one man at least would die tonight. But they were in no hurry to engage again, each uncertain as to the outcome. They had begun in confidence, but it had ebbed away as no advantage presented itself. So evenly matched were they that chance would determine the outcome of the fight, and this was a thing neither of them wished.

Suddenly Vorbald charged. He danced forward on light feet, but there was nothing light in the stroke of his sword. It was a mighty slash, leveled at his opponent's neck where helm ended and chain mail began. Many men wore a chain mail coif that trailed beneath their helm and protected this vulnerability. Not Gormengil. Nor did he need it.

Gormengil did not dance back, but rather he edged forward a half step. This threw his opponent's timing off, and parried the strike with a deft move for the full force of the blow could not be delivered. Then, with a second deft move, he drove the pommel of his sword direct into Vorbald's helm.

There was a crash as the blow landed, and Vorbald staggered back. He moved to lift his sword between them again, but he was not quick enough. Gormengil followed through, drawing in close and headbutting the other man before following up with another strike of the sword pommel. This one took Vorbald under the chin, and he toppled like a felled tree.

Gormengil was not done. As the other man sprawled on the ground he stamped on his sword arm, crushing the man's wrist beneath his boot and ensuring he released the weapon.

Vorbald screamed. Gormengil ground the heel of his boot in deeper. And then he let go his own blade and drew a fine-pointed dagger. Dropping to his knees and pinning the other man with his weight, he slid the point of the dagger through the eye socket of his opponent's helm.

Vorbald screamed again, and he thrashed in an attempt to dislodge his opponent. But Gormengil was no small man, and Vorbald was badly weakened. The blade penetrated, but stuck, and Vorbald cried out piteously.

Gormengil twisted the blade slowly, seeking a way through the eye into the brain. He hefted his weight upon the blade, and bone suddenly gave way.

Vorbald spasmed and then grew still, blood seeping down onto the ground from out of his helm. A moment Gormengil looked at him, and then he drew forth his dagger. It had snapped, and he stood slowly before casting the broken and bloodied blade near the feet of Unferth.

"Sire," he said softly, no emotion in his voice. "Death is loosed this night, and ere the war is over it will be loosed again."

Unferth knew it as a threat. Knew it as a threat against himself, and anger burned inside him. But he could not prove the words were directed so.

"Fetch my coin chest," he commanded the lord beside him. "A king always pays his debts. And he rewards those who serve him just as they deserve."

11. Word Spreads Like Fire

The rider sped across the slope and angled toward the road leading to the fortress. Whoever it was could ride with supreme skill, for the slope was uneven, steep and dotted with outcrops of rock and boulders. A mistake by either horse or rider was death. Yet the rider came on, weaving a course around all obstacles and somehow finding a safe path.

"He'll kill himself riding like that," Sighern said.

Brand did not answer straightaway. His attention was on the rider alone, and he was gripped by their skill and their courage. But he was also curious.

"Whoever it is," he said without taking his gaze off the scene, "has great skill. But why do it? What drives them? What danger lies behind?"

Shorty slowly shook his head. "There are men out there felling timber. And there are scouts. If the enemy was upon us, then we would have heard long since."

"I think so too," Brand agreed.

They watched as the horse gathered its legs beneath it, and then leapt a line of tumbled stones that would be waist high to a man. The rider bent low in the saddle, helping the horse keep its balance. It landed on the other side, slipping before righting itself, and then speeding on at a nudge from its rider.

But the jump had caused the rider's hood to fall back, and a tumbled mass of dark hair came free. A moment Brand looked, amazed and lost for words.

"Tinwellen," he cried after a moment, and even as he did so she turned the horse onto the road and raced along it, shooting toward the fortress like a dark arrow with a cloud of dust rising behind her.

The others looked at Band. "She was the daughter of the merchant who owned the trading caravans I used as cover to enter the Duthgar. But she shouldn't be here, or anywhere near here."

Explanations would have to wait. He leapt down the stairs at the rear of the battlement two at a time, and the others followed fast behind.

Brand came to the courtyard beneath the gate towers. The tunnel through the wall opened before him, but there he waited. Within the confines of that dark space the clatter of hooves roared and the movement of a rider could be seen speeding through the narrow way.

And then Tinwellen was there, all dark hair and curves, excitement in her eyes and a flash of recognition as she saw him there.

She pulled her horse to a stop. It was a fine animal, though worked hard just now. Its coat was black, but sweat frothed over its flanks and it drew in long breaths of air loudly. It trembled also, close to exhaustion. Even so, it stood proudly. Brand admired it, but it was not one that he had ever seen in the merchant's caravan.

But prouder than the horse was she who rode it. Tinwellen sat there, her eyes haughty and a look of calm on her face as though she had strolled in here by accident and now looked around with mild curiosity. Still, there was the faintest hint of a smile on her lips. She had enjoyed the ride, dangerous as it was.

Brand stepped forward and ran a calming hand over the horse's withers, but he was looking up at Tinwellen all the while.

"I hadn't thought to see you again, but I've missed you." She dismounted gracefully, and looked him in the eye. "Of course you have. I'm not easy to forget, am I?"

He grinned at her. She had not changed at all, except perhaps that there was a darkness in her eyes that had not been there before.

He signaled a soldier to take and care for her mount. "Who could forget you? But I wonder why you're here? And where is the caravan?"

"So, you care for me after all, city boy?"

Brand ignored the looks from the others. They seemed surprised that she called him that. And well they might be, but it was what she had called him when he was in hiding, and he did not mind it even now.

"You know I do," he answered quietly.

She arched an eyebrow at him. "Well, you have a strange way of showing it. First, you lie to me about who you are, and then you run off without even a hug, still less a kiss."

If the others were looking at him before, they did so doubly now. But he did his best to ignore that. She had made him sound churlish, but under the circumstances he did not mind. Perhaps, he had even earned it.

"None of this answers why you're here now. What's happened?"

She stood tall and proud, but that glint of darkness in her eyes was stronger now. She was not the same as she had been, and he felt that something terrible may have happened. Almost, she seemed to sway before him, but she steadied herself and fixed him with her gaze as though nothing had happened.

"Very well. I'll tell you. Much has passed, but in short this is what you need to know. Unferth has imprisoned my father. The king suspects that he knew who you were and helped you into the Duthgar."

Brand had a sinking feeling in his stomach. He had feared something like this, but it was still hard to hear. It did not matter that he had kept his identity secret and told no one. The old man may have guessed, perhaps, who he was and what his intentions were. But he had not *known*. But Unferth would not care about the truth.

"I'm sorry. That was one of the reasons I told none of you anything."

"Well, it's hardly your fault." The look she leveled at him indicated she was only being polite.

"What of the others?"

"The guards were taken by surprise one night. They had no chance to fight back. Laigern may have arranged that, but I can't be sure."

Brand fumed, but he tried not to show it. Laigern would be exactly the type to betray them. And again, it could be laid at his door. The two of them had a feud going, and that would have played a part in things. Perhaps he should have killed him when he had the chance.

Tinwellen seemed to read some of his emotions. She reached out and touched his arm. "It's not your fault. But will you help me? I have nowhere else to turn."

He held her gaze, wishing he had more time to think things through and decide what could be done, but her question demanded an immediate answer.

"Of course I'll help. Though it may be that the only thing I can do is win the war against Unferth. If I do that, then after they will be freed."

She gave a shrug. "That will be soon enough. They're safe for now I think, and nothing is likely to change until after the war anyway."

It was a somewhat cold response. Brand had thought she would be frantic for him to attempt a rescue, but he supposed that the situation had hardened her. She saw the practicalities of things, and that the best way to help really was to win the war. But then there would be a final reckoning with Laigern.

"How did you escape? And how did you know where I am?" he asked.

She looked at him with an air of mystery. "I can do what I can do, and I know the things I know, city boy. And better would you be if you didn't doubt it."

Brand was beginning to remember the manner of her speech. She always liked to keep an edge, so he merely looked at her thoughtfully and said nothing.

After a few moments she grew exasperated. "Very well! If you must know, I had made ... friends with one of the lords at the hall we were staying at. He hid me while the others were taken, and he gave me the horse afterward so that I could escape."

It seemed likely enough, although there was much that she glossed over. She was certainly more than friendly with the lord, but that was not important. Brand had other thoughts on his mind.

"And how did you know where I was?"

She seemed annoyed at him now, and she drew herself up. "The lord asked me to marry him, you know."

Brand grinned at her. "I'm not surprised. But that doesn't answer my question."

She narrowed her eyes, realizing that he was not going to play her game. Or worrying that he was, only that he was playing it better.

"The whole Duthgar knows where you are, city boy. Or it will soon enough. Word spreads like fire about what you've done, and rebellion rises like smoke from the ground everywhere. There's no place that doesn't smell of it."

Brand had thought as much. Still, it was good to hear news from someone who had traveled the land and who knew what was what and why it was so. There was little that Tinwellen ever missed.

He reached out and touched her hand. "You should go from here swiftly, then. You know what's coming, and this will be no safe place. I'll send a few men with you, and when the battle here is done, I'll get word to you to return. Then we'll free your father."

"Safety? Do I look like I need to be kept safe? I can look after myself, thank you very much! But at any rate, this much is true. The most dangerous place in the world right now is with you – but it's also the safest. Who better would I trust in a such a time?"

Brand did not know what to say, and she softened her tone.

"I'll not leave your side. I'm as safe as I can be, right here. And in turn, I offer my loyalty."

Suddenly, knives flashed in her hand, swift as a serpent striking, the points upright and the blades still. She knew how to use them.

"I'm not without defenses, and I'll guard your back as well as you guard mine."

A moment she held his gaze, and as though satisfied that she had made her point, she swung away and imperiously called a servant over.

"Take me somewhere that I can freshen up. On Lord Brand's orders." Even as the man led her off, she turned to Brand and winked at him.

They watched her walk away, her figure swaying just so slightly at each step, her every movement one of controlled grace.

"That's a whole lot of girl, right there," Shorty commented. "You do make some *very* interesting friends, Brand."

Brand did not answer. Tinwellen had been as she always was, but he had forgotten just how strong her presence was.

"I'm sorry," Sighern said into the quiet. "I don't like her."

Shorty shook his head. "What's not to like? And the way she pulled those knives. Very impressive."

"If you don't *mind*," Brand said. "We have things of greater importance to discuss."

Taingern tried hard not to show any amusement, but the corners of his lips twitched.

"See, Brand? I for one am always serious. I'd never talk about any of your female companions. Especially one so good with a set of knives."

Brand ignored him. If he responded, his two old friends would keep going all day.

"This much is what is serious," he said. "There's rebellion in the Duthgar. That's to our benefit, and to Unferth's detriment. Whatever he does, he must act quickly."

"True enough," Shorty replied. "If we thought he'd come to you and attack before, he has all the more reason now. If he doesn't stop you fast, he may as well grab a horse and ride for the hills. They'll be the only friends he has."

It was good news, in its way. But on the other hand, if Unferth defeated him then he could turn his army on the Duthgar. Whatever rebellion was arising would die swiftly then.

They talked a little while longer, and then Brand asked for some food to be brought out to them. They sat down at one of the rough tables that had been placed in the courtyard, nothing more than sawn logs for seats and a wide plank for the table itself, but it was comfortable enough.

Tinwellen returned, and Brand offered her a seat, which she took graciously. This much he liked about her; she was at home around a campfire in the rough company of men, or in the courtyard of a fortress surrounded by soldiers and the threat of war. But he did not doubt that she would be equally at home in the hall of a lord somewhere, or even the palace of a king.

"So," he said, "what's happening in the Duthgar? Tell me all you know."

She sipped delicately at some watered wine. "Rebellion, or the talk of it, is everywhere. Swords are sharpened in every hall, every cottage and every hut. And your name is on everybody's lips."

"And word of the battle?"

"Ah, yes. That too. Your victory is well known, and not just in these parts. Further south it's talked about as well. Unferth has a man … his name is Horta."

"Yes, I know about Horta."

"He's one to watch," she warned.

"You've met him?"

"I meet lots of people. And I understand those I meet well. He's a dangerous man, in his way. But maybe not so dangerous as you."

"And what of Unferth?" Sighern asked. "Does he march to war?"

She glanced at the boy, an eyebrow raised as though wondering what he was doing there, but she answered.

"He'll attack."

"But has he already marched?" Sighern persisted.

"Not when I left the south. But I left swiftly, and I traveled swifter still. He's coming, that much I promise you."

A man brought some food over. This was mostly for Tinwellen, as the others had eaten lunch not long ago. Whatever she thought of bread without butter and some dry cheese for a meal, she did not say.

"I don't doubt that Unferth will come," Brand said. "What I'd like to know is will he come with everything he has, or will he leave soldiers behind to help quell rebellion?"

Tinwellen shrugged. "I'm no soldier, Brand. But I know that when there's a fire in the camp all men come running to put it out. Else the camp burns down."

He thought as much himself. He would soon be facing everything Unferth could throw at him, and he felt gladder than ever to be behind these walls. But it nagged at him that they had fallen once, and he knew that it might be so again.

12. The Wise Man Reads the Future

Horta sat in thought. The goddess was gone, and his acolytes recovering from the form of possession that she had forced upon them. But Arnhaten were sturdy, and they would recover. If not, then the weakest of them would perish, thereby rendering those who remained a smaller, but stronger group.

She had demanded her price for help, and he agreed. He had no choice. That did not mean that he had to like it, but it was done now, and nothing would change it. He must accept the situation for what it was. Only then could he proceed with a calm mind to the next step. That was the important thing. He must think only of his great goal; all else was of little importance. And to achieve that, he must think clearly and act wisely.

What then should be his next step? He had sent word to the Kar-ahn-hetep, and within time an army would come to support him. When that happened, he would be strong. His enemies would be irrelevant, for though diminished as his people were, yet still they were far greater than the Duthenor. Even if they chose to resist, they would be felled like trees before a horde of woodcutters.

But until then, he was vulnerable. No, that was not what he was. For in truth, there was little chance of anything going wrong. There still existed the possibility of failure, though it was small. It disturbed him, but he knew he was one to remain uneasy unless success was guaranteed. It was a fault, and one that he had never remedied. He worried constantly, even when there was no call for it. Perhaps one day he would attain a higher state of thought. But wishing for that … was also a fault.

Horta sighed. He was unsuited for the great task fate had bestowed upon him. He was not great like the magicians of old. But still, he would not let that stop him.

What was to be done now? He must wait for the army to come. It was true that those who would respond to his call would only be the soldiers of his clan. But that was all that would be needed. The full army of his people would perhaps be enough to conquer realms and lands all through Alithoras. That would come later, when the god rose from his tomb.

Brand, and his tricksome army, small though it was, was what worried him most. Unferth should kill him. How could that go wrong? And yet Unferth was a fool, and that was becoming increasingly evident as he had been put under pressure.

But it was possible that Unferth might fail. Against that chance, Su-sarat offered protection. The goddess would *not* fail. She was wise and cunning. She could appear as anyone. She would insinuate herself into Brand's company, or kill a man or woman who already was and guise herself as that person. And once there, she would poison him with words and blind him to truths.

Certainly, he would prefer if she killed Brand. But under the influence of the goddess, in thralldom to her, it would be close enough to death that it did not matter.

Horta took a deep breath. Even so, dare he leave such a pivotal point of destiny to others? Should something somehow go wrong, could he stand before the shade of Char-harash, the god to be, and justify his actions?

He knew the answer to that. He could not, and he would not. He had no taste for battles, but he must go himself. There was risk in this also, for in the turmoil of war he himself could be slain. But that was a risk that he must take. Indeed, if it came to it, he must risk his own life to see Brand dead. But it would not come to that. Between Unferth and Su-sarat, Brand was finished.

And it would be just as well. Horta understood Brand's nature. He would not like being the hunted. He was one who would sooner become the hunter. And that meant he would come for him.

Horta shivered. He was under the protection of gods, but that would be a situation he would not care to face. But he was making fear where there was none. Brand *was* finished.

Yet still, the wise man read the future and used foreknowledge to act first before potential harm turned into actual harm. It must be so now. It was time once more to cast the Kar-karmun. The runes of life and death would show him the truth of his situation and guide him to what he must do.

13. The Runes of Life and Death

Horta waited until nightfall. The cave was a better place to cast the runes than the top of the hill, but the Arnhaten were tired and rest would do them good. If the omens were bad, they would need to be able to travel with great haste.

But night was a good time to cast the runes. The spirits of the dead were more restless then, more easily summoned. But not more biddable.

He had come to hate casting the runes. Summoning spirits was dangerous at the best of times, but these were the spirits of those magicians he had killed. Though constrained, their enmity was a palpable thing. Once, he had enjoyed that. In his youth, he had taken pride in it, had gloried in it as a sign of his power. Now, it just made him feel old and tired.

High on the hill top, sunlight yet shone. But down the slopes below, across fields and forests and flatlands, the long shadows of dusk had crept forth and stolen color from the land.

It was this time of day more than any other where the Duthgar reminded him of home. If he half closed his eyes, he could imagine himself on a ridge of the arid wastes somewhere. There would be goats instead of sheep. In the distance, there would be the calls of desert finches returning from their evening drink. Perhaps, there might also be the roar of a lion from afar. Certainly there would be the wailing bark of the most intelligent desert-dweller of all, the hyena.

His home was a dangerous place. But he loved it, and wished for a moment with all his heart that he was back there.

He bestirred himself, thinking that he must be getting old. He had a job to do, and nothing would stop him. Restless, he walked around the hill top as night fell. The Arnhaten left him alone. They always did when this mood was on him, and just as well.

The night fell suddenly. There was no lion roaring here, but he heard several owls. In the distance, a few cottage lights sprang up in the dark. The murmur of water came from close by, and the temperature fell quickly.

He would not wait until midnight. He had waited long enough, and though midnight was a better time to cast the runes, he was a magician of power. He was strong enough to compel the dead even during the day, if he must.

"Come to me, Arnhaten," he said. "We will delay no longer."

His acolytes moved to sit behind him, Tanata foremost among them as was proper. Horta adjusted his bearskin serape and sat also. And then he began to chant.

There was magic in his words, the magic his ancestors had learned long ago when the gods walked among men. He sensed that power infuse the words with vitality.

The cadence of his voice was harsh, yet the language he spoke, the tongue of a near-forgotten people who once contended to rule the world, was a harsh language. His dead ancestors would be proud of him now, for his power had waxed over the years and his dedication had brought near the arising of the new god. Yes, they would be proud, but they were as harsh as the land that bred them and the gods who tutored them in the mysteries of magic. If he failed them now, when victory was near, they would not forgive him.

Horta brought his mind back to the task at hand, and he lifted his chanting to a higher pitch. Through him, his people might yet rule the world as once they wished. Why did that prospect not bring him the joy that once it had? Was fear of failure disturbing him now that his goal was close to being accomplished? Or was something else happening?

He pulled his thoughts back to the chanting. A mistake during the invocation could be deadly. He continued to utter the ritual words, the power of his magic one with his voice. His disciples chanted with him, and their incantation drifted up and was lost in the vastness of the heavens.

The air around the hill top swirled and grew ice-cold, and the small fire the Arnhaten had built before the summoning gutted erratically. An acrid odor filled the air, and the spirits of the dead moved invisibly all over the crest of the hill. Could they have just now tried to distract his thoughts and cause him to make an error?

Horta ceased to chant, and his acolytes fell silent with him. The magic surrounded him, infused him, drew on his strength and gave form to his purpose. He sat motionless, eyes open but gazing only at the night-dewed grass before him. Those he had summoned were never visible, or at least they rarely were, but he felt their presence.

He shook the small pouch fastened to his belt ten times, fulfilling the ritual as it had been taught to him. And then he carefully dipped his right hand into the pouch and felt the dry bones gathered there. The finger bones of dead men, magicians every one of them.

His fingers slid among the rattling bones, and he took great care to grasp only some of them. To cast all at once presaged ill-fortune of catastrophic proportions. Such a thing rarely happened, but it had occurred to a few magicians over the ages. He would not let it happen to him, but then again, the runes had a life of their own. Or the spirits of the dead exerted control over them. The choice was possibly not within the control of the magician, and that was a sobering thought. Magic had a life of its own, also.

The spirits of the dead surrounded him, the possessors of the bones in life, and they drew in with glee his anxious thoughts. Their ill-will was a cold caress on the back of his neck.

He drew forth the bones, and with a quick but certain jerk of his hand cast them onto the grass. The runes of life and death tumbled and scattered over the ground, and then moved no more.

The future he sought to predict was now revealed by the agency of the summoned spirits, and though he felt their enmity the force of the rite constrained them to obey.

This was always a tense moment. Three bones had fallen, and each had landed cleanly, showing but one rune each. This indicated certainty of the future. But he must still study them carefully, for interpretation was everything, and the less wise sought to imprint their desires over everything. It was foolish. It was a risk. But he was wise enough not to do so. Wishing did not make reality. Deeds did.

The presence of the dead was a cold breath all around him, and their enmity was distracting. They should be released, and he did so.

Almost casually, he chanted again, this time only a few short utterances of command. The spirits were released, their task completed, and the power that had summoned them now repelled them. The small fire flared and then snuffed out. Horta felt the hatred of the spirits rage through the open sky above him, but their enmity was of no import. For a moment, the air swirled and eddied about him with invisible forces, and then the dead were gone.

Silence fell, deep and still over the top of the hill. Nothing moved nor stirred, and Horta turned his thought to the runes and studied them.

First, he studied the finger bone that had fallen higher than the others. This was *Harak*. It was the rune that signified the dualities for war and peace. This, he had been expecting, for war was abroad in the land. But what could he learn from it?

He drew deep of his wisdom, remembering the lore that went with the runes. War, he knew, could exist without peace. But peace could not endure without war, or the threat of war. There were always those who sought to steal or conquer. If not stood up to, the world would fall into chaos. So, what was the lesson for him here? How should he interpret it?

War was certain. And whoever won, peace would descend afterward. Only fools expected one state or the other to prevail without cessation. It was the cycle of nature. Should he win, how could he prepare the ground for the raising of a god? Peace would be beneficial then, for the nation that survived the coming of the god must be brought together to serve him. And after, it would march across the lands to war again. It was something to consider, and Horta knew he must do so. But not quite yet.

He turned his gaze to the next rune. It was lower, but sitting directly beneath the previous. This indicated a strong connection. The rune was *Rasallher*. It had the dual aspects of mountain peak and valley, but it was valley that showed.

Horta sighed. This was always a difficult rune to interpret. From the valley, a mountain peak looked beautiful. Yet so too did the valley from the peak. All life was about perspective, and the moral of the rune was that the wise man put himself in the perspective of his friends or enemies to better understand them or predict their actions.

This is what he must do with Brand, and he must focus on war due to the proximity of the previous rune. What then did Brand intend in terms of a military strategy?

Horta knew what *he* would do. But he was no general. He would gather as many men as he could and come against Unferth to grasp victory. He would use speed and surprise. He admired how Brand had moved his army with stealth also, appearing and disappearing. Was there any reason Brand would not continue exactly as he had been? No, there was not. And yet, perhaps that was the very reason to expect something different. Brand was clever. He would be looking to change his tactics so that they might not be guessed and countered.

Next, he turned his mind to the third rune. It stood apart, quite lower than the previous two and further to the right. *Hassah*. The water and dust rune. Surely one of the most obviously antagonistic runes in that nothing could be the more opposite of each other than water and dust.

Yet as the lore of the Kar-karmun taught, assumptions were often false. The ascendancy of one aspect gave birth to the nadir of its opposite, which in turn grew and became the stronger. Of dust, all life was made, and back into dust all life returned. Even the dry sands of the desert, parched beneath the blazing sun, held the seeds of future life in its dusty embrace. When the rains came, the golden sands turned green and then bloomed with color.

How then should he interpret the rune? It could mean many things. It might suggest that the old ways of the Duthgar were about to die, and the new ways of the rising god would grow. It could mean that. But it could just as easily mean that the established rule of Unferth was about to be overturned by Brand.

It could mean either of these things, but it stood apart from Harak and Rasallher, and that meant that, he thought, it applied more to him than the overall situation of war and the strategies of war the previous two runes revealed. What was he, personally, meant to learn from it?

Even the witless seed and the dumb animal understood when to act and when non-action was required. So the ancient lore taught. The wise man followed nature's example, and acted when it was propitious to do so. Or he held back and waited and showed patience when it was not. In this way, he turned the cycles of nature and the tides of human affairs to his advantage. So, the more he considered this the greater his certainty that it applied to him, and him alone. It was the answer to his most pressing doubt. Should he ride to war beside Unferth, or wait still in the shadows biding his time until his armies came?

The moment drew out, and he was undecided. Then he saw what he had failed to notice in the dark before. A fourth rune had fallen, and the Hassah rune covered it. One bone had fallen perfectly on the other, obscuring it. This had never occurred to him before, and though it was possible, and though the dark helped conceal it, he wondered if the malevolent spirits had played a part. It was possible if he had not chanted the invocation properly.

Gently, he reached out and removed Hassah to show the fourth. It was *El-haran*, which signified the wanderer and the farmer. The one sought adventure and thirsted for new things. The other grew deep roots and knew little, but what it did know it knew with unrivaled intimacy and understanding. The lore also said that people were likewise divided in their hearts. That they may say one thing, but mean another. Or that a thief may do a noble deed and an emperor steal from the poor.

That the two runes had fallen together tied them closely. Hassah, which was water and dust or life from death, and El-haran which signified duplicity of thought against action, might together mean that one close to him intended him harm but veiled his thoughts.

Horta shivered. His back was to the Arnhaten, but he did not think it applied to him now. It applied to Unferth. Someone near to him would bring him harm. And suddenly Horta understood.

Gormengil was one that he had cultivated. The man was cold as ice, and that was a good quality. He was an extraordinary fighter and a man of great courage. That was for the good too. But he was also the heir to Unferth, and for that reason it was prudent to befriend him. If something happened to Unferth, he must rely on Gormengil's goodwill. But the man was also ambitious. No bad thing in itself, but if he planned to usurp Unferth just now it could bring disaster while the land was at war. And with a sickening feeling, he realized that the runes were warning him of just that.

Horta leapt to his feet. He must waste no time. Already it may be too late, and his plans could yet fall to ruin if Brand won the war and controlled the Duthgar. Then, he might learn of the location of the god king's tomb and destroy his body. He did not know how Brand could learn such a thing, but it was possible. The man had surprised him before.

Tanata was instantly by his side. "What is it, master?"

"Trouble. Now move, the lot of you! We have far to go and little time."

He strode down the hill, all the while cursing how far it was from the village. It would take hours to walk there, and when they reached it there would be no rest. No, there would be no rest at all on a night like this, nor any until he caught up with Unferth.

He strode down the hill, and already some of the Arnhaten struggled to keep up.

"Stay with me!" he bellowed over his shoulder. "Or you'll wish that you were dead."

The Arnhaten hastened then, grouping together and trailing close behind. There was fear in their murmuring, but it soon ceased. At the pace he set, talking was difficult.

Tanata ventured a breathy question though. "What did the runes say, master?"

"Trouble, lad. Trouble for Unferth. But we may reach him in time."

"What sort of trouble?"

"The worst kind. Trouble of my own making. I was too friendly with Gormengil … gave him too many ideas. I did not think he was ready to act on it. But he is."

Even in the dark Horta noticed Tanata's expression. It was not in the least puzzled. The man understood straightaway what was going on, had probably long realized that he had been cultivating Gormengil with a view to the possibility that Unferth may die, or need to be removed. He understood, and kept his silence thereafter. All were admirable qualities and Horta began to think that he had found a student at last that was worthy of the full transmission of the mysteries.

But his mind soon turned back to Gormengil. The heir was in many ways a far greater man than his uncle. He was cool of thought and quick of mind. His courage was great, and he had fighting skill to match it. What he lacked though was experience. He was not ready to lead his nation to war. Nor would he necessarily be accepted by all the people. Certainly they were growing sick of Unferth. Even the Callenor seemed to hold him in low esteem these days. But were they ready for Gormengil? Doubt, hesitation and confusion were enemies. And, if even for only a few days, all three would run wild if Gormengil usurped the throne. Such a state Brand would be sure to capitalize on, and that could not be allowed. Not if he could help it.

The night wore on. It grew cold and cloudy. A patter of rain fell several times, but then it faded away. Horta hoped it would stay that way, but no weather was going to stop him or slow him down. Nothing would, but he did expect trouble ahead. Not that it would stop him either. Not now, not in these circumstances. And anyway, it was about time that the sullen villages saw a glimpse of the true power he wielded.

Horta was tired by the time he reached the village, and his arthritic knee ached. If he was not in a bad temper before, he was doubly so now.

He went straight to the king's stables. These were set well away from the hall, but they were guarded by a few soldiers. The horses inside belonged mostly to the king's messengers, but there were others there too. These were owned by lords too old to ride to war and to their wives. Horta needed them, for he needed speed. And as much as he hated riding, he would forget that now. Time was pressing and he would never catch up to the army afoot.

He swung open the doors, his weary acolytes behind him. The few men that were inside, young stable hands and soldiers stood up from where they had been playing dice.

"A dozen horses," Horta commanded. "Saddle them swiftly. We ride to the king."

The men before him looked uncertain, but the oldest of them answered. His hair was gray, but his eyes were steely. He was a man who had once seen fighting. Horta read that look about him, and he did not like it. He wanted no resistance now.

"These horses belong to the king's messengers. We have orders to guard them, and none but the messengers are allowed to use them."

"Stand aside, old man. In the name of the king."

"It's in the name of the king, and at his order that I guard them. I'll not stand aside. If you must have them, seek leave from Lord Hralfling who sits in the king's hall. He's in charge here."

Already this was taking too long, and Horta acted swiftly. The use of magic was his, but surprise would serve him well now. He swung a swift punch that caught the old man flat footed. He tumbled to the ground, but rose up again nearly in the same motion with a knife in his hand.

Tanata was already moving though, and he struck the man a second blow that felled him.

Horta kicked the knife away from his opponent's hand and signaled the Arnhaten through. "Find yourselves horses and saddle them swiftly!"

Some of the stable hands helped the old man up while the soldiers fled the building. They would return with others of their kind no doubt, but Horta hoped to be gone before then.

He found his own favorite horse and saddled it himself. It was beneath him to do servants work such as that, but the situation demanded it. He was ready more quickly than the acolytes. He at least had ridden from time to time, but the others had done so only rarely. But soon they were all gathering before the doors.

Horta saw vague movement through the crack where the two doors stood ajar. But there was room enough to ride through and nothing would stop him.

He urged his mount forward and the others filed behind him. With a kick of his foot he opened the doors wider and rushed through. There were soldiers gathering there, and he saw the glint of cold metal in the night. None of these barbarians liked him, and they would not likely hesitate to use blades, advisor to the king or no.

He kicked his mount again, and it leapt forward. Behind him came the thud of many hooves. Ahead, the soldiers were trying to group together and block his path. They were waving arms and swords now, trying to make the horses shy and stop.

Horta slipped a hand into one of his many pouches, and he drew out a large pinch of grainy powder. With a muttered prayer and a jerk of his arm he cast it out before him.

The powder turned to fire and smoke in the air. Sparks of many colors streaked toward the men and they jumped away in astonishment, opening a gap. Through this Horta charged, and the Arnhaten thundered after him.

He was on his way, and nothing would stop him, but fear rode in the saddle beside him. Would he be too late?

14. You Need Swear No Oath

Tinwellen had been right, Brand realized. The whole Duthgar knew where he was, which was what he wanted, and rebellion was ablaze through the land.

Since dawn, warriors had been coming to the fortress to join him. They looked warily at the old structure, but men on the walls rather than ghosts reassured them. That, and the Dragon Banner of the chieftains of the Duthgar that rippled lazily in the air.

They came at first by their hundreds. And then they numbered in their thousands. He had a true army now. This was no mere band of rebels, but a force to be reckoned with. Well led, they could achieve much. And they brought food and equipment with them.

They also brought tidings. Unferth was on the move. He had indeed commenced to march from the south, and he would not take long to reach here. If he knew yet that his enemy had secured a fortress, no word told. Still less what he thought about it. Brand wished he could see his face when he heard *that* news.

More pressing was the possibility that Unferth had sent spies ahead of him. It was possible. Even among the Duthenor there would be those who would serve an enemy for gold or the promise of status to come. Against this, Brand took precautions.

The new men were spread out. No larger group that came in together was allowed to stay together. They were watched, and Brand had his own men throughout them to listen and report back anything suspicious. This had not happened, but he would not expect it yet either. There was little any traitor could do for the moment, except perhaps to send word back to Unferth of numbers of soldiers and the state of the fortress. But now only trusted men were allowed to leave.

Against the possibility of the fortress's water supplies or food being poisoned, guards were set of trusted men. Against sabotage to the gate, men were also set to watch. If Unferth had sent agents for these tasks, he would likely be disappointed. But Brand doubted the man had the luxury of time to plan such things before he marched, and may only now be discovering the exact whereabouts of his opponent anyway.

One question worried him more than any of the many other concerns he had. Would Unferth attack the fortress? This was the center of his strategy. Despite the new men coming in, he was still at a numerical disadvantage. He needed the walls of the fortress to balance the odds. But that did not mean Unferth would do as expected. On the other hand, if he did not attack and win quickly, revolt could spread through the land. Then he would have to march to stamp it out, probably to several places at once. If he did so, Brand could leave the fortress and crush the enemy piecemeal.

No. Unferth would come. He had to. Having, for the hundredth time satisfied himself of that, Brand left his accustomed position on the battlements to see for himself the many tasks underway.

Tinwellen joined him as he came down the stairs.

"What now, O mighty warlord?" she said. Her eyes gleamed with humor as she spoke.

"Now, we check the gate," he said.

"I'm glad you said that. I've been fretting over the gate *ever* so much."

Despite her sarcasm, she slipped her arm around his and he led her through the gate tunnel.

"I know you're joking," he said. "But the gate is important. We'll not hold the fortress long without it."

She grinned at him, her teeth white in the dim light of the tunnel.

"I know, city boy. I know it well. But you drive yourself too hard. All work and no play is a bad way to prepare for battle. You need something to take your mind off things."

She slowed her step in the middle of the tunnel, at its darkest point. But Brand had seen the bones of dead men here. He knew how they had died, for he had seen men die in terror like that before. Arrow and spear coming through the walls. Nowhere to go except forward, and men waiting there to kill too. She had not seen that, and did not understand it. The remains had been taken away before she arrived.

He kept moving ahead, and he felt her reluctance. Almost, she seemed to stamp her foot, but he might have imagined that. It was dark. Nevertheless, she came along with him and did not let go. If she was offended, she did not show it. But he knew too well that she was not one to trifle with.

There was movement ahead, and the sound of men's voices. Suddenly Shorty loomed up out of the dark.

"Ah, perfect timing. We've just put the last finishing touches on things."

"Let's have a look, then," Brand suggested.

His old friend led them the rest of the way along the tunnel. The light grew swiftly, and the gate stood there, closed.

Brand was impressed. "The smiths have done a good job." It was hard to believe that this was the same gate that he had seen lying in ruin on first entering the fortress. The metal had been straightened, and the rust removed. "It looks like it's newly forged."

He stepped forward and gripped one of the thick bars. There was no weakness there, and he grinned. Unferth would not like this at all. A walled fortress with a good gate? He could picture the anger of the man building up. It would be one thing to learn that his enemy had encamped in such a place, but quite another that the fortress had been made sound and was no ruin of ancient and crumbling defenses.

"Want to see it in action?" Shorty asked.

"By all means."

Brand led Tinwellen back a little. The workmen came away from the gate too, some into the tunnel but most outside beyond the wall.

Shorty brought both hands to his mouth and hollered to the tower above. "Raise the gate, lads!"

A call came back in answer. "Raising the gate!"

Within a few moments a tremor ran through the metal, and the gate rose on two great chains that disappeared up through the lintel and into the gate mechanism above. The chains moved smoothly, and the gate rose steadily. For all that it must have been extraordinarily heavy, it rose as easily as a man might open a cottage door until the gate was fully open.

Shorty flashed him a grin. "Not a sight that Unferth will ever see."

"I should think *not*," Brand replied.

Shorty hailed the men above again. "Lower the gate!"

"Lowering the gate!" came the reply. This time there was a tremendous blast from several horns. It was a warning for all to keep clear. Then swift and smooth the gate dropped. With a mighty clang that boomed through the tunnel the metal rim at the bottom slammed home into its shallow footing of stone on the ground. It was likewise secured within parallel furrows on each side, greased in order to ensure the gate rose and dropped with ease.

Brand could not have been happier. The gate had worried him, but it was as good now as it was when the fortress had first been built.

"Good work!" he called out to all the men gathered there. "Excellent! Let Unferth crack his head against that!"

The men cheered and shook each other's hands. But Tinwellen gave him a sultry look and moved to press her back against the bars, arms flung out and a grin on her face.

"O, great lord! You have me prisoner now. What will you do with me?"

The soldiers erupted with laughter, and Brand tried hard to suppress his own grin. He moved in close and took her by the hand.

"I'll think of something," he said, winking at Shorty.

The men cheered again, even louder than before. Brand led Tinwellen back into the tunnel, and the cheering seemed to not only follow them but to get louder.

They walked ahead, but this time Tinwellen quickened her step as they went through the darker parts of the tunnel. Truly, he could never quite guess what she was going to do next. And maybe he liked that.

"There are quite a few things I need to check on yet," he said as they came back into the courtyard.

"Lead on," she replied, slipping her arm through the crook of his again.

The next few hours went well. If Tinwellen was bored of inspecting the many things that needed checking, she did not show it.

Brand went first to the various wells that had been found. Some were shallow and some deeper. This was good, because it indicated different sources of underground water. If one went dry, the others might keep producing.

He did not doubt that there had been a great quantity of water available when the fortress had been built. Otherwise, it would not have been positioned were it was. Water was critical to an army, and the original army that held this fortress was much larger than the one that occupied it now. But all of that was long, long ago. Since then, the underground water levels could have fallen. It was just as likely that they had risen too, but one was a problem and the other was not. Still, all the signs looked good.

Next, he inspected the kitchens. These had been cleaned and fires burned day and night. An army needed a lot of feeding, and soldiers manned the battlements in shifts day and night. Cooks had been selected too, and though these no longer wore armor or sword, both were piled neatly in corners and ready for use if needed.

The kitchens had been well designed. They were spacious, and there were stone-lined ovens and fire-pits. Each had a chimney too, and these drew the smoke well to send great plumes of blue-white clouds to hang above the fortress when the air was still. They had needed much clearing of debris though to unblock them, the cooks told him.

Brand toured the battlements as well. These were cleaned now, free of debris and little structural work had been needed anywhere. Long poles were stacked in many places, to be used to dislodge scaling ladders. There were axes also, for the severing of ropes thrown over the ramparts with grappling hooks. Fresh made timber buckets were there as well, some containing water and others sawdust. These were to clean the rampart floor of blood, and then to dry the surface once more so that soldiers could better keep their footing.

Away over the Duthgar everything seemed peaceful, but that would change. In the foreground, the land was barren now and clear of tree and shrub. It was a good killing area. Further out, the pine-clad ridges marched away. Brand's heart was in places like that, with the scent of resin in the air and the mysteries of forest paths that led to the high places or down into secret valleys. But war was his life now, and he drew his gaze, and his thoughts, back to his responsibilities.

In many places along the battlements mock battles were being fought to get the defenders used to siege warfare. What these men learned now as a game, Unferth's would learn later at a cost of blood. He could not pity them. The general who pitied the enemy lost. At least, he could not pity them until he won, if that came to pass. Truly, he had less choice in things than he had ever thought. Necessity drove him, as it always had and always would.

The soldiers were good with the long poles, dislodging ladders swiftly. It would be harder with the weight of people on them, and the fear of death breathing down their necks. But they were hard men, and they understood this.

In other places, groups of archers took turns to fire at targets below. There were too few archers for Brand's liking, but it was a skill that needed learning like all others. He could put bows into the hands of many other men, but ten who could shoot with accuracy and speed were worth more than a hundred without skill. He would make do with what he had.

There were more spearmen, and this too was a skill, but not so great as archery. Strong men, and athletic, as most Duthenor were, could hurl a javelin with great force. One by itself might be dodged and avoided. But thrown as a unit as these men were training to do, to dodge one was to step into another, and to raise a shield to protect the face was to expose the legs.

Tinwellen also took in the training, and seemed impressed by it.

"You leave nothing to chance, do you?"

"Not if I can help it," Brand said with determination. "But the chances of the world are many, and no general can foresee them all."

The expression on her face indicated she agreed with that, but she only nodded solemnly and did not reply. Brand led her back along the rampart to the gate towers, and there descended the stairs at the back of the wall into the courtyard.

Even as they reached the bottom a new batch of men was coming in, several hundred strong. Two lords led them. Their fine armor and jewel-hilted swords identified them as such, but their clothing was of a finer cut also. They saw Brand, and recognized him by the Helm of the Duthenor that he wore, for they strode over quickly and bowed.

"Lord Garvengil at your service," the first said.

"And Lord Brodruin, also at your service," the second added.

"Pleased to meet you, gentlemen." Brand only glanced at them. Most of his attention was on the men the lords had led into the fortress. They seemed well equipped, and they were all tall and strong. They would be a good addition to the defense, but Brand could not help wondering how young they were. Some at least would not yet have seen their twentieth winter, and it disturbed him. How many would die beneath the same Dragon Banner now marked by Haldring's blood? Too many, and every one would be on his conscience. But war gave generals few choices.

Garvengil drew his gaze off the Helm of the Duthenor down to the hilt of Brand's Halathrin-wrought sword. The blade was a legend, but it was a true fighting weapon and the hilt was not decorated in the fashion lords seemed to favor these days. But still Brand sensed a little of the man's unease, even awe.

Brand clapped him on the shoulder, and his companion as well.

"Thank you for coming. You and your men will make a great difference."

"It's nothing but our duty," Brodruin replied.

That much was true, Brand knew. But he knew also that these men might not have come at all unless they believed he had a chance of winning. It was only the recent victory against Unferth that had swayed them, but still, they were here, and that was what mattered.

"When shall we swear our oaths?" Garvengil asked.

Brand was confused. "What oaths?"

"Oaths of fealty to you as our chieftain, or our king if you wish. Unferth calls himself such, but you are more worthy. We hear many things here in the Duthgar, even from far away Cardoroth."

Brand hesitated, and he felt Tinwellen's eyes upon him. This was not why he had come back to the Duthgar. Not exactly. And yet it was his right by birth. It was the destiny stolen away from him. But what of his responsibilities as a lòhren? It was true that he felt more a chieftain than a lòhren, but it was not that simple. Or perhaps for a time he could be both.

"There'll be time enough for that later. In the meantime, you need swear no oaths of loyalty to fight for the freedom of your land."

The two lords seemed a little perplexed, but they bowed.

"As you wish," Brodruin said. "In that case, perhaps we had better see to our men."

Brand nodded. "Of course."

They left him then, but Tinwellen's gaze did not. He led her to one of the tables along the side of the courtyard, and there they sat and rested for a while.

All around him men were working feverishly on one thing or the other. It would not stop until well into the evening, and what work that could be carried out was done then by torch light.

"They know the enemy comes," Brand said.

Tinwellen gazed around, and nodded. "You can feel the tension in the air, thickening it."

It was a good way to put it. But if she felt any of that tension herself, she did not show it.

He thought suddenly of the archers that he had seen practicing earlier. If need be, a thrown spear could still do damage with only a sharpened timber point, but better if it had a metal head. The same could be said for arrows, but doubly so because arrows were more deadly due to their accuracy and the numbers that could be shot.

He signaled a man over. "Track down either Shorty or Taingern," he instructed. "Tell them, if it has not already been done, to find whatever scrap metal is in the fortress. Old door hinges, cutlery. Anything. Not all will have rusted away. Some must have been protected from the elements. Find it and use it to make arrowheads. We don't have many archers, but we'll make the most of them. At least they'll not run out of good arrows."

The man went away quickly to fulfil his task. Shorty and Taingern had probably already thought of it, but it may have been overlooked. The weapons and armor of the long-dead soldiers had rusted to dust, but there must be places in the fortress away from water and humidity where some useable metal had survived.

"Will you never rest?" Tinwellen asked, her dark eyes studying him.

His answer was bleaker than he intended. "Time enough to rest when I'm dead."

For once, she had no quick joke or rejoinder. But her dark eyes remained on him, weighing him up as though he were a piece of metal himself being tested for soundness.

15. Dark Dreams

Brand dreamed that night, and it was like no dream that he had ever had before.

His room was small, likely some sort of officer's quarters within one of the barracks of the fortress close to the courtyard. It was dark and windowless, but he had it to himself unlike the men outside who slept in long rows along the floor. Whatever beds had once been here were long decayed. The area had been cleaned though, and the roof was in good condition, considering. If and when it rained, it would prove a good place to be.

With a feeling of unease, Brand woke. Only, he knew that he was still asleep. He was dreaming, and yet his mind was conscious of it and capable of rational thought.

He was alone, and unarmed. He wore neither his helm nor carried a sword. But even as he realized this, enemies appeared all around him. And they each held weapons, drawn and ready for use.

That they were enemies, he knew by the looks in their eyes. There was hatred there. It gleamed in their gazes like a torch in the dark.

Worst of all was that among the many enemies were his friends. But they hated him no less than the others, and he felt the pain of that run through him like fire.

Shorty and Taingern were there, their eyes glittering. But it was Haldring that disturbed him the most. She was accoutered as the shield maiden that she had been in life, only he saw her as she had been in death – vacant-eyed and bloody. Those lifeless eyes still managed to look at him accusingly, and the end of her sword dripped blood.

She pointed it at him, and she spoke, her voice dripping with scorn.

"Here is the great king. Hail, Brand, murderer of friends and betrayer of nations."

Brand was as near to panic as he had ever been. What was happening to him? This was a dream, and the people here could not be real. And yet there was something real about it. Some substance and form that was not found in the drifting and random thoughts of normal sleep.

"What do you hold against me, Haldring? It was not my blade that killed you. I would rather have endured it myself than watch you die."

The moment he answered, he knew it was a mistake. His acknowledgement of their presence made them stronger, and their hatred for him intensified and rolled over him like a wave.

He stepped back, and Haldring immediately stepped closer.

"You did not kill me with a blade," she said, "but with your incompetence. You should have seen what would happen, and prevented it. You're a fool. And you're not fit to lead an army."

Was there truth to those words? A part of him believed so. A part did not. But none of that answered what was happening to him now, and that was what mattered most. Guilt could be addressed later.

Shorty pressed forward. He was a small man, but he moved with grace. He was a warrior born, and Brand would not ever like to face him in a fight. There was a deadliness to him, and a coldness in his eyes that Brand had never seen before, though he knew the man's enemies had. Before they died.

"I could be a lord in Cardoroth," the smaller man said. "With a manor and grounds and servants. I could be enjoying life. But no, you don't want that for me. Instead, you drag me to this barbarous land to face death for a people who mean nothing to me. And I'll die here, because you'll make a mistake. You sicken me."

Brand was not going to answer, but this time no answer seemed to be expected. Taingern lifted off his helm, and Brand saw a dagger jutting from his eye.

"You betrayed me," his friend whispered, but his voice rang loud enough inside Brand's head that he would have heard it across the other side of the world. "I gave up everything for you. I, who could have founded a school of philosophers to study the meaning of life and bring wisdom to humanity, died by your own hand. If this is what you bring to your friends, how do you think to lead a nation? You will bring your people to ruin."

It seemed to Brand that the number of his enemies was growing. Wherever he looked, they milled about and cast accusing gazes at him. But he could seldom recognize their faces.

Yet now another stepped forward to reproach him, and the face suddenly became clear, a face he would never forget though he was not yet grown to manhood last time he saw it. Unferth.

And Unferth wore the Helm of the Duthenor. Tall he stood, and proud, though there was an air of justice about him.

"I am the rightful ruler of the Duthgar. I have united two nations, and more will follow. What once was a petty chieftainship, I have raised to the status of kingship. The high seat is no more. Instead, it is a throne. The people prosper beneath my hand, and what do you do to disrupt things? You bring war. You are a warmaker. You are not, nor will ever be, a ruler. But I forgive your sins against me. You know not what you do. Though after this, that excuse will not suffice."

If his demeanor was one of justice before, now it was one of executioner. He drew his sword, and Brand saw that it was the Halathrin-wrought blade that was his own.

As though this were a sign, all his enemies turned their faces upon him at once. And they drew their weapons also, and death was in their eyes. They leapt toward him, and he turned and fled, but they followed swifter than he ran, and he saw that they flew through the air after him as the hawk hurtles toward the dove.

Anger shot through him. He was no dove, no prey for others. And whoever, or whatever, these others were, they were not real. Another thought ran fast on the heels of that. This was a dream, and if so, it was his. If his enemies could fly, then so could he.

He leapt up into the air, and in the manner of dreams the earth fell down behind him and his mind swam the currents of the universe.

With a thought, he was high in the sky, his enemies trailing behind. With another, he was in the deeps of the void with the brightness of stars about him. But still, his enemies followed.

With a silent laugh on his lips he dived down again, hurtling through their ranks and dispersing them. He plummeted back to the blue earth, and there he found the peaks of ice-clad mountains. In life, he had a fear of heights. But in this dream world he leapt from peak to peak with gladness in his heart. But still the enemy came after him.

At a thought, he descended into deep valleys below. It was dark and secretive. Massive pines grew all around blotting out the stars in the sky and even the mountains. But he could still feel those mountains, and their roots that delved deep into the earth, layer and layer of stone and minerals and water and caves. The world, the universe, was boundless. And his mind could take him anywhere.

Yet still his enemies found him, and their rushing presence drove the joy from his heart.

He fled again, this time slipping beneath the still waters of a great lake. It was dark and cold, but he breathed of the water as though it were air and he swam with the silver-scaled fishes that roamed the water, turning and twisting in silvery beauty, their scales flashing in the pale light when they came near the surface.

And even here his pursuers found him. They swam also, and their eyes bored into him with icy malice colder than either mountain peak or the depths of a lake.

He could not escape them. And even as he swam, they lifted bows that they had not had before and shot fiery arrows toward him. The fish were gone. The lake was dark no longer, but lit by orange streaks that darted around him and caused the water to bubble with heat.

Where had bows and arrows come from? If his pursuers could do that, then why not he? It was his dream, after all, and therefore he should be able to shape its reality. Even as the dream-thought came to him, he understood the truth of it.

He turned to face his pursuers. At a thought, the sword of his forefathers was girded at his side. He drew the Halathrin-wrought bade, and it flashed wondrously beneath the water. This gave the enemy pause.

Next, he set the Helm of the Duthenor on his head. He was the heir to the chieftainship of the Duthgar, and he had won this long-lost artifact at risk to his life. It was *his* to wear, and not Unferth's.

A moment later chain mail followed, gleaming silver like the scales of a fish. And finally the banner of the chieftains of the Duthenor floated above his head. The dragon appeared as though it were swimming in the water, and Brand knew also that if he wished he could give it life and set it after his enemies.

But the banner, even in his dreams, was stained by blood as it was in life. There were some realities that bound both the waking and the sleeping worlds, some events that could not be forgotten.

His pursuers halted. At his thought, their weapons vanished. It was his dream, and he would command things as he wished. The Helm of the Duthenor that protected Unferth's head vanished also, disappearing in a sharp burst of light.

And then Brand moved toward them. A moment they gazed at him, surprise on their faces, and then they melted away in an eddy of water and were gone.

Brand was pleased. But the feeling did not last long. Two new figures rose from the depths of the lake, and he cursed violently.

16. Char-harash

The figures drew closer. Brand knew them, and he remembered them well despite the years that had passed since he had last seen them alive. It was his mother and father.

Anger flared through him. This dream was his, and yet he sensed another power at work. The first attack against him had failed, and now his parents were the second. It was too much, and his anger increased even further, but he compressed it into a cold ball inside him. This allowed him to think.

The figures were no more his parents than his previous pursuers had been friends and enemies. They were imagined. And he did not think that it was him who had done so. The dream was his, but someone else, some other force, was using magic to draw out these thoughts from his mind and give them reality within the dream.

But it was a dream, and anything seemed possible here. And all the myriad manifestations of his fears and concerns must have an origin. That they came from him was true, but it was just as true that whoever was doing this to him must also be present, else they could not delve into his thoughts as they had and give them substance within the dream.

Whoever that person was, they were responsible for what was happening, and if they existed, which he was certain now they did, then they must also have a location within the dream, a point of entry into his mind. If he could find that, he could find them.

It was time for the hunted to become the hunter. That the dream was his own helped, for originating in his mind he had the power. He used it now.

He opened his senses. His mind encompassed the dream world, and all that was about him fell away. There was nothing now but the void, and the stars wheeled and spun in the inky sky. This was good, for everything revolved around him. It was his dream after all.

Except one thing did not. One lone star far away on the edge of the sky did not move. That was his enemy, and with a thought Brand, or the dream of him that his sleeping mind had conjured, flew through the vastness and shot toward him as an arrow from a bow.

Even as he felt the vastness of the void speed past him, Brand lifted high his sword and a white light glittered on its edges as a cold fire. It was the embodiment of his wrath, and he sensed the other light retreat away from him.

But Brand would not let it escape, or rather the person it represented. For he sensed the other presence now. It was a man, and one full of malice. He sensed surprise also, and he caught a flickering image of a cave.

The light he pursued vanished, but not quickly enough. Brand sensed the trail it left, and he followed it through the void. Dark was all about him now, without star or moon or the cold glory of the universe. He was in the void no longer. His dream-self had now entered a cave somewhere in Alithoras.

He waited in the dark. His enemy was close by, and unmoving also. But unmoving did not mean scared, or not dangerous.

The cave was not as dark as he first thought. There was a soft light casting faint shadows, and this came off both his helm and his sword. He wondered if he still had the powers of command that he possessed in his dream to alter its reality. Would that work in this place, given that it belonged to the real world and he was only a dream within it? There was only one way to find out.

He willed light to emanate from the sword, but nothing happened. The rules of the dream had changed, because what was happening was no longer solely within his mind. It was different now. Some part of his mind was in this place, and this place was the lair of his enemy.

Brand felt vulnerable in the dark, for he could be easily seen by the light his sword and helm gave off. On the other hand, without light, even dim as it was, his enemy could approach unseen. That would be worse.

Gradually, his eyes adapted to the light. He saw now that this was indeed a cave, though the walls had been smoothed and evened, what little he could discern of them. It was perhaps a man-made chamber.

He dwelled on that thought a moment. What sort of chamber would be hewn out of rock such as this? He did not like the conclusions that he reached. And the more that he began to see of this chamber, the less he liked it.

There was evidence of paintings on the walls, though all he could see was the occasional human shape and some brighter patches of color. It was too dark to observe more, and he was not yet ready to move closer to look. To move might be to die, if that was even possible in a dream. Best not to chance that, yet.

To his right, some bulky objects stood out. These were large earthenware vases, he decided at length. Some were waist high to a man. Some appeared to be sealed, while others were open. And from the open ones he could now see the faint luster of gold. It was confirmation of what he had begun to believe. This was a tomb.

He gazed a little to the left. There was a stone platform there, almost like a dais in a throne room. But it was no dais. Upon it something rested, and he began to wish for the dark once more. Some things were better not to see. But he steeled himself, for he had discovered his enemy, and having discovered him he must learn more. Knowledge was power, and ignorance death.

He stepped closer. The sword he held high in his hands, the point of it just below the level of his gaze. And that which rested on the stone platform became clearer.

It was a body. Ancient it seemed, for the skin, where it showed, was dried and leathery. But the hair that spilled from beneath a strange helm showed traces of color and little damage by time and elements. And the face was there also. No skull was to be seen, but rather the same dried skin as on the hands. It could have been a fresh burial, but it was not.

In the air were the fragrances of cedar oil, myrrh, cassia and frankincense. He had smelled their like once before. He had been in a tomb before, and one built in ancient days by the Letharn. They used such things as embalming agents to preserve the flesh of the dead. And he knew it was so here, also. But he guessed this was no Letharn tomb, but one that belonged to the Kirsch, the ancient enemy of the Letharn.

The body was armored, and a sword of strange design rested near the withered right hand of the corpse. The robes it wore were golden, and the color was evident even in the dim light. There was a suggestion of sorcery too. It lingered in the air, and he knew that some powerful spell had been worked here long, long ago. And it yet endured.

Brand gazed at the corpse. Could this be his enemy? Was it possible? Or was there some subterfuge in action that he had not yet laid bare?

"Speak!" he commanded. "You are discovered, and I know an enemy when I see one."

In truth, he did not expect what happened next. He had spoken only to hear the sound of his own voice amid the crushing weight of the dark and the suffocating sense of inevitable death.

And yet the withered hand twitched, gripping the sword. Some movement stirred the hair beneath the helm, and the face moved, lips forming words though the flesh was dried and the tongue a husk.

Hurlak gee, mishrak ammon hul. Far geru arhat!

Brand stepped back. Fear stabbed into his body like a lightning bolt, and his heart thundered in his chest. That it was only his mind here and not his body did not matter. He knew that these things were happening to him where he slept far away.

He did not understand the words, but he knew a command when he heard one. Here was a man who ruled others, and expected to be obeyed. And then the voice whispered in his mind, and he understood the meaning of the words.

Kneel, mortal. You are in the presence of a god. I speak, and you obey!

Brand felt a desire to obey. Like a weight over his mind it fell, and his left knee buckled. But then he remembered what the man, or god, or whatever it was, had done in his dreams. Invoking images of his dead parents was too much.

"Eat dust and die," Brand answered. "I'm not your subject."

The corpse shuddered, and after a moment Brand realized it was laughter. And then the dried-out mouth began to work again.

"In my time, it was said that you could judge a man by his enemies. There is truth to this, and you are a fitting opponent for such as I. Almost."

Whoever this was, he had a high opinion of himself. But Brand was not impressed.

"Don't enter my dreams again," he warned.

The corpse laughed once more, and it was as disturbing a sight and sound as anything Brand had ever encountered before.

"You are in no position to make threats. Your enemies far outnumber you. One of your allies, nay, one of the closest of your companions, will betray you. Horta will rise against you, bringing his magic to bear as a storm of destruction. And you think yourself safe in a fortress, but doubt gnaws at your soul for you know that it has fallen before. No, it is best that you do not threaten me."

Brand considered the corpse. "You know a lot. For a dead man."

"Dead? You are ignorant of the great mysteries. Who are you to speak of death, or life, or the boundaries between? You know little of what has been, or what could yet be in the future."

"Then tell me this. Who are you?"

"I am Char-harash. Once I led an empire. Once, I commanded powers of magic that would still Horta's heart. Once … but the past is an empty thing. It is a cup of memories sipped from at whiles while the mind contemplates the future."

Brand grew weary of holding his sword upright. But he rested its point lightly against the ground rather than sheath it.

"And what do you see in your future, Char-harash?"

"I see godhood. In life, I was on the brink. In death, I am on the brink of life. In but a little while I shall live again. This husk of flesh will be renewed, this body enlivened. I shall walk the world again, and I, and my brethren to be, will bend it to our wills."

A faint sense of unease stirred in Brand. It was not just these words, it was something else. Why should his enemy speak so freely?

Char-harash, or what was left of him, was not done.

"You are strong," his enemy continued. "But you are ill-tutored. Serve me, and I will educate you in the mysteries. Obey me, and the world will tremble at your thought. I can give you powers that you have never dreamed of. There is a place by my side for such as you."

Brand had heard this sort of thing before. It held little temptation for him. What more could a man want but a smile from the girl he loved and a hearty meal? Everything else was empty.

"What point is there in serving a corpse?"

The voice of Char-harash came in answer, cold as death.

"A corpse now, but a god to be."

Brand's unease grew. He had taunted this spirit, and it did not respond with anger. Yet if he was any judge of character, Char-harash was spiteful and vindictive. Or had been in life. Death was not likely to have improved him. Why then had he not reacted with violence?

"You should have left me alone," Brand declared. "No offers of power will sway me. No bribe will tempt me, for you have nothing of true value to give. Instead, you attacked me in my dreams and now insult my honor. And you threaten the land I love. For these things, you have made of me an enemy."

Char-harash laughed once more, and Brand felt his stomach churn. But something was wrong over and above that. What was it?

This much Brand knew. His enemy was willing to talk to him, to threaten or to tempt, it did not seem to matter which. For that, there must be a reason.

A wave of weakness overwhelmed him. At first, he thought his enemy had attacked him in some way, but it was not so. This was something that originated from within himself. And then he understood.

He was here, but it was only his dream-self. Perhaps what some would term a spirit. It was something that he knew was possible, but of which he knew little. And an echo of some instinctive fear ran through him. If the spirit was separated from the body too long, the body would die.

Char-harash was trying to kill him, and that it was not done with an open attack made the danger no less real.

17. Patience

Horta hated riding, but the Arnhaten that came behind him hated it more. They bounced in their saddles and cursed and moaned. Of them all, only Tanata endured the ride in silence.

Through the land they had raced, and ever Horta feared he would be too late. If Gormengil had killed Unferth, the army might already have fallen apart. If Unferth had killed Gormengil, it mattered less. Yet Gormengil was respected, and a king who killed his own heir might lose the support of those he led. Especially when that support had become tenuous.

All things were possible right now, and different destinies vied with each other. Horta could almost feel the land itself hold its breath. He had lived a long time, but seldom had he felt this way before. All hopes were on the cusp of birth, and all catastrophes hovered like a dagger at his neck, ready to slit his throat.

The High Way made the riding easier, if it could be called that. It allowed quick and sure progress, even at night. And it was nighttime now. A village lay on their left as they clattered past, all lit up with lights in every window while the occupants finished their meals and prepared for bed. They were oblivious of the need that drove him, and he kicked his horse ahead a little faster. They were oblivious, but he was not.

For two days they had followed in the wake of the army. But the signs indicated it was close now. Very close. There would be no stopping until they reached it, and if a horse died beneath them, ridden beyond what it had to give, so be it.

The night was not yet old when they saw lights in the distance. Campfires. Thousands of them, and Horta felt a surge of energy thrill through him. He must *not* be too late.

Despite the sense of urgency upon him, he slowed the column to a walk. There would be sentries, and to go rushing through in the dark was to risk being speared or shot by arrow.

The column, which had spread out hundreds of feet, began to bunch together now. Tanata drew alongside him.

"Master, there are men nearby."

Horta did not get a chance to answer. No sooner had Tanata spoken than a group of four men reared up before them, spears in hand.

"Halt!" came a quick command, and Horta sharply drew the reins of his horse in.

One of the four men stepped a pace closer. He did not lower his spear.

"Who comes towards the king's camp? What's your business here?"

"I am Horta, advisor to the king, and my business with Unferth is none of your concern."

The soldier stepped a few paces closer, but the spear remained poised to throw or jab. Horta held his breath, but it had nothing to do with the spear.

The man peered up at him. "I recognize you," he said, at last lowering his spear. "You and your men may ride through."

Horta gave a silent prayer of thanks to the gods, and relief washed over him. He had called the king by name, and stated that his business was with him. Surely, if Gormengil had killed Unferth, the soldier would have said something knowing who he intended to see.

Luck had favored him. Or the quick ride had been worth it. Or, possibly, the runes of life and death had been wrong. Of the three possibilities, he knew the first was the most likely.

He nudged his horse forward without answering the soldier. The man was nothing to him now. All that mattered was what lay ahead, for while Gormengil had not yet made an attempt to usurp the throne, he knew the danger was still there, for the runes were never wrong. And he must still find a way to avert that disaster.

Or had Gormengil made the attempt and failed? That was possible too, and the soldier may not have mentioned it. But he did not think so. There had been a certain amount of tension in the air, but that was natural for sentries stopping travelers entering the camp. Had some sort of assassination attempt been made on the king, the anxiety of the sentries would have been much greater.

They passed through several more guard lines. The smell of smoke and cooking meals hung in the air, and the light and noise of the camp was close to hand.

Horta dismounted. A camp was no place to ride in the dark. The Arnhaten did likewise, and he led them forward through the rows of men. The army seemed vast, and Horta felt as though every set of eyes was turned on him. They all knew who he was, and they all disliked him. Had it not been known that he was an advisor to Unferth, he and his men would long since have been accosted.

The ranks of men, and the fires, and the occasional tent seemed endless. So too the hostile gazes. Yet at length, Horta found his way to the center of the encampment. There were more tents here, for the wealthier camped closer to the king. There were more horses also.

Horta turned to Tanata. "You will come with me when I speak to the king. Stay on your guard."

"What shall I be on guard against?"

Horta hesitated. But the man had proved his intellect and worth.

"Watch the king. And watch Gormengil. See if you can discern how things stand between them. Watch Gormengil especially, for my attention must be only on the king."

Tanata inclined his head, and asked no further questions. He was proving to be the perfect disciple.

They came to the king's tent. Outside were long rows of picket lines for other horses, and Horta and Tanata handed their reins to two of the Arnhaten.

"Stay close by," he commanded them.

He led Tanata to the tent flap where a group of soldiers stood guard. "Tell the king that Horta has come," he commanded. "And I would speak with him."

The men gazed at him with cold eyes, but their leader moved through the tent flap and disappeared. He returned a few moments later. "The king grants you audience."

The tone in which the man spoke was superior, and Horta did not like it. But he swallowed his pride. Soon, if all went well, these men would learn what true power was, and who wielded it. He moved through the tent flap himself, and put such petty thoughts behind him.

It was lit inside by several braziers that gave off a ruddy light. The smell of smoke was strong, and the air was cloying. Horta saw Unferth straightaway, and relief washed through him. It was one thing to deduce the man was still alive, but another to see him.

But Gormengil was there also. Indeed, most of the Callenor war leaders were. They were seated around a crude trestle table. That, some sawed logs for chairs, and the braziers were the only furniture. But all over the ground lay various animal rugs.

Unferth glanced up at him. "I thought war was not to your liking, Horta. But you have decided to come and serve your king anyway?"

Horta bowed. "I am no soldier, and little used to the ways of fighting," he lied. "But it may be, in my own small way, that I can help."

"Then join us at the table. You wield no sword, but you have a sharp mind."

Horta understood what was happening here. It was a war council, and it was evident that they faced some difficulty, judging from the looks on their faces. He glanced carefully at Gormengil as he sat, for he was the one whose emotions must be gauged most, but typically for the man, he was the one who masked what he felt the best. His face may as well have been carved from stone.

Horta was not comfortable on a sawed log for a seat. He would have preferred to sit on the ground. This, at least, Tanata was able to do, and he took up a position close behind him. No one at the table even looked at him. It was a slight, but these barbarians knew nothing of civilized ways. To slight the servant was to slight the master.

Despite his discomfort, Horta listened carefully as the king spoke.

"Brand has dug himself into a hole like a rat." The words were for Horta, bringing him up to date with what the others in the room already knew. "He has occupied an ancient fortress called Pennling Palace. It's a wretched dump, falling apart and reputed to be haunted, but he thinks the walls will keep me from him."

Horta knew the place. His wanderings had taken him across the Duthgar, but he had never ventured inside. The place had a bad reputation, and there was something about it that triggered his instincts.

Gormengil leaned forward, resting his elbows on the table where he sat next to the king.

"The fortress is old," he said, "and I've not been inside. But the walls are still standing, and they are strong."

Unferth grunted. "I don't care about walls and gates. We have the greater army. We'll storm the walls and demolish whatever barricade they've put up for a gate."

"It's not that simple, my king," Gormengil said. "The walls are an advantage to the enemy. And it's clear that Brand isn't going anywhere, so we may as well take the time to gather more men. Then we can be sure of defeating him."

Horta understood. The runes had been right, and Brand had done the unexpected. He also understood that the king's advisors were divided in how they should react. Worst of all, Unferth and Gormengil were on opposite sides of that divide.

Unferth seemed angry. "It's as simple as I say it is. My army outnumbers his. The walls offer a barrier, but they'll not stop me from crushing him, and all who support him."

The reply Gormengil gave was softly spoken, and his voice was void of emotion. But still Horta's blood ran cold to hear him speak.

"You underestimate Brand. You always have, otherwise he would already be dead. I urge you, don't take his skill as a general cheaply this time. Gather more men. Take your time. Be sure of victory before you rush in, foolishly."

Unferth went white. Then his face blossomed red in rage. He stood, and with a casual movement backhanded Gormengil. It was unexpected, and the sudden violence caused men to reel back off their seats and stagger upright.

Gormengil fell to the ground, but then he rose in a smooth motion, his body swaying to and fro like a rearing serpent. It was not dizziness that made him move so, but a martial technique to help avoid being struck while rising from the ground. Horta knew a great fighter when he saw one, and he increased his estimate of Gormengil. And even struck down, the man's face showed no emotion, but his eyes were cold as death.

Gormengil had his right hand on his sword hilt. Unferth reached for the wicked-looking axe he now carried with him. The men around the table stepped further back.

Horta acted swiftly. He drew powder from one of his pouches, and cast it onto the table where it exploded in flashes of multicolored sparks. Then swifter than either the king or the heir he moved, leaping across the table and gripping Gormengil's wrist.

"Stay!" he commanded. "Discord among us is to Brand's favor. Are you all children to squabble while the realm falls around you?"

No one answered. Slowly, Gormengil released his grip on the sword hilt. Unferth seemed in a rage, but he blinked a few times and then his eyes focused on Horta.

"Children, are we? Is that how you speak to your king?"

"I speak the truth," Horta answered. "And you know it. If you wish lickspittles to serve you, too scared to voice an opinion, then strike off my head now. Otherwise, heed my words!"

A long moment Unferth looked at him. "You are more than you seem. But you're right. Discord among us is only to Brand's advantage." He deliberately avoided looking at Gormengil as he spoke, but his gaze flickered to the man at the last and his hands still tightly gripped the haft of the axe.

Horta bowed. "Let me take Gormengil aside, sire. I'll teach him of my wisdom. And then let me speak with you. I sense the magic of Brand at work, sowing disharmony among us." It was not true, but Unferth did not know that, and it would distract him from Gormengil.

Unferth gave a nod of approval, and Horta drew the heir to the throne away. They walked out of the tent and into the semi-dark of the camp. Horta hesitated, and then led the younger man to the picket line of horses where they could speak without being overheard.

Horta swung toward him. "Are you a fool? We've discussed much, and one day you'll be king, but you're not ready yet. If you're not careful, Unferth will have you killed and your dreams will be dust."

The dark eyes of Gormengil gazed back at him, unblinking. "We've discussed many things. Some of it treasonous. You know that as well as I. Yet all I did tonight was offer good counsel to the king."

"It's not what you said. It's how you said it. He knows you wish the throne. He knows you hold him in contempt. Wait. Bide your time. Strike when you're ready and sure of victory. That's what I counsel you. Is it not what you advised the king to do? If you'll not listen to me, will you not at least follow your own polices?"

Gormengil turned away. It was hard to read his face in the shadows, but Horta knew his words had struck home.

"I'm not a hasty man," Gormengil said quietly. "But my dreams are afire with thoughts of kingship. Unferth is a fool. I would be a far better king."

"And so you will be. But now isn't the time for a change of leadership. Not during the middle of a war. Wait until afterward. And who knows, the kingship may come to you naturally if Unferth is killed during battle."

"I too may be killed in battle."

Horta turned away now. He knew something of the future, and something of the plans of the gods, but not enough.

"Patience rewards us all, Gormengil. Wait on your destiny. It will come. Glory, riches and power will soon fill the Duthgar. A nation will rise here to conquer the world, and the leader of the realm will be a god."

Horta looked intently at the other man to assure him he was speaking the truth. It did not matter that he had once had the same conversation with Unferth. What he said was true, and if they believed themselves to be the leader he spoke of, it was not his fault.

18. If I Don't, Who Will?

The dream-spirit that was Brand leapt out of the tomb of Char-harash. But his enemy was guileful and full of malice.

With a flick of his withered hand, the sorcerer sent Brand tumbling into the void, lost and without bearings. The shock of the power used to do so was awesome, and Brand felt fear run through him.

In the void, all was dark and the glitter of faraway stars faint and unfamiliar. Somewhere, he felt his body grow cold, and the blood in his veins begin to turn sluggish. He was near to death, and panic took him.

But he was a warrior. Death, and the threat of death, were familiar feelings. He calmed himself and thought. One thing he realized straightaway. Char-harash, for all his power and seeming familiarity with this dream world, had not followed him. Could it be that he was scared? That was good to know.

Another thought occurred to him. He had no idea where he was, neither his dream-self nor his body, and yet he could still feel his body weakening. He was linked to it in some way. And if that was so, then did he have to find his way back by landmarks or reasoning?

He closed off all his senses and floated in the void, drifting in the great dark. But he concentrated on the vague sensations of his weakening body. Those sensations sharpened, and it felt as though some invisible current within the void had taken him. He no longer drifted aimlessly, but now felt himself pulled in a specific direction.

He willed himself to go that way, and suddenly it felt as though he was falling. The void exploded all around him in shifting colors and burning suns, and he plummeted ever faster through the dreamworld.

Consciousness sped from him, and darkness blanketed his mind. But he woke moments later, his body wracked by pain. He reared up from his makeshift bed in his room in the barracks, gasping for air and shivering with cold. The room spun around him, and he felt violently ill.

He lowered himself back down, shivering and trembling all over. But slowly, his breathing returned to normal and the cold sweat that slicked his skin dried away. All the while, he dared not close his eyes nor even blink except when he must for fear of slipping away into death. He had been close.

It was time to think, and he lay there, eyes open in the dark of his room, doing just that. It was clear now that he must do more than depose Unferth. The Usurper was almost irrelevant in a way. A much larger game was afoot, and greater enemies stalked him. But still, Unferth must be defeated first. Everything, even the greatest of tasks, was accomplished one step at a time. Especially the greatest of tasks. And Unferth was linked with these other threats. His power was the greater because of it, and not just because of the magician Horta. He had been confident in the fortress until now, but a battle was being fought and swords and courage and strategy were not the only factors. Magicians, and gods, and men who wanted to be gods were now a part of the game. How could he defeat them all?

He knew the answer. At least, he knew one way to try, one way that he might bring the odds back to something approaching even. Kurik had told him he would need help. The wizard-priest had offered it. Brand had wanted no part of help from a dead man, from a spirit bound to the world in torture and perhaps in lust for revenge, but now ... now he must needs take all the help he could get. If it was not too late. Kurik had warned him that his spirit would not remain in the world for long after his release from the spell that bound him.

It was a task that could not wait, though Brand did not relish it. He stood on shaky legs and dressed. His helm he left behind, but his sword he belted to his waist. Even in a fortress held by his own army it was wise to be prepared. Then he moved silently through the barracks and deeper into the fortress.

He was glad to have the sword, for he felt from early on that someone was following him. He should make his way back to the soldiers while he could and get help. But if he did that, whoever followed him might slip away and remain unknown. It was better to go ahead and see if he could trap them. Knowledge was power, and ignorance death.

He moved ahead. The ways were dark, but he found a torch in a corridor and took it with him. It provided not just light, but would also serve as a weapon.

Down he went, into the depths of the fortress. And his stalker came with him. Whoever it was moved near silently, but not quite silent enough. No one could move silently in such a place of stone and corridors that took sound and threw it around from wall to wall. He made no effort to move quietly himself. Doing so would only serve to warn the person who followed that he was being cautious.

He reached the underground cavern where the body of water lay to his left. There, on the softer ground, he could move silently, and he ran ahead, wedging the torch into some sand and then running back into the shadows. Whoever followed would pause, not wishing to get too close to the light but probably not being able to see that no one held the torch up.

Brand drew his sword and squatted low to the ground. He held the blade behind him so that no flicker of light glimmered from its surface, and he kept his head down. It was the skin of a man's face that often revealed him in the dark, for being paler than his clothes it was more easily seen.

He waited several tense moments, slowing his breathing as much as he could so that he could not be heard. Whoever followed him came forward more quickly than he had guessed. They were sure of themselves to follow so closely, and such confidence spoke of skill. Then again, it could be overconfidence as well.

A shadow moved before him, dark as the perpetual night in this cave. And then it came to a stop. A moment it hesitated, and Brand tensed.

But before he could act, he heard a slow laugh that he knew well.

"Stand up, Brand. I see you there. You would not attack me, would you?"

It was Tinwellen, and Brand was amazed at her courage but also angry at her following him.

He stood and moved toward her. "How did you even see me?"

She laughed softly again, and her hands moved in the dark, perhaps sheathing her knives. "Is it just me you underestimate? Or is it all women? Don't you know that girls see better in the dark than boys?" She hesitated, and then added, "I can show you exactly how well I see in the dark, if you like. That might be fun."

Brand could see the flash of her brilliant smile clearly amid the shadows and his anger evaporated. "Hopefully, I underestimate no one. But why on earth did you follow me? What I do down here could be dangerous."

"Why must I keep telling you this? I have your back."

It was a simple answer, and a powerful one. But she spoke again before he could reply.

"What *are* you doing down here, anyway?" She looked around distastefully at what could be seen of their surroundings.

He told her then all about Kurik, and what had happened here before. And especially about the spirit's offer to help, and why he thought he needed it now.

"You worry too much," was all she said.

"It's my job to worry. If I don't, who will?"

"Things will sort themselves out. You were right to refuse help the first time. Who wants help from a ghost? And how far can you trust him? Better to leave well enough alone. Come back up to the fortress with me and I'll take your mind off all your worries."

He did not doubt that she would do that, and more. But the stakes had grown too high now. He could not turn away an offer for help. Other people would pay for any such mistake as that, and he already had enough on his conscience.

"You go back up. I have business here that I cannot put aside."

She stamped her foot. "I'm not going anywhere, except with you. If you'll not listen to reason, then I guess I'll just have to keep watching your back. Otherwise anything could happen to you down here and no one in the world would know."

That much was true, and not for the first time he wished that he had found Taingern and Shorty before rushing down here.

But all he said though was a simple thank you to Tinwellen. "I appreciate your coming with me. But the night moves on, and I have a feeling that time is running out."

He led her forward then. Deftly, he picked up the torch and then proceeded along the edge of the water into the next chamber.

"This was where he was bound," he whispered to Tinwellen.

She looked around, and her eyes gleamed in the torch light, but she said nothing.

"Kurik!" Brand called. "Can you hear me? I would speak with you again."

He knew there were rites involved with summoning the dead, but he did not know what they were, or want to know. But what he did now was no summoning. Either the spirit of Kurik yet lingered in this world, or it did not. Either it would help, or it would not. Both were beyond his control.

For long moments, nothing changed. Then the dark grew darker, and the shadows thicker. The torch in Brand's hand still burned, but it seemed that its flame gave neither light nor warmth. The smoke coiling from it filled the air, spilling out to cover the floor of the chamber.

The smoke before Brand swirled and eddied. Then it took shape, forming the image of a man. It was Kurik, or the spirit of him at least.

"Hail, Brand of the Duthenor. You have called upon me, as I knew you must."

Brand gave a bow. "Hail, my lord. Your wisdom is greater than mine. You offered help, and I spurned it. Now I see better why it is needed. And, if you are still willing, I will accept it."

Kurik made no answer. It seemed as though he was deep in thought. Perhaps that was so. Or perhaps he saw some vision of the future. But after a moment his head came up and his eyes, dark shadows that they were, blazed.

"My help you have requested. And you shall have it, such as it is. My power is spent, and my time nearly gone.

Yet still I may avail you aid, though it is but the shadow of what once I could have done."

"And what will you do, my lord?"

Kurik gazed at him, and then he turned those shadowy eyes upon Tinwellen. A while he studied her, and she returned his gaze without fear. At that moment Brand was proud of her, for few in her position could have done the same.

The spirit turned again to Brand. "I will do what I can, little though it be. But it is best you don't know what it is. The future is dark and untrodden. A misstep now could put you on the wrong path. I dare not risk that. But remember my warnings from when first we met. Keep them close to your heart, and keep hope also. You will need it."

The spirit of the dead man faded away as a movement of air pulled apart the smoke. It was not reassuring to Brand. He needed help, but what help could be given by a dead person whose ghost was not able to withstand a breeze? Yet still, it did not pay to underestimate anybody.

Tinwellen sniffed. "He seemed a stuffy old man to me. He'll be no help to you at all. And why on earth do you call him lord?"

Brand grinned at her. "I call him lord because it seems to me that he deserves it. As for help, time will tell what form it takes."

She frowned at him. "Why are you smiling?"

"Because you're here. Who else would stare back at the spirit of a dead man and call him stuffy after he was gone? Others would have fled, screaming."

That was the type of thing she seemed to want to hear, for her eyes sparked and her smile dazzled him.

"I told you. I have your back. I'm not going anywhere."

"And I have yours."

They retraced their steps up into the fortress then. All the while Brand considered how lucky he was. His friends had always been few, but they were people of character and strength. None more so than Tinwellen.

19. The Breath of the Dragon

Horta slept, but it was a restless sleep troubled by strange dreams. And then the goddess Su-sarat came to him, and she spoke.

"Wake, Horta."

And he woke, yet still remained in the dream. He was in the desert, in a place that he knew of old as a youth. Here he had hunted and ridden his chariot. In this place he had met his first great love, and here he had lost her also. It was dark, and he could see little, but each ridge and hill, each sweep of arid land and stunted bush, he knew them all, knew where they were in the dark even if he could not see them. And the scent of the desert air at night was like wine that intoxicated him.

The voice of the goddess whispered to him out of that darkness. "Horta, Unferth does not sleep and I cannot enter his mind. But I must learn of his plans. Speak to me."

Horta cast his gaze about. The goddess was nowhere to be seen, yet she was everywhere. Never had one of the gods visited him thus, nor had he heard of something similar from another magician.

"I am your servant, Su-sarat. Ask, and I will obey."

He did not like this. There was no ritual to follow here, no way to know if he was saying or doing the right thing.

Her voice came again out of the night. "Will Unferth attack the fortress, or will he wait?"

"He will attack, Great Mistress. Fear drives him, and his hatred for Brand also. He will attack, and he will throw all that he has against the enemy."

The night was still, thoughtful almost. "And his army is great? It will succeed?"

"How can it not?"

The goddess did not answer that. But she did speak again.

"And how long before Unferth reaches the fortress?"

"Soon, O Holy One. It will be soon. If not tomorrow, then the day after."

To this, she offered no answer, but her presence remained all around him. The air throbbed with it. So he risked voicing a question of his own.

"Has Brand fallen into your thrall yet?"

The brooding air about him tensed, and he guessed his mistake. Maybe. He should have given her one of her titles. The gods liked them.

"He resists me, even though he does not know why he does so. It is … desirable. Yet I shall have him in the end and that end is close. I am nearly there."

"Who are you in his group, O Dancer in the Night?" He gave her the title the lore said she liked most. But the lore was not always right.

"It does not matter," she answered. "I could be anyone, and my influence is hidden. That is all you need to know, magician."

He pondered that answer. The word *magician* had been a rebuke. It was meant to put him in his place, and he knew it. His role was one of servant and not questioner.

"I am blessed, O Queen of Secrets," he intoned, "to hear your words. Your will is supreme, your desires will come to fruition. You are a god, and the world orders itself to your thought. I am but a humble servant, and I would draw on your wisdom if I may?"

"Sweet are your words, Horta. Even if they are flattery. But you have earned something at least from me. Ask, and I will give answer."

Horta bowed. But he spoke swiftly. When a god gave permission to do something, it was best to take them up on it straightaway.

"Gormengil, heir to the throne, is a man of immense ambition. I believe he will attempt to displace Unferth. This could be disastrous at the moment, but I fear he may act despite my urgings not to."

"And your question, Horta?"

"Simply this. Should I kill him?"

The presence around him stirred, as though in thought.

"You would already have killed him, had that been best. You keep him alive, because in the future he is one who would serve Char-harash better than Unferth."

She made it a statement, rather than a question.

"That is exactly so, O Holy One."

The night deepened around him. He sensed doubt, fleeting but present. Then it was masked. He hoped the goddess had not realized he sensed it, for that might be his own death. But it troubled him that there should be any doubt at all. The gods were always sure of themselves.

"This Gormengil feels it," she said at last. "The breath of the dragon blows over the land. Change lurks in every shadow. Possibility stirs everywhere, and none know for sure what will be. But in the end, who cares if it is Unferth who bows before the gods returned, or Gormengil? Kill him, or help him. It matters not to me."

Horta was surprised. That she cared nothing for Unferth or Gormengil was irrelevant, but that she had spoken of the gods returning rather than just Char-harash ascending to godhood, that was something that he had not considered. Yet the gods derived their power in no small part from those who worshipped them. If Char-harash was resurrected, if he led armies over the land as he would no doubt do, then the ways of the Kar-ahn-hetep would spread everywhere. And so too their gods. All of them.

"Did you not know?" the goddess whispered from the night. "You seek to raise one god, but with him shall come the others. The old ways are returning. The old battles will be new again."

And then her presence faded and she was gone. Horta continued to contemplate what she had revealed though. It was more, much more than he had anticipated. If the old gods returned, there would be catastrophic war among them as there was of old. It would wreak destruction across all the world. But he had proceeded thus far, and he could not turn back now.

20. Blade and Hilt

Brand was tired, for he had gotten little sleep the night before. But excitement banished his lethargy.

All morning he had watched from the courtyard as new recruits entered the fortress. Often, he spoke with them, or their leaders. He learned where they were from and what part of the Duthgar was home to them. He listened to their changing accents, for even in such a relatively small land there were changes, especially between the eastern and western districts. To the west were other tribes. The Callenor was one, closely associated with the Duthenor through a long history, but there were others.

And it was to his surprise that one group of soldiers, only twenty strong, were from one of these tribes. He heard them talking as they came in, and he knew those accents though he had not heard them since his childhood. They were men of the Norvinor tribe.

They looked skilled warriors. In appearance, they were slightly shorter than the men of the Duthenor usually were, and their hair was black. They wore chain mail that was longer than common, coming down to their knees nearly, and their swords were of a larger kind. They looked grim men, and proud, yet they sang as they marched and there was something jaunty about them despite their appearance. There was curiosity in their eyes too, for they would not have seen a fortress such as this, nor, maybe, even heard the rumors about it.

Brand went over to meet them, and they ceased to sing. Before he could introduce himself, their leader bowed. "Hail, Brand, rightful chieftain of the Duthenor."

Brand was surprised. "You know me?"

The man grinned. "No, but even in our land the legendary Helm of the Duthenor is spoken of in stories. We knew it for what it was the moment we saw you."

Brand wore it so often now that he often forgot it was even there. The man continued. "Bruidiger, I'm called. And I lead these men to your service."

Brand thrust out his hand, and Bruidiger took it in the warrior's grip, wrist to wrist.

"I thank you and your men for your service. But I have to say I'm surprised to see any Norvinor warriors here. You're far from home, and this isn't your battle."

Bruidiger shrugged. "Both of those things are true, and it's only chance that brings us here. We were hired by a merchant to guard his caravan as he came through our lands, and we saw him safely to your own, for he heads through them to Cardoroth. But then we heard what was happening here, and we lingered, intrigued. Then we heard you had returned, and there was friendship once between your father and mine. So I came to help, and my men came to help me."

Brand remembered his father speaking well of the Norvinor, but he had not known he had a friend among them. It was interesting, and he wished to talk to Bruidiger further, but this was not the time nor place.

"If it pleases you, later I'd like to have a good talk. But for now, you and your men must be tired. There'll be a man at the barracks to find you a place to rest and get you a meal. But I'll find you this evening, if I get a chance."

Bruidiger bowed again. Brand signaled one of his own men over, and he led the small band away. He wished he had a thousand more of them, for they had the look of hard warriors about them, men who had seen a fight or two and come out the other side victorious.

A little while later another group came through, and this one was several hundred strong. They were from the south of the Duthgar, lands near to the High Way and down into a valley famous for the quality of its cheese. Brand had been there once, and he spoke highly of their home, and they liked that he did. But they gave him sobering news in return. Unferth was close behind them. There would be no more warriors entering the fortress after them.

Brand sent word for all the captains of the army to come out into the courtyard, and there he addressed them when they had gathered.

"Men," he said. "War approaches on swift feet. Soon this fortress will be tested, our strategies probed and the thoroughness of our training examined. But this I know. The fortress is strong, and the hearts of those who defend it beat with courage."

Some of the men cheered. Some looked scared. But most tried to show nothing of what they felt, either way.

"But will we win?" called out one of the captains.

Brand wished he was better at delivering speeches. He always seemed to get this question, but he did not mind. And as always, he gave a truthful answer. Men who risked their lives deserved it.

"I think that we will, else I'd not have come here. But there are no guarantees in life. Victory is not assured. Not for us, but neither is it for Unferth. It will be earned, and the payment will be dealt out in blood and death. That is the truth." He paused, before going on. "And this also is the truth. We have no choice. A fight is coming, and men will die. I could have led Unferth a merry chase around the Duthgar. But I've chosen this place to make a stand. And I stand with you, ready to pay the same price of blood or death that you all are. But if there are any who have changed their minds, I give you leave to go now, freely and without hinderance. I'll have no man here against his will."

He normally offered soldiers a choice like that. It was fair, and it was true too. Better to have only warriors who believed in the cause and a chance of winning. But it was a double-edged sword. If too many took him up on the offer, morale would plummet.

There was silence. No one moved. That too was normal, but he knew by offering them the chance to leave he played on their pride and they were more likely to stay. He was a general, and it was his job to think like that, but he did not like it.

He spoke again to the men, this time infusing his voice with greater passion. He was no speechmaker, but he knew this was the time to rally them to a state of excitement. He had told them death was possible. He had given them the chance to leave. But they were still here, and this was now the time to offer them hope and heat their blood.

"This army started small. It was just a band of a few men. Back then, I called us the point of a sword. But I said it would grow, and it has. Now we have the blade, and edges, and a hilt and pommel. Now, we are complete. Now, we will smite Unferth and free the Duthgar!"

The captains cheered. All of them this time. But Brand could not help wonder how many would die soon. They were a sword in themselves, but Unferth had his own sword. The walls of the fortress would run with blood, and he had made them feel good about it. And he would do worse, yet.

"Captains!" he cried out into the noise, and it subsided. "Tell your men what I have told you. Tell them victory is at hand. The sooner Unferth arrives, the sooner will that victory come!"

The captains cheered again, and then they went back to the barracks talking boisterously. A small group remained, and he saw that this was made up of his friends. Taingern and Shorty glanced at him, and he read approval in their looks. He had done what was necessary. Tinwellen scrutinized him as though she was assessing the value of a gold ring. He did not care much for that gaze, but then she smiled at him and his heart lightened.

But it was Sighern's gaze that troubled him. The boy looked at him with dark eyes. There was almost hostility there.

21. Duels are for the Reckless

The next day dawned to a gray day. Fog marched down the ridges near the fortress, veiling the pine-clad slopes that Brand liked. There were no green trees to be seen, nor a blue sky. And though Brand loved mists and fog and rain also, he did not like this concealing blanket.

As the morning passed, the fogs thinned and drifted away. Yet the sky remained dull and overcast. Rain was coming, and perhaps a storm with it. The air was heavy and oppressive.

But with the parting of the fog came another sight, and it was not the marching of pines up steep-sided ridges that drew his eye, but the marching of soldiers. Unferth had arrived, and his army with him. And though Brand searched among the masses for sign of Horta, he was not visible. Yet still Brand knew he was there. The fog was of his making. It reeked of sorcery and had worked to conceal the coming of the enemy.

Unferth may have thought it a good thing to approach so. But it made no difference. Everyone in the fortress knew they were coming. The last men to join Brand's army had brought word, and his own scouts had been watching them for some time.

Brand stood atop the battlement, the gate tower just to his left. From it the Dragon Banner of the Duthenor hung limply. But that it was present at all would anger Unferth. He would have no liking for what it represented, and its very existence reminded one and all that he had usurped the rule of the Duthgar.

From where he waited, Brand had a clear view of all that transpired, but he kept his eye also on the men lining the ramparts all around. They were quiet and grim, but he saw no panic there. Nor should there be. Unferth's army was bigger, but the men here had grown used to the walls and their advantages. They had discovered by their own training how vulnerable an attacker was who sought to scale it.

Unferth came into sight. He was too far away to recognize by his features, and Brand had last seen him a long, long time ago. But there was no mistaking the armor he wore, for in its way it was as famed as the sword Brand himself carried and the Helm of the Duthenor on his own head.

The helm and armor of Unferth gleamed red as blood, and a shiver went up his spine. Then he smiled to himself. That, of course, was the intention of the color. It could as easily be black, or green or some other hue. But it was red to produce fear in the enemy, to remind them that they might bleed. It also served to highlight the wearer so that his men knew where he was at all times. That could be both a good and a bad thing. Much depended on the leader.

Unferth would be tested here. Would he lead from the front? Would he fight with his men and prove his courage to the warriors he led? If he did, he might die. If he did not, they would not so willingly follow him. It was a hard choice, and one that Brand had made many times. He did not think Unferth had ever been in that position. He was rumored to be a skilled fighter, but he had been involved in skirmishes only and never a war.

Brand knew he would fight. It was his way, but also circumstances dictated it. Unferth was in a more difficult position. The risk of scaling the battlement was great, and retreat was difficult. Not so atop the walls. Brand could fight up here himself, and then step back to let men take his place. All battles were fought in the mind as well as with weapons. Unferth's red armor was a tactic. Brand fighting himself was another. No one could expect a besieging general to scale the walls, but when the enemy leader fought with his own men it would make Unferth look the worse for not doing so.

Even as Brand watched, Unferth came forward out of his host with a small group of men. The warrior beside him held high on a pole the banner of the chieftains of the Callenor. The cloth was snowy white, and upon it was the image of the black talon of a raven.

The Raven Banner infuriated Brand. Who was this man who dared bring it here to Duthenor lands? But that it angered him also worried him. He must be above that. A general must not succumb to such things, but rather be cool and level-headed at all times.

Unferth would not be expected to come to battle without his banner. But that went two ways. Brand gestured to Sighern. "Retrieve our own banner and bring it here, close to me."

The young man moved away and Shorty grunted. "It seems that Unferth wants to parley. And what's going on with his armor? It looks like he's been rolling around in raspberries."

"So it does. But legend says it's dwarven-made. The color is unusual, but it's not lacking in quality. Nor his helm or axe."

"I think it's cute," Tinwellen offered.

Brand had to laugh at that. "Please tell him so when he gets here. No words could be more insulting to him."

"But you'll try to find some anyway?" Taingern asked.

"Of course. If I can upset him, he'll be more likely to make a mistake."

They did not have to wait much longer. Sighern returned, holding aloft the Dragon Banner even as the Raven Banner drew close below and Unferth stood before the wall.

Brand did not wait for the other man to speak. "Hail, Unferth, chieftain of the Callenor, usurper of the Duthgar and murderer. State your business."

The cold voice of Unferth came in reply. If the greeting had bothered him, he gave no sign of it.

"Hail, Brand, outlaw and bandit. You know my business here. It is to bring you to justice for crimes against the Duthgar. You have brought unruly war to the land, and you will be punished."

Brand slowly drew his Halathrin-wrought blade. "By this sword, and the helm I wear, and most of all by the name you have given me, I declare myself the rightful heir to the chieftainship of the Duthenor. Do you deny who I am, or my rights and responsibilities?"

"I deny nothing. I recognize your heritage, and for the proud lineage that is yours I will not hang you as a common criminal. But I am king here now, and your heritage is of no matter. Come down and surrender, and I will show you mercy. Fight, and I will see every man here dead. Either by sword in battle, or hanged as criminals if they surrender too late."

Brand could hardly believe it. Unferth was an idiot. It went against all the stratagems of war to suggest that surrendered soldiers would still be executed. It meant that once the fight began, there was only one way to live, and that was through victory. Without surrender as an option, his army would fight harder, and to the very last. Men with their backs to the wall were the hardest opponent of all to beat.

"You will have to take this fortress first, Unferth, to make good your threat. And that you cannot do."

A silence settled between them, cold as ice. But Brand was not done. He spoke into it, his voice even colder and thick with contempt.

"And you name yourself a king? Nay. You are no king. I once served a true king, and you are not his equal. You are a fool wearing a crown of straw."

Even as he spoke, Tinwellen whispered into his ear. "Don't go too far, Brand. There's a chance to make peace here, or he wouldn't have come to speak with you. Thousands will die for your pride if you don't make the attempt."

The weight of her words carried force. There was a truth to them that he could not deny, yet at the same time he felt the futility of it all. War was inevitable, because Unferth would never renounce his rule of the Duthgar, and he himself could not let the murder of his parents go unavenged.

But even so, he heeded Tinwellen, though it was not in the way she intended.

"Unferth!" he called. "At heart, this battle is between us, and us alone. Men will die here, by their hundreds or even thousands. But you and I can stop that. I will come down and fight you, man to man. Let that be an end to our hostility. Let that decide who rules the Duthgar."

Unferth did not answer at once, and the longer he waited the better pleased Brand was. His opponent had not dismissed the challenge out of hand, and the longer he delayed answer the more credence it had. Those who followed him would know he had considered the matter before saying no, if he did so, and they would wonder if it was a lack of courage that informed his decision rather than strategy.

At length, the usurper gave reply. "I am a king, Brand. Duels are for the reckless. I do not gamble the fate of my realm on a battle between two men. Surrender, and I will spare your supports. Fight, and I will kill you all. Choose!"

Sighern shook the Dragon Banner, and he hissed in Brand's ear. "The men who follow you won't ever surrender. They don't just fight for you, but for their own freedom. Send Unferth to hell, and his army with him."

Tinwellen looked at the young man, fury in her eyes. He returned her gaze with cold contempt.

Brand was about to answer Unferth when Hruidgar also whispered into his ear. The hunter had been the last scout to return into the fortress and give Brand news of the approaching enemy.

"Patience, Brand. Stall for time. No more Duthenor can enter the fortress, but that doesn't mean a small army isn't gathering somewhere behind Unferth. Stall, and let time work to your favor. If that happens, we can crush him."

Seldom in his life had Brand ever been indecisive. It seemed to him that all the advice given to him was good, and yet it was all contradictory. How was he to decide?

"Well?" Unferth called up. "What's it to be?"

Brand sheathed his sword, and then leaned forward over the rampart to answer.

"Attack if you dare, Unferth. You'll spill the blood of your men in vain."

The usurper did not seem displeased. "You are proud now, Brand. But when every last one of your men lies dead around you as proof of your folly, I will have you brought to me alive. And then you will kneel at my feet and name me lord. Only then, when you have drunk deep of the dregs of woe, shall I kill you."

Unferth swung away, and he departed with the men he had brought. The Raven Banner hung limply in the oppressive air, and the threat he had voiced hung in it also, more ominous even than the banner of an enemy nation in the Duthgar.

22. Battle and Blood

Brand watched silently as the enemy made ready, nor did anyone else speak.

Unferth's army had come prepared. The front ranks moved forward, burdened by hundreds of coiled ropes with grappling hooks tied to their ends. Ladders had been made also. These, as with all the equipment, had a makeshift appearance. All would have been made hurriedly by men who had not observed such equipment in use. None of the Duthenor or Callenor had attacked a fortress before. Not that they were inferior warriors, just that their lords built no fortresses. They were a small people, Duthenor and Callenor alike, and they had no need of fortified strongholds. That might change after this.

The enemy drew closer, plainly visible now. The last trailers of fog had gone. Brand watched them closely, assessing their discipline and how they were organized and how quickly they responded to orders. What he saw was what he expected. They were no match for a professional army of full-time soldiers, but they were not that far behind. The same could be said of his own force, only he had begun to train them well and they had an edge.

Unferth's numbers were more worrisome. Five thousand men marched beneath the shadow of the Raven Banner. It was not a king's army – it was a chieftain's army. Even so, it outnumbered his. Five thousand were set against three. The walls helped there, and Unferth was not the general Brand knew that he was himself. But though the fortress helped in many ways, in that respect it was a partial hindrance. Out in the field Brand's superior skill and experience would show. But the walls reduced tactical choices, and that stole some of his advantage. No matter. War was like that. It took and it gave, it surprised and it ran to expected courses. It was set in its ways and fickle. It was a gamble, and the commander who gambled least had the most chance of winning.

It became clear that Unferth intended a frontal assault. He was not going to try to surround the entire fortress and attack it all at once. Rather, he was going to concentrate on the wall that housed the gate. This was the weakest point, and the tactic made some sense. Other commanders may have acted differently, but Brand did not mind. He was prepared for such eventualities, and every tactic had advantages and disadvantages. This, he considered, worked to his advantage. Unferth felt the gate to be a weakness, but Brand knew it was well repaired and highly protected. The enemy would discover so to their cost.

Horns sounded. Signals were given. A mass of the enemy separated from the main host and began to march forward. As they closed on the fortress, they gathered pace. Finally, they ran with their shields above their heads to protect themselves from the rain of death they feared would come from above.

And that rain fell. Arrows were shot first, the hiss of them as they thickened the air was loud and frightening. Nor could men run, hold up a shield and also carry ladders and ropes well. Especially without training and practice. Arrows struck home, finding gaps and weaknesses. Men died, falling to the ground to lie still. Others jerked and spasmed. All were trampled by those who followed.

Then fell the javelins. These killed fewer, but still wounded many. Again, the wounded were trampled, though some managed to turn their backs to flee. Arrows killed many of these also.

The survivors reached the wall. Faces were visible now. Men with frightened eyes looked up. The wall seemed tall to them, the chances of reaching the top meagre. And when they did, swords still awaited them. Surely, there was no harder task in warfare than what they faced now, and the knowledge of it must have been bitter. So too their curses for Unferth, who had brought them to this.

But the men were brave. Callenor tribesmen may have been the enemy, but Brand admired their courage. They cast up their grappling hooks and pressed their ladders against the wall, and they scrambled up. Speed meant less time to be shot at. Reaching the top of the wall meant a chance to fight, sword to sword and man to man. And if enough of them did so, they might win the rampart and live. So they came on, desperately.

They were met with dropped rocks, many the size of a man's head. Helms were little defense against this. Shields offered better protection, but it was awkward to hold one and climb at the same time. Even doing so, many men were dislodged to plummet, screaming, to death below.

And yet the enemy came on, driven by a need to reach the top for a chance at survival and supported by their large numbers. It seemed that their attempts to do so were futile, but those who lived climbed with speed and those above who cast missiles must make space for the men who hacked away at scaling ropes and dislodged ladders with poles.

Brand watched, hearing the sounds of battle that he hated, seeing men's heads cracked open like melons or bodies broken in death below. He felt triumph at the difficulty the enemy had in even reaching their opponent, and he felt gut-wrenchingly sick at the terrible deaths meted out. He watched, and he heard, and he wished it to keep going and to stop all at once. It was war, and he had done this before, and if he lived, must needs likely do it again.

A warrior hacked away at the rope that held a grappling hook nearby. He used a large knife, and severed the fibers quickly. Men fell screaming below, and their deaths were a costly error on Unferth's head. The ropes had not been twined with wire at the end to make the severing more difficult.

Quickly the warrior bent and picked up the metal grappling hook. For a moment it looked as though he was about to cast it down at the enemy, and then he remembered his training. Instead, he threw it to the rear of the battlement. It was one grappling hook the enemy would not have for their next attack. It was metal that could be repurposed into arrow and spear heads.

But despite the appalling slaughter, the weight of numbers and desperation of the enemy carried through. They began to reach the top, and the clash of sword against sword rang in the air. This gave encouragement to those below, and they swarmed up in a wave.

The enemy surged through the crenels first, where the gap in the battlement allowed archers to shoot. Then they clambered over the merlons next, which gave protection to the archers. This was the more dangerous, for from that greater height they could leap into the defenders, and this they did with swinging swords and wild cries.

Most died. The swords of the defenders flashed in answer. Their own battle cries rose up. But in killing these men others were given opportunity to clear the wall and fight man to man.

A warrior thrust his sword at Brand. With a neat twist of his own blade, Brand deflected the point and sent a riposte back that tore away the warrior's throat. Sighern knocked the blade from the warrior's now weak grip and thrust him back against the battlement. A moment he staggered there, blood coursing from his throat, and then Sighern toppled him over the edge. He screamed, blood spraying from his mouth. A thump and more screams followed as he dislodged other attackers from rope or ladder.

To Brand's left, another warrior broke through, but Tinwellen was there before him, a knife in each hand and both flashing. The man died before her swift onslaught, and she pulled a bloody knife from the eye-slit of his helm and kicked him away.

All over the battlement the same was happening. If the enemy broke through a little more, the battle would be won. If Brand's men kept them at bay, the numbers of those climbing must diminish, and the defenders would hold. It hung in the balance, and Brand fought with a cold fire in his belly. More attackers came over the wall, more died at his hand and the hands of others.

There was a momentary lull. No new grappling hooks were thrown up, at least not where Brand stood near the gate, and he leaned through a crenel to look out at the enemy. They still came up the wall like spiders. In the distance, Unferth stood out in his red armor, arms waving and seeming to bellow instructions. He was sending a new wave of attackers.

The lull did not last long. In moments more warriors confronted Brand. They swarmed over the ramparts, screaming and slashing with their swords. Brand fought back, his blade cutting gleaming arcs through the air. Blood sprayed his face. Blood slicked the stone beneath his boots and made footing unsteady. On it went, and then out of nowhere a bright light flashed, dazzling his eyes.

He staggered back, killing the enemy who followed him by instinct alone and not by sight, for he could barely see.

Then Char-harash was there, his eyes blazing and a wicked sword flashing for Brand's throat.

Brand weaved to the side, and used his own blade to deflect his enemy's attack, but his blade struck nothing. Too late he realized this was in his mind, that some sorcery had planted the image there. He felt the mind of Char-harash nearby, and his own magic came to life pushing the presence of the sorcerer away.

It took only moments, but the distraction had its effect. Brand's attention had been taken from the real attackers that came for him, and a mighty blow from an axe crashed against the Helm of the Duthenor. Sparks flew into the air, and Brand staggered, dropping his sword.

Death was upon him. But Sighern was there, his sword killing the axe-man, and then Shorty and Taingern came to his side, their blades flashing and their eyes burning with a cold light. The enemy was repelled, but Brand felt his knees give way and he tumbled to the ground beside his sword. Darkness swamped him, and he knew no more.

His mind swam through the blackness, and everything was vague and unformed. Then slowly it seemed that he rose up. There was light again, and he knew who he was and where. His eyes flickered open.

He was not sure how much time had passed. Moments? Hours? It did not feel like it had been a great length of time. He was on the ground, his head in Tinwellen's lap. She was caressing his face. Nearby was Sighern, a bloodied cloth at his neck, wet with blood. He had killed the axe-man, but not without cost. The axe-man must have returned a near killing blow before he died.

Brand was not sure if he had not seen these things after the blow to his head, or if he just could not remember. And the dull throbbing in his head did not help, nor the sharp pain in his neck where muscles and tissues must have been torn or twisted by the mighty blow.

The Helm of the Duthenor lay nearby. It was unmarked and undented. The Halathrin wrought things well, with the skills immortality and magic lent them. It had saved his life.

A great cheer went up along the ramparts, and Brand tried to stand. A roaring pain filled his head and he fell back down, Tinwellen cradling him.

"What's happening?" he asked.

Taingern seemed to come from nowhere, and he knelt down with concern showing in his eyes.

"We've repulsed the enemy. And we don't think they'll come again today. They had thought to take us in one great rush, but that failed, and they've learned what it's like to attack a fortress. No, they'll not come again today. Their losses are great in equipment, men and morale. Unferth must be chewing his own tongue right about now."

Brand wanted to answer, but the blackness was coming up to swamp him again.

23. Gormengil

Night fell, but the mood of the camp had long since been dark. Men muttered under their breaths. Treason was in the air. Not just of Gormengil, but in the heart of every warrior. Unferth had been confident of swift victory. He had promised it. But the attack had been a slaughter.

Horta could not say he was overly surprised. Always Brand did the unexpected, but never anything without reason. If he chose to fight behind walls, he did so because it gave him an advantage. His every move was dangerous, but Su-sarat should have him in thrall by now. Or perhaps he was even dead. Men had claimed he had been struck a killing blow by an axe.

Warriors eyed Horta coldly as he walked through the camp. Unferth had summoned him, and the messenger looked frightened. Everyone looked frightened. There was a dangerous feel to the air, and a sense that the world was shifting. So be it. But Unferth was right to call another war council. He would have to be open to ideas now, and a new plan would be developed. They still had the greater number of soldiers, and the enemy must fall, especially with a better-planned attack.

He came to Unferth's tent, but tonight a fire was set before it and the king's men sat outside. He was the last to reach it, and the others had been waiting.

A thin drizzle of rain began to fall. It had been coming and going these last few hours, but still the stars could be seen at whiles through breaks in the scudding clouds. But his knee ached, and he knew heavier rain was approaching.

Horta took a place near the fire, turning his knee toward the heat. No one greeted him, and he offered none himself. Only Gormengil glanced at him, his eyes as unreadable as ever. But the man looked away swiftly, and Horta felt the stirrings of unease. At that moment, Unferth pulled aside the tent flap and exited his tent. He remained dressed in full armor, and the raven axe was in his hand. He intended to remind people of his authority tonight. It would not be pleasant.

Unferth did not take a seat. He stood to address them. "We gave Brand a bloody nose today. It may even be that he is dead. But tomorrow, we will take the fortress. Even as we speak, men are working, and will continue to work through the night, to make new grappling ropes and ladders. Tomorrow, the enemy will fall. Count on it."

It was a confident speech. But he had spoken like that before. Horta glanced around him, assessing the mood of the men. Had Unferth done the same, he would not have spoken as he had. The men were in no mood for false confidence and bravado. Too many had died today, and too greatly had they underestimated Brand and overestimated their ability to take a fortress. Unferth was responsible for that, only he was not accepting it. Where he should have been asking for advice, he was saying the same things he had been for days, and his men knew it for incompetence now.

No one answered him. Even Gormengil remained silent, staring at the ground as though no sight was more interesting.

"Well?" Unferth said. "Does no one here have a voice? I expect enthusiasm from those I lead. And I expect them to impart that same confidence to the army. That's your job as leaders."

"We were beaten today," Gormengil answered. He had raised his gaze from the dirt and there was shame in his eyes. "We were beaten, and we should not have been. Had we—"

"Enough!" roared Unferth. "I expect better from you. I expect better from all my captains. You must learn to be resilient. What use are you if you fall apart at the slightest setback?"

Horta could see that Gormengil struggled to maintain his mask of detachment. Emotions chased themselves over his face. Anger, resentment, disbelief and then finally determination.

"The fault is not ours," he said softly. "Almost, we had the enemy. Almost. But they rallied. Brand fought on the wall, and his men fought with him. But you? You stayed back from the bloodshed. Had you gone forward in the battle and given encouragement, had you climbed the wall yourself we would have overrun them. But you did not see the moment that you should have done so. Or you did, and you were too cowardly to act."

Unferth went pale. "You dare to—"

"I dare because it's true." Gormengil spoke in a steady voice, void of emotion.

The king gripped the haft of his axe tightly. "You're dismissed, Gormengil. Not just from this meeting. Leave. Flee! I exile you from the realm, and your life is forfeit if ever I see you again."

Gormengil slowly shook his head. "I don't think so. You're not fit to lead us. You're a coward and incompetent. I challenge you under our ancient laws. It is my right, as heir."

"You're no longer heir!"

"I am, and I challenge you to a fight, as the law permits, for the leadership of the Callenor tribe."

Horta studied the men gathered there, and he saw that Unferth did also. No one met his gaze. They would not intervene, for they saw Gormengil as someone who might lead them to victory and Unferth as someone who had led them to disaster.

It was for this reason that Horta had hurried after the king, to stop such a challenge. He *must* stop it, or at least he had thought so. But now? Now, he felt the dragon's breath blow across the land. Destiny was in the air. He would not intervene.

Unferth grunted in disgust. He must know that he had lost the support of the men, but he knew also that if he killed Gormengil he would remove any real alternative to leadership. And the armor of his forefathers gave him confidence. As well it might. Horta sensed the magic in it, though it was of a kind unfamiliar to him. And though Unferth had a tendency to cowardice, he now had his back to the wall. He would fight, and he might well win.

"Come and die then, boy," Unferth said. He moved away a little from the men to give himself room to move. He would need it, for wicked as the axe looked it was an unwieldy weapon.

Gormengil joined him. His sword hissed from his scabbard, and the cold gaze of his eyes was even more remote than normal. A block of ice gave off more emotion.

But Horta knew it was there. And often those who showed the least emotion were those who felt it the strongest.

Unferth struck first. The raven-axe flew through the air, and it whistled as it did so by some art of its makers. It was a lightning strike, and Horta was confounded. How had Unferth moved so quickly?

Gormengil darted nimbly to the side, but even so, he only barely avoided one of the blades of the axe that would have severed his head from his body in a single stroke.

If the whistling of the axe surprised him, he did not show it. Perhaps the Callenor knew that as one of its properties.

The king kept moving. His first stroke had missed, and now he was vulnerable because the weight of the axe meant it could not be returned to a guard position nor could a follow-up blow be delivered quickly. Yet Unferth surprised Horta again.

Either by great strength or a lightness to the axe that Horta could hardly credit, the blades twisted in midflight and swept back in a reverse cut.

For all his speed and nimbleness, Gormengil was caught out. He was moving in to drive his own blade forward in a killing thrust when the axe bore down on him again.

There was no time to retreat. The axe was angling downward, so he could not duck. Instead, he jerked his blade toward the axe where the head met the haft. There it caught it, deflecting the blow but not stopping it.

One of the blades of the axe sliced down into the heir's side. Gormengil staggered away, fortunate to only receive a glancing blow. Yet still his chain mail vest was rent there, frayed as easily as rope by a knife.

Even so, Gormengil showed nothing of the pain or emotion he felt. He was like a wall of stone, immoveable, and Horta admired him for it. Unferth, however, grinned, and he swung the axe leisurely before him in slow circles.

"Your pride has killed you," the king taunted. "You're no match for me."

Gormengil did not answer. He merely gazed at his opponent with dark eyes, and his lack of fear or reaction seemed to enrage Unferth. The king leapt forward again, his axe hurtling, and this time it did not whistle but moaned. It was an underhanded cut, unexpected and swift.

But Gormengil seemed to have anticipated it, for he stepped a little to the side with time to spare and his sword crashed into the dwarven helm.

This time, it was the king who staggered back. Gormengil was upon him, his blade flashing in cuts and thrusts quicker than the eye could follow. Three times Unferth would have died save for the quality of armor he wore, but Gormengil made one strike too many and overbalanced slightly in his haste. Unferth saw his opportunity and the raven-axe moaned again, this time thrust forward so that the spike at the head of the blades could pierce armor and then hook out entrails.

The heir to the throne dived and rolled. He avoided the thrust but a follow-up slash caught him a glancing blow to his helmet. But this time he did not retreat. He stepped in close, avoiding the sweeping danger of the axe and drove a knife deep into the king's thigh, then leapt back, the blood-wetted knife in one hand and his sword in the other.

Unferth screamed. It was not a fatal wound, but he would weaken swiftly and lose strength in his legs if it was not bandaged. The raven-axe flew once more, whistling even as Unferth screamed, and it cut the air like a streaking shadow.

But this time Gormengil was quicker. Perhaps he had held back before. Or perhaps the sight of Unferth's blood gave him hope of victory and purpose. Either way he stepped in to meet the attack. The axe whistled, but Gormengil's sword sliced, and it severed the king's hand in one blow above the black gauntlet.

The axe thudded to the ground. Unferth's severed hand fell silently, looking out of place on the grass. Blood spurted from the stump, and the king, wide-eyed, looked in shock at his own gauntleted hand as it lay before him.

Unferth fell to his knees. He screamed again, a terrible sound to hear, but Gormengil was deaf to it. Slowly, step by step he approached, his sword steady before him.

The heir to the throne, he who now would rule, struck swiftly at his uncle. His blade flashed, cutting between the bottom of the helm and the top of the chain mail coat, and it found the small gap there.

Unferth toppled over and stopped screaming, but Horta was not sure if he was dead. Gormengil reached down though, one hand dislodging the helm and with the blade in the other he began to hack.

After some moments, he held up the head of Unferth. "He was a fool, and look where it got him?" He cast the head aside. "I am not a fool. I will lead you better."

No one said anything. The men were stunned, but Horta knew instinctively what to do and acted quickly. He stepped over to the fallen raven-axe and picked it up. He marveled at the feel of it in his hands and the lightness of it. Of what metal the blades were made, he did not know. Yet still he felt the deadliness of the weapon. Nor could he see any nick or blemish on the metal, which there should have been.

He approached Gormengil. "Hail, Gormengil, king by blood, and by right, and by victory in battle. Take your axe, and if you will have it, my service also." He bowed slightly, and lifted up the weapon.

Gormengil wrapped a hand around the axe haft, and Horta saw his eyes widen a fraction when he took it. He, too, marveled at the lightness of it.

"Truly," Gormengil muttered. "It is a weapon of magic." His gaze fell on Horta, and his eyes were emotionless again. "I will accept your service." There may have been no emotion there, but there *was* a glint of knowledge. He understood that Horta had just set the tone of how to react, and Unferth's counselors all approached. One by one they knelt and swore their oaths of loyalty.

When they were done, Gormengil spoke. "Go forth among the men. Tell them that the Callenor have a new chieftain, and this one is not so craven as not to fight himself." Then he hefted the axe wickedly through the air, making it whistle and moan.

24. Two Battles

Brand woke. It was dark, save for the wavery light of a single candle. There was a roaring in his head, and a dull ache, but a soft hand touched his forehead, and Tinwellen's voice came to him, suddenly clear above the roaring. "Sleep," she commanded. And Brand slept.

When he woke again, the light of the candle was gone and the gray of dawn filled the room he had in the barracks. Of Tinwellen, there was no sign, but Shorty and Taingern were there, their faces grim.

"What news?" Brand asked.

"First," Taingern said, "how do you feel?"

Brand was not sure. The roaring in his head had lessened, but not gone. And the dull ache had receded, but not entirely. And there was a stiffness in his shoulder and neck that troubled him.

"Given that I could be dead, I feel well enough."

Shorty grunted. "Make light of it if you will, but it was a bad blow you took. Or that the Helm of the Duthenor took. A crown it might be to the Duthenor, but the skill of the Halathrin who made it saved your life."

Brand knew that was true. But his two friends had not come here to tell him so. Something had happened, otherwise at least one of them would be on the battlements.

A look passed between the two of them, and he knew they judged him well enough to hear it, whatever it was.

"There's good news ... and strange news," Taingern said. "First, and obviously, we repulsed the enemy yesterday. They did not attack again."

Brand nodded, and wished he had not. A wave of dizziness rolled over him.

"And the strange news?"

"Well, that's possibly tied to the first. Their losses were heavy yesterday, and it seems that Unferth paid the price for it. Just now, as it began to grow light, we saw the enemy had put his head on a pole just before the gate. Obviously, they have a new leader."

Brand was shocked. All his life it seemed had been wrapped up in the idea of deposing Unferth and avenging his parents. And now … the man was dead. It seemed that he no longer had direction or purpose. But there was an element of relief too. Vengeance was a heavy burden.

He closed his eyes and thought briefly of his parents. Justice had been done at last, and though it was not by his hand, it did not matter. It *was* because of him though, because if he had not pressed Unferth and made him suffer military losses, the usurper would not have been deposed. More importantly, whatever he had done in the past, whatever he did now, it was for the benefit of the Duthgar. That was the one thing that must guide him.

Brand opened his eyes. "Do we know who leads the enemy now?"

Shorty shook his head. "We know Unferth had an heir. The men say he's called Gormengil, and he's Unferth's nephew. Whether he's now in charge though, we don't know. But the enemy has certainly not left."

Brand considered that. A new leader could change everything, but it probably would not. Whoever had deposed Unferth was not likely to free the Duthgar and return to Callenor lands.

But whatever happened, he was needed now on the ramparts.

"Help me up, lads. I'm a bit wobbly."

They looked at him carefully but did not argue. Not even when he had to lean on them just to stand. But after a little while the roaring in his head subsided again and the dizziness passed. Mostly. He left the room on his own two feet, but Shorty and Taingern stayed close, lest he fall.

Dawn broke silently over the ancient fortress, and color leached through the gray remnants of night. But the air was oppressive with the threat of imminent rain, and no sound could be heard in all the vastness of armed men. This would be another day of death, and the start of it was right before them.

Brand had been ready for it, but still the shock of seeing a head on a pole near the gate was sobering. That it was Unferth's … was, in some way, worse.

Even in death the Usurper looked at him, somehow seeming to accuse him personally for such a horrible fate. And Brand felt sorry for him, and wondered that that was possible.

A lone horn blew, sending a wail up into the gray-clad sky. As though awaiting that signal, a horseman cantered forward from the enemy camp. He came to stop before the gate, and there he looked up at Brand. The head of Unferth close to his own.

"In the name of the new Lord of the Duthenor and Callenor tribes, I command you to open the gate and surrender. If you do so, Gormengil will let you live. If you do not, you will die. Unless you surrender during battle. Those are his terms, and no other. You have one hour."

The messenger did not look at Unferth's head. He gave no sign of what he thought of the fate of his old lord nor the prospects of the new. Neither did he wait for a reply. Skillfully, he eased his horse backward a few steps, his eyes locked on Brand's, and then he turned and cantered back to the enemy host.

"Not as talkative as Unferth was," Shorty commented.

"And yet an eloquent message all the same," Brand said. "And this time a better strategy behind it. The threat of death is balanced by the offer of life."

They did not discuss what action to take. For Brand, there was nothing to do but fight. Unferth had usurped the rule of the Duthgar, and Gormengil now the same. Nor was there sign any that the defenders felt differently. They wanted freedom from Callenor rule. They had fought for it. Some had died for it. And those who lived were committed to the same course, unwaveringly and with courage.

The hour passed quietly. The threat of rain deepened, and it grew darker instead of lighter as the day wore on. But at the end of the hour, movement rippled through the enemy host. A bonfire sprang to life, flames twisting high into the air, and many horns sounded all at once.

Brand recognized Horta near the bonfire. And there were others with him, dressed in the same type of strange garb that the magician wore. Slowly, Horta leading them, they began to circle the fire. Brand was not familiar with their rites, but he understood the purpose well enough. Horta would invoke some form of sorcery.

But at the same time the warriors of the enemy began to attack. Many were held in reserve, but a great wave of them, greater even than yesterday, rushed forward. They were better prepared for the onslaught that greeted them. Arrows thickened the air, and many fell. But they held their shields better this time, and fewer were killed. The same happened when the javelins were thrown. Men died, but not so many, nor enough. Yesterday, they had gained the top of the rampart with less men. Today, they would do so again, and the danger was greater.

But the defenders now had greater confidence. They knew what they were about. They would not be broken easily, and they knew the task of the enemy was harder and more dangerous than their own. They had learned the wall was their friend, and how to utilize it better to their advantage. And they had won the battle yesterday. No matter how hard things would soon become, that knowledge would buoy them.

Onward the enemy came, and the slaughter was terrible. But they gained the rampart and steel struck steel as blades flashed.

Tinwellen stayed near Brand, and Sighern also. Neither fought, for they acted as his guards. Dizziness had not left him, and the roaring in his head seemed to rise to match the tumult of battle. But he held his sword in his hand, ready to fight as best he could, if he must.

Shorty and Taingern were among the battling warriors. Even as they were of different temperaments, so too were their fighting styles unlike. Yet men fell dead where they went, and the enemy melted away before them.

Brand watched the ebb and flow of battle, trying to remain detached as a general must. But this was sometimes easier done fighting than watching. Too many times he saw men plummet screaming from the battlement. Too often he watched as a man's sword hand was hacked away, or his entrails spilled. Blood sprayed through the air, gore slicked the stone of the rampart, and the moaning and screaming was louder than the constant roaring in his ears.

It could not go on long as things were. One side or the other must gain ascendancy. And Brand sensed a change. The enemy were excited. Soon he saw why. Up over the rampart climbed a red-armored figure. Gormengil himself, and in one hand he held the legendary raven-axe of the Callenor.

This was the moment. The battle would turn one way or the other now. Brand must fight him, and on the outcome of that fight the greater fight would depend.

But even as he took a step forward, he saw the dead enemy on the blood-slicked stone begin to jerk. Dead hands grabbed once more for sword hilts. Dead throats screamed a war-cry in a language that no Callenor tribesman had ever spoken.

Horta had unleashed some foul sorcery, and Brand must combat it. The defenders would not long stand if those they killed rose from the floor and slew them in turn.

But he could not fight Gormengil and counter Horta at the same time. But which could he ignore? The answer froze him to the spot. To ignore either was to lose the battle, and swiftly.

25. The Prophecy of the Witch

Brand was frozen in doubt. The roaring in his ears rose to a shrieking gale. The world seemed to spin, but he steadied himself. Yet still, he did not move. Some other power had risen also, and he felt the force of it threatening to tumble him into blackness again.

The very air filled with a sense of malice. The hatred was so strong that it turned his stomach. But it was not sorcery of Horta's making. That much he knew instinctively. It had a different feel to it, a feel both distant and yet somehow familiar.

Mist rose from the stone of the rampart. From that vague turning and twining of tendrils figures emerged. They were men. They were warriors, though they looked different from any Brand had ever seen. Their armor was strange. So too their swords. But they had the look of the eagle about them, of warriors who knew how to fight and had endured all that the world, and battle, and life could throw at them.

Even as Brand understood what was happening, the figure of Kurik, wizard-priest of the Letharn appeared before him. The man seemed taller than the warriors he led. He seemed stronger, more life-like. And the sense of malice that came from him was overpowering. His hatred had endured through the eons, and though his true enemies were dead, their descendants yet lived in Horta and his followers.

A moment Brand held the gaze of Kurik. No words passed between them, but the spirit of the dead man seemed to swell and grow. His eyes flashed and then he shot like an arrow of light, arcing over the battlement and toward Horta.

Brand looked around again. All over the battlement the dead Horta had raised were being hacked by the ghost-warriors of the Letharn. The Duthenor had crowded back, pressing themselves against the rear of the rampart, and no harm came to them.

Through the turmoil Brand's gaze met Gormengil's. Hatred burned between them, fierce as the sun. Yet the fray swept between them, and though each was ready to fight the other, desperately wanted to fight the other, it was not fated at that moment.

The press of men around Gormengil drew him back to the rampart, and there, taking hold of ropes and ladders they fled. Few warriors stood up to an onslaught of ghosts, though to Brand's eyes it seemed that the spirits only attacked the sorcerous dead that Horta had raised.

The ghosts of the Letharn faded away as the Callenor retreated. Their spirits were free at last, tied no longer to this world nor the last tragedy that they had endured here. But they had won a final victory for themselves, though Brand knew not for him. The enemy would regroup. They had failed yet again, but they were not defeated. A third time yet they would try to take the fortress.

He moved to the edge of the rampart, and all along the wall the Duthenor did the same. Out over the field the enemy sprinted back to their own host, fearful of what had happened on the wall but still alive. And the crimson figure of Gormengil was among them.

"He runs as fast as his men," Shorty said, his gaze on the same figure.

"But he is a man of pride," Brand answered, "and all the harder will he come against us again when the time comes."

Shorty did not dispute it. Nor anyone else. The army below them was in disarray, but it was not broken. The bonfire was scattered into burning debris across the field, scattered sparks and coils of smoke. Of Horta and his followers, there was no sign. Brand hoped he was dead, but did not think it would be so.

Almost Brand ordered a sortie, and he saw the question in the eyes of Taingern and Shorty. They had both thought of it, but he shook his head. The confusion of the enemy was momentary. The ghosts of the Letharn were gone and Gormengil was alive to regroup his men, and he would do so quickly. And still the enemy outnumbered him.

They watched from the walls, and Brand decided what he had to do.

"Gormengil is the key," he said quietly.

The others looked at him, and Sighern voiced their question. "The key to what?"

"To victory. To saving lives, or trying to. He wants to fight me. I want to fight him. If I kill him, the Callenor will have no true leader left. Gormengil binds them better than Unferth, but without him, they have no one."

"A duel then?" Sighern said.

Tinwellen shook her head. "No. I won't permit it. You're still injured. You can't beat him. You need just a little longer to—"

"It's the right thing to do," Sighern interrupted her. "You must fight him, and you must beat him."

Tinwellen turned her dark gaze on the young man, and her look was cold as death. But then she ignored him and swung back to Brand, placing her hands around his head.

Brand felt the coolness of her touch, and he marveled at the joy she brought him. But the roaring in his ears seemed to rise and swell, and the dizziness that was with him ever since he had been struck in the head weakened his legs. Almost he fell, but not quite. And as though from a great distance he heard Sighern's voice again.

"Let him go, witch!"

Abruptly her touch was gone from him. He opened his eyes and realized Sighern had pushed her away. The cold light in her eyes was bleaker than he had ever seen it, and amazed he watched as two knives appeared as if by magic in her hands and she darted at Sighern.

But Sighern acted quicker than she thought. His sword was still drawn from the battle, and reflexively he lifted it and thrust as she came at him.

Tinwellen drove herself onto the point, and then staggered back. The blade slid out of her belly, and Brand knew it for a mortal wound.

No one moved. Shock gripped them. But instead of falling Tinwellen hissed. And Brand wondered that there was no blood, but at the same time he sensed the presence of magic, of a spell unraveling.

Tinwellen swayed, and her figure blurred. In her hands the knives dissolved into the air and were gone. Her lustrous dark hair grew longer still, but paler. The complexion of her skin darkened. Taller she stood, more queenly, and her eyes were black pits of malevolence.

A moment she stood thus, as surprised as any. But her disguise was gone, the magic that transformed her broken. It was the Trickster of which Kurik had warned him, and had never been Tinwellen at all.

Brand raised his sword and summoned his magic. Before him stood a goddess of the old world, and who knew what powers she commanded.

But she made no move to attack. "Fool! You could have had endless joy. Instead, you will die in a meaningless place in a forgotten land."

"All men die," Brand answered. "Now begone, Trickster. Or we shall see if cold steel can find the colder heart of a goddess."

She gazed at him, seemingly in surprise. "How do you know me? No! Never mind. Now I know. He that led the spirits of the dead told you." She drew herself up, and now she looked like a queen to whom all other queens would bow. "Put away your sword. You will not need it against me. This game is up, and another begins. You will die here soon, and even if you do not, then know the futility of all you do. An army of the Kar-ahn-hetep marches even as we speak. Great warriors are they, and their numbers will overrun the Duthgar. And then the Dark God will rise, and on his conquest of lands and realms the old gods will return from memory to stride the lands that are theirs once more. Die, Brand. Despair, and die!"

So speaking, the goddess raised her hands and the figure that was hers, or one of her many likenesses, turned to pale smoke and then vanished.

Brand lowered his sword and rested his weight upon it. His gaze fell to Sighern. "Once more, it seems, you have proved your worth. Your eyes saw deeper than mine, and I thank you."

Brand wasted no time. Nothing felt right, but it rarely did.

He feared he was not fit for what he intended, but he must do it and he must win. Else the bloodshed would be catastrophic. And he knew one thing more, for he believed what the Trickster said about the army marching toward him, but he dare not think of that. Not yet.

He walked through the gate of the fortress and past the pole topped with Unferth's head, his stride seemingly sure, but he knew how weak his legs were, how close to falling he was, and that the roar in his head continued. He kept his gaze off the head, lest he vomit. Nausea accompanied the roaring.

With him came Sighern. He carried a flag, but it was not the Dragon Banner. Instead, it was a red cloth, the sign of parley in the Duthgar, and a light drizzle fell that dampened it. With him was also Hruidgar the Huntsman. Shorty and Taingern remained inside. They would lead the Duthenor if Brand fell.

They did not ride. They walked in order to be sure nothing they did could be taken as an attack. And, although Brand told no one, he feared he would fall dismounting from a horse.

"Are you sure this is a good idea?" Hruidgar asked. "Do the Callenor even know what the red flag means? Can we trust them?"

"It may not be a good idea," Brand answered. "But it's the best I have. And I don't know what the red flag signifies to them. But the Callenor are men like the Duthenor. They have honor, even if Unferth did not."

Hruidgar gave him a long look, but the man said nothing.

Brand liked him for that, so he offered something more. "Regardless, they know who I am by my helm. They will let us pass through until we reach Gormengil."

"And what then?"

"Then what will be will be."

Ahead of them, the faces of the enemy became clear. They were hard men, and war had treated them harshly. But they said nothing, and offered no word of scorn nor greeting. They simply gazed silently, showing nothing of what they felt, and parted to allow Brand and his small entourage through.

It remained the same as they walked through the heart of the army. Men stared at them, but said nothing. Yet a ripple of movement was always ahead of them, opening a way. Until they reached the center of the camp. Once there, the enemy closed around them again, and it was not a comfortable feeling.

But Brand had found what he sought. Here was a tent, and a makeshift table before it. Men were gathered there, and one of them was Horta. He had wished the man dead, but he was not. Yet still, he seemed haggard and his eyes held a hint of fear. The ghost of Kurik had treated him as harshly as war had treated the Callenor. Brand met his gaze and allowed himself the faintest of smiles. The other man looked away.

There was no more time for such games. One figure, and one figure alone, now drew his gaze and held all his attention. Gormengil stood from where he had sat at the table and faced him. In his hands he held the wicked-looking raven axe. It had two blades, and each was swept back like wings but there was a stabbing spike in the middle, curved slightly to resemble a beak. It could be used to stab, but also to hook and gouge. Brand knew the weapon, or at least some of the legends of the Callenor about it. A shiver of fear ran through him.

The red-lacquered chain mail he wore stood out. Supposedly, it was invincible to blade or dart. Time would soon reveal the truth of those stories. But it was the helm that stood out most of all. This, like the rest, was fashioned by the dwarves, and spells were cast upon it. Engraved into the same red-lacquered metal as the chain mail was a single dwarven rune: karak. Legend said it signified victory in their language. But whose? In a fight, always one lost and the other won. The rune would not change that, nor give the wearer of the helm advantage. Even so, it was an unlucky omen to see borne by an opponent.

Through the grim-looking eye slit of the fabled helm, Gormengil's dark eyes gazed out, cold and implacable.

Brand shivered again. Had he at last met his match? Had he finally risked too much in overconfidence?

Gormengil spoke, his voice cold as his eyes and strangely shaped by the metal of the helm.

"Have you come to offer surrender?"

"Not that. Never that. And why should I when the ghosts of the fortress serve the Duthenor?" It was a lie, but the enemy did not know that.

Gormengil nodded gravely, as though he expected such an answer and approved.

"Then why come at all?"

"To give you what you want."

There was a silence then, deep and undisturbed. Eventually, Gormengil moved, tilting his head slightly to one side.

"I want many things. As many as there are stars in the sky."

Brand laughed, but he was not sure how loud. The laughter and the roaring in his ears seemed one and the same thing.

"Life will teach you, if you live it long enough, that less is more. As it is in all things. But no matter. I have come to give you that which we nearly had on the rampart. I have come to fight you, man to man."

The dark eyes of Gormengil gleamed. "I had feared that fight would not come. Some said you were killed by an axe blow."

"I'm a hard man to kill."

"That I know. But no man lives forever." Gormengil's dark eyes studied him, boring into Brand like a force of nature before he spoke again. "And what terms do you propose?"

"Terms? We have no need of terms. You will not surrender, though I offer you peace if you do. No. We have no need of terms. Let the victor discuss such things with whomever leads his opponents when our fight is done. All I ask as that the men with me be allowed to leave unharmed to return to the fortress."

Gormengil nodded. "That I grant."

They said no more, for no more was needed. Brand drew his Halathrin-wrought blade, and the faint drizzle covered it in an instant sheen of moisture. In the distance, thunder rumbled and a wind picked up, scattering rain-scented dust into the air.

Gormengil adjusted his helm and stepped forward. The axe he carried lightly, and every move he made was one of the true-born warrior. Had Brand been well, he knew he could still kill this man. But he was not well.

A space was cleared for them. Silence fell so deep that Brand thought he could hear his own heart thud in his chest. Or perhaps that was thunder growing closer. He could not tell over the roaring in his ears.

Brand struck first. The quicker he finished this fight, the better. The longer it went on, the worse he would fare.

His blade flashed. Like lightning it shattered the gloomy air, but no thunder followed. A strike that should have hit his enemy's head merely cut air as Gormengil dodged to one side.

"You disappoint me, Brand. I had heard that you were a great warrior. It seems that your legend is nothing more than words."

Brand stood still and fought off a wave of dizziness from his sudden movement. "The blow I took to the head nearly killed me. I'm not at my best."

Let Gormengil make of that what he would. No warrior would admit such a weakness in the middle of a fight. But Brand knew his opponent was good enough to see some of the difficulties he was having. Let him wonder then if what he said was truth, or a ruse.

Gormengil began to circle him warily. The axe was held high, yet not so high as to deter another slash at his head. For that reason Brand made no such blow. Instead, he dropped low and sent a wicked strike at his opponent's knees.

The sword was always going to be quicker than the axe. It was the nature of the weapons, so Gormengil nimbly leapt back. Yet still the axe dropped low to block the blow, and it did so swiftly. From this, Brand learned two things. His opponent was unused to fighting with an axe, else he would have trained his reaction to simply be one of retreat, still holding the axe high and ready to strike. And that the axe was lighter than it looked.

But Gormengil had learned something too. Even as Brand slashed at his legs he had struggled to rise. His legs felt weak, and even when he regained his normal stance he swayed where he stood. Gormengil had learned his weakness was likely not feigned.

The Callenor warrior came at him then, the raven-axe flying through the air. It moaned and whistled strangely. Brand paid that no heed. He had expected it. He had *not* expected the speed and power of his opponent though.

Gormengil fell upon him like a toppling mountain. Brand dodged and weaved, using his feet to move away rather than blocking with his sword. Swords did not block axes, yet still he should have had time to see a gap and strike back. Yet no such opportunity came.

Gormengil wove the axe through the air in deadly arcs, but they were tight and narrow. Where the weight of the weapon should have slowed him at the end of a slash and made it hard to change direction and send back a reverse cut, it did not.

Brand saw no opening to attack. Instead, he was forced to strike at Gormengil's gauntleted hands in the hope of injuring him. This was a lesser tactic, for no death blow could be delivered that way.

Gormengil stayed his attack, and grinned at Brand. "Not easy, is it? I found a way to defeat Unferth, though. But now I know I'm better than you. Better than the fabled—"

The axe was light, but it still tired his opponent's arms and he was stalling for a rest. Brand gave him none, driving forward in a straight thrust that had killed people before. But he was not as fast as he could be, nor did the power of the strike drive up from his legs as much as it should have. Gormengil brushed it aside with a sweep of the twin blades, and held his ground where he stood. He was an image of supreme confidence, and once more Brand felt a cold shiver run up his spine.

"Your head will sit upon a pole next to Unferth's soon," Gormengil taunted. Then he came forward to attack again. This time he did so carefully, driving one deadly swing after another at Brand, but only one at a time, meting them out judiciously so as to preserve his strength.

Brand backed away. The rain began to fall now, no mere drizzle but a heavy torrent that fell in waves, lightened, and then came again heavier than before. Thunder rumbled with it, and a bolt of lightning slivered through the air to strike a tree on the pine-clad ridges above them.

Nothing stopped the combatants. It seemed that the whole army watched them, and no storm nor danger would force people away to seek shelter. They all knew that Brand had been injured on the battlements. They all knew Gormengil was a great fighter. And a battle unfolded before them the like of which they had never seen. For though Brand was disadvantaged, yet he always seemed to avoid the deadly blows directed at him. Though he stumbled and fell, he righted himself at the last minute. Though he swayed with dizziness, he dodged blow after blow that should have killed him. And though his knees buckled beneath him, yet still he somehow stayed on his feet and defied his opponent. The Callenor admired that, for they saw there was no give in Brand. But they knew it could not last.

Nor were they wrong. Brand knew it, and knew that it was all he could do to just defend himself. Attacking was beyond him, for he had neither the strength nor the speed. The roaring in his ears grew so loud he was not sure if it was him or if thunder rumbled continuously. But he must go on, and he *must* find a way to win.

The raven-axe whistled through the air. Brand was not quick enough. He was struck a mighty blow on his helm and toppled to the ground. Yet still he did not give up. Even as Gormengil came in for the kill, he thrust upward with his sword. The strike was fast, but his enemy was quicker. The axe whistled again, and Brand's sword was caught between one of the blades and the stabbing beak. Gormengil gave a sudden twist, and the blade was stuck fast.

Too late Brand realized what Gormengil had done, and the true purpose of the axe's beak. It was like a sword breaker. The work of the dwarves was cunning, and his sword was trapped.

Gormengil pushed both axe and sword to the ground, and then he stomped upon the blade. Great as it was, Halathrin-wrought and imbued with magic, it could not endure such force from that angle. The blade broke. The hilt was ripped from Brand's hand. A sudden light flashed, blindingly bright and lightning arced from the sky to strike a tree on the ridge. Thunder rolled across the field, and Brand's heart lurched at the loss of a weapon that was sacred to his people and that had been borne by his forefathers since the founding of the Duthgar. He felt also the shadow of death fall upon him.

Gormengil towered over him, the axe raised high. The roaring in Brand's ears rose to a crescendo. The axe whistled down, cutting for his neck, and Brand could not escape it.

But it was not in his nature to give up. His sword was broken, yet the helm he wore was Halathrin-wrought also. One final gamble he took. Tilting his head he took the full force of the blow on his helm. He felt the weight of it crashing down, and he felt his head knocked to the side. His vision faded out so that he saw nothing, yet still he drew a dagger and stabbed upward.

The blade hit something, but he did not know what. He rolled to the side, far too slow to avoid another blow, but it never came. He staggered to his feet, and his vision swam. The blackness receded, bit by bit, and he saw Gormengil before him.

But his enemy made no move to attack. He had dropped the axe and instead clamped both hands against a wound in his thigh. Even so, blood spurted and Brand knew his dagger had struck the great artery in his enemy's leg. It was a killing blow unless a tourniquet was applied immediately.

Summoning the last of his strength and trusting to luck, Brand dived and rolled. All in one motion he dropped his dagger, grabbed the haft of the axe and rose again. There he swayed, half seeing his enemy, but suddenly one stroke away from victory.

Gormengil seemed a man little given to showing his emotions, but fear and shock showed on his face. He was going to die. Victory had turned to defeat, and all his dreams were ash.

Brand had little liking for him, but he could not just watch him die. Still less did he wish to strike him down with the axe, though he knew Gormengil would not hesitate to do the same. But he was not Gormengil, and though what he was about to do could prove costly, he saw no other choice.

Brand lowered the axe, resting it upon the ground and leaning on it like a walking stick to keep his balance. "Quickly!" he called. "Get this man a tourniquet!"

For a single moment, nothing happened. All that moved was the rain falling in sheets. Then men were running to the tent. There would be cloth in there, or clothes, or rope. Something to try to stop Gormengil bleeding out where he stood.

But even as the men moved the air sizzled. It was a strange sound, and frightening. The hair on Brand's neck stood on end. Light flashed near the tent as a bolt of lightning hit the ground and the crack of thunder came with it like a blow.

Warriors reeled away. Dirt flew into the air. Steam hissed and spurted, and Brand watched, stunned, as a figure formed amid the roiling turmoil. It was the Trickster. And as she strode forward Brand heard a moan from his left. It was Horta.

But the Trickster ignored him. She ignored everyone. Like a queen she walked, her gaze on Gormengil only. And when she reached him, she placed a hand upon his shoulder. Only then did she deign to look at anyone else and speak.

"Thus I claim what is owed to me," she said to Horta. "The chieftain of the Callenor." And then her gaze turned to Brand. "Even if it is not what I sought."

She flung up her arm, and lightning sizzled again, stabbing up from her fingertips into the cloud-dark sky. Light flashed, searingly bright, and when Brand opened his eyes once more neither the goddess nor Gormengil were there.

Brand leaned wearily on the axe and gazed around him while the rain fell. Of Horta, there was no sign. Had the goddess taken him, or had he fled? Probably the latter.

"Well," Brand said, "the fight is done, and I am the victor. Will you honor the pledge to let us go freely back to the fortress?"

One of Gormengil's captains stepped a few paces forward. He was older than the others, with a short gray beard. He had the look of a lord about him, but most if not all Gormengil's captains would have been.

"We of the Callenor have as much honor as the Duthenor. You are free to go."

Brand nodded in acknowledgement. But he made no move to step away.

"There's much that the Callenor and Duthenor share in common. Not just honor, nor our distant ancestors."

The lord looked at him curiously. "So it is said, and it is said with truth."

"For instance," Brand continued, "our laws are mostly the same, especially those that govern the rights of the people, and succession to the chieftainship. So much alike, that I believe in challenging Gormengil to a duel and then defeating him ... Perhaps I have a claim to the chieftainship of the Callenor tribe. Is it so?"

There was a long silence, and the rain fell about them almost unnoticed.

"There are some who would say so," the lord answered carefully.

"Let me be clear," Brand said. "I may have a claim to the chieftainship, but I would never try to enforce it. In truth, I cannot. But I have heard that Gormengil was the only true heir. And he is gone, leaving your tribe leaderless. So, I propose this. Take me as your chieftain, if even only temporarily. In that way we can avoid war and bloodshed amongst ourselves. But what happens between us is only a part of what is afoot." He paused then, thinking his next words through carefully. About them, the rain began to diminish.

"You have seen the goddess. She took Gormengil, but she is not alone. Horta, whom you know, serves her and her like. And there is now, even as we speak, an army marching toward us. You have only my word for this, but I give it with honor. I speak the truth. Enemies gather. Not just of the Duthenor but of the Callenor. And of the world as we know it. Lands and realms will fall before them. Ours will just be the first. But, perhaps, we can stop it. If we cease our own battle and unite. What do you say?"

If the silence had been long before, it was longer now. The lords regarded him with troubled eyes. But the gray-bearded warrior paid them no attention. His gaze on Brand only, he eventually shrugged and then knelt.

"I believe you. You are a man of courage and strength. If I am a judge of men, you are worthy. And the truth of your warning is in your eyes. I will serve you."

This swayed the others. They too knelt and offered their service.

Brand raised the raven-axe in salute. But as he did so, his gaze fell to his own broken sword. The sight of it weighed heavily upon him, and he remembered the prophecy of the witch in the swamp. If she was right, there was more yet to come.

Epilogue

This was no desert land. It was green, and bird and tree and animal were all different. But no matter the changes to the landscape as they marched, one thing would remain unalterable. Warfare. The stronger, the better trained, the smarter led would prevail over the weaker.

Wena turned his head from side to side and surveyed the army he led. Footmen were the greater part, but there were charioteers too. Swords hung at the sides of men. Spears were in their hands. And the bright look of battle-lust shone eagerly in their eyes. They marched to war, and a cloud of dust rose behind them. Soon, fear would press ahead of them, and the enemy would tremble.

The long days of marching were good. It brought them closer to battle and victory. But night was better, for in his dreams the long-foretold god came to him and urged him forward with promises of glory.

And of late, Wena had begun to hear Char-harash in his waking moments. Even now, he heard the god's voice whisper in his mind. *Come to me, my children. Hasten! A new day is dawning. The old gods will rule again, and the Kar-ahn-hetep will conquer the world!*

Wena strode ahead, and his army followed after him.

Thus ends *The Crimson Lord*. The Dark God Rises trilogy continues in book three, *The Dark God*, where Brand must face his greatest enemies ever: not just men, nor sorcerers … but gods.

Amazon lists millions of titles, and I'm glad you discovered this one. But if you'd like to know when I release a new book, instead of leaving it to chance, sign up for my newsletter. I'll send you an email on publication.

Yes please! – Go to www.homeofhighfantasy.com and sign up.

No thanks – I'll take my chances.

Dedication

There's a growing movement in fantasy literature. Its name is noblebright, and it's the opposite of grimdark.

Noblebright celebrates the virtues of heroism. It's an old-fashioned thing, as old as the first story ever told around a smoky campfire beneath ancient stars. It's storytelling that highlights courage and loyalty and hope for the spirit of humanity. It recognizes the dark – the dark in us all, and the dark in the villains of its stories. It recognizes death, and treachery and betrayal. But it dwells on none of these things.

I dedicate this book, such as it is, to that which is noblebright. And I thank the authors before me who held the torch high so that I could see the path: J.R.R. Tolkien, C.S. Lewis, Terry Brooks, David Eddings, Susan Cooper, Roger Taylor and many others. I salute you.

And, for a time, I too will hold the torch as high as I can.

Appendix: Encyclopedic Glossary

Note: the glossary of each book in this series is individualized for that book alone. Additionally, there is often historical material provided in its entries for people, artifacts and events that are not included in the main text.

Many races dwell in Alithoras. All have their own language, and though sometimes related to one another the changes sparked by migration, isolation and various influences often render these tongues unintelligible to each other.

The ascendancy of Halathrin culture, combined with their widespread efforts to secure and maintain allies against elug incursions, has made their language the primary means of communication between diverse peoples.

For instance, a merchant of Cardoroth addressing a Duthenor warrior would speak Halathrin, or a simplified version of it, even though their native speeches stem from the same ancestral language.

This glossary contains a range of names and terms. Many are of Halathrin origin, and their meaning is provided. The remainder derive from native tongues and are obscure, so meanings are only given intermittently.

Often, Duthenor names and Halathrin elements are combined. This is especially so for the aristocracy. Few other tribes of men had such long-term friendship with the immortal Halathrin as the Duthenor, and though in this relationship they lost some of their natural culture, they gained nobility and knowledge in return.

List of abbreviations:

Cam. Camar

Comb. Combined

Cor. Corrupted form

Duth. Duthenor

Hal. Halathrin

Kir. Kirsch

Prn. Pronounced

Alithoras: *Hal.* "Silver land." The Halathrin name for the continent they settled after leaving their own homeland. Refers to the extensive river and lake systems they found and their wonder at the beauty of the land.

Anast Dennath: *Hal.* "Stone mountains." Mountain range in northern Alithoras. Source of the river known as the Careth Nien that forms a natural barrier between the lands of the Camar people and the Duthenor and related tribes. Also the location of the Dweorhrealm, the underground stronghold of the dwarven nation.

Aranloth: *Hal.* "Noble might." A lòhren of ancient heritage and friend to Brand.

Arnhaten: *Kir.* "Disciples." Servants of a magician. One magician usually has many disciples, but only some of these are referred to as "inner door." Inner door disciples receive a full transmission of the master's knowledge. The remainder do not, but they continue to strive to earn the favor of their master. Until they do, they are dispensable.

Black Talon: The sign of Unferth's house. Appears on his banner and is his personal emblem. Legend claims the founder of the house in ancient days had the power to transform into a raven. Disguised in this form, and trusted as a magical being, he gave misinformation and ill-advice to the enemies of his people.

Brand: *Duth.* "Torch." An exiled Duthenor tribesman and adventurer. Appointed by the former king of Cardoroth to serve as regent for Prince Gilcarist. By birth, he is the rightful chieftain of the Duthenor people. However, Unferth the Usurper overthrew his father, killing both him and his wife. Brand, only a youth at the time, swore an oath of vengeance. That oath has long slept, but it is not forgotten, either by Brand or the usurper.

Breath of the dragon: An ancient saying of Letharn origin. They believed the magic of dragons was the preeminent magic in the world because dragons were creatures able to travel through time. Dragon's breath is known to mean fire, the destructive face of their nature. But the Letharn also believed dragons could breathe mist. This was the healing face of their nature. And the mist-breath of a dragon was held to be able to change destinies and bring good luck. To "ride the dragon's breath" meant that for a period a person was a focal point of time and destiny. The Kar-ahn-hetep peoples hold similar beliefs.

Brodruin: *Duth.* "Dark river." A lord of the Duthgar.

Bruidiger: *Duth.* "Blessed blade." A Norvinor warrior. Brand's father once saved his father's life during a hunting expedition.

Brunhal: *Duth.* "Hallowed woman." Former chieftainess of the Duthenor. Wife to Drunn, former chieftain of the Duthenor. Mother to Brand. According to Duthenor custom, a chieftain and chieftainess co-ruled.

Callenor: *Duth.* One of several tribes closely related to the Duthenor. This one inhabits lands immediately west of the Duthgar.

Camar: *Cam. Prn.* Kay-mar. A race of interrelated tribes that migrated in two main stages. The first brought them to the vicinity of Halathar, homeland of the immortal Halathrin; in the second, they separated and established cities along a broad stretch of eastern Alithoras. Related to the Duthenor, though far more distantly than the Callenor.

Cardoroth: *Cor. Hal. Comb. Cam.* A Camar city, often called Red Cardoroth. Some say this alludes to the red granite commonly used in the construction of its buildings, others that it refers to a prophecy of destruction.

Careth Nien: *Hal. Prn.* Kareth ny-en. "Great river." Largest river in Alithoras. Has its source in the mountains of Anast Dennath and runs southeast across the land before emptying into the sea. It was over this river (which sometimes freezes along its northern stretches) that the Camar and other tribes migrated into the eastern lands. Much later, Brand came to the city of Cardoroth by one of these ancient migratory routes.

Char-harash: *Kir.* "He who destroys by flame." Most exalted of the emperors of the Kirsch, and a magician of great power.

Dragon of the Duthgar: The banner of the chieftains of the Duthenor. Legend holds that an ancient forefather of the line slew a dragon and ate its heart. Dragons are seen by the Duthenor as creatures of ultimate evil, but the consuming of their heart is reputed to pass on wisdom and magic.

Drunn: *Duth.* "Man of secrets." Former chieftain of the Duthenor. Husband to Brunhal and father to Brand.

Duthenor: *Duth. Prn.* Dooth-en-or. "The people." A single tribe (or less commonly a group of closely related tribes melded into a larger people at times of war or disaster) who generally live a rustic and peaceful lifestyle. They are breeders of cattle and herders of sheep. However, when need demands they are bold warriors – men and women alike. Currently ruled by a usurper who murdered Brand's parents. Brand has sworn an oath to overthrow the tyrant and avenge his parents.

Duthgar: *Duth.* "People spear." The name is taken to mean "the land of the warriors who wield spears."

Elù-haraken: *Hal.* "The shadowed wars." Long ago battles in a time that is become myth to the Duthenor and

Camar tribes. A great evil was defeated, though prophecy foretold it would return.

Elùgai: *Hal. Prn.* Eloo-guy. "Shadowed force." The sorcery of an elùgroth.

Garvengil: *Duth.* "Warrior of the woods." A lord of the Duthgar.

God-king: See Char-harash.

Gormengil: *Duth.* "Warrior of the storm." Nephew of Unferth. Rightful heir to the Callenor chieftainship.

Halathrin: *Hal.* "People of Halath." A race named after an honored lord who led an exodus of his people to the land of Alithoras in pursuit of justice, having sworn to defeat a great evil. They are human, though of fairer form, greater skill and higher culture than ordinary men. They possess a unity of body, mind and spirit that enables insight and endurance beyond the native races of Alithoras. Said to be immortal, but killed in great numbers during their conflicts in ancient times with the evil they sought to destroy. Those conflicts are collectively known as the Shadowed Wars.

Haldring: *Duth.* "White blade – a sword that flashes in the sun." A shield-maiden. Killed in the first great battle between the forces of Brand and the usurper.

High Way: An ancient road longer than the Duthgar, but well preserved in that land. Probably of Letharn origin and used to speed troops to battle.

Horta: *Kir.* "Speech of the acacia tree." It is believed among the Kar-ahn-hetep that the acacia tree possesses magical properties that aid discourse between the realms of men and gods. Horta is a name that recurs among families noted for producing elite magicians.

Hralfling: *Duth.* "The shower of sparks off two sword blades striking." An elderly lord of the Callenor.

Hruidgar: *Duth.* "Ashwood spear." A Duthenor hunter.

Immortals: See Halathrin.

Karak: The dwarven rune for victory. Famous in the Shadowed Wars, where also the dwarves came to prominence for the crafting of superb weapons and armor.

Kar-ahn-hetep: *Kir.* "The children of the thousand stars." A race of people that vied for supremacy in ancient times with the Letharn. Their power was ultimately broken, their empire destroyed. But a residual population survived and defied outright annihilation by their conquerors. They believe their empire will one day rise again to rule the world. The kar-ahn element of their name means the "thousand stars" but also "the lights that never die."

Kar-fallon: *Kir.* "Death city." A great city of the Kar-ahn-hetep that served as their principal religious focus. Their magician-priests conducted the great rites of their nation in its sacred temples.

Kar-karmun: *Kir.* "Death-life – the runes of life and death." A means of divination that distills the wisdom and worldview of the Kar-ahn-hetep civilization.

Kirsch: See Kar-ahn-hetep.

Kurik: A wizard-priest of the Letharn. Cousin to the emperor, and ruler and protector of a large military district.

Laigern: *Cam.* "Storm-tossed sea." Head guard of a merchant caravan.

Letharn: *Hal.* "Stone raisers. Builders." A race of people that in antiquity conquered most of Alithoras. Now, only faint traces of their civilization endure.

Light of Kar-fallon: See Char-harash.

Lòhren: *Hal. Prn.* Ler-ren. "Knowledge giver – a counselor." Other terms used by various nations include wizard, druid and sage.

Lòhrengai: *Hal. Prn.* Ler-ren-guy. "Lòhren force." Enchantment, spell or use of mystic power. A manipulation and transformation of the natural energy inherent in all things. Each use takes something from the user. Likewise, some part of the transformed energy infuses them. Lòhrens use it sparingly, elùgroths indiscriminately.

Lord of the Ten Armies: See Char-harash.

Magic: Mystic power. See lòhrengai and elùgai.

Norhanu: *Kir.* "Serrated blade." A psychoactive herb.

Norvinor: *Duth.* One of several tribes closely related to the Duthenor. This one inhabits lands west of the Callenor.

Olbata: *Kir.* "Silence of the desert at night." An inner door disciple of Horta.

Pennling Palace: A fortress in the Duthgar. Named after an ancient hero of the Duthenor. In truth, constructed by the Letharn and said to be haunted by the spirits of the dead. At certain nights, especially midwinter and midsummer, legend claims the spirits are visible manning the walls and fighting a great battle.

Pennling Path: Etymology obscure. Pennling was an ancient hero of the Duthenor. Some say he built the road in the Duthgar known as the High Way. This is not true, but one legend holds that he traveled all its length in one night on a milk-white steed to confront an attacking army by himself. It is said that his ghost may yet be seen racing along the road on his steed when the full moon hangs above the Duthgar.

Ruler of the Thousand Stars: See Char-harash.

Runes of Life and Death: See Kar-karmun.

Shadowed wars: See Elù-haraken.

Shemfal: *Kir.* "Cool shadows gliding over the hot waste – dusk." One of the greater gods of the Kar-ahn-hetep. Often depicted as a mighty man, bat winged and bat headed. Ruler of the underworld. Given a wound in battle with other gods that does not heal and causes him to limp.

Shenti: A type of kilt worn by the Kar-ahn-hetep.

Shorty: A former Durlindrath (chief bodyguard of the king of Cardoroth). Friend to Brand. His proper name is Lornach.

Sighern: *Duth.* "Battle leader." A youth of the Duthgar.

Su-sarat: *Kir.* "The serpent that lures." One of the greater gods of the Kar-ahn-hetep. Her totem is the desert puff adder that lures prey by flicking either its tongue or tail. Called also the Trickster. It was she who gave the god Shemfal his limp.

Tanata: *Kir.* "Stalker of the desert at night." A disciple of Horta.

Taingern: *Cam.* "Still sea," or "calm waters." A former Durlindrath (chief bodyguard of the king of Cardoroth). Friend to Brand.

Tinwellen: *Cam.* "Sun of the earth – gold." Daughter of a prosperous merchant of Cardoroth.

Unferth: *Duth.* "Hiss of arrows." The name is sometimes interpreted to mean "whispered counsels that lead to war." Usurper of the chieftainship of the Duthenor. Rightful chieftain of the Callenor.

Ùhrengai: *Hal. Prn.* Er-ren-guy. "Original force." The primordial force that existed before substance or time.

Vorbald: *Duth.* "Wolf warrior." A great warrior among the Callenor.

Wena: *Kir.* "The kestrel that hovers." Leader of a Kar-ahn-hetep army.

Wizard: See lòhren.

Wizard-priest: The priests of the Letharn. Possessors of mighty powers of magic. Forerunners to the order of lòhrens.

About the author

I'm a man born in the wrong era. My heart yearns for faraway places and even further afield times. Tolkien had me at the beginning of *The Hobbit* when he said, ". . . one morning long ago in the quiet of the world . . ."

Sometimes I imagine myself in a Viking mead-hall. The long winter night presses in, but the shimmering embers of a log in the hearth hold back both cold and dark. The chieftain calls for a story, and I take a sip from my drinking horn and stand up . . .

Or maybe the desert stars shine bright and clear, obscured occasionally by wisps of smoke from burning camel dung. A dry gust of wind marches sand grains across our lonely campsite, and the wayfarers about me stir restlessly. I sip cool water and begin to speak.

I'm a storyteller. A man to paint a picture by the slow music of words. I like to bring faraway places and times to life, to make hearts yearn for something they can never have, unless for a passing moment.

THE DARK GOD

BOOK THREE OF THE DARK GOD RISES TRILOGY

Robert Ryan

Copyright © 2019 Robert J. Ryan
All Rights Reserved. The right of Robert J. Ryan to be identified as the author of this work has been asserted. All of the characters in this book are fictitious and any resemblance to actual persons, living or dead, is coincidental.

Trotting Fox Press

1. The Broken Sword

Brand walked silently through the sacred woods of the Duthenor, and the magic within him grew restless. It sensed something, and responded.

He stepped carefully and reverently, for this was not a place to move fast or to speak. And those few with him did the same.

Shorty and Taingern were among them. What they thought of this place, he did not know. But they each had seen strange things before, and knew there were powers in the world beyond the understanding of people. This was such a site where those powers were strong, and the ancient Duthenor had known it.

The Duthenor seldom came here. It was a place of ancient ceremony, and usually it was left alone except for certain times of the year and certain occasions.

This was one such occasion. The sword of the chieftains of the Duthenor was broken. It was a link between father and son from a time out of memory and into myth. It was a part of the Duthenor people themselves. It was a symbol of them, and its breaking was like the dying of a chieftain.

And there were rites that went with that, born from a past older even than the Duthenor habitation of the Duthgar. They went back to the dark days, the time of the elù-haraken. The Shadowed Wars.

One of those rites was the offering of something of great value back to the land from whence all life sprang. In this case, it would be the sword itself.

Brand carried the broken shards reverently in his hands, held palm up before him. No steel blade was allowed in the sacred woods, and none of his companions carried a weapon. But the broken sword was the offering itself, and there was a tradition of giving swords back to the land when their owner died. This was in that spirit.

Though it was early morning, the forest was dark about him. The trees were mostly pine, and the scent of resin sharpened the air. To all sides the trunks marched away, dark and mysterious. Branches creaked, and strange sounds of wood rubbing against wood disturbed the quiet.

It was an eerie place, and Brand sensed foreboding tickle the back of his neck. Was that the natural effect of the strange woods? Or were his instincts warning him of something?

It did not matter. They were nearly at their destination now, and there was no turning back. With him and his two oldest friends came Sighern and several of the highest-ranking lords of both the Duthenor and Callenor tribes.

Brand paused. Then his gaze found the hidden path that he remembered of old, and he turned down it. Overgrown by ancient trees it was, and the sense of eeriness increased. Here, he remembered coming once as a child with his father. It had been eerie then too. Strange that it should be even more so now as an adult.

Furthgil, the gray-bearded lord of the Callenor, preeminent among his tribe now that Gormengil was dead, cast a wary gaze about him as he followed down the dark trail. Well he might. No Callenor had been here before, but they too would have their sacred place. Behind him, for there was only room for one man at a time, came the lords Brodruin and Garvengil. These were the most senior surviving nobility of the Duthenor. They hid their unease well, but they had been here before and knew what to expect. Last, but not least, came Bruidiger. No lord at all, but a warrior of great presence. He represented the Norvinor tribe, and Brand thought it fitting. Here he had gathered, against tradition in such a sacred place, not only the Duthenor but representatives of all the peoples that faced the great threat to come. It was the beginnings of binding them into a single force, and that was needed. Without it, they would not survive.

The path wound downhill now, and the steepness made each step treacherous. It grew darker, and the trees leaned over them, looking down like sentries, scrutinizing those who passed.

But pass they did, and they came to their destination. The trees gave way, grudgingly. The land leveled, and a patch of clear sky, blue-purple as it seemed looking up through the dark tunnel of tree trunks that formed a circle around them, gazed down unblinking like an eye.

Here of old the chieftains of the Duthenor made offerings to the land to honor it. Here was the *Ferstellenpund*, a tarn of still water, mirrorlike, its surface still and the bright-colored sky reflected in it. At night, there would be stars, but no offerings were ever made save by daylight.

The banks were too steep to walk, but the end of the trail had led down a rocky path to the water's edge and a flat shore. The path was cut into the rock by the hand of man, but no Duthenor would ever have done that. To the shore Brand came, the others behind him. And here, by the very edge of the tarn, they halted amid a heavy silence. This was where he would commit the sword back to the land. This was the sacred heart of the woods.

Tendrils of mist reached up from the water, creeping into the trees. No sound came to Brand's ears. The whole world seemed watchful, as though it awaited some event. It was a dreary place, and Brand's heart was heavy. He began to think that the eeriness of the woods was caused by his own emotion. Grief washed through him. So many had died recently. So many more yet would. And the sword of his forefathers was broken, even as his parents were dead. The hopes of his youth were ash, and the reality of the world was hard to bear.

But bear it he must. He straightened. For now, he would do what was required of a chieftain. When he left these woods, the combined army of the Duthenor and Callenor tribes would be waiting nearby. He would lead them, and he would wield them like a weapon to do what had to be done.

A movement caught his eye. It was a trickle of water running down the stony bank at the other side of the pond. But there was no sound of running water, nor did it disturb the surface. It was strange. Yet there were many strange things about the pond. Another was that no one had ever plumbed its depths. And it had been tried, at least according to legend.

Brand gave no more thought to it. He uttered the sacred words of the Duthenor, the words handed down from father to son, from chieftain to chieftain, since days beyond memory. They were the words spoken at an offering. They were the words spoken at a chieftain's funeral. And he heard an intake of breath from the men of the other tribes with him. They would have their own such sacred words, and they would know the sanctity of such things. They would know that Brand was treating them as lords of the Duthenor, letting them hear what only lords of the Duthenor had ever heard before.

And when he was done, he cast the shards of the broken blade into the center of the pond. The still water shattered. The image of the sky shuddered, and the water showed the flashing image of the surrounding trees, leaping and striding like warriors drawing swords to attack.

The shards of the blade slid into the water, disappearing from sight, though even that made no noise, and it troubled Brand.

Yet the offering was made. That which was drawn from the earth was laid to rest within it again. The land had been thanked, and the rite completed. It was time to turn and go.

But Brand did not move. Where the water should be going still again, it did the opposite. It trembled, and then seethed. The tendrils of mist turned to billowing exhalations, and vapor rose in a sudden fog. This had never happened before. Not that Brand's father had ever told him, nor that any rumor of legend whispered.

Brand waited. But for what, he did not know.

2. Will You Serve the Land?

A feeling came over Brand, and it was one that he had experienced before. But at all other times it was vague and slight, a hint of things that could be.

Now, it washed over him as a mighty wave. It was awesome, and it was a wonder. It was both joy and terror. For it seemed that his mind opened and expanded, or else a veil had been withdrawn that had dimmed his perceptions. He stood where he did, and he gazed upon the churning water of the Ferstellenpund, but at the same time he had a sense of other lands and other places. Deep into the earth his mind plumbed, and it also streaked high into the thin airs above the earth. North, south, east and west it sped also. And it seemed to him that he heard whispers of joy and far-off wailing, as though the land itself spoke to him of what was happening to the people who dwelt upon it.

The water of the pond began to still again, but now there was a presence in it. He saw nothing, but he felt it. And the sense of awe that overwhelmed him before redoubled now. The others fell back behind him, but slowly, reverently, Brand knelt upon the stony shore.

He looked into the water, and there was a face there. Human it appeared, but he could not be sure. Nor could he tell age, for the face was ageless, and in her eyes, for it was the face of a lady, it seemed to him that all the woe of the ages was caught, but also all the joy. Wise was her gaze, and tranquil, yet behind it lay an indomitable will, stronger and more enduring than mountains.

And the lady spoke, her voice clear but coming from no one place. Rather, it seemed as though the woods about him spoke, and the very air thrummed with her voice.

"Hail, Brand. Do not be alarmed. No harm can come to you here."

Brand remained kneeling. "This I know, Lady, for you are the land itself, and ever have I striven to protect the life to which you give rise."

She smiled at him. And it seemed that sunlight bathed the dark woods.

"Yes, you have done this. And I thank you. Yet I must now ask more. Will you devote your life to me? Will you serve the land?"

"I will, Lady."

Her smile deepened, and it was like sunlight on a winter's day. Brand gazed into her eyes. They seemed at times brown, and hazel and then green. They were wells into which a man could fall forever.

"I have watched you, Brand. I have felt you move across the earth. Your deeds are great, and your fame grows. All over the land I hear rumor of your name."

"Fame is fleeting, Lady. This you know better than I."

"You are powerful too."

"All power grows old and withers, Lady."

"You could be an emperor, for you could conquer realms and gather armies. The riches of kingdoms are yours for the taking. Who could stop you?"

"I stop myself, Lady. I have no desire for those things. The riches I truly seek are now forever beyond my reach."

The image within the water paused then. It could have been for a heartbeat, or for eons while the sun tracked the sky and the stars wheeled in oblivion. Brand did not know which, for he still gazed into her eyes and he knew that in this place time had no meaning.

"Then will you serve the land?"

"I will serve you."

"I am pleased. Take back your sword. You will have need of it, lòhren."

Brand knew what she had meant when she asked if he would serve. But this puzzled him.

"You call me lòhren, but lòhrens wield no sword. They carry rather a staff."

If it were possible, he would have thought her expression amused, though perhaps it was some shimmer of water that altered her face.

"You are not as other lòhrens. Your talisman is not a staff, but the sword. Take it."

It was then that he saw the rest of her body, for the water seemed to move and clear. She stood within it, upright, and in her hand she held the hilt of a sword. His sword that he had cast into the tarn broken.

She rose then, and all the while that she moved, still she fixed him with her gaze. Up, out of the water she ascended, and it trailed from her in streams and yet her skin was dry and so also the cloth of the simple white dress she wore. But the sword dripped water in her hand when she held it before him, now by the blade with her two hands, the hilt pointed at him.

He reached out, reverently. His right hand took the hilt. It felt good in his grip, but suddenly his sense of connection to the land strengthened even further. Something of her passed into him, for now both held the sword together and he felt one with her, one with the land.

And then her hands were off the blade. The world seemed dimmer, and for the first time Brand remembered he was in the woods, and the strange sounds of the forest came to life around him once more, reminding him of where he was and drawing him back to it, and back to the tasks he had yet to accomplish in this small, small part of the world.

"I will serve you well, Lady."

"This I know, Brand. And this I say to you. You will be like no lòhren that has gone before, for you will be a warrior, and a lòhren, and a king all. You will sire kings, and of your line will spring the hope of the north." She paused and her eyes glittered with thoughts beyond what Brand could discern. "Know also," she continued, "that the enemy comes. And with them, gods. It falls to you to defeat them."

Brand held her gaze. For her, he would risk his life. He had done so many times in fighting for the land.

"I am a mere man, but I will contend with them as best I can."

"This also, I do not doubt," she answered. "They will kill you if they can, but you are resourceful. And though they be gods, yet still they fear you. Let that give you courage and confidence. Your task is very hard. Perhaps your hardest yet. But you are Brand, and you do not die easily. You may yet prevail."

She reached out and touched his cheek gently, as though in blessing. Then she sank noiselessly into the water and was gone. The surface of the pond was still again, reflecting the purple-blue sky as it had earlier.

For a few moments Brand stayed kneeling. He did not trust himself to stand, such were the emotions that roared through him. A warrior, lòhren and king he would be. And of his line would spring the hope of the north. What did it all mean?

But he would get no more answers waiting here. What answers he would have would come fighting men. And gods. But only if he survived those battles. Yet the sword in his hand would help him, and he rejoiced that it was whole and his again. It did not matter how. The land had given it to him. It was both a sword and the symbol now of his stature as a lòhren. It was subtly changed, too.

He gripped the sword tightly and stood, turning to face the men he had brought. They remained kneeling, and were pale-faced and trembling. They looked at him with wide eyes, and he wondered if they would ever look at him the same again. Even Taingern and Shorty.

"Rise!" he commanded. "We have work to do."

3. The Tomb

The shadow of fear was upon Horta, and he did not like it.

How had things gone so wrong? Only he and Tanata had survived the wrath of the old Letharn spirit that Brand had somehow summoned or loosed upon the world. The rest of the Arnhaten were no more. The thought of it shamed him. But what followed had been even worse.

It was with disbelief that he had watched Brand fight Gormengil, and win. And in winning somehow sway the Callenor to join him. One moment they had been at war, and the next Brand led both tribes. *It was the breath of the dragon.* For the first time Horta understood exactly what that meant. Brand was touched by fate.

But so too was Horta. He had a task to complete. He had been chosen for it, for out of the countless searchers through years unmeasured, it was he who had found the tomb of Char-harash. It was he who would draw him back to life. And nothing could interfere with that now that he was so close. Not even defeat and the ruination of all his plans.

It still burned him like fire. He would never forget slipping away like a thief when Brand usurped control of the Callenor. He had found Tanata, taken horses and fled before they could be found and stopped.

For long years Horta had schooled himself to harden his heart. He had done things that would shrivel the soul of an ordinary man, but the shame of defeat had done something. Emotions flowed through him all the time now. Anger. Fear. Grief. He liked none of them, but stronger than they, and more welcome, was lust for revenge and the knowledge that it would come to pass. An army of Kar-ahn-hetep were on the way, and not even the combined forces of the Duthenor and Callenor could stop it. And when they conquered the land, the resurrection of Char-harash could begin. Then his own life could begin anew again also, for he would be the right hand of the god-king.

They rode down a steep bank. Tall pines grew to the left. To the right, the lights of a faraway village twinkled palely. Too close, Horta knew. Yet this was a populated land and even traveling at night there was a risk of being seen.

"Where do we go, master?"

Tanata had followed him loyally, never questioning him until now. But it was a good question, and it needed an answer.

"Where we must. Where our duty requires us to go. And where we will be safe from prying eyes."

In truth, Horta had not known where to go. It was only when the question had been asked that he understood the answer. Until then, he had just been getting away.

"Is anywhere safe for us now?"

"No, lad. Nowhere is safe. But some places are safer than others. We need the wilderness to hide us. And we have a place to guard until our army arrives. We go now to the tomb of the god-king."

Tanata accepted that news in silence. Although, perhaps he thought one place was as good as any other. Or perhaps he was still in shock from all that had happened. Horta would not blame him for that. He felt it himself. But his disciple had learned other things in the few nights of fleeing that at least Horta had known before. He had learned that the tomb of the god-king had been found, and that his time of resurrection approached. That had been as great a shock as anything Brand had done.

They slipped away into the dark. The slope was behind them, and the tall pines just a clump of darker shadows. Somewhere in the distance a dog barked, and Horta felt fear upon him.

He resisted the urge to gallop. The dog was far away, and no one would come to investigate. He might be on a farmer's field, but the Duthenor went seldom abroad at night. They preferred the warmth of their hearth fires, and the comforts of home. Things that Horta did not have, and anger replaced his fear.

He wondered again how it had come to this. His plans lay scattered. The men who followed him lay dead. The barking of a dog caused him fear. Nothing, it seemed, had gone right since last he had cast the Runes of Life and Death.

At least he had supplies. Enough to last a good while, and he would need them because there was nowhere he could go to buy any. He must disappear from sight until the army he waited on arrived.

So it went for the next several days. Traveling by night, and avoiding the habitations of men. Riding well clear of roads, and hugging the shadows like a thief. He liked none of it, but eventually they arrived at the tomb of the god-king one night in the gray hours before dawn.

Tanata deserved to see what he had risked so much for, so they dismounted and tethered their horses at the base of the hill. Together, they walked up the slope and then cleared away by hand the soil that Horta had left there to obscure the man-made stone of the tomb entrance.

Quickly, the cartouche of the great king was revealed. Three stars, one ascendant over the other two. They gleamed in the shadowy air, and Tanata trembled.

"That is enough for now," Horta said. "When our people arrive, the resurrection will begin."

He began to push dirt back to hide the stone once more, but the stars gleamed with sudden light. The earth trembled, and he lost his footing.

Even as he tried to stand, the earth groaned and roosting birds all around screamed into the night. Something was very wrong, and with a feeling of dread he began to understand.

4. Homecoming

Brand was at the fore of his army again. His Halathrin-wrought blade was sheathed in its old scabbard, and it felt good at his side once more. Better than ever.

Less welcome were the looks people gave him. Word of what had happened in the sacred woods was spreading. It could not be helped. But few now spoke to him, or looked at him as just a man. He had become more in their sight. He was a leader who spoke to the Lady of the Land, and one destined to contend with gods. No wonder they did not look at him straight. Even Shorty and Taingern seemed distant. With them, he knew it would pass. But the rest? He was not so sure.

The army marched down the High Way, and all about were lands that Brand knew well. This was where he had grown up. If the Duthgar was his home, then here was his home within a home. He knew every cottage, every copse, every stream and field.

Then came the moment he had yearned for nearly all his life, and yet also dreaded. The hall of his parents came into view. The hall of his ancestors into antiquity, and the seat of power within the Duthgar.

A road wound down to it from the hills on the other side, but the hall was also set on a hill, the highest for many miles around. The stone-crafted terrace before it was as he remembered. Up and down those stairs and platforms he had run and jumped as a child while his father's hall guards watched from their seats near the doorway above.

Brand's gaze turned to the hall. Proud it stood, the largest and fairest in the Duthgar. The broad gables were decorated, and the long-sloping roof designed to shed snow gave it the characteristic shape of any hall, even if bigger. The doors he could see too, huge slabs of oak bound by black iron.

But he would not pass through them, and the thought of that was grievous. He wanted to, but destiny, if there were such a thing, made no allowances for his wants and wishes.

The enemy was coming, and speed was critical. He must meet them before they came to the lands he loved. Not just the Duthgar, but all the tribes of the greater Duthenor people. He would not see the enemy ravish them. He would give them no opportunity to burn fields and homesteads. Nor to destroy villages while he waited and gathered more men. Those same men could come to him while he marched, and already riders had been sent ahead to give warning and to ask for help.

He thought that help would come. Though the tribes were different, once they had been closer. In times of war, before even they came to these parts of Alithoras, they had banded together under a war leader. They would do so again. They *must* do so again.

They drew level with the hall, and his gaze lingered on it. Would the chance ever come again to see it? He was not sure. The Lady of the Land had foretold he would be a king. But of whom? Of the combined Duthenor tribes? Perhaps. But she had also said that of his line would spring the hope of the north. What did that mean? And yet he had always yearned to explore the northern mountains of Alithoras. They drew him like a moth to light. But for any of that to happen, he must live. At the moment, that did not seem likely.

The hall passed from view. He set his gaze forward, and forced himself to think of the task at hand. He had not had the homecoming that he dreamed of, but he had something else. The sword of his forefathers was at his side. So too his friends, and an army at his back. And the memories of his youth would be with him all the days of his life.

The High Way soon began to take on a downward slope.

"What's ahead of us?" Taingern asked. "The land seems to be changing."

Brand was grateful for something to take his mind off things. He wondered if Taingern guessed that, and asked the question to distract him. He was always sensitive to other people's moods.

"The high plateau that runs through the Duthgar comes to an end here. Pretty much, the Duthgar ends with it. Beyond, and to the east, lie the lands of the Callenor."

"And what of the road?"

"It begins to deteriorate quickly from here. At least it used to, and I doubt that has changed."

"Does it still head southward?" Shorty asked.

"No. Soon, it'll turn south-west. It hugs the end border of Callenor lands, and of the tribes beyond them. Truly, it's not much of a road, but it must still have been traveled by the Letharn. Better to say really that those lands border it, for the road was built long before any of our people came here."

They walked their horses ahead. The going was easy, for the road was still good and the downward slope helped. But soon the way narrowed, and the road ran in half loops instead of a straight line. This was to find the least steep gradient and to help stop the road from eroding.

At each corner, the land below came into view. It was lush like the Duthgar, but flatter. Yet soon the expansive view disappeared. A great forest grew up, all of tall pines and shades of green mixed with shadows.

"You didn't mention *that*," Taingern said.

Brand knew what he was thinking. The way ahead was a good place for a trap or ambush. He did not believe the enemy was here yet, but he could not rule it out. And he trusted the Callenor, more or less. At least those with him, but he was entering their lands now, with an army, and he could not be sure of the reception he would receive.

"Time to send out scouts," he said.

"Time to proceed slowly," Shorty answered.

5. A Time of Change

Horta and Tanata fell back a little way down the slope. It seemed that the hill itself had buckled and moved.

"Earthquake!" Tanata yelled.

Horta wished that were true, but he knew it was not. Dread gripped him. Fear such as he had seldom felt stabbed at his chest, and his breath came in painful gulps. This was no earthquake. It was what he had striven to achieve, but it was too early, and he was not prepared. Nor did he understand how it was coming to pass without the proper rites and invocations of power.

"Stand back!" he yelled, but even though he did so, he never took his eyes from the flat stone of the tomb entrance.

The earth stilled. But the birds in the dark treetops continued to shriek. Then came a sudden booming, muffled by dirt and stone. It thrummed through the air and Horta felt it beneath his feet.

Three times that dreadful sound tolled, like a mighty bell beneath water. And on the third, fire darted from the cartouche and smoke rose, greasy and black.

The stone of the tomb entrance cracked, and then it fell into rubble. A dust cloud rose, and the air became choking, but neither Horta nor Tanata moved.

Before them lay a gaping hole in the side of the hill, and in the darkness of that pit something moved.

Horta knelt, and seeing that Tanata stood motionless and dazed, he grabbed him and pulled him to his knees.

"Kneel," he whispered, "and pray for your life. Glory is now ours, or death."

Out of the pit a figure emerged, and Horta slipped a norhanu leaf into his mouth and bit into it to release its powers. This was all wrong. It should not be happening. Not like this.

The figure clambered into view. Dirt covered it. A once-white burial shroud clung to it like a husk, and even above the smell of dust Horta caught the strong odor of oils, herbs and resins used in the preservation rites of the dead.

"O Great Lord!" he cried. "Your humble servant is here to aid you."

Horta bowed his head, even though he was kneeling, but still his gaze looked up. It was never wise to take your gaze off kings or gods.

Char-harash towered above him. In his right hand he hefted a mighty war hammer, blackened by the blood of ages past. His left was a claw of withered flesh.

The god-king looked down as though upon a beetle, deciding whether to ignore it or crush it beneath his feet. Or to use it for some menial purpose. Horta did not care for that look at all.

"I know you," rasped Char-harash. His voice was hollow, and it smelled of the tomb. "You have served me. Rise! Rise and live. You will walk in my shadow and serve me still in the days to come."

Horta stood. He beckoned with his hand for Tanata to do the same, for the god seemed to ignore his presence. Better to have company to face what was to come than to be alone.

"O Great Lord," Horta answered, and it was a sign of his shock that he could think of none of the ceremonial titles that he should use. "How have you risen from the dead? Your people come. An army marches to aid you. I, with my own hands would have performed the rite of resurrection. But you bestir yourself of your own will, without rite or ceremony or invocation. How is it possible?"

Char-harash fixed him with his hollow eye sockets. It seemed that there was a glimmer of light within their dark recesses, but Horta knew the eyes were removed during the embalming process. Yet still, that stare pinned him just the same.

"Am I not a god? Do not even fate and destiny learn to bow before me as the long years pass? These things are true, yet also the stars and planets shine upon me from the void. Even now, in their endless trek across the skies, they align and the powers that form and substance this world shift. Some forces wane. And others, myself and my brother and sister gods, wax. Our power begins to increase, and the world trembles!"

Char-harash flung out a skeletal arm, though still the bonds of muscle and tendon and ligament held it together. "See!" he cried, and his bony claw of a hand pointed. "There is Ossar the Great, and there shimmers Erhanu the Green, and brighter than them all shines blessed Murlek. These give me strength. These sustained me through the darkness, and they draw me into the light once more as their forces twine and spill down upon this world. As water they are to the parched throat. They are the blood in my veins and the beating heart in my chest."

Horta had heard those names before. Though the names had changed through the ages since last Char-harash had seen them. But he had no heart in his chest. That, and the rest of his internal organs were removed to stop his body rotting. Yet here he stood, and Horta feared him. If the god spoke, who was he to deny the truth of his words?

This much also Horta knew. There was power in the land, and there was power in the light that shone from the distant void. And well might it be that some change there had woken the ancient spells laid upon the corpse of the king who would be a god.

Char-harash was not done speaking though. He hefted his war hammer high. "Life begins to run through my body once more. Strength returns. And even as I wake from the long sleep, so too do my brothers and sisters stir. The light of the void and the breath of the dragon touches us, calls us, beckons us towards the destiny we have chosen for ourselves. The time of change is here, and all things are possible."

"All the gods grow in power?" Horta asked.

"All," answered the god-king. "The gateways of the universe open and close. But now, safety! I grow weary."

Even as he spoke the first rays of the dawn sun shone over the land, and Char-harash flinched as though they stung him. He seemed less like a god now, the more he could be seen. And evidently the clear light of day hurt him.

"Follow me, Great Lord," Horta asked. "I know a place of safety nearby."

"It must be a place of shadows!" hissed Char-harash.

"It is such a place, Great Lord."

Horta signaled Tanata to gather the horses, and when that was done they mounted. Almost he offered the god-king a horse to ride, but the horses were restless in his presence, shying away from him. For his part, Char-harash eyed them with disdain.

So Horta led the strange procession away, and they traveled in silence. This he liked, for it gave him time to think. Much had happened, and many things that he did not understand, at least fully.

He led them along a winding trail that climbed higher among the hills. Char-harash kept up with them, striding beside the horses, and he looked at everything he saw with arrogance. Or contempt. Truly, the gods, old or new, were in some ways the same no matter their differences. And at heart, Horta was sick of them. They demanded so much, and gave so little in return. If he had his youth again, he would walk a different path down the ways of his life. He would abstain from magic and gods and plotting. He would stay in the desert lands that he loved. The wild lands where no man walked, for that was the place to live a life.

But his youth was spent, and his choices diminished. Now, all that was left to him were the ways of Horta the Magician.

6. The Witch

Brand led the army forward into the forest. Hruidgar headed the scouts, and he had sent men forth to investigate. They had not returned, but the army could not delay. At any rate, the men left signals that the hunter could see. The stem of a certain plant broken and bent one way or the other signaled safety or danger. There were others, but the hunter alone knew them. And so far, all was well.

But Brand went slowly anyway. He led, and he kept watch. He also kept one hand near his sword in case of threat. It was not wise for the general to ride before the army. He could fall if there was an ambush. He could be targeted by a bowman from far away. Certainly, he would be known as the leader by any eyes that watched secretly, because men came to him to report and left to carry out orders. Yet, balanced against this was the example he set the men. He was not afraid. And for the whole army to see, with him rode men of both the Duthenor and Callenor tribes. So too the few men from the Norvinor tribe that had joined him. It was a display of unity, and it would help bind the tribes together. Until recently, they had been at war.

"It's a gloomy place," Sighern muttered.

Brand glanced around. They had now entered the forest, but the road still descended, and at this point quite steeply.

"Gloomy, perhaps. And yet I like it all the same. The forest is a world to itself, and I like the feel of them. Better to me than a city, any day."

Hruidgar glanced at him. He did not speak himself, but if anyone knew what Brand meant, it was him.

Yet it *was* gloomy in this forest, and it was large enough to swallow an army. Or a hundred armies. That the men who followed were nervous also was evident. They did not speak much among themselves as they marched, and all that could be heard was the tread of thousands of booted feet.

Brand was confident though. If an enemy was ahead, the scouts would find them.

For some while they continued, slowly but surely. Then scouts began to return. They reported no enemy. This was good news, and the leadership group that rode with Brand was relieved. Yet somehow unease grew within him, and he did not know why.

It was possible that an attack, if it came, would not be with swords but with magic.

"Stay alert," he said. His mood infected the others. They saw no reason for it, but they had learned to trust his instincts. Their hands were never far from their sword hilts, and if their gazes lingered in shadowy patches of the woods before, they stared twice as hard now.

But nothing happened. The road dropped down further, seeming to plunge into the forest that it cut through. More scouts returned, easy in their manner and reporting nothing ill.

Brand led his horse, still holding to the practice of walking as his men must walk. They seemed to like it, and he thought of them now. Stretched out along the winding road and vulnerable. He was their leader, and everything he did influenced their lives. Even their deaths, for surely many, many would die. It was his task to see that the fewest of them paid that sacrifice as was possible.

Fate was not his to control, however. If there was such a thing. But he knew he would blame himself for the smallest of mistakes, for any life lost that wasn't necessary, and perhaps even for those that were. Who was *he* to decide what was necessary and what was not? Yet someone had to, and he trusted himself more than any other to make those decisions.

And he trusted himself now. The sense of unease increased. He lifted high his hand in a clenched fist, and behind him the army came to a standstill. Nothing moved within the woods. All was silent. But he waited, and the silence deepened until the air grew heavy with it.

"What is it?" whispered Taingern in his ear.

Brand gave the only answer he could. "I don't know. But something comes."

He drew his sword then. The leadership group around him did the same. And the hiss of thousands of swords leaping from the scabbards of the soldiers echoed them like muted thunder.

And still, nothing happened.

The tension deepened, and Brand embraced it. The army was forgotten. The people around were forgotten. There was just him and the forest, and the sense of a presence within it. He knew then that the Lady of the Land had changed him in some manner, or woken something within him. He was not quite as he was. He *knew* there was something coming, even before it was there.

Ahead, on the road, a figure came into view. The darkness of the forest shrouded it, and it held its head down. But Brand perceived who it was.

"It is the witch from the swamp," he whispered.

Shorty peered ahead. "Last time we saw her it was some creature of the gods pretending to be her."

"This is her," Brand answered confidently. "At least, what she was."

Shorty gave him a strange look. "What does *that* mean?"

"You'll see."

The figure glided toward them, not seeming to walk but coming closer anyway. Brand knew she had no need to walk. She was not there at all.

She came to a stop before him. Slowly, she raised her head and studied him a moment. If her lank hair and bushy brows worried her, she gave no sign. But her eyes were less rheumy than they were, and the warts were gone.

"You will have learned now that my foretelling is true, lòhren."

Brand inclined his head. If she gave no greeting, nor would he. "I didn't doubt them, not really. But you also said we wouldn't meet again."

She cackled then, hoarse and throaty. But there was an edge of bitterness to it. "I did say that, didn't I? And yet here I am. But my foretelling is never wrong. Quite the mystery, isn't it?"

"Not really," Brand replied. "You lied. Or you are dead, and not really here at all except as a vision."

She looked at him sternly a moment. "Aye, you have the right of it. Not much slips past a lòhren, eh? But which is it?"

"You are dead, lady." Even as he spoke, he moved his hand through her image and it passed through unobstructed. Gasps came from behind him, but Brand ignored them.

"How rude!" she said.

Whether that referred to his calling her dead, or moving his hand through her image, Brand was not sure. But he had no time to play games.

"Why have you come, lady? What troubles your spirit?"

She stood taller then. Almost she looked him eye to eye, and her hair was less lank than it was, and her face younger. The spirit of a dead woman could appear however it wanted to, and apparently she was tired of looking like a crone.

"Well, I'm certainly dead. And I didn't think we'd ever meet again. I think that prophecy was close enough. The truth is, I should have helped you. Perhaps if I'd joined forces with you, I'd still be alive."

"Perhaps," Brand answered.

She stood even taller. "Too often I thought only of myself. I had reasons. But now. Well, now I will help you, just a little. It's all I can."

"Why?"

The witch grimaced. "Sooner hide a strange scent from a dog than hide the truth from a lòhren, as the saying goes. Well, if you want the truth, it's this. It's not for you. What I say now is for revenge. And if I get it, it'll be sweet."

Brand nodded. "That, I can believe. Nor do I spurn it. Speak, and I shall listen."

The witch seemed surprised at his ready acceptance, but she should not have been. Brand knew himself to be practical. He also knew he needed help.

"Three things I shall say," the witch replied after a pause. "I can do no more. First, this. Your enemy may yet be your friend. When despair grips you, hold tight to that thought."

Brand did not know what that meant. He had too many enemies, and none would ever be a friend. But still, he committed the foretelling to memory.

"Second," the witch continued. "The breath of the dragon blows across the land. All things become possible. Change comes, and change can be shaped. Make it yours. Seize opportunity from your enemies before they seize it from you."

Again, Brand did not know what to make of this. It was good advice though. Fortune favored the bold, and he knew it.

"Third," the witch stated, and her voice had grown strong and her visage that of what she must have been in youth. "Self-sacrifice is victory. Offer yourself up in order to grasp victory from defeat."

Brand considered her, and she returned his gaze silently.

"Good advice all, I'm sure. But how am I to use it?"

"Ask no more! I can say nothing else. But remember my words. They won't help you now. They won't help you in the future. That's not what foretelling is for. Hold onto hope, that is all. And you will see by the end."

Brand knew this was true. Her talent was real, but that did not mean she could tell him what to do and what not to do. Her words would not change anything, and would not really help. But perhaps they would shape his thoughts in those critical moments when the time came. Perhaps they might make a difference. It would be a fool who did not heed her.

He offered a slight bow. "Thank you, lady."

She swept a hand through her hair. It was luxurious now, and longer. Nor were her eyes as they were. They were sharp and bright, and they bored into his own as if that was the way she read the future.

"I have done what I can, small though it is. This time, truly, you will see me no more. Good luck. You'll need it."

Even as she spoke the image of her began to fade. He caught a faint whisper of her voice. *I come*, she said. But she was not speaking to him. In moments, she was gone.

All around, the forest seemed to grow a little lighter, and the calls of birds and the chirping of insects seemed suddenly loud.

"Did you make any sense of her foretelling?" Shorty asked.

Brand sighed. "Not a bit. But I wasn't meant to. As she said, it was to give me hope. And hope we have. The task at hand isn't doomed, else she would have said so. Victory is possible, though it will be difficult."

That was not quite what she said. He had put a more positive light on it, but it was still the gist of things.

He signaled the army forward, and the sound of swords being sheathed in scabbards was like a raspy rush of wind. Then, once more, the soldiers followed as he stepped ahead.

7. All the World is Yours

Horta came to the woods he was looking for. They were not large, but the growth of pines was thick and old. They cast deep shadows, and within their concealment the god-king would find respite from the sunlight that hurt him.

Char-harash shuddered when they entered the shadows. It was a strange sight. A dead man walking, or a god coming into his own. A being of great power, and yet one scared of sunlight, even hurt by it. Why should that be?

There were no answers to such questions, but Horta would ponder it anyway. That was the way to discover hidden truths.

"Just a little further," Horta said. Char-harash seemed ready to lie down where he was, but there was a better place ahead.

The god-king had grown weak. The war hammer seemed in danger of dropping from his hand, and the long strides that he had started with a little while ago were now a decrepit shuffle.

But they came very soon to the place that Horta sought. It was just below the highest part of the hill, yet still the tree-growth was thick. The god-king had the cover he wished, but there was a glade at the very top where Horta could go to study the lands about and see what was happening.

A spring seeped away from beneath a boulder, and it would supply them water, if they used it carefully.

Char-harash wandered a few paces off the dim trail, and there he lay down beside another boulder. It seemed that he slept, and Horta had no desire to disturb him.

In silence, he and Tanata established a camp. They tethered the horses nearby, and fed them a little of the oat supplies they had. Later, Tanata would take them to the clearing at the top of the hill to graze.

While Tanata replenished their water bags from the spring, Horta himself built a ring of stones around a slight depression, and there he gathered dry timber for a fire, which he lit. The timber would not smoke much, and what smoke was given off would be dispersed by the tree canopy above. No one was likely to discover them because of it, and he was tired of cold meals and a cheerless camp.

For the first time in a while, he felt a sense of relief. If Brand hunted him, the pursuers he sent would struggle to find him. This was not his land, but he was no novice at hiding his trail. Nor would they be discovered here by chance. It was an isolated spot, and farmers and hunters must come only rarely.

He allowed the sense of relief to wash over him as Tanata sat nearby. But then his glance fell to the sleeping god-king, and his heart was troubled again.

Tanata followed his gaze. "I did not know that gods slept. Do they?"

Horta shook his head slightly. It might have meant that they did not. Or that he did not know himself. It was the latter, but Tanata did not have to know that. It, too, was troubling. Was Char-harash a man, or a god? The legends said he would *become* a god. If so, what was he now? Was he even alive or was he dead? What were his powers? Would they grow? Surely they must, but then again he had shrugged off the sleep of death and risen from the tomb himself. That was power beyond any mere man or magician. Truly, the forces of the universe must be in flux and the god-king attuned by his own talents and the spells of his funeral rites to draw on them.

He talked a little while with Tanata, softly so as not to wake Char-harash, and then they too lay down near the fire and slept. The last few days had been tiring.

It seemed that Horta had just drifted off though, when the voice of the god-king rang through the camp.

"Wake!" commanded Char-harash. "Wake!"

Horta rose from the ground, his head turning and his eyes darting about seeking some enemy. But there was no one. Tanata staggered up as well, fear on his face and his eyes wild. Yet they were alone with Char-harash, though evidently the god-king had rested. For he had risen and stood over them, though he stayed clear of the fire and took turns staring at them as though they had done something wrong.

Char-harash, having got their attention, stepped away from them and the fire.

"I must know what transpires in the land," he said.

Horta gave a bow, or at least the suggestion of one. He was not best pleased, and still his heart hammered in his chest.

"I will tell you what—"

"That is not what I want. I would speak to a fellow god, and I shall summon one. Stay silent, but be ready to serve."

Horta bowed again. This time he did so more deeply. He had recovered, and it would not do to displease his new master. Death would come of that, swift and sure. He had no doubt about it.

Char-harash began to chant, and Horta understood the words. It was the rite of summoning, but here and there the phrases were different and the inflection altered. Horta had been taught by his masters, every one of them, that the words must be spoken exactly the same. He had learned that the words were said just as their ancestors said them long ago. But it was not true. Toward the end, the words became quite different indeed, and Horta wondered what else he had learned that was not correct.

Even so, he slipped a norhanu leaf in his mouth and began to suck upon it. That at least was sure knowledge. The leaf eased fear and gave strength. Both of which he might need. But his store was growing low, and that disturbed him. He would have to begin to eke it out until he could replenish his supply, but he had a feeling he would need more of it than he ever had before.

The gods appeared in fire, smoke and mist. Shemfal came first, bat-winged and terrible. Su-sarat followed, in her human form rather than serpentine. And last came one Horta had never summoned. But it was Jarch-elrah, human-bodied and jackal-headed. Black was the fur over his dog-like face, and his long ears twitched. He was the god of the grave, and rumor claimed him mad.

Horta sucked harder on the norhanu leaf. These were gods who hated each other, and the thought of summoning more than one at a time frightened him greatly.

"Hail, brothers and sister," intoned Char-harash. "We must speak and plan, for the hour is come foretold in antiquity."

But the gods did not look at him. Instead they studied each other with hooded eyes. Jarch-elrah barked, although Horta soon realized it was a laugh, if a mad one. Shemfal gazed at Su-sarat, and there was murder in his eyes. Su-sarat grinned at him, licking her lips as though testing the air with her tongue.

Horta knew the history between these two, and he groaned. But Char-harash looked sternly upon them.

"Heed me!" he commanded. And the two gods stepped away from each other and turned to face him, even if they kept glancing warily at their enemy.

"You do not yet have the power," Su-sarat said. "You have no right of command."

"I *will* have it," Char-harash claimed. "Soon. And then you will obey me. Learn to now, or it will be harder for you then."

Shemfal stood taller, and a pale light glimmered in his eyes. "The powers flux and alter. No one knows yet who will ride on their flows to ascendancy. Prophecy says it will be you, but prophecy is words in the air. Empty until the deed follows. The witch is right. You have no right of command."

"Then heed wisdom," Char-harash answered. "The prophecy is true. I shall ascend. But so will we all. Your time comes again, and my first with it. But an obstacle stands in our way that will hinder the conquest of our children. Will you let this stand? Will you let ancient enmity destroy your future as well as your past?"

The gods did not answer. Silent they stood, brooding powers like a storm ready to burst over the land. Among them, only Jarch-elrah moved, his ears twitching and the teeth of his snout bared in a snarl. Or perhaps a grin. The mad god was hard to read, and Horta held his breath.

"I will listen," Su-sarat replied at length.

Shemfal glared at her, hatred burning like cold fire in his eyes. "I also shall listen."

Char-harash turned to the jackal-headed god. He did not speak nor demand an answer. He merely looked at him.

The god of the grave gave answer. "I also shall listen, but I care not who rises to ascendancy. I care only to run and to hunt, and to find and to eat. And to voice my thoughts upon the wind."

The god lifted high his head and loosed a screeching howl.

Horta shuddered. The sound chilled his blood, and there was a thread of madness twining through it.

Char-harash spoke as though he found none of this strange. Perhaps that was fitting. He was stranger than them all.

"Set me free," he said. "Death still chains me, but my children come. Blood and slaughter will follow in their wake, and I shall gather strength. All of us will prosper and gain worshippers as our name spreads across the lands. Our children are the key. When they come, truly I shall be born again. But Brand stands in their way. He and a ragtag army. Destroy him. Destroy his followers. Then the future will be ours."

Su-sarat hissed. "You make it sound easy. But Brand has power. Defeating him is like attacking a mountain."

Shemfal laughed. "I hear your words, but I sense the true meaning of them. He has not fallen to your wiles and tricks. But where duplicity fails, might succeeds."

Jarch-elrah did not speak. But he grinned, and his black ears twitched.

"It does not matter how it is done," Char-harash said. "Destroy Brand, and then all the world will be yours to grow in and play with. Even to fight among yourselves, if you wish. But destroy his army. Aid our children that come. Lend strength to their sword arms. Give wisdom to their commanders. Put courage in their hearts and victory in their minds."

Shemfal gave a sharp nod. "I shall do so."

Char-harash turned to Su-sarat. She grinned at him. "I shall do so."

Next, the god-king turned to Jarch-elrah. The god of the grave gave no answer, save that he lifted his head and howled once more. It was answer enough.

The three gods disappeared in fire, smoke and mist. Char-harash slumped as though the energy had gone out of him. A thing of skin and bone he seemed, which in truth he was. He ignored Horta as though he were just another tree in the forest or a piece of rock, and he walked warily around the fire and cast himself back down in the deep shadows to rest again.

Horta kept sucking the norhanu leaf. He was addicted, but it did not matter. He had the strength of will to overcome it, but not in these circumstances. Unfortunately, he only saw things getting worse. How could they get better? He shook his head and sat down wearily by the fire.

Tanata joined him, but they did not speak. Horta did not mind, for he had much to ponder.

Clearly, much more was going on than he understood, and he did not like that. Char-harash had great powers, for to summon three gods at once was unheard of. But he was dead, and he was strange too. All the gods were. But dead was dead, and obviously great magic must yet be needed to resurrect him fully. Once, Horta thought he understood the process. He had delved deep into the dark arts and ancient lore of his people. He knew things that would burn the souls of others, even an acolyte like Tanata. But he knew less than he thought, and what he did not know was troubling.

And if Char-harash were rebirthed, how great would his powers be then? Could he really ascend above all the gods? What strife would that cause among them? Would there be wars, of gods and men, as there had been in the ancient past?

One thing was clear though. The army coming to their aid was key. Through this, other lands and realms would be conquered. Blood would be spilled, and worshipers converted by the sword. Nor would the god-king stop.

Once the Duthgar fell, the next realm would follow. And the next.

It was the path to glory for his people. But the price in blood would be high.

8. Is it True?

The army moved forward, and Brand was the head of it, the Helm of the Duthenor marking him as leader, if not king. Though he allowed no one to call him that. Time enough to make choices like that later. For the moment, deeds counted more. And the task at hand was to travel swiftly and try to surprise the enemy.

They left the forest, and entered a different type of land. It was flatter here, and green fields and farmhouses dominated the scenery. Many of the houses had turfed roofs, which Brand found a little strange. But they existed in the Duthgar too, and he knew they were effective.

The Duthgar was behind them though. Now, they had entered into the lands of the Callenor. At least the edge that bordered the wild country to the south.

There was no one in the fields. No farmer worked, tending cattle or sheep. The land seemed deserted, but Brand knew it was not so. They were in those houses, watching and waiting and hoping the army passed without incident.

The road was no longer the High Way. It was dilapidated and narrow. But it served their purposes and the army moved quickly along it. So too the scouts, and they began to bring word of an armed force ahead.

This was not unexpected. They were Callenor warriors. But how they would react to a joined army of Duthenor and Callenor warriors was another matter. No word had yet come back to Brand in reply to the messages that had been sent.

Brand turned to Furthgil, the gray-bearded lord of the Callenor who accompanied him in the leadership group.

"What will these warriors ahead be thinking?" he asked.

The man stroked his beard carefully. "They'll have heard of events. They've not replied yet, but my messengers will have reached them. How they'll respond is impossible to say. I think they'll join you, but they'll be uncertain."

That was what Brand thought himself. All they would really know was rumor. They would doubt what they learned, but they would know one fact for certain. An army had entered their land. The way ahead was dangerous.

The news did not alter Brand's plan though. The army continued, though he gave strict instructions that no one was to leave the road. He did not want any incidents, and the tenseness in the air told him there would be if his warriors trampled fields, some with ripening wheat, oats and barley, or if they helped themselves to a stray pig or fattened steer. Farmers didn't take kindly to that, and he didn't blame them.

Soon, the road wound around in a loop to avoid a scattering of hills, and on the other side the gathering of Callenor warriors came into view.

Brand studied them. They were arrayed for battle, yet there were only a few hundred of them. They could not intend an attack. Not unless it was a trap. Yet his scouts had reported no other gathering of soldiers.

Warily, Brand went ahead. His gaze missed nothing of the countryside round about. Every copse was scrutinized, every fold of the land studied for potential enemies. It was not that he doubted his scouts, it was just that a man was a fool if he left his life unnecessarily in the hands of others.

He drew the army to a halt a quarter of a mile away from the gathered Callenor warriors. To go further was to invite battle. Now was a time for diplomacy. It was a time for words, not a show of arms.

Sighern felt nervous. He was not sure why. The Callenor warriors ahead were not a threat. There were too few of them. Yet it was an important moment. How they acted might determine, probably *would* determine, how the remaining Callenor warriors throughout the land acted. It was important that hostilities were avoided. It was even more important that every single warrior capable of fighting joined Brand's army and fought with him. How else could he have a chance of winning the great battle to come? How else could he hope to defeat gods, as the Lady of the Land said he must attempt to do?

At just that moment, Brand had called him over and he did not know why. Furthgil was already there, and it was plain that he would be sent to speak to his countrymen. What need had either of them for him?

"I have a job for you, Sighern."

"Name it, and I'll do it," he replied quickly.

Brand grinned. "You're always so quick to agree. I like that, but it could see you in trouble before the end."

"No man gets through life without trouble."

Brand sighed at that. "True enough. Hopefully there'll be none now. I want you to go over to the Callenor tribesmen," he gestured with his hand toward the warriors ahead. "You're my spokesman. Tell them I want their help. Tell them why. And answer any of their questions with honesty."

This was not what Sighern expected. Why on earth would Brand send *him*? He was barely old enough to fight as a warrior, though he had accounted himself well lately.

"As you wish."

Brand studied him. "You have no questions?"

Sighern shrugged. "Your instructions are clear enough. Do I go alone?"

"No. Furthgil will go with you. He'll represent the Callenor that have already joined my army. But you represent me."

"Very well." He glanced at the Callenor lord. "We might as well get going."

But Brand was not quite done. He went to his horse and retrieved the Raven Axe of the Callenor. "Take this with you."

Sighern took the weapon, and he felt the hard gaze of the Callenor lord upon him. He understood. It was a symbol of the Callenor, and it should not be in his hands. And yet it was Brand's now, and he had given it to him, at least for a little while. Furthgil would just have to accept that. The why of things did not matter, although Sighern would certainly try to figure it out. It seemed strange to him.

"Good luck," Brand said. "And remember. I need these men, and all the others like them. If they join me, the rest will more easily follow their example."

Sighern gave a bow. It was not something that he normally did, and Brand never encouraged it anyway. The Duthenor were free men, although it was said that men groveled to kings and lords in the cities far to the east such as Cardoroth.

He left then, Furthgil leading his horse by his side, until Sighern mounted his own. Then they nudged the horses forward toward the Callenor warriors.

Furthgil said nothing. The man seemed upset, and Sighern did not blame him. Possibly, the lord had more claim to the Raven Axe than any other. Certainly more than he did.

He hefted it in his hand. It was much lighter than it looked. A careful inspection revealed that the handle was not even wood. It was some sort of metal, strong but very light. It was hollow too. This was why it was so light, and there were slits in it. This was what caused the strange sounds when it was swung through the air. Ingenious.

They merely rode the horses toward the gathered warriors at a walk. Anything faster could give the wrong impression, and that might end badly. But it gave him time to think, too.

Why had Brand sent him? Why had he given him the axe? He could not be sure, but it seemed to him that a leader accrued authority by others doing his bidding. Had Brand gone over himself, it would have lowered his status. That much was easy enough to see. But anyone could carry out such a task, and most were better trained and more experienced than he was.

That was a line of thought that yielded something. Brand was not stupid. He knew all this better than he did himself. So, was there a benefit in sending someone over to accomplish the task who was young and inexperienced?

It took him a few moments, but then the answer became clear. Brand had picked him for exactly those reasons. He was young and inexperienced. He was no trained negotiator. The warriors he was going to talk to would know that instantly. They would discern quickly if he lied, exaggerated or tried to manipulate them. Not something he would have tried, but he also had Brand's only advice to go by. *Answer their questions with honesty.*

Sighern was a lesser figure than the warriors he would talk to. He posed no threat. He would tell them the truth, and he would be trusted more than anyone else. The warriors would believe what he said more than anyone else, even Furthgil. He was one of their own, but he was old and wise enough to lie without being caught. Brand might have given him inducement to do so, in gold or some other reward.

It made sense. The worst choice was the best, and Sighern's estimation of Brand went even higher than it was. But why give him the axe? Might that not cause animosity? The warriors would not like to see it in Duthenor hands.

For this also there would be a reason. It was just a matter of working it out. What would Brand achieve by it? No. That was the wrong way of thinking. It was not about Brand or the Duthenor. Everything was about the Callenor.

The Callenor warriors were clearly visible now, just a few hundred feet away. Soon, they would recognize the axe. What would they make of it?

One thing Sighern knew. It would not intimidate them. Not in his hands. Not when there was just he and Furthgil facing hundreds of them. That was surely not the purpose Brand had in mind. Was it intended to surprise them? Certainly it would. But was surprise an advantage? He did not think so. It would not achieve much.

There was no answer to the question. Giving him the axe served no purpose that he could see. But again, it was not about him, Brand or the Duthenor. It was all about the Callenor.

The warriors ahead would be surprised by it. And uncertain. They would not be able to decipher its meaning any better than he could.

He considered that. Uncertainty. It was a powerful mental state. It made people pause and think. It stopped them from rash actions. And more than that. It showed that Brand was *not* undecided. Rather the opposite. It showed that he knew what he was doing, and why, and all the more so because he was making decisions they did not understand themselves. As well, it showed that he was in complete control of not just the Duthenor but the Callenor with him.

Sighern grinned, and Furthgil gave him a strange look. But there was no time to explain what he thought now. Perhaps the other man already knew. Afterall, Brand had spoken to him first.

They drew their horses up, and dismounted before the line of warriors ahead of them. Sighern gazed at their faces. They were hard men. They were true warriors, and they carried themselves with that sort of casualness that could burst into deadly action in the blink of an eye.

Sighern admired that. Brand, Taingern and Shorty were like that as well, only more casual and more deadly. But he was used to it. He held it in the highest of esteem, but it did not scare him. These men would not attack him. It would be a cowardly act, and he knew just by looking at them that however violent they could be, it was controlled and directed only toward protecting themselves and their land.

He led his horse forward a few paces, holding the reins in one hand, while in the other he held the haft of the Raven Axe. He gripped it high, near the double-bladed head to indicate he had no intention of swinging it, but still the eyes of the warriors flickered between it and him, and their gazes were hard. They knew it for what it was.

Tension filled the air, and Sighern spoke first, before Furthgil who was both his elder and one of them.

"Hail, warriors. My name is Sighern, and I've come here at Brand's bidding to talk."

He was met with a wall of silence from all these men, but one stepped forward a pace and answered. He was, perhaps, a little older than the others. Certainly his armor and clothes were of a better quality. He was of the nobility and their leader.

"Hail, Sighern of the Duthenor. My name is Attar, and I lead this band. Hail also Furthgil, who once dwelt in Callenor lands."

Furthgil grimaced. "I know you, Attar. Why do you say that I once lived in Callenor lands instead of calling me a Callenor? Do you truly believe my allegiance has changed?"

Attar looked him in the eye. "You've been gone from us a long time. And you come here now, you and other men who once lived here, joined to a Duthenor army. What am I to make of that?"

"You know why your countrymen are here," Sighern said. "And why the Duthenor are as well. You'll have received messages. But if you doubt them, then speak to us. Ask questions. I'll hold nothing back, and answer you truly."

Attar studied him, surprised again that he took the lead over Furthgil.

"We've received the messages. Interpreting them is another matter."

"It makes sense to be cautious," Sighern replied. "I don't blame you. But now you have a chance for more than messages. I've been with Brand since first he returned to the Duthgar. I've seen everything with my own eyes. Where you have doubts, ask me and I'll tell you what I know. Truthfully."

The other man seemed thoughtful. It threw him that Sighern was in charge, and that Furthgil did nothing to try to change that. But he showed little of this on his face, even if a glimmer of uncertainty gleamed in his eyes. But it too was quickly suppressed, and he asked an unexpected question. Sighern was prepared to talk of gods and foreign armies, but Attar appeared to have other concerns, or at least was not yet willing to go direct to the heart of the matter.

"What's Brand like? What sort of man is he?"

Sighern was not sure how to answer that. "What can I say? He's like no other man I've ever met. There's no one braver than he is. Time and again he's risked his life for his people. I don't think there's anything he wouldn't do for them. And the rumor is that he could have been king of Cardoroth had he wanted. But he kept his word and stayed regent only. He returned to the Duthgar, when he could have been a king, or lived like a king. That says it all."

Attar pursed his lips. "So, Brand would die for his people, you think?"

Sighern didn't hesitate. "He would. I believe that."

The Callenor warrior nodded. "And what of you? Would you in turn die for Brand?"

Again, it was not the sort of question Sighern expected. But he answered it truthfully.

"No one knows for sure what they're made of until they're tested. But yes, I think I would. At the least, I hope I have the courage for that."

Furthgil looked at him, then at Attar. "The boy has courage. Whatever else you doubt, don't doubt that. He and one other accompanied Brand and walked into our camp to speak with Gormengil. Three surrounded by thousands. That took guts."

Attar raised an eyebrow. "Guts indeed. I don't doubt it." He turned his gaze on Sighern again. "Tell me of this army that supposedly comes against us."

"We know it's coming. We don't quite know where or when, but it'll be near here and soon."

"And who is this army made up of? What do they want?"

"They're the Kirsch. They want to conquer the Duthgar and wake … I'm not sure. A long-dead king of theirs who is buried somewhere in the Duthgar.

Supposedly he'll be a god, and he'll conquer the world if he isn't stopped."

"And you believe these myths? For surely that's what they are."

Sighern held himself tall. "If someone had just told me, perhaps I wouldn't. But I've seen one of the gods of the Kirsch. She was real enough to me."

"I saw her also," Furthgil stated. "And sorcery besides. The times are changing, and the world shifts. There's danger in every action, but the greatest danger is to do nothing and hope things pass us by."

Attar looked at them long and hard. Then he glanced at the leaders of his men. What passed between them, Sighern could not tell. None of them spoke, but they still seemed to have arrived at a decision, or supported what decision they knew Attar had made.

He turned to Sighern. "Then we will join Brand and fight."

Sighern slowly raised the Raven Axe. "I expected nothing else. You're Callenor."

9. A New Banner

Brand was pleased with what Sighern had done. Hundreds of Callenor warriors had joined his army, and Attar now rode in the leadership group. He was a minor lord, but he looked a hard man, and used to fighting. More importantly, he sent his own messengers out. Word of his joining Brand would spread. It would convince more to do the same.

The army pressed forward. A sense of urgency descended, and though Brand did not know where the enemy was or how close, he felt that soon the scouts would bring him word.

They moved across the edge of Callenor lands. It became flatter still, most unlike the Duthgar, and the turf-roofed houses became bigger. This was a more prosperous area, and Brand could see why.

There were many fields, and they were quite large. But each grew a good crop of some kind of cereal. Oats dominated in the Duthgar, but here it seemed to be wheat. The grain heads were filling, but harvest was still some way off.

Almost it seemed peaceful. The late summer sun shone warm and hot, but autumn was at hand. The fields rippled to every breeze, the grain heads nodding. It was drawing on to harvest time, a period of hard work and then celebration. There would be many barn dances, and beer would be drunk while sausages were made and hung from kitchen ceilings to smoke. It was a defiance of the hard winter to come. But this winter would be harder.

War was coming. Blood would be spilled and lives lost. Men who should reap wheat and thrash grain would instead cut and stab at an enemy. Women who should sing harvest songs would weep. And many would die, perhaps all, if he failed.

He must not fail. The land needed him, and he served her. It was a pity that all his skills related to war, and the fighting of men in groups and single combat. Even magic was a weapon, though only against sorcery. But a man learned what life forced him to learn, and he acted according to the deeds that were required.

There was more to fighting though than the cut of a sword, and more to leading warriors into battle than being the best fighter among them.

He glanced at Sighern. He had asked the young man to keep the Raven Axe a little longer when he had returned and offered it back. No one was quite sure what to make of that, least of all the lad. Perhaps Taingern knew, for he was a deep thinker and he missed nothing, least of all what was hidden from plain sight. But no one else.

"Sighern," Brand said. "Do you still wish to be my banner bearer?"

The young man nodded enthusiastically. "Of course." The banner was not on display now though. Brand had ordered it taken down when they entered the lands of the Callenor. It was his birthright, and he was proud of it, but it would be provocative to them.

"Then I have something for you. Keep the old one in your saddle bag for the moment, but for now, use this instead. I've had it specially made these last few days."

He dug into his own saddle bag and handed the banner he had designed and ordered made to Sighern.

"Attach this to the old staff, and carry it proudly."

The young man withdrew the staff from a leather loop attached to his saddle, and he tied the new banner to its end by the cloth strips attached to it.

But it was only when he held it higher that it properly unfurled, and the design upon it became visible. The cloth gave a white background, and on the banner's bottom left was embroidered a red dragon, the emblem of Duthenor chieftains. But on the top right corner was the black raven claw of the Callenor tribe.

There was silence as Sighern held it high, but the young man merely glanced at it, giving a small nod of approval after a few moments of consideration.

"Of course," he said, almost to himself. "We're no longer just the Duthenor. This army is of Duthenor and Callenor warriors combined. Neither takes precedence over the other. This is a banner all can fight beneath, and die if they must."

Attar responded solemnly. "You are right."

Brand gave no answer. Yet again, the young man impressed him. His insight and understanding of situations and events was greater than could be expected from someone his age. Shorty and Taingern knew of the new banner, and they approved. But they had no sense of patriotism to either tribe. Their loyalty was to him.

It had been different with the Duthenor warriors he had found to make the banner itself. He had located men within the army who had some skill at sewing and embroidery, if mostly with thin leather for decorative saddles, reins and the like. When he had told them of the design he wished, they had resented it and even argued. Brand guessed that most of the Duthenor felt that way, but he knew it would change.

Sighern understood better. When the fighting began, warriors would not care much if it was a Duthenor or a Callenor beside them. All they would want was that their comrade held the line with them, fighting shoulder to shoulder and helping to protect one another. They would be one army then, and one people.

The army halted for a rest soon after. The leadership group wandered to the shade of an apple orchard by the road. The fruit was not ripe yet, but the skins of the apples were beginning to show color. The shade was good though, and it was a relief from the late summer heat.

But though he enjoyed the shade, Brand had work yet to do. He called over Bruidiger, the leader of that handful of Norvinor tribesmen who had joined his army.

10. Like Whey from Curds

Wena led his army forward, and pride filled him. The days of blood and glory were coming again. He was a magician and a battle leader, and the gods would favor him for his diverse skills.

Dust rose behind the troops, but not as much as previously. The dry lands of his home were behind him. The new green lands lay all about. Fat, luxuriant and soft.

Even what dust rose in these green lands would be less now. A cold rain had begun to fall. It was little more than a shower, but it would dampen the earth and settle the telltale haze. If there were any enemy eyes in this wilderness, it would help hide the passage of his soldiers. Other than that, he hated the rain.

He hated the land more though. So green and lush, and the wind always blew. It was late summer, but it seemed cool to him. How then would it be in winter? The thought chilled him. Snow and ice and razor-sharp winds, according to legend. The prospect of campaigning for years in such a place did not appeal. But the thought of the bloodshed to come warmed his heart. He would show Char-harash what he was made of.

Horta was a concern though. The man was soft. He had a reputation for treating his Arnhaten well, rather than as the slaves they were until they had endured years of hard service and learned the craft of the magician properly. A state few achieved. But worse, he was the discoverer of the foretold one's tomb. That would lift him high in the eyes of Char-harash.

And Horta would use that. Oh yes, he would use that. He would seek dominion of all the Kar-ahn-hetep eventually, but certainly in the first instance the army that came now to free and serve the god-king. That could not be allowed.

Wena grinned to himself as he marched. He would not confront Horta, nor challenge him for authority. He would greet the other man as a brother, and when opportunity arose, he would slip a knife into his back. That was how situations like this were handled. But Horta was powerful, very powerful indeed, so it must be done carefully.

Despite the weather, he was in a rare good mood. His mind flitted back to earlier this morning. He had ridden in one of the war chariots. It was an exhilarating experience, but not one that he ever had much opportunity for. The chariots were few in number, only some five hundred in total. And they were instruments of war, reserved for highly trained specialists. One driver and one warrior to each. Only they and kings were allowed to use them, and there had not been a king for a long, long time. That might change.

The savages ahead of them would not know proper military tactics, still less the means to face horse-drawn chariots that moved at speed and broke enemy formations. No, they would be surprised at that, and they would fall back in dismay.

The battle to come did not disturb Wena. He grinned to himself as he walked, but between one pace and the next that grin was gone.

Something was coming. The hair on the back of his neck prickled as it did when he performed the rite to summon a god. Only he had done no such thing.

He signaled the army to a stop, and drew his short sword. Was this some attack by the enemy? He felt magic at work, and that was always disturbing.

But it felt familiar also. It could not be the enemy. Unless it was Horta? Could he be launching a preemptive attack? It was possible, but he did not think so. He would need all the help he could get for the Rite of Resurrection that must yet be performed.

Smoke writhed up from the ground as though the earth itself was afire. Fire seethed in the air, and mist twined through it, turning instantly to vapor.

Three figures sprang into being, and Wena stumbled backward a few paces. Then he knelt. For he knew who these figures were. Shemfal, Su-sarat and Jarch-elrah. They were gods, and not just gods but leaders among gods. Nor was that alone what intimidated him.

It was unprecedented for three gods to appear at once. It had not happened in living memory. Perhaps not even in legend, but he could hardly think.

A shadow fell over him, and he knew Shemfal had stepped closer. His great wings moved and shimmered, and a terrible light was in his eyes.

"Stand, mortal," the god said. "If you have no courage, we will find another in this army to lead."

Wena rose. His legs were unsteady, and his heart pounded in his chest. Death filled the air, or at least the possibility of it, but he forced himself to look into the eyes of the Lord of the Underworld.

Shemfal gazed at him the way a man might study the fruit of a tree to see if it was ready to be picked.

"That is better," the god intoned. "If you would serve, you must have courage and wit."

Wena did not hesitate. "I have both, O Great One. Command, and I shall obey." He gave a small gesture to his Arnhaten, and they stumbled toward him. A sacrifice may be called for, and he had no intention of facing that request alone. Dying was for lesser servants, but the gods did not always know that. Better to have all his options close to hand.

Jarch-elrah gazed at him, as though reading his very thought, and those eyes pieced him for there was madness in them.

But it was Su-sarat who spoke. "Courage will be needed more than wit. We know your task, and we have deigned to help you. Our thoughts will be your thoughts, and you will have little need of your own."

Wena was not sure what that meant, exactly. But it revealed one thing at least that he liked. They did not intend to kill him. That was what mattered above all else.

It was time to try to take some initiative. "We hasten across the lands, O Great Ones. This Duthgar that we seek is getting close, according to my guide. Soon we will unleash war, and find the tomb of the god yet to be. Then—"

Shemfal towered over him, but as he stepped closer Wena observed the famous limp.

"We know this, mortal. You will do these things or die. But there is more you must do."

Su-sarat leaned forward now. "Peace, Wena. We have felt your tread on the earth, and the gods know you for a man of distinction. You are marked for greatness, and truly the days to come will allow you to shine. But there is more for you to accomplish in this fight with Brand."

She reached forth with her hand and touched his cheek then. The thrill of it ran through him.

"O Hunter of the Night, I am your servant. Command, and I obey. My guide has brought word of this Brand who leads the enemy. I will crush him for you."

Su-sarat smiled at him, and her gaze was kinder than the shade of an *uzlakah* tree in the desert.

"You will crush his army, but for that man ... I have a plan of my own. Leave him to me, but as for the battle with his forces, this is what you will do."

She bent near him, and her soft breath was upon his cheek. Just as well to remember that she was the Trickster, and honeyed words could swiftly become a venomous bite. But as she spoke, he liked the strategy that she outlined.

"First, travel swiftly," she advised, "for Brand himself hastens. Keep your main army with you, and make no attempt to hide. His scouts will find you quickly enough. But pick a man of judgement, and let him take a smaller army, one of three thousand men, and task him with flanking Brand in secret. This will not be easy. Let him have your best scouts in order to kill Brand's. Tell him also that failure is certain death, for should Brand become aware of him too early, his small army will be destroyed before you arrive."

Wena nodded slowly. He would not interrupt, for he liked the plan, and he knew what was coming next.

"When you approach Brand's army," she continued, "slow down your advance. Give the second army time to maneuver, for it must needs travel wide and further than yours to escape detection. Then when you have joined battle, the second army will descend upon Brand's in surprise and fury. Caught between two forces, the enemy will be destroyed."

It was as Wena thought. But he was not so sure of the outcome.

"Yet still the enemy may retreat," he said. "If so, and if well led, they may salvage the situation and surprise will be lost."

"And what will you do then?" Su-sarat's voice was a whisper.

"Then I shall follow with speed and force, harassing him all the way. He must turn and fight, else be destroyed piecemeal. But in the end, by force, or surprise, in one hour or over days, he *will* be destroyed."

Su-sarat nodded. "Let it be so, but you will find that he does not retreat. Be wary that he does not attack just when defeat is likely. He is that sort of man."

Wena noted that. He was surprised that there almost seemed to be admiration in the voice of the goddess. But likely he imagined it. The gods did not admire men.

Su-sarat withdrew, for Shemfal loomed closer. Wena felt the enmity between them, and it seemed they did little to try to hide it. She sneered at him, and he pretended that she was not even there, assuming a lofty arrogance befitting a lord among gods.

Jarch-elrah growled deep in his throat, but after a moment Wena interpreted that to be a laugh. It sent a shiver down his spine, but he ignored it. His attention was on Shemfal only.

"The Duthenor are soft," the Lord of the Underworld declared. "When the time is right, slaughter them in blood and fury. It would please me. And all the better will those who remain alive come to serve their new masters."

Wena bowed, and when he looked up again the shadow of the god had passed from him, and Shemfal and the other two had their backs to him, walking away. In a moment, they disappeared in roiling smoke. But the limp of the bat-winged god had been obvious.

One of the Arnhaten nearby laughed nervously. "The legends of the feud between the snake and the bat are true," he said. "And the snake had the victory."

Wena did not hesitate. In a single motion he drew his sword and decapitated the man. The head rolled on the dirt, and the body stood a moment, blood gushing. Then it fell in a heap.

Wena casually bent and cleaned the blood off his blade with the man's cloak. Then he stood.

"Bury the man," he ordered the other Arnhaten. "Make it a narrow hole, and place the head in first with the body after, feet up."

Wena moved aside and issued orders for the detachment of the second army. He would squeeze the blood from these soft northerners like whey from curds.

11. He Would be a King

Bruidiger came over to Brand, as requested. His every step was casual poise, and he had the look about him of a warrior born. The grace of a dancer was needed to be a swordsman, and a will of iron harder than any blade. This man had both. But it was more than a look, for Brand had seen him fight. Even so, the man smiled now with good nature. The Norvinor, Brand had discovered, were a happy and laughing people, quick to joke and quick to make light of themselves. It was a trait Brand admired, and all the more so in deadly warriors.

"Can I do something?" Bruidiger asked.

"Yes. I have a job for you, if you're willing," Brand answered.

"Name it, and it will be done."

"You're like Sighern – always agreeing to things before you know what they are."

"Guilty as charged, my lord. But then again, I can always try to back out of things afterward if I don't like them."

"True enough," Brand said. "But I don't think you'll want to back out of this. We need more warriors, and your homeland is on the further side of the Callenor lands. It's getting closer. So, would you be willing to go to your chieftain, and to tell him what's happening? And then, on my behalf, ask him for help?"

"Of course," Bruidiger replied. "But I can't guarantee what he'll say. But if rumor of events in the Duthgar has already reached him, it'll help."

"I can ask no more than that you try."

"When do you want me to go?"

"Now. I'll have a fast horse given to you. And one for each man in your small band if you like. They may prefer to go with you."

"I don't think so. Their place is here, even if I'm not with them. What comes is a threat to us all. But I'll ask them."

It was not long after that Bruidiger sped away on a black mare. It was a fine horse, though not as good as Brand's roan. Just as well that Bruidiger's men had not gone with him – the army had few horses and fewer still that could keep up with the black.

Brand turned his thoughts away from Bruidiger. He would succeed in convincing his chieftain to send warriors, or he would not. There was nothing more Brand could do about it. But his own army was a different matter.

For all that he was trying to create a sense of unity among the two tribes, it was not easy. The lords of either tribe seemed to bicker among themselves, and they were quick to feel slighted at an accidental word. To be sure, there was mistrust there, but it was more than that, and Brand knew it.

They all sought power. It was what lords did. And the current situation created a void. For the moment, all power came from Brand. He was careful to assign tasks, responsibilities and praise equally, but he also made choices based on merit. It was a concept they did not understand. They had come to power through networks and connections and the luck of being born to certain parents.

They knew though that war was at hand, and battle and death. If he himself was killed, a likely enough possibility, someone would have to take charge. Most of them wanted it to be themselves, and they fought for power now to make their rise easier in such an event.

A few of them had also seen what he had long known. The new banner had made it clear, for those with the eyes to see. The Duthenor and Callenor had once been a single people. They could be so again. They could become powerful, and have a powerful king to lead them.

Brand knew he could do that. But should he? The Lady of the Land had said he would be a king, but not of whom. And always the mountains of the north beckoned him. Why was that? And how did it fit into anything?

The army was on the move again, but Brand found an opportunity to talk to his oldest and most trusted friends, without others listening in.

"Should we win the battle ahead," he asked, "what future do you see for the two tribes?"

Shorty scratched his head. "You always like to plan ahead. Me? I'm only thinking about the fight just in front of us and how to win it."

Brand laughed. "Pretend all you like, Shorty. But you see things as clearly as the finest strategist, and you're as wise as any philosopher."

The other man grunted. "If you say so. But alright, this is what I see. You're already forging the two tribes into one nation. And you know as well as I that if we win the battle ahead, these men who have fought together will draw close as brothers. Suffering together does that. You'll have them all in the palm of your hand, and a kingship beside, if you want it. And if you're alive."

Brand thought on that. Shorty had said it bluntly, as he always did. But his insights were correct. He wondered how long Shorty had seen his plan to unite the tribes into one kingdom. Probably from the beginning.

"What do *you* think?" he asked Taingern.

His other friend answered quietly. "The kingship is yours, if you want it. But you don't. The Duthgar was your home, but it isn't any more. More than you ever dreamed of is within your grasp, but it has been before, and you left it behind. You have another destiny. But you also have a problem. Only you can unite the tribes. The lords quarrel among themselves for precedence, and without you, hostility will break out. Who else is there that can unite them all?"

Brand knew that was truly the question. There was no one. But then again, he had given thought to it before. Nothing was impossible, and he had a few ideas. But Shorty was right. They had to win the battle ahead first. When that was done, *if* it was, then things would be clearer.

His musings were interrupted though. Hruidgar, that strange hunter he had made head of the scouts, approached.

"What news?" Brand asked.

"Nothing. To the south my men report empty wilderness, as expected. So too the south-west. To the north, well, we don't go too far because they're Callenor lands. But we've seen no forces there, hostile or friendly."

"The Callenor will join us I think, but just as the Duthenor in the Duthgar it will be smaller groups at a time. Keep the scouting up there, because I don't want any surprises, but I don't fear they'll attack us." He swept his hand out to the south-west. "Out there is the true enemy. Somewhere. They're coming for us. Time to send the scouts further afield, I think."

Hruidgar nodded and ambled away. He never was one to speak much, but he knew what he was about when it came to organizing the men he had picked and been given charge of.

The army went ahead. The land changed again, and northward rose in a series of sweeping slopes. They were not steep, and they caught the sunlight. Here was established vineyard after vineyard, and the place was famous even in the Duthgar. This was the origin of the wine the Duthenor drank. They had a taste for it, even if they preferred beer and mead more.

The vineyards were not as grand as what Brand had seen in Cardoroth, nor of the same quality. But with time and attention, they could be.

It was rumored the people here were prosperous, for they profited well off the expensive wine. But profit or not, they had a good life and it was said their autumn harvest festivals were the best in the lands all around.

Not for the first time, Brand wished he made a simple living like that. For all his power, they lived the better life.

12. The Old Masters

Horta had rested through much of the day, for the flight from Gormengil's army, or the army that had become Brand's depending on how he looked at it, had been wearying in the extreme.

It was night now, but only just. He felt fresher than he had for days, and though the exhaustion of physical effort had fallen away, the mental strain of fear of pursuit had not left him. But it was reduced. He and Tanata had taken turns through the day to climb to the open glade at the crest of the hill and observe the countryside for miles all about. There had been no sign of any search.

Dusk had just given way to full night. Tanata had woken too, and he threw more wood on the fire. It was time to cook some dinner. This was a chore for the acolyte, but in truth Tanata had proven a surprisingly good cook. Even with the limited supplies he had to work with, he turned out edible meals. And he liked doing so. How unusual that someone who was learning the great mysteries of the universe should also like the mundane.

But Tanata had proven a surprise in so many ways. Not least his acceptance of their new situation, and his seeming lack of anxiety. The man was confident, although part of it was an act. His brethren had been killed around him. He now served a dead man, not quite come back to life, who would yet become a god. He took it all in his stride, as the Duthenor would put it. But there were shadows under his eyes and he whimpered in his sleep without knowing. The fear was there, but masked to near perfection. It was an admirable trait.

In the shadows, Char-harash woke and stirred. The god seemed to stumble upright, and then he strode over.

"Food," he said, his voice harsh and dry. "I must have food."

"We have supplies, O Great One. Tanata will prepare something."

The god-king seemed to consider that, then he shook his head. To Horta, it seemed the gesture was filled with frustration.

"I need more than you have. Stay by the fire, and do not go out into the dark."

Char-harash ignored them then, and he moved away into the night and disappeared from sight.

Horta felt the eyes of Tanata upon him, and he knew the unspoken question in the other man's gaze, but he ignored it.

"Prepare something for us," he said, turning his own gaze back toward the shadow-haunted forest.

Tanata did not answer. He merely went about his task quietly and efficiently, but Horta, despite not answering the unspoken question, could not ignore it in his own secret thoughts.

He put more timber on the fire, leaving a section of embers alone so that Tanata could use it to heat their cooking pot. It was a night for a large fire, but he could not risk making it any larger than it was for fear of being seen, however unlikely that was.

Unwillingly, his thoughts turned to Char-harash. Could he not eat normal food? Would it not sustain him? That seemed to be the case, else he would have eaten in the camp. But why go out into the dark? Had he need of living flesh to eat? Would he hunt some beast and eat it raw, thereby increasing his life force?

A still-beating heart, and the blood pumping from it, of a sacrifice was part of the Rite of Resurrection. It was said to help bring the dead back to life. But there was great magic involved in that rite also, and he had always taken the blood to be symbolic rather than necessary. Yet he could be wrong. It was possible Char-harash, having exited the tomb by himself, now undertook what was necessary to sustain himself in his own way.

But no magic had been invoked at the tomb, at least that Horta had sensed. That must still be to come. Or, possibly, the god-king had worked his own spells and used the influence of the heavenly forces to fortify himself before anyone arrived.

Anything was possible, and Horta did not like not knowing the answers. Was Char-harash alive in any true sense of the word? Could he really become a god? And if so, what kind of god would he be? If he needed to feast on living flesh now, would that always be so?

Horta had no answers, and he ate the food Tanata prepared in a melancholy silence. The answers to all his questions would come, eventually. But still, the urge to use the Runes of Life and Death pulled at him now. If ever there was a time for foretelling, this was it.

They finished eating, and Tanata cleaned up. The night wore on about them, and Char-harash did not return. But it seemed that the dark was alive with unseen eyes all about them.

Horta made up his mind. "I shall cast the runes," he said to Tanata.

The young man merely nodded. He had expected it. Perhaps it was what he would have done, or maybe he had come to know his master well. Whatever the case, Horta was pleased, and glad that at least one of his acolytes still lived. Serving a god by himself would be a lonesome task.

Horta moved a little way from where he sat so that he did not look directly into the fire. He motioned Tanata to join him, and allowed him to sit level with him rather than behind. It was not something that his masters had ever done with him, but the times were changing, and the old ways were not always the best.

He began to chant, and his words flitted up into the night the way that smoke and sparks from the fire rose in a swirling plume.

Forces gathered around him. Dark forces fit for summoning only at night. He felt their presence disturb the natural air. He could not see them, but much of magic was like that. The unseen was the most powerful.

And despite not seeing them, he could still put names to them. All his masters that had gone before him, and no few of his enemies as he had risen through the ranks of magician society. Ten there were, and they came now at his summons to do his bidding and reveal the future, as they were constrained to do.

But with their presence they also brought hatred. Enmity thrummed through the magic that bound them. He felt them strain against it.

He continued to chant, his voice louder now and the strength of his will greater. Each word he uttered with perfect clarity. Last time he had cast the runes, there had been some mistake. He would make none now.

Certain that all was well, he exclaimed the last words of the invocation in a commanding voice. Then he sat in silence. A moment he hesitated, for fear came upon him every time he was about to cast the runes. Knowing the future was a dangerous business.

He did not pause long though. This was a task that he did not like, but one that he had performed many times. He knew the pattern of it, and the ceremony that had come down of old. None among the Kar-ahn-hetep knew it better than he.

He slid his hands into the pouch that contained the runes. They were cold to touch, which disturbed him.

Normally that was not so. They were fashioned of bone, not metal.

It did not matter. He would cast them and read the future, whatever it was. The wise man looked forward to nothing, and the wise man feared nothing. What would be would be.

He shook the bones in the pouch ten times, as ritual demanded. This was to ensure the caster could not choose certain runes deliberately.

His fingers seemed numb from the cold now, but he took hold of the bones that he felt and withdrew them from the pouch.

All around him the spirits of the dead flew, but they were hushed and invisible, nothing more than a whisper of pressure somewhere on his mind.

Then he cast the runes, flinging them to the ground as he always did, careful to let them fall where they would and not try to guide them in any way. But no sooner had he done so than a great tumult broke out.

The spirits screeched through the air, and the flame of the fire dipped and wavered. Even Tanata gasped, and Horta glanced at him quickly. The man was pale as snow.

Horta did not understand what was happening. It was then that he saw the runes, and the blood drained from his own face. The spirits raged all about him, but he was heedless of their presence. He had eyes for the runes only.

He studied them. The finger bones of dead men lay there, and nothing in all the world mattered save them. He counted them. And then he counted them again. There were ten, and there was no mistake.

A cold fear settled into the marrow of his bones. His heart thrummed, and his mouth worked silently. He had no words to express his dismay.

Ten bones. It signified one thing, and one thing only. Catastrophe of the highest order. The ten bones must *never* be cast at once. Never. And if they were, which legend recorded only perhaps once before, it meant, death, destruction and calamity. Had the sky fallen upon him in a ruin of shattered stars he would not have been more surprised.

But he was Horta, a magician of power. Let fate be what it would be, he would face it with courage. He stood up slowly, drawing Tanata with him, and guided him to stand further back.

Then he drew powder from one of his many pouches, and cast it at the bones. Fire flared and sparked to life, flashing brilliant white in the dark, making the campfire seem pale. Twice more he did so, uttering words of power.

Smoke rose, dark and acrid, and the very earth seemed to melt and roil. The bones were destroyed, what they revealed blotted from his sight, and the spirits of the dead that the runes entrapped were loosed. No more would they be constrained to serve him, and their faces billowed up in the smoke and leered at him.

Then, with cries of glee, the images of the old masters faded away on the night. The fire died, but tendrils of smoke still rose from the blackened patch of ground. Horta watched them, silently.

He felt a hand on his shoulder. "Come away, master."

With slow steps, Tanata led him to the other side of the campfire, and then he urged him to sit down and rest. When he had done so, the acolyte fetched him a cup of water.

"Drink, master. All will be well."

It was a lie, and they both knew it, but it was well meant.

Horta sipped from the cup. The water tasted like ashes in his mouth, for that was what his life had become. Catastrophe was coming, and he would be at the center of it. But what shape would it take?

Something of his old spirit returned. If catastrophe was to be his lot, so be it. He would still make the most of it. The true man endured disasters and came out the other side. This is what he would do, no matter what.

He straightened, and took another drink of water. Then he looked at Tanata.

"We will not speak of this again. Erase it from your mind. Banish it from your thoughts."

"Yes, master," Tanata replied. But Horta saw from the look in his eyes that he would never be able to do so. He knew the meaning of ten runes all at once, just as well as Horta himself did. And what man could foreknow coming disaster, and ignore it?

They sat in silence after that, sheltering close to the fire. Horta built it up into a blaze, for it was a night where warmth and light were needed. He would take the risk of being seen by any of the Duthenor that searched for him.

In truth though, he did not fear the Duthenor. Had Brand sent men after him, they would have found him by now. Or else they searched, but had found no trail to follow. And if they had not found one in the first few days, then they would not find one now.

Whatever disaster was to come, Horta did not think it had anything to do with the Duthenor. It would come from the gods.

Even as he thought that, Char-harash moved stealthily from the shadows and entered the camp. He sniffed at the air, as though he smelled the unnatural fire that had burned here.

He seemed to dismiss it from his mind though. With a glance at his two servants, but not a word of greeting, he strode over to the other side of the camp where he had slept before and lay down.

Horta exchanged a glance with Tanata, and he saw that the other man had observed the same thing he had.

Char-harash was stronger than he had been when he left.

Horta should have been happy with that knowledge. The coming of the god had been all that he had striven to achieve for years. But instead, he wished only for the tranquility of the desert wastes. All the more so, because he feared he would never experience it again.

13. Nothing is Destined

The vineyards became larger as Brand led the army forward along the road. They covered the slopes, and the neat rows of vines continued for mile after mile. But eventually, they came to an end.

The land changed soon after, and steep hills rose all about. The road turned and twisted, climbing the steepest, and at its top were ruins.

"Those are *old*," Shorty said.

It was true. Brand noted the collapsed walls and piles of rubble. The stone itself seemed weathered, its surfaces roughened by wind and rain and cracked by frost.

"It was here before the Callenor ever came to these lands," Furthgil advised them. "We stay away from them, but there's no rumor of ghosts as with Pennling Palace."

The reference to Pennling Palace was apt, and Brand guessed this building was constructed by the Letharn too. It was not so large, or grand, but from what remained of it there was no doubt it was a fortification too. And one that was perhaps older, when the Letharn border stretched deeper into foreign lands.

They kept going, for Brand knew that haste would serve him well. It always had in the past. Travel quicker than the enemy expects, was his motto. It was advice given to him by his father, but he had also studied it in the records of the great campaigns of Cardoroth, and other nations whose wars were recorded in Cardoroth's libraries.

Give the impression of the expected but execute the unexpected, was his other favorite motto. This too had been used to great success in many campaigns, but for the moment at least, he saw no way to implement the tactic. The Kirsch were coming, and he was going to meet them before they had a chance to ravish the Duthgar or its allies. It was a simple strategy, and its best chance of success was to bring battle to the enemy before they anticipated it.

But for all that speed was necessary, he raised his fist and halted the progress of the army as he had done at the coming of the witch.

But this was no witch. Now, he felt the presence of a god. Su-sarat was nearby, even if she had not revealed herself yet.

How Brand knew this, he was not sure. But his instincts were sharper since he had met the Lady of the Land, and he trusted them.

A fine mist rose from the ground before him, and it formed into the image of Tinwellen, the guise the goddess had used to trick him in the Duthgar.

After a moment, she stood there, dark hair gleaming and eyes smoldering, but she was not alone. Gormengil stood next to her. He had once been a chieftain. He had once been a man. But he was something more now, or less. He gazed at Brand with dead eyes that did not blink, nor was there any expression on his face.

Su-sarat spoke, and her voice was high and clear.

"We meet once more, Brand of the Duthenor. Have you brought all these men to worship me, as you should? Have you come to worship me yourself?"

"Neither," Brand answered. "We have come for battle and victory."

The goddess laughed, and the sound of it was a joy to hear.

"I speak of love, Brand. And you speak of violence. Is there a future for humanity if that is your true nature?"

Brand grinned. "Pretty words. And from a pretty lady. But they disguise reality, and I have better things to do than bandy words with a trickster."

Her eyes smoldered even more, and there was a sudden anger in them, cold and sharp.

"Pretty? Is that the best compliment you can give me? I suppose you would call the ocean a mere drop of water?"

She turned slightly to face Gormengil. "What do you say, my lord?"

The man who had been Gormengil immediately knelt on one knee before her.

"O Goddess, you are fairer than the sun, and I bask in your glory. When you look away from me, the cold of winter grips my heart. When you gaze into my eyes, I am a drowned man who wishes only to plunge deeper."

Gormengil did not move, except that he swung his head to look up at Brand. "Shall I kill him for you, O Goddess? Speak the words, and I will fulfill them."

Brand held the gaze of his former enemy. There was no emotion there, no spark of life. He *had* been his enemy. But now he was like a dead man, moving to the unseen strings of his mistress like a puppet.

"Not yet, my pet," Su-sarat said to him, bending slightly to lay a hand on his head as a woman patted a dog.

Brand sensed Furthgil tremble beside him. Gormengil had once been his lord. He was thought to have been dead, but he was not. Su-sarat had somehow saved him, but in that saving he had been changed. His body lived, but his *mind* was dead. Yet still, he had been the chieftain of the Callenor, however briefly. Would they want him back again?

But Furthgil made no move and spoke no words. He saw who Gormengil served now, and what he had become.

"What do you want here?" Brand asked the goddess. "Time presses, and I have better things to do."

The way he spoke was an insult. It was intended to be. How she reacted would reveal more of her character.

But she merely smiled, and her eyes sparkled. "Oh Brand, how I would have enjoyed breaking you to my will. But no matter. The past is the past. And in remembrance of the good times we shared together, I shall give you this warning."

She gestured for Gormengil to stand, and he rose smoothly at her touch, but she did not take her gaze off Brand.

"Leave these lands," she said, lifting her chin and speaking proudly. "Gods conspire against you, and you cannot challenge our might. Leave warfare behind you. Leave bloodshed behind you. I know you better than you know yourself. You are no warlord, nor heartless warmaker. Each drop of blood spilled is as a tear in your eye. This I know, and thus I give you opportunity to prevent it, and a chance to forestall guilt that will weigh down your very soul. Brand, leave all this behind, and go wherever else your heart takes you. But do not stay here."

The goddess spoke with power, and even Brand felt the force of her words. All eyes turned to him in expectation. Many seemed worried and anxious, for if he left there was no hope to fight off the Kirsch.

"Lady," Brand answered. "I hear your words. Even, I would say, they are well meant. But if you truly knew me, you would know that the guilt of betraying my people would weigh me down more than all else. With a clear mind and a patriotic heart, I answer you. And not just for the Duthenor, but all the tribes threatened by your coming. I will not go. Rather, I bring us all together in defiance of your army and your magic, and even of your gods. Shall I defy it all? If I must."

A deep silence fell, and no answer Su-sarat gave. Instead, she bowed her head as one in deep thought, or perhaps sorrow.

"So be it," she said at length. "I have given warning, and you have given answer. I can do no more for you, and truly, I regret your passing."

"I have not passed yet, my lady."

"But you will, and the world will mourn you for a while. As will I."

"Don't mourn me yet, goddess. I'm a hard man to kill."

"And yet, you are just a man, if a powerful one. You possess a warrior's skill, and a king's bold heart. Even, you possess the magic of a lòhren. But these things will avail you nothing. Change sweeps over the land. The starry void spins and turns, and the gods come again. You cannot prevent it. You can only fall before it. Even the mountains topple when the ocean rises in fury. It is destiny."

Brand laughed. "Destiny? You are wrong. Nothing is destined. Nothing is fixed. You and your kind have a chance to return, and I have a chance to stop you. That is all. And I *shall* stop you."

Su-sarat sighed. "Such courage. You could be one of us, but you never will be."

"I do not wish to be."

"Then there is nothing left to say. We will not meet again."

Slowly the image of the goddess turned to mist. Brand watched, wary to the end for she was the Trickster. But she spoke no more, nor made any attack.

Gormengil was another matter though. His body was vague, shifting vapors disappearing in the air, but his face was still clear. And he spoke, his voice void of emotion, but somehow still filled with a cold desire.

"You will not meet her again. But you *will* meet me. Dread that day, for it will bring ruin to your army and spill your blood upon the earth even as mine was spilled."

Then the Goddess and Gormengil were gone, but a chill remained in the air.

14. Only by Chance

Hruidgar was sick of the army. Too many people, and too much noise and talk disturbed him. He was a loner, and did not really like people at all. But Brand was different. When he spoke, it was to a purpose. And where he led, others followed.

But for all that Brand spoke seldom, his gaze was never far away, and those eyes seemed knowing. It was not possible for him to *know*, and yet there it was. As uncanny a thing as Hruidgar had ever experienced.

Few remembered the days of his youth. He was older than he seemed. But once, he had left the Duthgar. Three years he had been gone, and when he returned men questioned him where he had been, and he refused to answer. That had given him a reputation, and afterward he was avoided.

That was for the best. And for his part, he became a hunter, roaming the wilds and bringing meat into villages in harsh winters and furs for trade at other times. He had never grown rich, but he had avoided people as much as they avoided him.

They were dead now, most of them. Few knew his name, still less that he had ever been away from the Duthgar.

But he had. And it was the best time of his life. Seeking adventure, and to forget a girl who had spurned him, he joined a merchant caravan heading south. He had wanted to go to Cardoroth, but the merchant was going to Esgallien.

One destination was as good as any to him though. And anyway, it had not been the destination that mattered. It was always about the journey, and the strange lands and wild places of Alithoras that lured him. That merchant had a knowing gaze as well. He was a man who understood.

So it was that Hruidgar fell in with men in Esgallien who understood him too. The *Raithlin* they called themselves, a last offshoot of a legendary scouting organization. Their skills were extraordinary, and their courage just as great. They taught him, and he trained with them. Even, he undertook missions with them. But he never became one of them.

Learning what he could, reveling in their skills, he formed a camaraderie with them that he had never felt elsewhere. But eventually the call of his own homeland came to him again.

He returned home. And if he was a loner before then, he was more so afterward. But Brand had drawn him out, given him authority and responsibility. He recognized his skills, but he had no way of knowing how they were acquired. Yet still, those blue eyes fixed him at times as though they saw all secrets.

Hruidgar would serve that man well. It was almost a vow. Seldom had he contributed to his community. You could not contribute to something you were never really a part of. But Brand had picked him out and trusted him with a task. He headed the army's scouts, even if there were not enough of them and he was sick of all the people and noise.

But he *did* contribute now. At the same time, he knew his own character. He needed time in the wild by himself. The scouts would report directly to Brand for a while, and all would be well. He would return refreshed and ready for the last stage of the great events he had been caught up in.

He rode a slick black mare, though he would have preferred to be on foot. It was easier to scout that way, and to remain unseen, but he was getting older now, and the horse would allow him to cover much more ground.

But where should he go? He had sent scouts out in all directions, but most had been sent to the south-west. Only a few had gone south, so he turned his mount in that direction. Those men needed his help more than the others. There were fewer of them, and they were the less skilled. In truth, all the scouts were no more than hunters. They were crafty in the wild, but had they known the true skills of the Raithlin they would have been in awe.

He nudged his mount down a slight slope, and once more checked that his assortment of throwing knives, daggers, short sword and bow were all in place. A man could never be too careful, but there would be nothing to find where he went. Still, old habits died hard.

He slipped away into the night, and it welcomed him like a long-missed friend. The army camp was perhaps a half mile away now, but it was invisible. The noise of it, a low rumble in the distance pierced by high-pitched shouts and laughter, still came to his ears though. But soon that would fade. So too the scent of smoke in the air. And when they were gone, he would be truly alone.

He moved south, a shadow in the night. Not only was he leaving the army behind, but the populated edge of Callenor lands. Ahead was the wild. There were no farms and fields. Even hunters would be scarce. He eased forward at a walk, letting his mount choose a path and keeping his own senses alert to the surrounding dark.

He was alone now, and he began to think like himself once more. Almost, he was like another animal that roamed the land. He scented the air. He lingered on the higher points of ridges, looking further afield to see if there were campfires in the darkness ahead. He never moved too far along a straight line, because he had no wish to be predicable.

But even here in the wild, he would not be quite alone. Some few of his men had been sent this way too. They would be out there, somewhere. Though he doubted they would see him or he them.

Brand had allowed him quite a few men. More than he would have thought, but it was still not enough. Maybe that was just as well. It gave him reason to leave the camp and have a look at things for himself. It would only be for a day or two, but that would be enough for him to regain a sense of his own self. When that was done, he could return to the bustle of the army and the milling together of all those men.

The night drew on. He rested at times, even dozing a little now and then. At other times, he led his mount by hand. He did it where the ground was rough and he feared the mare might make too much noise or break a leg. Brand did it all the time, and he had no such reason, though still a practical one. He did it to show he was one of the men. If he walked where they walked, he would fight where they fought. Warriors respected that. A single gesture such as that was worth a thousand words.

Dawn began to break. It was a quiet time, that period where night gave grudgingly way to day. It was a dangerous time too, for a man's thoughts could drift and ebb, and the tiredness of a long night could catch up with him.

That was particularly dangerous for a scout. That was when an enemy would spring a trap. Not that there were any here, yet still it seemed just that little bit too quiet.

Hruidgar sat taller in the saddle. Just thinking of enemies gave him the sense that he was being watched. The wilderness always did that, but the man who ignored his instincts in the wild might soon be dead. And those instincts sparked to life now. Even the mare seemed a little uneasy, flaring her nostrils nervously as if catching the scent of something that she did not like.

He rode on, but warily. Even so, it was only by chance that he discovered the body.

15. Not my Heritage

The army was on the move again, and the scouts had brought in word of a great gathering of warriors ahead. Five thousand strong it was, but it was a Callenor force and not the enemy.

The Callenor had gathered more quickly than Brand had thought. It was a good thing, yet it still made him nervous.

The two forces drew closer, and out of the Callenor a small group detached and came to Brand. They would be lords, and their gazes swept over the bigger army, but came back to rest again and again on the banner that Sighern carried.

Brand gave the reins of his horse to Taingern, and stepped forward to meet them.

"We've come to join you," one of them, a silver-haired man, said simply.

"You're welcome, and you're needed," Brand replied.

They shook hands and greeted one another. But their gazes kept going to the banner. Brand said nothing, waiting for them. And one of them at last mentioned it.

"What does the banner mean? I've not seen its like before."

"It means this. The Duthenor and the Callenor fight together. For a time, we'll be one army with one purpose under one leader."

The silver-haired lord spoke. Hathulf, Brand had learned he was called.

"For how long a time?"

"Until the threat we face is beaten. And after? Only as long as you wish. I'll not forge a kingdom by force. I'll not make the Duthenor and Callenor one people. Not unless they want it."

The older man seemed thoughtful. "And what if they *do* want it?"

"Then all things are possible. But let's not ride the horse until it's caught and saddled. We have an enemy to beat first. Nothing else matters until that's taken care of. Nothing at all."

Hathulf seemed to accept that. But his gaze, when it was not on the banner, was on the Raven Axe that Sighern now carried through a loop in his belt.

"And what of that?" he asked, gesturing toward it but not naming it. "Why does a boy carry it and not you?"

Brand was not sure if Sighern appreciated being called a boy anymore, but no insult was intended and the words seemed to roll off him.

"I don't carry it because it's not my heritage." Brand said no more, but he waited. Another question would follow soon after.

Hathulf grunted. "According to the messages I received, you won it and it's yours. So too the chieftainship of the Callenor. At least according to ancient law. But if you don't want the axe, why not give it to a Callenor lord? Why not give it to someone whose heritage it belongs to?"

There it was. And it was a dangerous question in its way.

"The axe is temptation," Brand answered. "It's mine by right, but if I give it to a Callenor lord, what then? Would he not begin to wonder, holding that axe, if he could unite the Callenor beneath him? Would not the thought arise in his heart that he could be a chieftain? And what then of our alliance?"

"So, you mistrust us then?"

Brand replied swiftly. "I trust my understanding of the hearts of warriors and lords. Tell me. If I gave you this thing, would you carry it and not be tempted?"

Hathulf grinned at him. "You've been honest with me, so I'll be honest with you. I'd be tempted. Very tempted indeed. So I agree. Best that it shouldn't be in my hands, nor any other lord of the Callenor. Yet still, why give it to a boy and not one of your great warriors? I see men with you who seem no stranger to the press of battle."

"I give it to Sighern because he also, despite his youth, is no stranger to the press of battle. He has the courage of a true warrior, and wits as sharp as a well-kept sword. But most of all, I give it to him because he's young. He thinks little about the Duthenor and the Callenor, and all about fighting and beating our enemy. I can trust him with it. To him, it's an implement of war rather than a symbol of leadership."

The eyes of the Callenor warrior studied Sighern anew, and silence fell.

At length, Hathulf spoke, and it was to Sighern. "High praise indeed. But now that I look at you properly, the words ring true. Sighern I'll call you, and boy no longer."

Sighern answered him. "Too high praise I think, for I'm just a simple farm lad. But I'll swing this axe in the battle to come, and I'll fight for the Duthgar because that's where I was born, and I'll fight for the Callenor because I have the great honor of carrying this axe for them. I'll do my best to be worthy of those who wielded it before me."

Hathulf nodded slowly. "I believe it. Though not all who held that axe before you were men of honor. But most were, and I don't think they'd be displeased for you to carry it now."

He turned again to Brand. "I'll serve you, and my men with me. Lead us well, for if the messages are true, you'll need to be the greatest war leader our peoples have ever known."

"Sadly," Brand answered, "that's exactly what I am."

16. A Long Night

The light was a little stronger, for the sun was close to breaking over the rim of the world, and Hruidgar could see better.

And he did not like what he saw. Scattered around were the prints of wolves or wild dogs. They had spent time here, for their spoor was everywhere. But most of all, they had gathered at the base of an oak tree, ancient and hollowed in its lower trunk. Save there was no opening. This had been blocked by a mighty branch fallen several years ago.

It all looked natural, but he knew it was not. That branch, large as it was, had been moved.

Carefully, Hruidgar dismounted and tied his reins to a sapling. He studied the branch, and one side was paler than the other, and the darker side showed signs of dry rot. Until recently, it had lain on the ground.

No animal moved a branch that size. Still less to place it against the opening of a hollow tree trunk. Men had done that. Hunters maybe. But a cold twist in his gut told him that was not the case.

Something lay hidden in the hollow, and he guessed what. It must be a body, and the effort of concealing it was for one purpose. It was not meant to be discovered.

Had it been left in the open, crows would gather. They would draw any scout in the vicinity like moths to the flame, and whoever had done this did not want that.

Hruidgar spat. Theories, he knew. They were worth nothing. He must have the facts, and that meant pulling aside the branch. He had to know, for if the enemy scouts were here, then the army was not far away, and Brand would be flanked and surprised.

He took a grip of the branch and heaved. It moved with difficulty for oak was heavy, and it was near as thick as his body.

With a grunt, he let it fall. A faint smell of decomposition met his nostrils. And he forced himself to look inside the hollow. He knew what he would see, but he had to confirm it.

Inside was a corpse. Ants covered it, and glazed eyes stared up unseeing. Eyes that he knew. Durnheld, a hunter the army had picked up after the battle with Gormengil.

Hruidgar cursed under his breath. The dead man was little more than a youth, all eager for adventure. He had skill and talent, but he was also young and inexperienced. Hruidgar had sent him to scout out here to protect him. Better this than where the army was expected.

How wrong he had been. The man's throat had been cut, and dried blood showed on his tunic where he had been stabbed at least once. He had been killed, and then his body hidden.

Why?

Murder, perhaps. Anything was possible. But he knew in his heart it was an act of war. Durnheld had been killed by enemy scouts. And that meant one thing. The enemy was close. Two things, actually, and Hruidgar cursed again. The enemy was close, and Brand did not know.

But what should he do now? Seek confirmation, or return to Brand swiftly and give warning?

It was not an easy problem to solve. But first things first. Regretfully, he must hide the body again. Durnheld would get no decent burial. There was no time for that, and without putting the branch back up wild animals would devour his corpse.

Hruidgar muttered a few words, long forgotten he had thought them, but they were the Raithlin funeral creed, and they came unbidden to him now.

Well did you serve and protect
High was your honor, low your hate
Your love for good was a beacon of light.

Then he reached out and pulled the man's cloak up over his head. There would be no funeral shroud for him. No mourners and no ceremony. The hollow of a tree would serve as his tomb. But at least he would rest for eternity in the wild lands that he loved.

Hruidgar heaved the branch back into place, and then he turned and leaned his back against it, thinking hard.

Durnheld had not been dead that long. If enemy scouts had done this, then how far away were they? He could not know, but they might still be close. Close enough that they may have seen his coming and followed him. They could, even now, be stalking close and setting him up for a kill.

He studied the landscape around him. He saw nothing out of place, but nor would he. Durnheld was young, but he did have skill. To kill him, the enemy scouts must be good. Perhaps very good.

His gaze fell to the ground close by. The tracks that he had seen were from dogs rather than wolves. The middle toes of dogs were slightly larger, whereas the four front toes of wolves were the same size. The bare ground beneath the massive oak was soft from years of falling leaves, and the sun was now fully up. The dog tracks were quite clear, but he spotted more marks that he had not seen before.

There were no human tracks, except for his own. But there were signs of disturbance, nonetheless. A leafy branch had been used to smooth over the surface. This had removed all trace of the people that had been here, but it left its own tell-tale signs. Whoever had done this was taking no chances.

It was not reassuring. It spoke of skill and determination. Neither of which he wanted in abundance in an enemy. Nor did it make his choice of what to do any easier. Should he return now and warn Brand? Or should he discover the enemy and learn their numbers?

It was the first that he wanted to do. He was never very brave. And as much as he hated large groups of people, the army offered safety, of a sort. At least until battle was joined. Moreover, Brand needed to be told that the enemy may be flanking him.

But really, what good would that news do him? Was the entire Kirsch army here? Had it split into two? Was this only a small expeditionary force? These were all things that Brand would need to know. If he did not, he would be forced to send out more scouts to discover that information, and more young men like Durnheld would be killed.

No. He wanted to go back, but he must go forward. He must find the enemy, tally their numbers and discern their intention. That was his job as a scout. That was the job of a Raithlin.

He spotted a fallen branch, and used its leaves to hide his own boot marks. If the enemy scouts returned, and they might do on purpose to see if anyone had discovered what they had done, they would not know their presence had been revealed. But they would certainly know that he was here, for he could not hide his horse's tracks.

There was nothing he could do about that. His presence alone was reason enough for them to try to kill him, but if they knew he was aware of them there would be a greater sense of urgency. Far greater.

He rested the branch down on the ground when he was done, trying to make it look like it had fallen there naturally. Then he turned and surveyed the scene. It was just as it was when he discovered it, and he could do no more than that.

Next, he turned his gaze to his backtrail. A long while he studied it, seeking any signs that he was being followed. He saw nothing. But that did not mean much. A good scout, or even a group of them, would not allow himself to be seen.

Still, there were no other indications either. Bird calls were one thing he listened for, and so too the sight of birds rising up from trees which might indicate something moving below them. But there was nothing like that.

Yet the thought would not leave him that someone was there, and perhaps more than one. Instinct? Fear? He was not sure, but there was nothing else to do but get on with his job.

He loosed the reins of his horse from where they were tied, and mounted swiftly. If need be, he could gallop now and cover a lot of ground, but that was the last thing he would do. Only an attack would bring that on. Otherwise, it was best to move slowly and carefully. In that way, he might escape detection. But the horse would make it harder.

He knew he left tracks, and he could not hide them. But he moved ahead, being careful to change direction often so that he took no predictable path. He avoided good places for ambush too, and tried to keep himself from being highlighted on open ground on a rise.

Everything he did was designed to avoid being found, but deep in his heart he knew the enemy were out there, and they were good. He had sufficient skill to avoid them, but that alone was never enough. He needed a touch of luck too.

So he moved through the day, and though he saw nothing out of place nor heard anything out of order, his anxiety only grew.

The land about him began to change. There were less pines and more oaks. It flattened too. This was, perhaps, an advantage. Without high points that would serve as lookouts, he would be harder to see from a distance.

If he had the opportunity, he would have hidden during the day and traveled only at night. That would have been safer, but there was no chance for that. Time pressed, and the sooner he found out what was happening, the sooner he could return to Brand and give him an opportunity to develop a counter strategy.

Brand was a canny man, and a war leader the like of which the Duthgar had never known. He snatched victory from the hands of defeat, again and again. What was to come though, that would be a greater test than all that had gone before. All the more reason that he *must* have accurate knowledge of what the enemy was doing. Without it, he was doomed.

Hruidgar guided his black mare down a slope at an angle. And when he was halfway down, he changed direction. This sort of maneuvering was costing him time, but being predictable could cost him his life.

To the west, the sun sank low on the horizon and shot the scattered clouds through with pinks and reds. The oak trees, scattered across the land like the clouds scattered in the sky, cast long shadows.

Night was coming, and he breathed a sigh of relief. He had not liked traveling through the day, but it had been necessary. Now, he would travel through the night. It would be safer. But it would be a long night without rest. He was too old for this kind of work, but there was no one else to do it for him. If one of his scouts had been killed, likely enough the others had too. Durnheld was the best that he had sent out this way.

He reached the bottom of the slope, and angled south again through a small cluster of trees. The light was fading fast now, but even so he saw the track in the grass.

It was a boot mark, and it was fresh. Very, very fresh. Even as he watched, he saw a blade of grass within it spring upright again. It was only minutes old. Perhaps not even that.

17. Ambush

Hruidgar knew he was a dead man. Only chance had taken him at this angle down the slope, but it had caught his enemy by surprise. Had he not come this way, he would never have known the danger.

But knowing the danger did not necessarily help him. Not much at any rate. If more than one scout was stalking him, he certainly was dead. But, perhaps he had a chance if there was only one of them.

He lifted his gaze off the boot mark. It was best just now not to give away any indication that he knew the man was somewhere close by. If he did so, the scout would be twice as wary. If he thought that he remained undetected though … that would make him complacent. Hopefully.

It was a chance Hruidgar had to take. He had no others.

He moved ahead slowly, letting the horse pick its own way forward. The option was there to kick his heels in and gallop. That might swiftly take him away from danger. Or straight into an ambush.

No. It was best to continue just as he was, and to allow himself an opportunity to see the ambush that would be sprung on him rather than gallop blindly into it.

Dusk was covering the land in a shadowy blanket, but there was still enough light to see by. If an ambush was coming, it would likely be soon. No scout would want to try tracking him in the dark. It would be hard to do except by staying close, and at night that meant a much higher chance of stepping on a branch in the dark that would give away his presence.

No. He would be ambushed, and it would happen very, very soon.

He moved ahead slowly, trying as hard as possible to show no sign of anxiety. All the odds were in favor of his enemy, but at least one thing might work to his benefit. The enemy would expect him to be surprised when the attack came, but if he was ready for it, he just might be able to turn that surprise around by acting quickly.

Another thing was advantageous too. Durnheld had not been killed by arrows but by blades. It seemed the enemy scouts carried no bows, and that was a stroke of good fortune. Had they done so, he likely would already be dead.

He tried to determine where the ambush would be laid. He had seen where the enemy scout had been, so he put himself in the man's position and tried to work out where he would go.

There was lower ground ahead and to the right. A man could lie there unseen, and then rise and attack with sword or knife when his target came closer. It was a possibility.

But ahead and to the left was a clump of straggly trees. That too was a good hiding spot. But which would it be?

His life depended on guessing correctly, for he could not guard well against both sides at once. And things would be even worse if there was more than one enemy.

He made his choice. Had it been him, he would have avoided the lower ground to the right. The grass was taller there, and the chances of leaving a visible trail were higher. The clump of trees to the left offered shorter grass that would leave no trail, and also the chance to remain standing behind a tree rather than lie down. This would mean a quicker attack when it was time to act.

Hruidgar let out a slow breath. He wished with everything he had that he dared to string his bow and notch an arrow, but then his element of surprise at not being surprised would be lost.

He licked his lips. An irrational urge to laugh came over him, for the idea of surprising someone by not being surprised suddenly seemed ludicrous. But on such a situation his life now turned.

He could not string his bow, but he did have throwing knives up the sleeves of both arms. Surreptitiously, he let the one on his right inner forearm slide out of its sheath and into his hand. That would enable him to throw better to the left. But if he was wrong, and the attack came from the right, he would be disadvantaged. He wished he could feel the hilt of a knife in each hand, but he had to control the horse, and when the attack came that might be needed for the horse would surely shy at sudden movement.

He drew close to both likely ambush places. His heart raced, but nothing happened. Had he been wrong about them? Was the man somewhere else?

He had nearly gone past the places when a man rose suddenly from the grass on the lower ground to the right. Hruidgar had chosen badly, and yet had his knife been in his left hand he would now have to try to turn back and throw, which would be too slow. As it was, he was able to fling the knife in his right hand in a quick backhand motion.

But the other man was throwing too. Hruidgar dropped low in the saddle, and the horse leaped forward in surprise. One of those things saved his life.

He did not even hear the noise of the passing knife. It must have missed him by a good amount, but his own had struck home. The man, fully behind him now, reeled backward.

Hruidgar pulled hard on the reins, turned his horse around, and kicked in his heels. He would charge his attacker down.

The scout staggered, and then he leapt to the left, but the black mare's hooves caught him, and Hruidgar, still bent low in the saddle, drew his short sword and swiped.

He hit nothing. It was too short for a cavalry blade, and not meant for striking a man while mounted.

Cursing, Hruidgar leapt from the saddle. He could not let this man escape, for then he could give warning to his comrades and a whole group of them would be after him.

He hit the ground running, but the scout had no intention of fleeing. Blood showed on his tunic, but whatever wound he had did not seem to slow him down much. He charged himself, and the two of them met in a crash of steel blades.

It was not a pretty fight. Neither were great swordsmen. Hruidgar wished he had a tenth of the skill with a blade that Brand had, but he had to settle for what he possessed.

What he possessed might be enough. Maybe. He hacked and blocked, and the other man did the same. There would be no fleeing now. To turn was to invite a sword blade through the back.

The other man was younger. Much younger. But he was wounded, and his breath came in ragged gasps. It evened out the age difference.

Suddenly the other man stumbled back. Hruidgar drove forward, his blade seeking the scout's life, but it was a ruse. The man had drawn a knife and he flung it hard.

Hruidgar dodged to the side. This time, he heard the knife pass close to his head and even felt the wind of it. He moved to attack again, but he had been thrown off balance and the other man leapt forward, his blade thrusting at Hruidgar's heart.

Hruidgar stumbled back in his haste, and while he escaped the killing stroke, he also lost his balance. He fell down, landing badly.

The sword came for him again, this time a wild slash at his neck. Somehow, Hruidgar fended it away, and the smash of steel on steel was loud in his ear. But the other man was standing over him, and Hruidgar kicked him in the groin with all the strength he possessed.

The enemy scout groaned and staggered back, bent over. Hruidgar rolled to his feet and struck. The man was little able to defend, but grunting and lurching backward he fended off the blows. Most of them, at any rate.

One slash hit his left shoulder, and there was the grating feel of metal against bone. Hruidgar had hoped for a killing stroke, but this was not it. Nor was it debilitating, for it was not his opponent's sword arm.

A moment later, the tip of Hruidgar's sword nicked the man's thigh. It drew a yelp of pain as well as blood, but again it was not a killing blow.

Hruidgar pressed forward. He had the advantage now, and he tried to take it. But the other man was facing death. And he knew it. He fought back with tenacity born of desperate fear.

Once more Hruidgar nicked him, this time a shallow slice across his stomach, and it seemed to enrage the other man. Either that, or the desperation of his situation drove him to one last attempt at victory. He crashed forward, screaming and slashing wildly.

Hruidgar was forced to retreat. This time he kept his footing, and blow after blow smashed against his sword until the hand that held the hilt grew numb. But he blocked all the attacks, and the other man grew weary. A great lethargy seized him. And Hruidgar realized his enemy must have lost a lot of blood. Death was creeping up on him, and that had lent the man desperation.

But it was nearly over now. The man swung slowly, and the power of his blows was much reduced. Yet still determination set his face in a grimace, and he advanced with a fierce expression that did not match what his body was able to deliver.

Suddenly, Hruidgar felt sick. He was going to kill this man, and he did not want to. Not like this. But he steeled himself. The man had probably been the one who killed Durnheld.

Before he knew what was happening, his own blade turned from defense to attack. It drove forward and up, slipping into flesh and seeking toward the heart.

The blade tip found it. Blood sprayed from the man's mouth, splattering over Hruidgar's face. He wanted to jump back, but instead he stepped closer, forcing the blade higher and twisting it.

His enemy fell, dead, and Hruidgar reefed his sword free, with difficulty, and then turned and vomited.

For some while he emptied his stomach, and in moments between he used a rag he carried to clear the blood off his face. But all the while he kept his sword drawn, and his gaze swept the countryside seeking other scouts.

At length, he recovered. Standing, he surveyed the countryside all around again, but there was no sign of any enemy. Not that he could see much anyway. Dusk had nearly given way to night.

He walked over to the man he had killed, and he knelt next to him. In the last of the light he studied his clothes and weaponry. All were different from anything in the Duthgar. They were different from anything he had seen before. Without doubt, he was of that race of men that the stories called the Kirsch.

But what amazed him most was the man's footwear. They were not boots, but something he had heard of in stories. Sandals.

He stood and shook his head. The clothes and weapons were well made, but sandals were foolish.

Perhaps they would serve in hotter climes, but when summer faded, which it nearly had done, frost and snow would set in. Sandals would lead to frostbite. But not only that, a sandaled foot was vulnerable in battle compared to a booted one.

Hruidgar gave a low whistle. His mount was some way off, having been scared by the fight. It was no war horse, nor ever would be. But its ears pricked and it studied him. Then it shook its head and the reins dangled down loosely.

He needed that horse. It was speed, which was the one thing he required above all else. He had much yet to do before he returned to the camp and gave Brand warning.

The horse looked at him, but it did not trot over. No matter. He would go to it. But slowly and carefully. He could not afford to spook it.

He took a few steps, and spoke quietly. Night was all around him now, dark and dangerous. The black mare was one with it, and though she was no warhorse, she stepped quietly when walking and had a turn of blistering pace when pressed to it. Both might be needed in the long hours to come.

He stepped closer again, talking softly and calmly. The blood that was on him would not help. He had cleaned it off as best as possible, but she could smell the stain of it on him, and she did not like it.

But she responded to his voice and took a few halting steps toward him.

He paused himself. "That's right, girl. Come over here. We have a long way to go, you and I, but I'll see you there safely if you do the same for me."

She shook her head again and stepped closer once more. He stayed where he was. She was a quiet animal and well-trained, but if he scared her now he could end up searching for her half the night.

He kept talking and she stepped over to him, stretching out her neck and sniffing at him.

Slowly and carefully he reached out and gripped the reins. When they were in his hand, he breathed a sigh of relief and patted her shoulder.

"Good girl," he said. "Remember our bargain. I'll look after you, and you look after me."

He mounted then, and looked around into the dark. There was little to see. Even the corpse of his enemy was just a darker shadow among many on the ground. Best not to think about that. It could have been him. And it might yet be if he was not careful.

What to do next? It was a pressing question. His goal must be to find the enemy encampment, for surely there must be one. Where the scouts were, the army could not be that far behind. His task had not changed. He must estimate their numbers and try to deduce their intent.

He nudged the mare forward, staying clear of the corpse. His thoughts were all about the enemy somewhere ahead, but a part of him knew there would be other scouts out in the dark. Perhaps there was no one around for ten miles. Or perhaps there were a dozen moving in on him now. It was impossible to tell.

He did what he had done before though. He moved quietly, or rather he allowed the horse to pick her own way and move at her own pace. It was slow, but it was near silent. And now and then he guided her to a different angle to avoid being predictable. But all the while he moved southward.

The enemy was in that direction. If they were more to the south-west, it did not mater. His scouts were roaming that territory, and they would discover the enemy if they were there. But here, it was just himself and those other few men he had sent this way. But of them, there had been no sign and he feared they were all dead.

The night grew cool. Autumn was drawing on, and though the days were still warm the night made promises of the winter yet to come.

He scented the air often for smoke, for surely the enemy encampment would have cooking fires. But he detected nothing. That did not mean much. The air was near still, and the scent of smoke would not travel far. And if anything, the breeze was coming from the north. Not that there was much of it.

Instead of smoke, he must listen carefully for the dull noise of an army ahead. He would hear them before he saw them. But the closer he drew, the greater his danger would be. Once he was in proximity to any encampment, it was not just scouts that he had to look out for but sentries. If he stumbled into one by accident, he would be dead before he could blink.

He could not slow the horse further, but he pulled her up often just to stare into the dark and listen. But he heard nothing save the hoot of owls and the scuffling of small animals in the leaf litter beneath trees. He did not fear the noise came from scouts. A scout would be silent until the attack came.

It grew even cooler, and he drew up the hood of his cloak. It was a risk, for the cloth dulled his hearing and reduced his sight. But all life was a risk, and he felt that his luck was in. He had, after all, survived the ambush by the enemy scout.

The oaks about him began to grow thickly now. It was nearly a forest here, and he did not think the enemy would establish a camp in such a place. The commander would prefer a spot in the open where a view was obtained of the surrounding countryside. Trusting to his luck again, he urged the mare forward at a faster walk. The night was wearing on, and better for him if he found the enemy at night. He could get closer that way, undetected. During the day it would be harder.

The oaks loomed over him, and the shadows were deep. It was the middle of the night, and drowsiness set in. He wanted to lie down and sleep beneath the cover of the trees, but duty pressed on him. Brand needed to know what was going on here, and swiftly.

The yearning for sleep passed. The oak wood around him thinned, and the glitter of stars lit the sky again. They were old friends to him, and he knew them well and the stories that were told of them in the Duthgar. Different stories were told in Esgallien, and other lands between. But some of those stars and the stories of them had been the same wherever he traveled.

He did not look at them tonight though. His eyes searched the shadows ahead, and his ears listened to his backtrail. But it was smell that told him what he wanted to know.

The air was perfectly still now, and the scent of old smoke was suddenly heavy upon it. The enemy camp was close, and though he had thought to hear it first, he had been wrong.

But if he could smell it, it must be close indeed. Not even the faintest breeze blew now, and there was nothing to bring the smoky air to him. Gently, he pulled the mare to a stop.

If he were afoot, he would have hunkered down here in the grass and waited. But he must trust to the night and the dark coat of the horse to hide him. Yet still, he did not know where the enemy was, only that they were close.

Dimly, he saw the land ahead of him slope downward. Where he waited now must be some sort of ridge, though he had not known it in the deeps of the trees. He knew it now though, and knew also that it was a likely spot for an enemy lookout.

Nothing moved. Nothing stirred. And he could not wait here until first light revealed him to the world. He nudged the horse forward again, and soon he came to the edge of a drop.

It was not steep. But spread out below was a vast area of flat lands, blanketed by the night. Except for many hundreds of fires. Here, at last, was the enemy he had sought.

But how big was the army? Certainly, there would be many more men than fires. But how many?

The only way to find out was to go there and see at close range. But he did not move. Fear gripped him. There could be scouts anywhere. There *would* be sentries. The stupidity of trying to go down there undetected overwhelmed him.

But that was the shadow of fear upon him. In truth, he had skill. He could do what was required. He *must* do what was required.

He nudged the mare forward. It was colder than before, but he flipped back his hood. He would need his every sense to survive this, and he could not afford to dim them.

Quickly, he checked his knives and made sure they were all in place. He had many of them, and he was a good thrower. But preparation was king. So he strung his bow for the first time. Almost, he notched an arrow, but that was going too far. If he needed to act quickly, it would be at close range and the knives would serve him better.

Lastly, he drew a leather pouch from his belt and dipped his fingers into it. It contained powdered charcoal, moistened by oil. This he smeared onto his face. It was the most likely aspect of him to be seen, for the horse was black and his clothing dark. It was the face of a person that glimmered palely in the shadows, revealing them.

For good measure, he smeared some on the back of his hands too. It never harmed to be too careful. Then he gave all his attention to the night around him as he moved down the slope and toward the enemy.

18. The Enemy

Far away the approaching dawn colored the horizon gray. But daylight was still a long way off. Even so. Hruidgar hastened as much as he dared. He had to get close to the army, and then back into the trees before first light. Otherwise, he would have a whole regiment sent to kill him. Or worse, take him prisoner for questioning.

Travel was easier once he reached the flatter land below the slope. But there were few trees here and not much that offered cover. He relied on the soft walk of the mare to make little noise, and his senses to detect the presence of anybody in the dark with him.

The glittering stars were not quite so bright. The horizon had become grayer. Even, he thought that he could see further through the dark than he could before. He wanted to urge the horse into a canter, for time was running out on him. But that would be foolish. He gritted his teeth and pressed on as he was.

Suddenly, he paused. Drawing the mare to a standstill, he waited in silence. Had he heard something? Had some sense warned him of hidden danger?

He felt vulnerable atop his mount. Being higher, there was greater chance of standing out against the lighter sky and being seen. He wanted to dismount. Yet if he did that, and he was attacked, he could not flee.

And flee he would have to try to do if detected. There would be no fighting here, if he could avoid it. To fight here was to risk alerting others, and in a matter of moments he could be fighting a hundred men.

So he waited where he was, and listened, while his gaze swept the mysterious night.

Then a noise came from off to his left. It was a man clearing his throat. It was not loud, and perhaps the man was not even conscious that he made the noise, but he did, and it had saved Hruidgar's life. On such chances turned his fate.

Hruidgar continued to wait. It was several minutes more before the man once again cleared his throat. The noise came from the same place as it had before, and there was no sign of anyone else. How far away were the sentries placed? Would there be one line of them or two?

He had no answers to any of his questions. The only thing to do was move forward again. But now, he dismounted. He could not risk being seen. Being heard was already likely enough.

But the horse moved quietly, and the grass here was short and soft. Somehow, he moved ten paces, then twenty and finally fifty without any sign of being detected.

He realized that a cold sweat had broken out over his face, and his hands were clammy. His face did not matter, but clammy hands were dangerous. The bow could slip in his grip when he needed speed and strength.

Wiping his hands dry, one at a time on his trousers, he mounted again. Moving forward, he saw the army begin to take shape before him. The fires had died down, but they gave off a cumulative light, and he could see the silhouettes of tents and the rough shapes of men that lay beside the dying fires.

The tents were few. The men by the fires many. He drew closer, his gaze taking in everything that he saw. There were banners held high by spears stuck into the ground, but they were too distant and the night too dark to see any detail. Of cavalry, he saw no sign. It was an army of infantry, which was a good thing for Brand, and something he would wish to know.

Then he set to counting. He was close enough now, as close as he dared go. He eased the mare to a stop, but he did not dismount. He needed his higher position to see better.

He divided the army into eighths, and counted one portion. Then he did the same again, using a different portion. His count was close to the same, both times. Then he multiplied by eight. Three thousand of the enemy were gathered here.

It was an army. By the standards of the Duthgar, a great army. But was it all of the Kirsch, or just some of them? He did not know, and had no way of finding out.

It was not likely to be all of them though. It was not a large enough force to take on Brand by itself, though stranger things had happened. Probably, the enemy had split into two. This was supposed to be a surprise flanking force. That meant that the real army was likely to the south, as expected, and that it was bigger than this.

The realization was not comforting. Once again, Brand would be outnumbered. Yet at least he would not be surprised. So long as word made it back to him.

That was his job now, and Hruidgar knew it. Nothing else mattered. He *had* to reach Brand. But he had made it safely this far, and going out should be easier than coming in had been.

But he had to hurry too. Movement in the camp had begun, and preparations for a meal started. The fires were being fed the remainder of the dry wood that had been collected last night. Soon enough, the enemy would be on the move again.

Worse, the eastern horizon was lit orange by the rising sun. Daylight was close to hand, and he would have to hurry to make it back to the relative safety of the woods before he could be seen.

He used his knees to signal the horse to turn, and then he nudged her forward. Safety lay ahead, but to get there he must pass through the sentry line again.

Following the same path that he entered, he left. It did not seem as though the sentries patrolled the perimeter of the army. They stayed in place where they had been stationed. This would help him, or at least so he hoped. He could not be sure he was taking precisely the same path.

He eased ahead, conscious of the lightening sky behind him. All was quiet. Shortly, he reached the place where he had heard the sentry clear his throat on the way in. But there was no sign of him now. He brought the horse to a stop and waited, surveying the dark, but he could not wait long.

Satisfied, as best he could be, that he had retraced his route exactly, he nudged the mare forward again. But even as she moved a figure loomed up out of the dark.

It was the back of a sentry, but the man must have heard something for he turned even as Hruidgar watched. A moment they each looked at the other, both shocked to see what they did.

The sentry fumbled for his sword. It was a mistake, for he should have yelled. Or better, dived away and shouted a warning.

Hruidgar lifted his bow, notched an arrow and drew and fired in one motion.

The sentry wore armor. He was no scout, sent into the wild to find and observe the army. He was a warrior, and well-protected. There had been only one killing shot, and that was to the neck.

The arrow flashed, a dark streak in the dawn shadows. It hissed through the air, and then struck with a thud. The sentry reeled back, blood gushing from his torn throat, and then he toppled and lay still.

Hruidgar swiftly notched another arrow and then waited, perfectly still, listening for other sentries. Had they heard anything?

His heart thudded in his chest. The horse stamped restlessly, but no call came from another sentry asking if all was well, nor any sign that someone walked across to investigate.

But still, Hruidgar waited. Fear gripped him, but after some while a greater fear took over. He had to get out of here, and swiftly. Dawn was at hand.

He slipped the arrow back into his quiver, and he dismounted. Walking the horse forward, he came to the man he had killed. He knew what he had to do. Should he be left there, his body would soon be found and an alert given. That an intruder had seen them would be known, and it was best for Brand that the enemy thought themselves undiscovered.

It would be best for him to. If they knew he was here, men would be sent after him.

Quickly, he bent down and pulled the arrow from the dead man's throat. He cleaned it, and returned it to his quiver. Then he lifted the man over his horse's withers ahead of the saddle.

There was blood on the grass, and this he washed away as best he could with some water. He tried to leave no sign that a man had been killed there. It was possible that the other sentries would think he had deserted during the night.

It was the best he could do. He mounted again, and nudged the horse forward. He did not notch an arrow again. If he were discovered, he would kick the horse into a gallop and escape that way. However, he did slip a knife into his hand in readiness.

But he passed through the sentry line without further trouble. Yet still the knife remained in his hand for several hundred feet. He looked ahead to see any sign of the enemy, and he looked behind for any pursuit. There was nothing, and his nerve gave out at last. He heeled the mare forward into a trot, hoping to reach higher ground and the shelter of the oak trees before daylight revealed him to all the world.

The dead man draped over the shoulders of the horse before him bounced to and fro. It made Hruidgar sick, not least because in dying the man had soiled himself. But it was necessary to hide his body. This was war, and it was kill or be killed.

And yet the Kirsch had begun it. They had no business here, and Hruidgar hoped with all his heart that Brand could defeat them. If anyone could, it would be him. Even so, he would be outnumbered, and he would face gods. Could a man prevail against such odds, no matter who he was?

Hruidgar looked back. It was light enough now to see the army, albeit dimly. Fear gripped him, and he kicked the mare into a gallop. A chance gaze could reveal him now.

He sped along. The horse labored slightly under the weight of two men, but the animal was all class. In moments, it was climbing steeper ground, and soon after it had cleared the crest of the slope and entered the shelter of the oaks.

Hruidgar drew the mare up and turned her around. From within the shadows of the trees, he looked back and observed the enemy.

There was no sign of anyone separating from it to hunt him down. Not on horseback nor on foot. It seemed strange to him that they had no cavalry at all, but it was an advantage to Brand and he liked it. Even more did he like that the army showed no signs of agitation. It seemed that the missing sentry was either unnoticed or caused no great concern.

The tracks of his horse were another matter. They would be visible for anyone with the skill to see. But those with the skill were probably out scouting and not nearby. At least he could hope so.

Finally, he turned the mare around once more and nudged her forward into a walk. Now that the surge of fear had left him, he felt exhausted. He had gone a long time without sleep, and he knew he would have to rest soon. But for that, he would have to find a well-hidden place deep in the woods. There also he could hide the body of the sentry.

He moved on, fighting sleep and trying to stay alert to the woods about him. The army was no danger anymore. Certainly, their scouts had found the edge of the woods and they would march near there and in open country. But that did not mean that scouts were not infesting this wood, ensuring no enemy lay concealed within it, nor that they would not stumble across his tracks.

The morning passed, and the warmth of the day grew. It was cold nights and warm days this time of the year. But soon it would just be cold. These foreigners and their sandals would struggle then. But if they were here at that time, they would have beaten Brand.

He managed to stay awake and travel until noon before weariness overtook him. But when he dismounted, deep in a stand of oaks, he hid the body in a hollow tree just as the enemy scouts had done themselves. So too he covered the opening with a large branch and hid his tracks as best he could.

Finally, he cast himself down and slept. If there were scouts around, they could kill him for all he cared just now.

But he slept undisturbed for several hours, and when he woke, dusk was settling over the land and he felt somewhat refreshed.

He did not bother to eat. He mounted the mare and set off. He still had a long way to go, but the dark offered concealment now, and he was far enough from the army that enemy scouts would be few and far between.

19. Five Tribes

Brand had led his army onward, and others had gathered to it. Now that it was known that several Callenor lords had joined him, others who had hesitated did likewise.

The army swelled, but his fears did not lessen. The task ahead was too much for him. He was a man, and not a god. Yet the Lady of the Land had charged him with the task, and this she would not have done if there were no hope. She had said as much herself.

So he went on, gathering warriors, building morale and establishing a sense of unity. None of it was easy, and there was no let up at night.

Dusk had fallen, and he had picked a place to encamp. He now had a tent, large enough to fit his entire group of commanding officers, but he did not use it. Instead, he sat outside on some logs before a blazing fire and listened to the reports of the scouts as they came in.

And for the first time, they brought word of the enemy army.

The third scout to bring news of it that evening sat before him now, close to the fire. Brand had given him a chunk of bread and goblet of mead as he made his report. The scouts were always grateful for that kindness. They came to him to report as soon as they entered the camp, and they did not tarry to eat or drink first.

"How large is the army?" Brand asked.

The scout sipped at his mead. "Seventeen thousand strong, in infantry. But there are five hundred chariots."

This was very close to the figures the previous two scouts had given. The numbers were a concern, but even more so the chariots. Brand had heard tales of them, but formulating an attack or defense against such a novelty was not easy.

"These chariots," he questioned, "how do the enemy use them?"

"Most are drawn by a single horse, but a few by two. Behind is the chariot itself, and for this there is a driver and a warrior."

This also Brand had heard before. "And what weapons does the warrior have?"

"He's armed with a sword, but also with a short bow. Possibly they could skirmish, but I think more likely they'll approach our lines, fire volleys of arrows and then wheel away again."

That too, Brand had heard before. He deemed it most likely himself, but it never paid to be sure of things that were not proven.

"And the driver?"

"He carries a shield, likely used to protect them both, and a sword also."

Brand offered the man another chunk of bread, which he took. "You've done well. And your tally of the enemy's numbers matches the other scouts so far. Rest well tonight, for no doubt you'll be needed again tomorrow."

The man nodded and walked off.

"They don't say much, those scouts," Shorty commented from where he sat nearby.

"No, but they never do. Scouts are quiet men, as a rule. But what he said was enough."

"Do the chariots trouble you?" Taingern asked.

Brand shrugged. "All things trouble me, until they don't. But the short bows of the charioteers won't shoot as far as the longbows of our archers. They'll think to swing past and soften us with volley after volley before sending in the infantry. But they'll get better than they give."

"I think so too," Shorty answered. "But they'll be a moving target while our men will be standing still."

Brand knew that was true, and he did not like it. "Agreed, but even so I think we'll at least match them. And we can hope they'll be surprised by the power and range of our bows."

Attar stretched out his legs where he sat on a log. "You Duthenor think too much. When they come at us, we'll shoot them down. It's that simple."

Brand grinned. "I like things simple, and you're probably right." He did not add that time would tell, but despite his simplistic approach, he knew that Attar did not underestimate the enemy. He just did not believe in worrying about things he could not change.

It was not much longer before another scout came in. Brand gave him the customary goblet of mead and a chunk of bread.

"What news," he asked.

"I've been to the north," the man answered. His voice was the deepest Brand had ever heard. "There's an army there."

This was something new. Brand studied the man as he sipped at his mead. He was one of the few Duthenor to wear a beard, and it was thick and black.

"How large," Brand asked.

"A thousand strong," the man answered without hesitation. Brand liked that. It spoke of confidence. And certainty that he had seen what he had seen and made the correct calculations.

"Who are they?"

"I don't know. Callenor, I expect. But they flew no banners."

"Cavalry?"

The man shook his head. "They're all foot soldiers. And they're close. Less than a day away."

It was interesting news. Brand had thought all the Callenor who were going to join them had done so already. They were nearing the end of their lands.

The scout had little else to report, and left soon after.

"Do you think they're Callenor?" Brand asked Attar.

"They'd better be. They're on Callenor lands. But in truth, I wish I was sure. I would have thought that all the Callenor who were going to join you had done so already."

Brand was uneasy about the whole situation. It was not a large enough force to threaten him, but he did not like mysteries. Not when it came to war and battle. In the game of swords, the unknown was a greater threat than blades.

But the mystery was solved not long after. Bruidiger returned from his mission to the Norvinor tribe. He came straight to Brand, and Brand shook his hand in the warrior's grip.

"I bring good news," the man said.

Brand poured him a goblet of mead and handed it to him. "Let me guess. You've led a thousand men to join me?"

"Ah, I see. Your scouts have spotted us. I'd thought to surprise you."

"Well, it's still a surprise. We knew a force was out there, just not who it was. But surprise or not, it's good news. Better than I'd hoped for, and quicker."

Bruidiger quaffed his mead in one go. "Things went better than I expected. Still, these are only men from the southern regions of our land. There'll be more to join us from the north later."

Brand refilled the man's goblet, and filled one for himself too.

"I'll drink to that."

Bruidiger quaffed the second goblet as fast as the first.

"There's something else too. With me I have a hundred men. Most are from the Waelenor tribe. But a few are from the Druimenor tribe."

Brand had heard the names of those tribes growing up, but he had never met anyone from them. He grinned, and quaffed his own mead.

"That's fitting. They may be few in number, but all five tribes will now be represented. I like it, and their swords will be welcome."

Brand called over a soldier then, and he sent word to the men who had made the last banner. He wanted a new one, and this time to represent the emblems of all five tribes.

"If men will die fighting in this army, however many or however few from each tribe, they should at least fight under a banner that means something to them," he said to Bruidiger when the soldier left on his errand.

Bruidiger did not answer, but he looked knowingly at Brand. He was another who thought a kingdom was being forged here, but he did not seem disturbed by the notion.

Taingern leaned forward and pointed. "Over there, Brand."

Brand looked. Walking toward him through the camp was Hruidgar, and he looked the weariest man Brand had ever seen.

"That man has been through it," Taingern said.

Whatever *it* was, Brand had no idea. But he agreed. Something had happened. But underneath all the weariness of the hunter, something else showed. Determination.

Hruidgar reached them, and once again Brand poured out some mead.

"You look like you need it," Brand said.

Hruidgar took the goblet. But he merely held it in his hand and did not drink.

"The enemy are close," he said.

Brand nodded grimly. "Yes, they are. But your men have already warned me of it."

Hruidgar seemed confused for a moment. Then he shrugged.

"What have my men told you?"

"Seventeen thousand in infantry," Brand answered.

Hruidgar considered that. "And they're coming in from the south-west, as expected?"

"Exactly so."

"Well," Hruidgar said softly. "I haven't been out that way. I went south instead."

Brand felt his stomach sink. This would not be good news.

"I saw an encampment there of three thousand soldiers. They had no cavalry."

Brand did not show any surprise, though he felt it. A commander must be seen to take all news in his stride.

"What about chariots?"

"Chariots? No. Nothing like that. Does the other army have them?"

"They do."

"Well, that's some luck then. Nasty things according to the tales I've heard."

Brand posed his next question carefully. "You're the first to report this second army."

Hruidgar dropped his head, and then for the first time sipped at his mead.

"I thought I would be. The enemy has good scouts. I found one of my men. Dead. Dead, and hidden. That was what warned me. So I went ahead, but carefully. I had a feeling I was the only one to see the army. Or at least the only one to make it back to tell you. But I got lucky."

Brand knew that was an understatement. The hunter had certainly been lucky, but luck was one of those things that the harder you worked and the better your skills, the more of it came your way.

He filled the hunter's cup with more mead, and gave him some bread.

"Rest, Hruidgar. You've earned it. But if word comes in of any other scout from the south, I'll let you know."

The hunter left, and Brand's mood soured. But such were the ups and downs of war. A little while ago he was happy that more were joining his army. Now that good news was overshadowed.

"Your thoughts, gentlemen?" Brand asked.

"They'll try to flank us," Shorty said. "When the main battle comes, they'll drive in from the side."

Taingern nodded agreement. "But they'll try to keep their presence hidden as long as possible. Even, if they can, right up until the moment of attack."

That was certainly true. Hruidgar had said their scouts were good, which was no easy feat in foreign terrain. These lands must be nothing like their homeland.

But even so, surely some of Hruidgar's men would have avoided them. The enemy had deployed not just skilled scouts, but many, many of them. And for the purpose of ensuring their flanking army was *not* observed. That indicated they intended to launch a surprise attack, just as Taingern thought.

But knowing what the enemy planned was one thing. Countering it was another altogether.

He knew what needed to be done though, even if he did not like it.

Brand looked at the men gathered around him. He trusted them all, but who had the skills to do best what would be required?

Only Shorty and Taingern. But which one of them, both great friends, must he send into terrible danger?

20. There Goes a Good Man

Brand spoke into the silence. "You know what needs to be done."

He did not direct the comment at anyone in particular, but both Shorty and Taingern nodded.

"I'll do it," Shorty answered.

"I'll go," Taingern said at the same time.

Sighern swung his gaze from one to the other. "*What* needs to be done?"

Brand turned to him. "The enemy is out there, preparing to flank and attack us when we engage their main force."

Sighern considered that. "So you'll send a force to oppose them? And either Shorty or Taingern will command it?"

"Exactly. But we're outnumbered. So against three thousand, I can only spare one thousand. But, despite their superior numbers, this might be enough. They hope to catch us by surprise. Thanks to Hruidgar, they've failed in this. But they probably don't know it. So, in our turn, we can hope to catch *them* by surprise. A smaller force can more easily achieve that. And we have Callenor warriors who know the country. That's an advantage to us."

"But it'll be dangerous?"

"Extremely. If the force is observed and surprise lost, they'll be in great jeopardy. But they won't be able to retreat. They *must* engage the enemy as the enemy is ready to engage us. Or our whole army will be at risk."

Sighern answered quietly. "I see. I'm no great warrior, but I offer my services. I'll go with either of them."

That took Brand by surprise, but he knew he should be used to it now with Sighern.

"You're a better warrior than you know, but I think I'll keep you here. You're my flag bearer, and I have plans for you."

He turned to his two oldest friends. "Which of you will it be?" he said simply. "I can't choose."

Shorty grinned at him. "Then you go, and we'll both stay here." He finished this with a wink, showing he wasn't serious.

Taingern laughed. "I'm not sure that going is any riskier than staying. But I'll flip you for it."

He withdrew a gold coin from his pocket, and turned it side to side. The image of Unferth was on one aspect, and two crossed swords on the other.

"Take your pick," Taingern said.

"Swords," Shorty answered.

"Then I'm heads," Taingern said, and he flipped the coin high with his thumb.

Brand watched as the coin turned and tumbled through the air, reaching a high point and then falling. How it fell would determine the fate of one of his friends, but in the end all life was chance such as this.

The coin landed with a thud. They all bent lower to look.

The gold visage of Unferth gleamed back at them.

"I never did like him much," Taingern muttered. "But maybe dead, he'll bring me more luck than he ever did alive."

Brand sighed. "Let's hope so. But you make your own luck Taingern. You always have."

Taingern retrieved the coin. He weighed it in his hand a moment, and then handed it to Shorty. "Keep it for me until I return."

Shorty took it. "I'll do that."

"We'd better discuss a few things," Brand said.

Taingern sat again. "It seems simple enough. Take a thousand men. Move swiftly, but undetected. Attack the enemy force just as they're about to attack you, and turn their attempted surprise on its head. This will not only nullify their flanking move, but also throw out the main force from the south who'll be relying on the chaos caused by the flanking to drive forward their own thrust."

Brand sat down as well. Taingern always did have a quick grasp of strategy, and he showed it here.

"It's the *undetected* part that concerns me."

"How so?" Taingern asked.

"The whole plan depends on it, but it's the hardest part to actually do."

"I don't get it," Sighern interrupted. "I'd have thought a thousand against three thousand was the hardest part?"

Taingern answered him. "Numbers count less in battle than you might think. Morale and preparedness are worth more, any day. If I catch them by surprise, their superior numbers won't mean much at all."

Brand agreed. "What he says is right, and it's a lesson worth remembering. But to move undetected will mean taking Hruidgar with you. He's our best."

"He's tired now, but he'll have a full night's sleep. He'll be right to go."

"He can take the majority of scouts with him too."

"The majority? What if you need them yourself?"

"You'll need them more. To catch the enemy by surprise, you'll have to kill any scout that might find you. Besides, I have a feeling the army coming from the southwest won't maneuver too much. They'll make themselves obvious and draw us in to battle quickly so that our attention is on them. That's what I'd do to draw focus away from scouting in other directions."

Taingern thought about that. "You're right. And I'll need the scouts, but with a bit of luck I'll be able to fully circle this flanking force. Their scouts will be ahead of them, between them and you. They'll not expect someone coming up behind them."

"Exactly, but that raises a point. Their scouts will already have observed us. But they don't need to see you going. Leave just before dawn, and head north first."

"Into Callenor lands?"

"I think that's best. If any scouts *should* mark your going, let them think you're abandoning the army. Let them think anything but the truth."

Taingern grinned. "A good idea. And perhaps better if they do see us go. Then they'll take word back to their leaders that there's discord in our camp."

"The greatest weapon in warfare is deception," Brand quoted.

They fell silent then. The plan was made, and it was up to Taingern and the men he chose to fulfill it. But all plans were fragile, and subject to the tides of chance.

"Good luck," Brand said.

Taingern stood, and Brand shook his hand in the warrior's grip.

"Best of luck to you also."

Taingern left then. He had much to organize, but he shook Shorty's hand also before he departed.

"Keep that gold coin safe. I'll want it back."

"I'll try not to gamble it away," Shorty said.

Then Taingern disappeared into the dark of the camp. As he left, Sighern watched him.

"There goes a good man."

"The very best," Brand agreed.

Brand issued orders then. First, he sent word to the scouts in the camp that they were to go with Taingern.

And then he sent a man to Hruidgar, if he was still awake, to tell him what had been decided.

21. The Golden God

Char-harash paced to and fro, and anxiety evidently gnawed at him. He muttered to himself also, but Horta did not catch the words.

This much was evident though. He was stronger than he had been, and the previous night's hunt had sustained him in some manner. But also, he did not like the sun, and he was careful even as he walked to avoid any patches of light that shone down through the gaps in the tree canopy above.

But why should a god be anxious? What did he know that might make him so?

Char-harash spun upon him. "How powerful is this Brand who leads the enemy?"

"In magic, O Great One?"

"Yes, in magic. But in all things."

"He is not like others I have known. He has strong magic, but it is not like the magic of the Kar-ahn-hetep. I don't understand it well. The power seems to come directly from the land without working through a god. He uses no rites or ceremonies. But he is powerful. Perhaps a match for me."

"Can he fight gods?"

Horta felt a stab of fear. How could he answer such a question? The gods were powerful, yet they had failed several times trying to kill the man. But he could not say that, nor should he lie. Char-harash was likely to detect it.

"He has the courage to fight gods. And he always seems to be lucky. But luck runs out for all men, eventually."

Char-harash gave a brisk nod. "Luck can run out for gods too." His leather-dry hands clamped over his belly, and Horta remembered the legend. It was said he was killed by a spear driven into his guts and up into his heart.

"What else is there to tell of Brand?" the god-king demanded.

"He's a skilled leader of men, both in a military sense and a political. He has courage and determination. His people ... like him."

Char-harash grew agitated. "It seems as though you admire this man?"

Horta thought on that. "I do. What is the point of enemies if they don't test you?"

"That may be so. But gods do not have enemies. They crush them like a man squashes a beetle beneath his foot. And I would just as soon that Brand did not exist. He vexes me, and he defies my brothers and sisters yet."

Horta began to have an idea of why Char-harash was anxious. It seemed he had a way of communicating with the other gods, and that they had not defeated Brand yet. But the army of the Kar-ahn-hetep could not be far away. Battle would be joined soon, and his people would be supported by gods. How could they lose?

The god-king was not done speaking though. He raised his voice and lifted high his withered arms. But it seemed to Horta that he spoke to the universe rather than him.

"I shall prevail," he said, and his hands clenched into bony fists. "I shall be the Golden God, bright as the sun and my benevolence will make the earth prosper wherever my armies have conquered. But winter I shall call down upon my enemies. The grains of the earth will shrivel and rot. The rivers will stagnate. The frosted earth will bear no fruit. These things I will command, and the earth will obey, or she will perish in defiance."

A moment the god king stood, still as a statue, his gaze cast upward, and then he swung again to Horta.

"I feel the strength of star and planet run through me. I am invincible!"

Horta had long since given over his belief that the gods were invincible. But it would not do to say as much. Nor did he think this creature before him would be a Golden God. Rather, he would be a Dark God. But that thought he crushed lest it showed on his face.

He bowed. "You need no servant, Great Lord. Yet still I offer my talents, such as they are, for your use."

"All will be well," Char-harash answered. "My children come to me, and my brother and sister gods work to one purpose, as they rarely have before."

"Yet still," Horta found himself daring to say, "Brand is an opponent of strength and cunning. He seems to find a way to defy powers greater than himself. How it is so, I don't know, but it is something of which to be wary."

The god-king showed no emotion. Instead, for once he seemed to consider the words rationally.

"He is the champion of the land. That is why. And that is all. It need not concern us."

Horta had heard of such a thing before. It was said that in ancient days the Letharn had such champions. Then it occurred to him that the Letharn prevailed in those times against all the might of the Kar-ahn-hetep. Could it be so again? Could his people and his gods be defeated once more? All things were possible under the sun, but that was hard to believe. Brand really was just a man. He could not continue to defy gods.

Char-harash leaned in close, the dry sockets of his eyes boring into Horta.

"You said you are my servant?"

"Yes, O Great One."

"Will you do anything I require?"

"Of course. You are my god."

The dusty gaze of the god-king turned to Tanata.

"And you? Are you prepared to give whatever your god requires?"

"Yes," Tanata said simply. But he trembled as he spoke, and his bow did not cover it.

Horta saw the way that the god looked upon his Arnhaten, and he had a feeling Tanata's days on earth were growing short. There was a burning hunger in that long-dead gaze. The god would consume him in sacrifice. A poor fate for one who had served so well, but it was not his place to question. He was a servant, and it was his role to obey. But still, he was sick of such waste.

22. Let Them March to Us

Brand led the army forward, and it marched into uninhabited places now. No tribe claimed this area, though the road of the Letharn built long ages ago continued.

But even the road seemed little more than a path now, for it was narrow and rutted and grown over in places by bushes and trees. Yet still it took them south-west, whence the scouts reported the Kirsch were located and were hurrying on themselves, as expected.

That morning the thousand that Bruidiger had brought joined Brand, and Brand had met Arlnoth, chieftain of the Norvinor tribe. So also he had met representatives of the few among the new warriors who were of the Waelenor and Druimenor tribes. These were strange men to him, at times much like the Duthenor but also different. Yet they looked good fighting men, and after the initial reserve of their first meeting was gotten over, they seemed at ease and ready to fight for their lands with the others.

Brand had given Sighern yet another banner to carry, and this had the emblem of all five tribes upon it. The red dragon of the Duthenor, the raven claw of the Callenor, the radiant star of the Norvinor, the crossed swords of the Waelenor and lastly the eagle of the Druimenor. Sighern carried it proudly.

For the first time, Brand felt the army was coming together as one. All the tribes were represented, and with word of the enemy ahead the lords had stopped bickering. There was only one thought now. Fight together as one, and turn away the enemy.

They stopped for a noonday rest atop a hill with a long view. They could not see the enemy, but the scouts kept coming in reporting their movement. The Kirsch hastened toward them.

The Norvinor chieftain approached Brand. "Battle will be joined soon," he said.

Brand liked the man. He reminded him of Taingern, because he was red-haired and freckled. But his manner was always thoughtful too.

"Soon," Brand replied. "Soon indeed. But there's no need to hasten it. Let the enemy come to us if they will."

"You think they'll attack us on a hillside?"

It was a question Brand had given much thought to. "I think they will. They know the longer they wait the more chance for their flanking force to be discovered. I think they'll attack quickly and try to employ the advantage they believe they have."

The existence of the flanking force had not been kept secret. Better that the men knew and were prepared for it. All the more so if Taingern's counterstroke was defeated.

"They have the advantage of numbers," Arlnoth said. "Even so, they'd have to be confident of beating you to attack uphill."

"I agree," Brand said. "But they *are* confident. The scouts report they march straight toward us, and swiftly."

The Norvinor chieftain ran a hand through his red hair. "It sure looks like they'll attack. But they might change their mind when they see us. They might have the greater numbers, but the five tribes gathered together is no small force."

Brand turned his gaze to the south. At the base of the hill lay a large wood, and it was this more than anything that gave him confidence the enemy would engage. It was perfect cover for their flanking force, and he did not think they would let that chance slip by. At least, so long as

Taingern remained undiscovered. If he was able to do so, then the trap would be turned around on those who sought to snare him.

Shorty had been listening. "Of course, there's another tactic available."

"Go ahead, Shorty."

Brand knew that what would come next would question his own tactic. But that was good. That was Shorty's job.

"This is a good place to fight. The hill is to our advantage, and so too the creek to the north." He swept his hand out in that direction, and Brand knew what he meant. The enemy would be funneled toward them, uphill all the way.

"But numbers still matter. We're fifteen thousand strong, less now the one thousand that Taingern leads. The enemy is seventeen thousand strong, with five hundred chariots, the effect of which we don't properly know."

"That's correct," Brand agreed. "We're outnumbered, and we have no way to factor in exactly how the chariots will be used against us."

Shorty continued. "The standard rule in warfare is to avoid engaging a greater force. And here, we do have the option of avoiding battle. We know where the enemy is, and we can retreat from them."

It was an option Brand had considered. "We could, but that would expose our lands and people to the mercy of the enemy."

"It would. But it would also allow time for more forces to join you. Perhaps in a few days or a week, you could match the enemy force warrior to warrior."

"Perhaps," Brand said. "But there's no guarantee of that. But this much *is* certain. Winter is coming on. The enemy is far from home. To whom will they turn for supplies of food?"

Arlnoth folded his arms across his chest. "They'll turn to Norvinor lands. Or Callenor lands. Or whoever is nearest at the time. They'll ravish farms and towns, seeking food and supplies and killing indiscriminately."

The Norvinor chieftain seemed certain of this, and he had made up his mind that it was best to make a stand here.

"We don't know any of that for certain," Shorty countered. "The enemy will have a supply route, linking them to their homeland. No army would march without one."

"Agreed," Brand said. "But supplies for an army are never enough. Even our army, so close to home and support, is struggling. Supplies are *always* fewer than needed, and likely the enemy would do as Arlnoth suggests. And if not for supplies, perhaps just to spread terror before them."

Shorty shrugged. "What you say is true. All of it. For myself, I'd pick this place for the fight as well."

Arlnoth scratched his head. "Then why did you argue against it?"

Shorty winked at the chieftain, but it was Brand who answered.

"That's his job. The job of all in my leadership team. I don't want followers. That's a sure way to find defeat. I need people willing to speak their mind and offer alternatives. Even if they agree with me, I want them to suggest other ways of doing things. That way all options get considered."

Arlnoth raised an eyebrow. "That's an interesting approach. You Duthenor sure like to make things complicated."

Brand grinned. "That's something I may have picked up in Cardoroth. Things are not so simple there. But they're not simple here either, I guess. The only thing we know for sure is that people will die. That's our only guarantee. As for tactics and strategies, the only true test is the battle."

23. I Will Not Kneel

The army encamped, and threw up ditch ramparts to fortify its position. It was wasted work if the enemy did not attack, but if they did, it would go some way to balancing out the numerical superiority of the Kirsch.

The work went well, and the army ate well overnight and rested, enjoying a break from Brand's fast-paced marches.

By dawn, more scouts returned. The enemy came on, unswerving. It was a beautiful day, but marred by the threat of war and the pall of anxiety that hung in the air. No army was ever free of that. Not when a hostile enemy was nearby.

The night had been cold again, but the day warmed swiftly. The sky was cloudless, and it seemed the height of summer weather was here. But winter was approaching, and with it snow. The Kirsch, even if they won this war, would be ravaged by it.

Brand turned the possibility over in his mind. If his army lost, the five tribes must fend for themselves. There would be few warriors left. The Kirsch would move to confiscate food and shelter. But what would the people do?

It would be hard, but they would flee into the hills and remote places. They would take what food and livestock they could with them. The rest would be destroyed to deny it to the enemy.

It was a grim thought, but if the Kirsch won here, they would face a harder battle later. But it was not something to dwell on. It was Brand's task to ensure the enemy did *not* win here. That was what he must concentrate on.

And he had made a good start. He had a favorable position, now further fortified beyond what nature had provided. The creek protected them well on one side. The woods on the other were a deadly trap, but for him or the enemy was yet to be decided. The prospect of it would draw the enemy to attack when perhaps they would not otherwise. But there were three great unknowns that troubled Brand.

The first was the gods arrayed against him. He had seldom known defeat before, but they were a force above him. The second was the chariots of the enemy. Against them, he could take steps, but not with certainty. The third was Taingern. He trusted no one else except Shorty to do the job that was needed, but it was a hard task. If Taingern failed, Brand knew he would face a superior enemy on two fronts.

The enemy was not visible, but soon the dust cloud of their passage showed. It hazed the air, and then it grew thicker as time passed. This, perhaps, was due in part to the chariots. The horses that drew them and the wheels of the chariot itself disturbed the ground more than marching men.

No doubt, it was a reason that the flanking force did not have them. It would have been much harder to try to approach in secret.

Eventually, the army itself came into view. That it was large, Brand already knew. But it really did seem to hasten.

Attar noticed the same thing. "They're keen to join battle," he said.

"Or trying to give the *impression* of being keen to join battle," Sighern offered.

Brand turned that thought over in his mind. It was entirely possible. The enemy may yet hasten toward them only to halt a distance away and fortify a camp of their own. Or they may skirt his force altogether and force him to leave his advantageous ground. All things were possible, and he was glad that Sighern had considered such a thing.

But his instinct was that the enemy was supremely confident. This, perhaps, was the influence of their gods. They would come, and they would attack, and they would expect to win. Why should they not?

The enemy drew closer. Flashes of metal shot through the air. The movement of a great mass of men was visible. And the chariots also. These were deployed as cavalry often were, broken into two units and forming the outer wings of the force.

Brand, once again, set his mind to how they would be used. Their disposition was a clue. There were only two hundred and fifty to each side. Was that enough to use separately?

He did not think so. Despite being placed to each flank of the army, they would both be used in the same manner. Just like cavalry, they would charge, draw close to their opponent's ranks, and send forth volleys of arrows. Then they would be on their way again. Moments later, the second group of them would do the same thing. In this way they would take turns at harassing his army and intimidating it. When their general thought they had been softened enough, he would charge with the infantry and try to destroy all opposition.

That would be their plan. But how to counter it?

The enemy might suppose the speed and movement of the chariots made them harder to hit with return fire. This was so, and that the chariot driver also carried a shield would work into this. But they would not be expecting the stronger longbows of the five tribes.

Brand could use this by ensuring his archers shot the moment the enemy came into range, and before they expected attack. This would go some way to unbalancing their own attack. Also, the Duthenor and other tribes were skilled with shields. They would raise them high as a protective roof when the enemy finally drew close enough to shoot. They would not be as harassed or intimidated as the enemy general hoped.

The enemy would drive home their full offensive then, and that would be the real test. Against this, Brand arranged the Duthenor at the center of his defense. They had fought much lately, and they were hard men who would not be broken easily. The Callenor and other tribes he placed on the wings, but some also in the center. That way all the tribes fought together.

Under a warm noon sun, the enemy drew to a halt half a mile away.

"Will they attack or send an envoy first?" Furthgil asked, stroking his silver beard.

"It would be normal practice to send an envoy," Brand answered. "But who can say? These warriors are not like us."

They did not have long to wait. Five chariots came forward, and the lead one held a banner. It was a black scorpion, tail raised, against a white background.

The chariots drew up a hundred paces from the army, and two men dismounted and stood before them. The one on the left wore simple clothes. He was not dressed as the other Kirsch, and appeared taller and of another race. The one on the right was a commander of some sort. His bearing said as much, and his armor, though strange to Brand's eyes, was expensive and trimmed with gold as was the scabbard of his sword.

The tall man on the left spoke, casting his voice loudly and speaking in somber tones.

"The Kar-ahn-hetep have come," the man declared. "These lands are now theirs. Who speaks for you, and leads you, conquered thralls?"

It was not a gracious speech. And the accent was strange, dominated by whatever language the Kirsch spoke, but there was a hint of other accents in it too, some not unfamiliar to Brand's ear. He also noted how he had been placed in the position of one answering to the names of conquered and thrall.

"I lead this army," he replied. "This army of free men, unconquered. And if you think words alone can make us thralls, you are mistaken. The price for that will not be foolish boasts voiced into the air, but paid in spilled blood. If you have the heart to try."

There was silence for a moment, and then the tall man spoke again.

"Proud words, but in vain. You cannot stand against us. Surrender, and offer yourselves up to the mercy of the god-king to be. That you may know him, his hallowed name is Char-harash, Lord of the Ten Armies, Ruler of the Thousand Stars, Light of Kar-fallon and Emperor of the Kar-ahn-hetep! Kneel now to his emissary, Wena, and he will intercede on your behalf."

Brand did what no one expected. He laughed, and the shock of it showed on the faces of the foreigners.

"Char-harash? A god to be? You set a lot of store in a dead man. Yes, I've met him, or his spirit at any rate. He's a thing of dried rags and half-rotting flesh in a tomb. You can kneel to the shell of a man if you want, and pretend he's a god, but I'm a free man and I will not. Nor will my people. They are free also."

Brand drew himself up. And he cast his voice back over to the enemy, carried on a thread of magic that made it loud and deep.

"You are not welcome. Go back whence you came, and take your bickering gods with you. We will not endure them here. Should you not heed this warning, blood will flow in rivers and the might of your army will be crushed. Heed my words, for they are no threat but prophecy."

Brand fell silent, and he let the threads of magic that had supported his voice drift away. His concentration was on the second man on the right. So far, he had been silent. But unless Brand missed his mark, he was the commander of the enemy host.

The emotions on the other man's face were hard to read because of the distance, but even so Brand thought he saw shock or outrage at his reply gradually turn to anger.

The herald would have spoken again, but the second man stopped him with a swift gesture. He stood forth a few steps, and he laughed.

Brand knew it was false. This was a man of show, and not very good at it. But that did not mean his military leadership was poor.

"You will see," the man replied haltingly, and with a heavy accent. "You will see, and you will regret."

That was all he said. But his voice was confident, and Brand knew the man believed what he said. But even as he turned and remounted the chariot, his head swiveled to the south and the woods that lay there. All was silent there now, and nothing moved. But Brand sensed his enemy's expectation.

The chariot turned and sped back to the army, and the four chariots with it followed in its wake. When the commander reached its ranks, trumpets blew and a tumult sounded.

Shorty grunted. "That Wena doesn't say much. But what he has his herald say, I don't like. He'll please me better when I thrust a sword in his guts."

"Which one – Wena or the herald?" Brand asked.

"Both!"

Brand did not really listen to the reply. He knew Shorty only spoke to relieve the tension of the men. His thoughts were on the wood, and especially on Taingern. So much depended on him.

24. First Blood is Spilled

Char-harash sat atop a boulder in their forest camp, and Horta watched him carefully. For some while the god-king had been excited, muttering to himself and shaking his head. Horta began to wonder if he was sane.

But that was a stupid thing to ponder. He was to be obeyed, no matter what. And if he was not sane? What dead person come back to life in a far later age than he had lived would be? Horta considered it all. Why should he care one way or the other? So long as he remained careful, he would enjoy the spoils of victory at the side of a god.

The god-king turned to him, and fixed him with those dry sockets that served as eyes.

"The battle prepares," he said. "Listen, and learn, for I shall show you now of the old magic."

Char-harash turned away then, and fixed his gaze to the south-west, though there was nothing to see there but trees. But in moments, he began to chant.

His voice was different. It was softer, almost as though he mumbled. It was not a summoning of a god or a beseeching of divine aid. That would not be fitting anyway for one that would be a god himself. Horta did not know what it was, for it was not like any rite that he had ever heard or read of.

Yet there was magic in the words. He felt the power of it build and grow. He tried to memorize what he heard, but Char-harash continued to mumble and he could not catch all that was said.

That too was a difference. Most of the rites that Horta knew rose to a crescendo as the power was unleashed. Yet not so here. It was almost as though the god-king drifted away to sleep. And, after a little while, his mumbling grew so soft as to be inaudible. Then it ceased altogether.

Nothing happened. Char-harash continued to sit there, but now his head was bowed. Perhaps he was meditating.

But suddenly his head snapped up and his back stiffened. He spoke again, his voice strong now, though with a faraway cast to it.

"The Children attack!" he proclaimed. "The Sons of the Thousand Stars bring war as once they did of old. These lands that once were nearly ours will assuredly fall this time."

Horta exchanged a glance with Tanata. Could the god somehow sense what was happening elsewhere? But they dared not speak, for Char-harash was not done.

"I feel the rush of blood in my veins, and what it is to be a man in battle. The battle cry that rises in their throats, rises in mine. The thrumming of their hearts sets mine afire, and the hatred in their minds as they charge is as kindling to my spirit."

Horta understood now. Somehow, Char-harash saw events exactly as they were transpiring elsewhere.

This was the final throw of the dice, and the culmination of everything that Horta had so long worked for. His people were coming, and his god had wakened and walked the earth once more. Yet he felt empty inside, for he knew what was to come.

"Horses and chariots fly over the earth," Char-harash declared. "The hooves are thunder and the wheels rumble. Sharp are the points of the arrows to be shot, and they glitter with the fire of the sun. Ah! The glory of battle is here and the earth will be wetted with the blood of my enemies."

This now was the hour of Brand's downfall, and Horta should be pleased. Yet he was not. Had he been in Brand's place, would he not have done the same things?

"First blood is spilled!" Char-harash proclaimed, and there was excitement in his voice. "Now also my brothers and sister come, and they lend their wills to mine."

The god-king sat even more upright, as though his back were a rod that had just been thrust upward, and his bony hands clawed at the stone of the boulder. It seemed that he struggled, either living out the battle being contested or striving for the strength to maintain the magic that he wrought.

"Now I see afar," Char-harash said, and there was hatred in his voice, "he who leads the enemy. Brand! How I hate him! But his day has come. He shall be as dust beneath the sandaled feet of my children."

Suddenly Char-harash sprang upward to stand upon the boulder. He was a towering figure, and menace and power radiated from him. For once, he appeared to be the god that he claimed.

"The enemy is struck. Ah! The glory of it! Blood flows, and yet it is but a taste of all that is to come. Kingdom after kingdom. Nation after nation. Land after land. All will fall to me!"

The god-king stood there, radiant in his power, but in the blink of an eye he seemed lesser again. He fell to one knee and held up his hands imploringly. "No! My strength lessens, and the vision fades."

With head bowed once again, but his dark eye sockets still visible, he turned his dead gaze on Tanata.

"Come to me, my child."

Horta looked at his acolyte. Tanata trembled all over. There was fear in his eyes, and had he been able he would have run. Yet some power held him, and he stepped, slow pace after another, toward his god.

With certainty, Horta knew what would come next. Life gave power. Sacrifice nourished the god, and this was the first of many.

25. Worthy of That Axe

Brand watched, and it seemed that the very earth trembled at the charge of the enemy host. No trial of strength and resolve was this. It was a full attack, and no reserves were left behind. This was army against army, steel against steel and man against man. The stronger would prevail. The weaker would perish.

Afar, he heard the trumpets of the enemy. But they were drowned by the rushing of the chariots. They would strike first, unleashing their arrows, but such was the confidence of Wena in victory that the army followed. One attack only the chariots would launch, and Brand, despite the cold that had seeped into his bones, rejoiced at the mistake. The enemy did not know the danger of his archers and their longbows, and Wena would not learn of it until it was too late to halt the charge.

But still, though the longbows would take a great toll, it would not stop such a charge as this.

The chariots roared closer. They came from each wing of the enemy, but the left group had begun sooner and would reach first. When they had passed, then the right group would take their place.

The faces of the chariot drivers were visible now, and so too the warriors standing beside them. Hard men all, and skilled. Brand marveled at the horsemanship and the balance of the men to ride such a vehicle and yet still be able to use their weapons.

Closer they came, and Brand studied the small recurve bows they held. He glanced at his own archers. They had moved, according to plan, to the front rank of his army.

There they stood. Proud men, and hard also. No less than the enemy, nor suffering from lesser skill. Arrows they had notched already, and in moments death would flash through the gap between opposing forces.

Brand waited. Fear thickened the air all around him. It was always thus in battle. A horn blew in his front ranks, and others took up the note. The archers did not draw their bows. Rather, they kept their right hand at rest and pressed the weight of their body through the left. This bent the limbs of the great bows that only strong men, trained since their youth, could shoot.

And then they shot. Long arrows hissed through the air. One hundred yards. Two hundred yards. Further still, and the enemy, unready, rode into a storm of death.

Hurriedly the drivers raised their shields, protecting them and their passenger. But caught by surprise, many shields were not well placed. Arrows slew men. Armored horses died also. Chariots and beasts fell in tangled wrecks, and screams ripped the air.

The enemy came on. Arrows flew again. The charioteers were better prepared now. Not so many died, yet still screams roiled up into the heavens. A litter of dead and dying lay behind the wheeled charge, and this would do little for the morale of the infantry that followed.

Three times the archers shot, sending death to the enemy. Then they raced back between the ranks of the army. Now, the charioteers were in range with their own bows, and these they fired as the chariots wheeled in a part circle.

Shorter arrows, less deadly, now flew. Less deadly, but deadly enough. Despite the raised shields men still died. But fewer than among the enemy.

Brand watched, calm as ever. He would die today, or he would live. Victory would be his, or loss. His army would conquer, or be vanquished. All he could do, as with all his men, was try.

He glanced to the other group of chariots. These, coming in a little later, had not been so devastated by his archers. But he saw fear on the faces of drivers and warriors. Their charge was not so swift. They too drew close and unleashed their attack. More of Brand's men fell. But not many.

The chariots raced away. Brand's archers, having sheltered behind the last rank of infantry, sprang forward again. They would have little time, but the enemy infantry came on, and they would receive at least two flights of arrows.

Brand willed speed to his archers. And they did not disappoint him. They moved with alacrity and precision, coming to the front once more and firing a hail of arrows at the charging host.

Men went down, only to be trampled by those who came after. It mattered not if they were dead or alive. But many were dead, for the arrows found targets between lifted shields. No shield wall could be properly held during a charge, and it was yet another mistake of this Wena. The enemy should have approached at a steady march, thus protecting themselves better.

Three volleys Brand's archers managed before the enemy was nearly upon them, and they withdrew once more through the ranks of their comrades.

Those ranks closed swiftly, shield to shield and man to man. Then, with a mighty roar, the two forces came together in a deafening clash. Men died on both sides. Blood spurted and guts spilled to the earth. The dying screamed and the living yelled their defiance.

The center of the army where the Duthenor mostly stood began to buckle back, ceding the advantage of the ditch rampart. This was where the enemy attacked the most fiercely, and Brand surmised that Wena had done as he had also done, placing the most experienced warriors in the center.

Sighern held the banner of the five tribes higher. He looked at Brand, and Brand read the question in his eyes. He wanted to know if it was time for Brand and his leadership group to bolster the men by joining them.

"Not yet," Brand told him above the din of battle. "The men will hold this charge."

He hoped it was true. The line buckled further. But if he joined in now there would be nothing to give later. And also, he must keep an eye on *all* his enemies.

The three gods of the Kirsch that he had met before were there now, behind their army and urging it forward. What plan had they concocted? What sorcery would be sent against him? He must keep himself free as long as possible to face that threat.

The buckling line steadied and then, slowly, pushed back. The Kirsch screamed their battle cries, fighting inch by inch, for they sensed how close they had been to overrunning their opponent.

But they had not. And the quick victory they had sought, even expected, did not happen. Almost, Brand could feel Wena's chagrin.

The three gods were not still. They moved about behind the ranks of the Kirsch, urging them ahead and filling them with purpose. If not, with fear, for the men redoubled their efforts.

Again, the line began to buckle. This time it was the left wing. Brand's gaze flickered to the woods. Should the second army of the Kirsch attack on that flank now, all was lost. But there was no sign of movement there.

Shorty too was looking in that direction.

"We hold!" Sighern cried. "We hold and push them away again!"

Brand turned back to the battle. The left wing was creeping forward once more, and a great shout went up from those ranks. The joy of battle was upon them, for they had faced death, defied it, and now turned it onto their enemies instead.

Brand knew that feeling. But such was always the ebb and flow of battle.

So it proved. On and on the battle raged, and no quarter was asked nor given. Again and again Brand's lines buckled, but always some hero stood forth and rallied the morale of the men, bringing them with him to straighten it. Sometimes, though much less often, the defenders pushed forward beyond the earth rampart, opening a gap among the enemy.

Whether this was a tactic of the enemy to draw them into a trap or not, Brand did not know. But he never gave an order to capitalize on it and try to break the foe. If it were a trap, this was what the enemy wanted. If not, and he thought not, his army was not big enough to rout the enemy in that fashion. If he were to win, it must be by holding and wearing the opponent out. Only when they retreated might they be vulnerable to attack.

And always, the gods were there. Vague glimpses of them from behind the enemy. Moving. Cajoling. Perhaps threatening. They used no magic that Brand sensed. Their presence alone was a kind of magic that gave purpose to the enemy and offered support.

But that could not last. The gods would make their own move against him at some point, and even as he watched his men straighten the line once more and stand resolute, Brand knew that moment had at last come.

The gods acted. A spell was loosed. It drove the Kirsch to a frenzy of attack, and hatred was in their eyes and an absence of fear in their hearts.

Brand did not wait for the lines to buckle against this new threat.

"Now!" he cried to his leaders. And the lords of the five tribes and the chieftain of the Norvinor sprang forward with him. Before them all Sighern lifted high their banner.

"Now!" Brand cried again. "To battle and war and the defeat of the enemy!"

And some in the ranks of his men heard his great voice above the tumult, and they called out to others to tell them, and his joining of the fray and that of the lords lent strength to weary arms and courage to desperate hearts.

Brand moved forward, and a way was made for him and those with him to enter the ranks and come up to the battle line itself. Above them Sighern held the banner of the five tribes, but not for long.

He drove the spear point into the ground and stepped forward into the front rank also. Brand saw him on his left, and he was glad that he was there. The young man had courage, and he wielded the light Raven Axe with skill, using it to stab with its spike like a sword.

Brand was glad also that Shorty was on his right, and together they fought with sword and shield, firming the line against the frenzy that came against them.

The Kirsch were maddened. The influence of their gods drove them, and some even threw down their shields to swing their swords two-handed.

This was an error, and the power of the gods turned against them. For these warriors were swiftly cut down, though they died slowly, clawing forward over the ground even as they perished to try to deliver one last strike against their foe.

Others of the enemy were not so careless of their lives. They fought with skill and determination, and the power of the gods did not make them reckless, yet still it gave them heart and purpose, driving them forward implacably.

The line began to buckle once more, despite Brand's presence. He fought with cool skill, stabbing and blocking, blocking and stabbing. Shorty did likewise beside him, and the dead enemy filled the lower ground before them.

Had Brand not ordered an earth rampart dug that gave his men an advantage, already they would have been routed. Even so, it would not be long now and Brand knew it. He thought desperately of what he might do, but even as he did so Sighern yelled a battle cry beside him.

To the lad's left fought Furthgil, that gray-bearded lord of the Callenor who once had been Brand's enemy and was now his ally. The man was older, yet he still fought well. But a blade had torn into his thigh from a near-dead warrior on the ground before him.

Half into the ditch Furthgil had fallen, and about him the enemy gathered for the kill. But Sighern dropped his shield and jumped down among them, swinging the Raven Axe of the Callenor wildly but to deadly effect.

The foe shrank back from him, and a Duthenor warrior heaved Furthgil up to safety. With a roar Sighern swept in among the enemy, causing them to scatter, for his axe severed arms and cut heads off the enemy in single strokes. Then the young man leaped back up to the line again and picked up his shield once more.

Brand looked on with pride. The boy had become a man. And a great one, for he had risked his life to save another.

Furthgil rose to his feet. A moment he held Sighern's gaze. "You're worthy of that axe, boy. Thank you."

Sighern nodded. There was no time to answer for the enemy came forward again. But a great cheer rose up round about for the courageous deed. And for all that the enemy pressed home their attack once more, thereafter they were wary of the young warrior with the deadly axe and tried to avoid him. Their drive had diminished.

The battle wore on. Here and there, Brand had an opportunity to glance southward to the woods. What was happening there? Had he miscalculated and the second Kirsch army would attack from another direction? And what of Taingern?

The gods tried a new tactic now. Or, more accurately, the Trickster did.

Brand noticed movement among the back ranks of the enemy, as though they made way for something or someone. He had an idea what this would be, and he was proven correct.

Gormengil pushed his way forward. He was clad in black, and a black-bladed sword was in his hand. He stalked through the Kirsch like a hunting animal, all litheness and deadly force ready to pounce. Yet his face and eyes were visible below his helm. And for all the liveliness and grace of his every move, they remained flat and dead.

Those eyes fixed Brand, and he felt a chill run through him. Magic was at work, but they gleamed with single-minded determination also. He had come to kill one person, and one alone.

Like a wolf after prey he came straight toward Brand, and it seemed that the battle raging all around them slipped away into oblivion. There was only the two of them in the world now, and nothing else mattered. The fight that they had not quite finished back in the Duthgar would be ended here.

But if Gormengil was already dead, how could he be killed and defeated? It was a haunting thought, and one that Brand suppressed. Doubt fed weakness, and here in this fight he must be at his strongest. Nothing else would serve.

But the thought remained. Even his strongest might not be enough. As a man, Brand knew he had Gormengil's measure, but as some magic-enhanced warrior it was another matter.

Gormengil drew up before him, shouldering aside Kirsch warriors, and his voice came cold and clear, a match for his dead eyes.

"Hail, Brand. Chieftain of the Duthenor and Callenor both. Are you ready to die?"

"Were you?" Brand answered swiftly. "For I killed you once before and I shall again."

Gormengil gazed at him with those dead eyes, and Brand knew this was a man beyond taunting or unbalancing. Perhaps even beyond fear and pain.

"Words," the one-time leader of the Callenor said, "are a poor weapon for warriors. Come! Let us put blade to blade and dance the one true dance."

Brand nodded. His shield he cast down, for Gormengil had none, and around Brand the men in the line made space. The black-clad warrior leaped nimbly up to the top of the earthwork rampart and there faced him.

Brand made no move to stop it. Single combat was an honored tradition among all the tribes, even in the midst of battle. Had he tried to stop it, men would have thought him scared and weak. This, he could not afford.

But single combat was a two-edged sword. Should Gormengil lose, the five tribes would rally all the harder behind Brand and try to emulate his example.

About the two combatants the battle went on, yet neither side fought with full attention. Every man tried to catch a glimpse, here and there, of the fight between the champion of the gods and the leader of the defenders.

Gormengil held forth his black sword, and Brand touched it with his Halathrin blade. A cold note rang out, and the duel commenced as if no battle existed but theirs.

Brand struck first. His sword swept low, aiming for his opponent's thigh where he had wounded him before. He had thought to remind him of that blow and perhaps cast over his enemy the shadow of doubt and a memory of pain.

But Gormengil seemed beyond such things. He stepped casually out of the way, a smile upon his lips for he understood what Brand had tried. But his eyes remained dead and void of all emotion.

Then the black sword flickered. It swept through the air and cut and stabbed. Gormengil seemed to make no effort, but the blade flashed with speed and power.

Brand retreated. He blocked and deflected, getting the feel of how his enemy moved. But he blocked and deflected clumsily, or so it seemed to him, for the other man was *fast*. Too fast for mortal skill. But this thought Brand put from him. He had faced deadly opponents before. Some that were better than him, and they were dead now. Skill was important, but courage was too, and a belief in victory. Not because it was deserved, but because others depended on it. That drove him on, and kept fear from his mind. He would not lose, because others needed him to win.

Gormengil dropped low and swept his blade out. Brand stepped back from a cut that would have crippled him, but the black-clad warrior was not done.

From his low position, Gormengil sprung upward into the air like a striking serpent, the tip of his blade flashing before him.

Brand stumbled back, surprised. It was a move that required incredible strength in the legs to perform. But to perform it so quickly was beyond human ability.

The blade nicked Brand's throat as he reeled away, and the fear of death was on him. How could he beat such an opponent?

But he must.

Anger coursed through him now, and he regained his footing and turned from defense into attack. His bright sword swept out, flashed and cut in glittering arcs and lines. Cold flame, pale as winter moonlight gleamed along its edges.

Gormengil merely gazed at him with those dead eyes, and he danced away and out of harm's way with ease. But Brand did not relent. He pressed forward, and his blade sliced the left arm of his opponent and his right leg also. Not deep, but enough to draw blood.

There was no change in the black eyes of his enemy. Neither fear nor pain showed. And soon Brand knew something else, also. The wounds did not bleed.

Was Gormengil dead? Did his heart pump hot blood? Or was he caught on the very cusp of death and held there, even unwillingly? The Kirsch seemed to have some fascination with death, and perhaps their gods shared it.

Brand feigned, ever so slowly, tiredness. Everything in battle and war was based on deception, and he feigned it well, for like lies the best trap was the closest to the truth, and his arms and legs were weary.

At the last, he stumbled for just a moment, the tip of his sword drooping lower than it should have. It was a snare. Well set and cunningly deployed. A thousand warriors would have fallen for it and rushed in to try to land a killing blow.

But not Gormengil. He stepped back instead, that smile on his lips again that was cold as the gaze of a hunting animal. But his eyes were not cold. For the first time they showed some faint glimmer of emotion. And it was contempt.

"Is that the best you can do? I had thought you a better fighter than that."

"Then come kill me, if you can."

"I can and I will. You know it. I see it in your eyes."

"And I see nothing in yours save what the goddess puts there. You are her puppet. Pulled on her strings. I had thought you a man, but you're a toy for her instead."

The black eyes hardened. Brand had guessed right, for there was chagrin there, and ever so faintly he felt the presence of the Trickster. But there was some other glimmer in those eyes as well. For just a moment he saw hope, and that was no emotion the goddess would be feeling now. Some part of the mind of the man that had once been Gormengil remained.

What that meant, if anything, Brand had little time to consider. His enemy swung a mighty blow at his head, and though he jumped back, still the edge of the blade glanced off his helm and a line of sparks flew, leaving a glittering trail.

Once more Gormengil attacked, and once more Brand defended, fighting for his very life and the hopes of five nations and lands unnumbered beyond them.

Steel rang against steel, and the thrum of the strikes traveled up Brand's arm and into his body. This was now no duel of finesse and skill, but a fight of hammer blows.

And Gormengil seemed not to tire. But Brand did. He tried to spare his body, but threatened as he was he must use all his strength and speed just to stay alive a little longer.

This was not a fight that could continue much longer. Brand knew he was outmatched, and sought now to use his magic to discover why. He could not, or would not, use it as a weapon against a man who did not threaten him with sorcery. Nor did he think that would work. The goddess would have given him protection against such a chance. Yet that did not mean that the means by which Gormengil was kept alive and given strength could not be sought out and considered.

Even as Brand retreated and the blade in his hand snaked out in defense, so too his magic slipped into the air and probed around his enemy.

The black blade was of steel, and no magic was in it. So also the armor Gormengil wore. Yet around him was cast a net of power, hugging him like water dripping from a man climbing out of a river.

And like a river, that power had a source. Fast as light Brand sent his magic probing along that current, seeking its origin to see if he could sever it.

Brand found it. He sensed at that place the joined minds of the three gods, and one other. This was Char-harash, the spirit that had hunted him in his dreams. He knew it, and recognized it, and anger flared even brighter. He was the root cause of the problems that had beset Brand ever since he returned to the Duthgar.

But with anger came frustration. The will of these four kept Gormengil alive, if life it could be called. Their magic animated his corpse, and kept his mind within it, trapped. He was like an insect frozen in ice, and the magic required for this was great.

Brand sensed the combined power of his four enemies, and it was greater by far than his own. The gods brooded behind the army, pressing them on and lending their strength to the Trickster whose will drove Gormengil. Yet also, from a great distance, the spirit of Char-harash strived the hardest. Somewhere in the Duthgar he stood upon a boulder in a forest and joined his will to that of the others.

The strength of Char-harash seemed to Brand to be greater, and upon him was focused a power of magic beyond Brand's experience. It was not of the earth as lòhrengai and elùgai were, but born of the cyclic powers of the universe itself.

Together, the gods were by far too much for him. And the instrument of their will, Gormengil, was thus beyond his skill and strength.

But he fought on, somehow avoiding the relentless death strokes Gormengil hammered at him. And he remembered the words of the witch. *Your enemy may yet be your friend. When despair grips you, hold tight to that thought.*

But none of these enemies were his friend, and all along the line the five tribes were pressed harder than they ever had been before.

26. Like A Torch

"Come to me, my child," the god-king repeated. And Tanata went to him, one slow step at a time, fighting each movement with all his will, but failing.

Horta watched. Tanata was but a puny thing compared to Char-harash. The one was a god, or a god that could be. The other only a man, and young at that. Nor deeply trained in the sacred mysteries. Not that training would have made much difference. But still he struggled, and valiantly. The instinct to live was strong, and the will of Tanata great.

Annoyance flickered across the leathery visage of Char-harash's face. He did not like it that his chosen sacrifice resisted. He did not like it at all.

From somewhere within the foul burial shroud the god-king wore, he withdrew a dagger. Hilt and blade were of gold, but dried blood darkened its luster. Last night Char-harash had caught prey to sustain himself, and now it was the turn of Tanata to lend his power to the gods.

Horta did not move. The sacrifice might as easily be his own. He did nothing to draw attention to himself, for that would be folly of the greatest kind.

But it seemed pitiful to him that one who would be a god looked as such. Dead. Dried to a husk. Smelling of corruption overlaid with the oils, resins, wood tar and sacred herbs of preservation. The hand that held the knife was a bony claw, and upon the boulder next to him was the war hammer with which he had broken from the tomb. Dead, but alive. Weak, but powerful. Hungry for power, but insatiable.

Of the two, Tanata was the nobler figure. The lesser fought the mighty, without hope of victory. But he did not give up, and Horta admired that.

His heart swelled. Tanata would be worthy to learn the sacred mysteries. But that chance was denied him. All chances were denied him. The god would consume his life to grow stronger, to see the battle that might decide his fate.

Tanata was close to the god-king now, and somehow he wrenched his head, so very slowly, to face Horta. He could not speak. He could do nothing but walk stiffly toward his own sacrifice, but his gaze silently implored help, and a single tear glistened on his cheek.

The god gestured impatiently with his knife, and Horta looked away. Some things did not need to be seen.

The forest was empty around him. No beast nor bird stirred. All was silent, and his heart was empty.

Had he served the gods for this? Death and destruction? Had he served them so that good men could die? Did he grovel at their feet, hoping to gather the scraps of their power? He did, and the voice of his heart that had long been silenced spoke.

He was a man. And he would live or die as such. Better to die thus than to live and know shame all the days of his life.

He swung around. His acolyte stood before the god-king, his head tilted up to expose his own throat. Charharash bent toward him, the gold knife in his hand held high.

Time ceased to move. Horta watched, transfixed. Not by the sight before him; he had seen men die before. But by the thought in his heart. It was blasphemy. It was death, for a man did not defy gods. It was an overturning of all that he had ever believed and striven for. If he acted on it.

Time moved again. The gold knife began to descend in an arc of cold death. The hollow eyes of Char-harash fixed on Tanata like a hawk on a mouse, and the dry tongue in his withered mouth licked his leathery lips.

Horta's hand was already in one of his pouches, and he had drawn a fistful of powder. Shouldering Tanata away and uttering a word of power, he flung what was in his hand straight at Char-harash.

Dust filled the air. It enveloped the god-king, but did not cover the surprise on his face.

Horta dived away. Char-harash made to leap from the boulder after him, but a thunderous boom rang out, and light flashed as though lightening tore at the earth.

And then Char-harash screamed. It was a horrible sound, as though all the agony the world had ever known was given voice all at once.

Horta lay in a heap on the ground. A wave of heat rolled over him and away, and he looked up through watery eyes.

Char-harash was like a torch. The white shroud of his burial was gone, but his body had caught alight and burned. All of it, from the stubby toes to his leathery face. The oils and resins and tar used to preserve his body in ancient days was flammable.

The god-king screamed, and fell to his knees on the blackened boulder. Greasy smoke coiled from his eye sockets, and sparks flew from his mouth.

Horta rolled away. But Char-harash screamed and leapt from the boulder, a streak of flame and roiling smoke billowing behind him. The earth shook as he landed, and he came for Horta.

Staggering, the god-king moved toward him. Horta got to his knees, but Char-harash towered above like a bonfire. And in his hand he still held the gold knife, heated red-hot as an ember.

The knife rose to kill him. This was the price of disobedience. He would be sacrificed himself. Yet still it would not save the god-king. Nothing could now. Those flames could not be put out, and already the corpse was falling apart.

The knife fell. But Tanata had come up beside them, and he held the war-hammer of Char-harash. With a clumsy movement he smashed at the god-king's arm and fended the blow away.

Char-harash turned on him and screamed, his open mouth gushing flame. But the hammer struck again, this time an overhead blow. It took Char-harash on the shoulder and sent him spinning. But the head of the hammer tore through his body also. An arm fell away. The head twisted at an unnatural angle. The torso was a ruin like a split tree trunk, and newly exposed embalmed tissue was fresh fuel for flames.

Char-harash tottered. He screamed again, though there was no sound now except the roar of flame. And he fell into a writhing heap.

There, on the forest floor, the god burned. And he did not cease burning, for the substances used in embalming did not flare and go out. Rather they would burn and smolder for hours.

Warily, Horta stood. Together the two men looked down on the remains of the god they had killed. If indeed Char-harash was yet dead. The body still moved. Whether that was the residue of life within him, or the heat of combustion, Horta did not know.

But there was magic to account for also. Chemicals had preserved the body, but magic had bound the spirit of Char-harash to it. That magic had endured through long ages, and Horta thought it would endure fire also. Until the body was consumed by the flames and become ashes scattered on the wind.

"Not a good way to die," Tanata said quietly.

"Neither was a spear through the body," Horta answered without pity. "But he suffered that. And he will suffer this."

27. The Hunter Becomes the Hunted

Taingern took his thousand men north into Callenor lands before the sun rose. With him were many scouts, and chief among them Hruidgar.

Much depended on the hunter. But more on Taingern himself, and he knew it. If he failed in his mission, Brand would likely die. And his army with him.

That was intolerable. The world needed Brand, and therefore it would not happen. He knew it for a vain thought, but thought was the root of action, and he would prove it.

He did not go far into Callenor lands. His task was to come around behind the flanking force and surprise them. That could be achieved in two ways. He could head north, traverse a great loop and come around again, all the while traveling at forced marches. Then, spent, engage the three thousand soldiers of the enemy's flanking army.

Or, he could wait where he was, resting and preparing, then when sufficient time had elapsed, and Brand's army and the flanking force had moved on, cut at a direct angle behind them. This meant covering far less ground and keeping his soldiers fresher. But it was also riskier. If he mistimed his march, the scouts of the flanking force would observe him.

But he chose this option. Decisively. He would take that risk, because he must face three thousand enemy with one thousand. For that, his men would need to be fresh.

Additionally, he knew his men liked the thought of resting while the enemy marched. It gave them a sense of superiority. It deepened the idea that they would outthink the enemy, and thereby outfight them.

Victory, just like thought, occurred in the mind first. Actions followed later.

Taingern knew others thought him cautious. The men were surprised at this plan, even if they liked it. But he knew himself better than all others. Only Brand and Shorty understood him. He was neither cautious nor adventurous. He merely did what was required. No more and no less. Usually, that gave him the appearance of caution.

But he could risk everything at need. And seldom had he, or those he cared for, had a greater need.

Hruidgar, perhaps, was beginning to understand him. But he knew better than most what was required here, and how it could be done.

The scouts were pivotal to everything. They must advance ahead of his force, identify where the enemy lay without being seen. Or, if seen, kill the observers. Without fail. All it took was one man to return to the flanking army with news of his presence, and surprise would be lost and with it the chance of success.

He waited until noon. The scouts were out long before that though. Giving a hand signal to the men, for nothing would be announced by horn in their current situation, he led the men back the way they had come this morning.

It did not take long to reach their old camp of last night. It was an empty place now, the army gone ahead with Brand toward the enemy and the destiny that awaited them.

Taingern turned that word over in his head. Destiny. If ever a man had one, it was Brand. But he denied it. A person made their own future, he always said. Perhaps that was so. But personal skill and courage only took you so far. The rest was design, or luck. But if there was no such thing as destiny, how then did prophecy work? And he had seen foretelling after foretelling come true about Brand.

His thoughts were disturbed as Hruidgar came and reported to him at the old camp, as arranged.

The hunter was not one for formalities. There were no bows or greetings. Taingern did not care. He had been on the receiving end of them for years, and knew them for empty gestures. The informality of Duthenor warriors, even to their leaders, was refreshing.

"So far, so good," Hruidgar said. "My men report seeing scouts following Brand."

"And the flanking force?"

"They're too far away yet. But they'll know their main force approaches. They'll want to stay as close as possible to Brand now. They'll go as close as they dare."

That was certainly true. Taingern did not think the main enemy host would delay. The battle was coming soon. It would be tomorrow.

"And have any of our scouts been seen?"

"Three, that I know of. But the enemy scouts who did so are dead." He gestured backward with his thumb. "The land out there is alive with my men. For the most part, the Kirsch scouts are staying between their flanking force and Brand. They're not concerned by the possibility of anything behind them."

Taingern nodded. "Let's hope we can keep it that way. Until it doesn't matter anymore."

Hruidgar grinned. "We just might pull it off. Then we'll see how they deal with a surprise attack themselves."

Taingern was not so keen. Once Hruidgar's work was done, his own would begin. And though surprise was a great advantage, he still had to lead his group against an enemy three times its size.

"It's safe for you to move out and cross the enemy's backtrail now," Hruidgar said. "But don't hasten. If there's any real catching up to do, it's better to do so with a night march."

"Of course," Taingern agreed. He knew the men would not like it, but they knew as well that the night would hide them. And they knew too that everything depended on surprise.

"Are you going back out now?"

Hruidgar looked grim. "I've got a personal score to settle with these Kirsch scouts. I'm going back out, and if I find any stragglers, they'd better watch out."

He said no more then, but just turned and walked away. Taingern liked it. The man had no sense of etiquette at all, but so long as he did his job, that did not matter. In fact, it reminded him of Shorty.

Taingern led his men on. They marched at an easy pace, in no hurry. But he made sure word was passed around that there would be a night march.

It was late in the afternoon, very late, when they finally crossed the trail of the flanking army. The signs of their passage were clear, and it confirmed that they were heading after Brand. Not that this had ever been in much doubt, but the possibility existed that their purpose was something else.

Night fell slowly, but Taingern did not halt the march. He followed the trail of the enemy, and he increased the speed of travel, bringing him closer to those he pursued. Ahead, his scouts were now concentrated. They ensured, or tried to ensure, that no enemy scout saw them. But as word continued to come in, it appeared that although the enemy was not watching closely behind them, further scouts had been observed and eliminated. Taingern just hoped that none had seen his approach unobserved.

The night grew chill, but the men did not feel it. He hoped that lasted, for there would be no campfires when they finally rested. Nor would there be any meals. There would be cold rations only. He made sure the men understood why this was so. Secrecy would preserve their lives. It was worth some minor discomfort, and the word back was that they agreed. This, and the secrecy of a night march, fed into the feeling that they were outthinking and outmaneuvering the enemy.

After some while, the dark grew ominous. Taingern ordered that the men walk quietly, and only spoke in whispers. It was an excessive precaution, but he felt it wise. The chances of the world were many, and all it took was one unseen enemy scout to hear a noise in the distance and come to investigate for the fate of realms to change.

It was a strange countryside, shifting between flats and small hills, alternating between woods and open ground. But the enemy had been careful to move as much as possible through the trees and had stuck to lower ground to avoid being seen.

Taingern followed in their trail, and he felt like a fox hunting a scent through the night. So it went, save for the regular rest breaks. But he was in no hurry. Word came back to him from the scouts that the flanking force was close ahead. But from Hruidgar, there was no word, and this was a worry.

Toward midnight Taingern called a halt. The battle would follow tomorrow, both his and Brand's, and the men needed sleep. They encamped in a creek valley, overgrown by trees. And the enemy was only a mile away, themselves in a wood, but one that bordered the ancient road whence Brand would be traveling.

It was a restless sleep, what sleep the men could even get. The camp was nervous, for everyone knew that battle and death, for them or the enemy, would play out tomorrow. But though they were fewer, and though they had marched part of the night, yet still their presence was a secret. If they could preserve that, then victory was possible when daylight came.

Daylight came swiftly. The scouts brought word that the enemy remained where it was. This indicated that they had found the place where they would launch their flanking attack on Brand. Soon after, word came that Brand was himself encamped on the road. Nor was he moving.

The three armies were coming together now, and Taingern felt the shadow of war and battle upon him. But it was good news too. Had they been forced to march again, during daylight and this close to the flanking force, the chances of being observed would have greatly increased. Now, they could rest and gather their strength. And they could do it close to the enemy in a good place of concealment. All that concerned Taingern was that Hruidgar still had not returned. If he had been taken prisoner, all their plans might be at risk.

They ate a cold meal for breakfast, but still a good one. No one went hungry, for that was a bad way to face a day that would bring a clash of arms. But they laid low, keeping quiet as possible. No one was allowed to leave camp except for scouts, and these now had been reduced to the bare minimum.

Only the best scouts now kept an eye on the enemy. The fewer there were out and about the less chance of them being observed. But that did not mean the remainder of the scouts were inactive.

These guarded the camp. And just as well. Two enemy scouts had been located and killed as they approached. Taingern could have wished otherwise, but it was what it was. They may not have seen his army and taken word back to their commander, but by their absence, and those who had been killed before them, suspicion would be raised. Taingern just hoped that the battle commenced before the enemy commander had time to consider the issue and act on it.

So it seemed to prove. For, at last, Hruidgar returned. He had been wounded, though not badly, and obviously at least one more enemy scout was dead. More fuel for suspicion, because the enemy must sooner or later realize their scouts were being killed and wonder why, but the news he brought was otherwise good.

"It's time, Taingern."

"The enemy is on the move?"

"Not yet. But soon. And they won't be going far. Everyone is converging on this spot, and the battle is about to be fought."

"How soon?"

Hruidgar glanced skyward. "It's noon now. At best, you have an hour to make your move."

Taingern considered that. It was enough time to cover the distance between the two armies. If only they could do it unobserved.

"How sure are you the flanking force is ready to attack?"

Hruidgar grinned, but the look on his face was a very grim amusement.

"They look as nervous as a rabbit caught in the open by a fox, and hoping he isn't hungry."

It was good enough for Taingern. If Hruidgar said the enemy were close to moving, it was high time he did as well. He trusted the hunter, but the enemy, even if nervous, were not rabbits.

He gave a hand signal, and the men, awaiting this, stood and fell in behind him. Taingern looked at them as they did so. They, too, seemed nervous. And no wonder.

Odds of three to one were very bad indeed. But they trusted to his leadership, and so far he had not let them down.

He vowed that it would remain so, and led them forward. As best he could, he tried to keep them out of sight, but the trees thinned in places, and any enemy could see his force, if they happened to be there. But Hruidgar, walking beside him, seemed unconcerned. Taingern matched his look, and slowly and surely they covered the distance. Then, faint and far away, came dim noises of battle.

Taingern quickened his pace, and he led his men on. Today would be a day of victory. Or of death. He was not sure which, but if needs be, he would die as close as he could get to Brand.

28. Advance!

Brand staggered, and the black blade of Gormengil whispered past his throat. But then Gormengil staggered too.

Through his magic, Brand still sensed how his opponent was supported by the gods, and by faraway Char-harash. The god-that-would-be stood upon a boulder, and he hungered for blood. His strength had weakened, and he drew a man toward him. And Horta was there also. But the magician had done the unthinkable, and attacked him. The pain of fire roared through Brand.

He withdrew his magic. But he had seen enough. Char-harash was mortally wounded, though it would take a long time for the magic that bound him to scatter, and all the while he would suffer unendurable pain.

The witch, once again, had been right. *Your enemy may yet be your friend.* Brand steadied himself, but Gormengil was still under the shadow of Char-harash's pain, and the dismay of the other gods had momentarily left him uncontrolled.

Gormengil swayed where he stood, and for once his eyes were not so dead.

"Free me," Gormengil pleaded softly, but Brand heard it above the din of battle and his Halathrin-wrought blade leaped out, severing the head of his enemy from its body.

Gormengil collapsed before him, but there was no blood. A great roar rose among the five tribes, and Brand thought it was for his winning of the duel. But only for a moment. He soon saw that battle had at last broken out in the woods to the south, and the flanking force had been attacked and driven into the open. There they were trying to make a stand, and yet some had already begun to flee to join Wena's force.

Taingern had fulfilled his task. But he still needed to win that battle. And Brand still needed to win his own.

It was not just the gods that felt dismay. The Kirsch must also feel it, for their secret attack had been foiled and their plan was unraveling before their eyes. On such chances and such moods the fate of battle rested. This, if ever there was one, was the time for Brand to grasp victory from defeat.

"Advance!" he cried. "Advance!"

Horns blew, sending his order all along the lines of his army, and they began to step forward. They would leave the advantage of the earthwork rampart behind, but that was a defensive position. Victory required attacking.

And attack they did. They rolled forward as a vast unit, pushing, fighting, killing. The enemy, surprised by the failure of their secret weapon, resisted less than they should have.

The balance had shifted. Both sides felt it, and Brand's army moved forward, down the ramp and beyond, harassing the Kirsch without mercy. Too late the enemy commanders saw the danger. Too late they tried to steady their ranks.

But the balance could shift again. If the enemy commanders regained their discipline, they could halt the slide. And surprise would not last forever. It was a momentary ally. Also, the enemy still outnumbered Brand.

Already there were signs that the advance was slowing. No soldier liked being beaten back by an inferior force. The battle still hung in the balance.

Brand knew what he must do then. It was a final throw of the dice, and a surrendering of trust to the words of the witch. She had not betrayed him so far, and he hoped it would stay that way. *Self-sacrifice is victory*, she had said. And he gambled on her prophecy.

Steeling himself and drawing on his well of courage, he spoke. And he enhanced his words with magic so that they carried across all the field of battle, back even to where the three gods of the enemy stood.

"Hear me!" he proclaimed, and his voice boomed like thunder. "I am Brand, and I challenge the three gods who lurk behind their army while soldiers, braver than they, die. I am Brand, and I would contend with you. All three at once, if you have the courage!"

A silence fell, vast and strange for its suddenness was unnatural in the midst of battle. But the battle had ceased. This was something beyond the reckoning of ordinary men, and shocked, they watched and waited in silence and fear.

Brand knew he must go on as he had begun. There was no choice. This was the moment to take advantage of the enemy's dismay. Char-harash had fallen, and if ever gods felt vulnerable, it would be now.

"Do you hear me, you three? Come forth and do battle, or be known as craven. Come forth and die, as your betters have done already."

The silence now was profound. Brand stood proud and tall, and there was certainty in his voice. It did not matter whether he felt it or not. Leadership was an act, and he could play his role. Let the gods wonder if he was mad or confident.

But the men near him trembled in fear. They backed away, leaving an open space around him. They wanted no part in what would happen if gods took offence.

Yet even so, three men came to stand beside him. Shorty first, and he glanced at Brand, his gaze unreadable. Sighern second, and though his face was pale he lifted high the Raven Axe and shook it defiantly. Third was Bruidiger, his sword wet with blood and a smile upon his face as though all the world were a joke.

An eternity seemed to pass. Brand did not move, and neither did the gods. They were wary of him, for their power had been lessened and the fate of Char-harash troubled them.

And then the gods were gone. Smoke, fire and mist swirled where they had been, and then drifted away on the air. He had called their bluff, for surely had they accepted his challenge, they would have killed him. But it seemed that gods were unused to exposing themselves to the chances of life and death. They did not have the heart for it, as ordinary people must, and their courage failed them.

Out of the silence a pitiful noise grew. It was the moaning of the enemy soldiers. Their gods had deserted them.

Coldly, for stricken as they were the enemy remained a superior force, Brand did as he must.

"Advance!" he cried, and there was no need for horns to carry the signal, for his voice, still buoyed by magic, carried across all the field of battle.

And the army of five tribes advanced, slaying the enemy before them and routing them.

Many of the Kirsch tried to flee. Some tried to gather together and retreat in order. Some fell in behind Wena, their commander, and these fought hardest. Or most desperately. In battle, it came to the same thing, and it was toward them that Brand came, his sword dripping blood and a cold fury in his heart.

No matter the doings and plots of gods, it was this man, Wena, who had led the enemy and sought to overrun and conquer lands not his own. It was Wena who had threatened to bring ruin to the five tribes and had asked for nations to kneel to him as their overlord.

Shorty and Sighern were with him, as ever. And suddenly Taingern was there also, blood smearing his face from a shallow cut to his head, his helm dinted, but a grim smile on his face.

There was no time for greetings, but a look passed between them. Then they were up and against the picked bodyguard of the enemy commander. These were tall men, dark-haired and broad of shoulder. Axes were their weapon of choice, and they bore no shields.

But swords and shields would have served them better. Brand's men beat them back, blocking deadly attacks and thrusting with their swords. These men, though brave, fell.

Then suddenly Brand was face to face with Wena. Hatred flashed in the other man's eyes, and Brand met it with his own implacable gaze.

Wena drew a sword, and he made to thrust with it, but then his other hand gestured and he uttered a word of power.

Brand felt the force of it. Magic was at play, and the taint of dark sorcery filled the air. His own powers stirred in response, but he saw nothing untoward. Yet still he felt something, and he leaped back.

Where he had just stood the earth crumbled in on itself and a fissure opened in the ground. Flames darted within it, and noxious gases rose.

Wena began to incant some further spell, but Brand was done watching. It was time to act, and to end this last battle. If Wena fell, all resistance would fall with him.

Brand discarded his shield, and leaped the fissure, his Halathrin-wrought blade glittering. Red tongues of flame twisted up to meet him, but he passed over them, and his sword flashed down and clove Wena's helm.

The enemy commander lurched backward, his split helm falling away and revealing his shattered skull. The white of bone showed through a mess of gore and brains, and then he collapsed.

The fight of the enemy collapsed with him, and the Kirsch fled the field.

"We have won!" Sighern cried, but he looked around at the ruins of the battle and the wreck of war, and the triumph on his face died.

29. Free of Ambition

The Kirsch fled, and the five tribes harried them until the sun set red in the west and a cold wind blew from the mountains of the north.

When dark fell, the fire went out of the hearts of the warriors, and Brand ordered a camp to be established and fires built. Tonight, they would eat and drink and revel in the life they yet lived. But also, they would remember who had died.

And there were many. Fields would lie fallow next spring that should be turned by the plough. Many were the warriors who would never tread the land of their farms again, nor milk cattle, grow crops nor harvest the golden ears of wheat as the seasons turned. Sons, husbands, fathers – the dead were many and the grief was great.

Simple warriors had fallen, but also lords. The names were given to Brand as news passed among men, and of those he knew he mourned the lesser and the greater alike.

Arlnoth, the red-haired chieftain of the Norvinor had fallen to a spear driven through his body. Yet in dying he slew his killer and two others of the enemy. Brodruin and Garvengil, both lords of the Duthgar had perished. The first killed early in the battle by a sword thrust to the groin and the second by an axe even as the battle was nearing its end.

The Callenor payed a price in blood also. Attar and Hathulf had both fallen, one to arrow shot and the other to a spear in his leg. It had not been considered a dangerous injury, but on moving back through the ranks to be bandaged, he had collapsed and died.

Brand knew he would learn more names of the dead as time passed, but for now he must care for the wounded. These had been gathered together and helped as much as possible. Brand went among them, but he saw that here and there men still died. Yet most, if they could, shrugged away their pain as he talked to them pretending that nothing troubled them though their skin was pale and blood seeped through bandages.

The long night passed in a strange blend of joy and grief. Few slept even a little, and Brand none at all. Yet the next day he felt strong. His task was accomplished, but there was still work to do and decisions to be made.

He ordered timber to be cut to burn the dead and stop the spread of disease. This was done, and long rows of biers were fired just before noon.

The fallen warriors of the five tribes were kept separate from the Kirsch, but the reek of smoke merged and drifted skyward together. The dreams of dead men went with it.

When this was done, the army rested again. Not yet were they ready to travel, and wagons and litters were being made ready to carry the wounded that could not walk.

But Brand and the lords of the various tribes met. Shorty, Taingern and Sighern were with them, and Sighern still bore the banner of five tribes proudly. He and the banner went wherever Brand did.

From the Waelenor and Druimenor warriors, few as they were, there were no lords. But the two most senior men were invited. Brand wished that all the five tribes be represented in any decisions made.

Small matters they discussed first, but needful. The care of the injured was uppermost in their minds, and the transporting of them to the nearest villages where they could sleep beneath a protective roof and feel the warmth of fires while healers were gathered to tend them.

But when this was organized, Furthgil, that graybearded lord of the Callenor spoke.

"Brand. You are chieftain of the Duthenor and Callenor by right. Yet you could be king, and I would have it so. And the people need you. If you announce this thing, it will give them heart and take their minds off the tragedy just past and turn it toward a brighter future."

Brand did not answer straightaway. And before he could, Thurlnoth, the most senior Norvinor lord there, for he was the son of Arlnoth with his same red hair, bowed. But Brand noticed that Furthgil had looked to him before the other man moved, and he knew this had been discussed before in private.

"I would swear fealty to you also, Brand. And call you king. I would serve under your kingship as a chieftain."

At length, Brand spoke. "To the lordship of the Duthenor and Callenor, I have a claim. But it is not so with the Norvinor. Why would you serve beneath a king?"

Thurlnoth answered without delay, and Brand knew again that it was a matter he had considered previously.

"Because the Norvinor are a small tribe, and as recent events have shown, the chances of the world are many. The Kirsch are defeated, but may they not come again? We have enemies in the north also. It is a world full of foes and uncertainty. A king, and being part of a larger realm, would offer us better protection against such things."

Brand thought on that. Then he turned to the men of the Waelenor and Druimenor tribes.

"What do you think of this? How would your chieftains react?"

It was a difficult question. If the Norvinor were a smaller tribe than the Duthenor and Callenor, then the remaining two were far smaller. They would fret at the thought of a kingdom forming on their borders, one that might annex them if they were not willing to join freely.

"We've discussed this with the others," one of the men said. "For our part," and he gestured to his companion, "we're just warriors. We can make no agreement nor say with certainty how our chieftains will react."

"But you can guess," Brand suggested.

The second man nodded. "It seems to us that our lords will see the advantages that Thurlnoth described. But at the same time, they would wish to retain their chieftainships over their own land, and rule there according to their own ancient traditions."

It was as good an answer as Brand would get without the chieftains themselves there. And he was sure these men would speak favorably. They had seen what the combined force of the tribes could do.

Brand took a deep breath. All his life it seemed had been driving him to this point, but having reached it, having kingship within his grasp, he did not want it. He was a lòhren, and the land needed him. And though the Lady of the Land had foretold that one day he would be a king, he knew now it would not be of the five tribes. His fate lay elsewhere.

He sighed. "All that each of you say is true. Truer even than you know. Our enemies are many. In the mountains north of us dwell evils untold. South, far, far to the south, a great darkness stirs. It grows and prospers. This I feel in my bones. The lòhren Aranloth has gone thither, and in time we will hear of great events. Hopefully, we will hear that the champion he will raise to stand against it is victorious."

He held back a moment on the last thing that he must say, assessing their mood. Everyone looked at him strangely. They knew that he was more than a normal man. They knew that he was changed since the Lady of the Land had appeared to him. But not by how much. He was a lòhren now, and he *felt* the land. He sensed the evil in the south as a man sensed a cloud drifting between him and the sun.

At length, he finished speaking. "You should form this kingdom of the five tribes. It is needful. But I will not be king. I am a lòhren, and I have other duties."

At that, they fell silent. Their faces showed they were aghast, but they had no words.

Brand glanced at Taingern and Shorty. They at least did not seem surprised. And strangely, nor did Sighern.

Furthgil found voice for his thoughts. "But lord, everything you have done has … seemed to me to position yourself as king of all the tribes. And we think it a good idea. Will you not reconsider?"

Brand knew he must be decisive here. "I have worked to bring the tribes together. They need a king. But it will not be me. My time in these lands, even the Duthgar, grow short. I am called elsewhere."

Furthgil shook his head sadly. "Then all your labor is in vain. Without you, the tribes will go their separate ways."

"Do you really think so? I don't. The leaders of the five tribes know better than that."

"I fear not," Furthgil replied. "At least, they might know better. But they won't act on that knowledge. Instead, personal ambition will rule. We'll bicker and fight among ourselves to try to take the throne. And when no one can gain acceptance and trust from all the others, we'll go back to chieftainships and tribal lands."

It was Brand's turn to shake his head. "If you cannot rise above that, even seeing the *need* for a king, then you deserve what you get. But there is another choice beside me or bickering among yourselves for ascendancy."

Furthgil accepted the rebuke, for he knew it was true. But still there was a trace of bitterness in his voice when he answered, though Brand thought it stemmed from the truth of his words rather than from anger.

"What other choice can there possibly be?"

"Take for yourself as king one who is not a lord nor even a noble. Choose a man free of ambition. Pick a warrior both wise and courageous. Let him be young, so that he is not steeped in old prejudices, and yet able to learn and appreciate the customs of different tribes. Find someone who will rule all and treat all fairly. Was that not how our ancestors chose their first chieftains?"

Furthgil stroked his beard as though deep in thought, but Brand guessed his mind had already grasped the obvious.

"Who would you propose for such a thing?"

Brand pointed at Sighern. "There is the man I described. Has he not fought for all of us? Has he not shown wit and courage? Does he not still stand before you, even now, carrying the banner of the five tribes? And has he not always been proud to do so?"

The suggestion caused a stir. But Brand removed himself from it. He had done what he could, and now the leaders spoke to Sighern, asking him questions and weighing things in their mind. It would do no harm that the lad had saved Furthgil's life. Furthgil was the most powerful lord left alive among the five tribes. If he accepted Sighern as king, it would sway all the others greatly.

Brand left them to it. His part was done. He had returned to the Duthgar and achieved what he had wanted, but events had grown and shifted.

The Duthgar was not what it was. *He* was not who he had once been. The past was a dream that could be relived only in the mind, and the future was what called him now. It would be bright and new. But also dangerous.

Shorty and Taingern had followed him. They knew better than all others what he had done, and how he felt.

"Where to now?" Shorty asked. "Back to Cardoroth? Elsewhere?"

Brand did not answer immediately. But both his friends saw his gaze turn northward.

Epilogue

Brand did not return to the Duthgar. He wintered in Callenor lands, occupying a hunter's cabin high in a range of forested hills. But he was not alone.

Taingern and Shorty had cabins nearby, though they spent most of their time in his before a hot fire in the hearth during the day or close to the red coals late into the evening.

Sighern had been declared king, and the Banner of Five Tribes went with him wherever he traveled. He had his own bannerman now to carry it. Also, he now wore the Helm of the Duthenor that Brand had given him as well as carrying the Raven Axe of the Callenor.

Even the Waelenor and Druimenor chieftains had acknowledged him as king.

Brand was pleased. And though he enjoyed the solitude of the forested hills, he was not idle. He sent out word for what he intended in spring, and word came back from those who would join him.

The deeps of winter came. And they passed. Snow bound the roads, but still word went to and fro over the lands of the five tribes.

Spring approached, and men gathered. Hardy men and true. Warriors all, fierce and proud. And it mattered not to Brand from which tribe they came, and it mattered not to them.

They were one band now. A thousand strong. Well-armed, provisioned and thirsting for adventure.

Adventure they would have. Upon a spring morning, fine and sunny yet where it had rained during the night, they gathered to leave.

Brand, Taingern and Shorty led them, and they headed northward, leaving their homeland behind. The mountains of the north had always called to Brand, and he never knew why. But he had learned.

Auren Dennath the Halathrin called the mountains. Creatures of evil lurked in the valleys and stalked the high places. But Brand would forge it into a fair kingdom. Or die.

The High Lady had said that he would be a king, and sire kings, and that from his line would spring the hope of the north.

But Brand did not believe in destiny. Nor did the men who went with him. They trusted instead to the courage of their hearts and the true blades they bore.

They would need both.

Thus ends *The Dark God.* It brings the Dark God Rises trilogy to a conclusion. Yet elsewhere in Alithoras ancient evil stirs, and a hero rises to contend with it. Destiny touches him. Prophecy foretold him. But sorcerous forces seek his death.

More will be told in *The Seventh Knight.*

Meanwhile, learn Brand's history in *King's Last Hope,* the complete Durlindrath trilogy.

KING'S LAST HOPE

THE COMPLETE DURLINDRATH TRILOGY

Amazon lists millions of titles, and I'm glad you discovered this one. But if you'd like to know when I release a new book, instead of leaving it to chance, sign up for my newsletter. I'll send you an email on publication.

Yes please! – Go to www.homeofhighfantasy.com and sign up.

No thanks – I'll take my chances.

Dedication

There's a growing movement in fantasy literature. Its name is noblebright, and it's the opposite of grimdark.

Noblebright celebrates the virtues of heroism. It's an old-fashioned thing, as old as the first story ever told around a smoky campfire beneath ancient stars. It's storytelling that highlights courage and loyalty and hope for the spirit of humanity. It recognizes the dark – the dark in us all, and the dark in the villains of its stories. It recognizes death, and treachery and betrayal. But it dwells on none of these things.

I dedicate this book, such as it is, to that which is noblebright. And I thank the authors before me who held the torch high so that I could see the path: J.R.R. Tolkien, C.S. Lewis, Terry Brooks, David Eddings, Susan Cooper, Roger Taylor and many others. I salute you.

And, for a time, I too will hold the torch as high as I can.

Appendix: Encyclopedic Glossary

Note: the glossary of each book in this series is individualized for that book alone. Additionally, there is often historical material provided in its entries for people, artifacts and events that are not included in the main text.

Many races dwell in Alithoras. All have their own language, and though sometimes related to one another the changes sparked by migration, isolation and various influences often render these tongues unintelligible to each other.

The ascendancy of Halathrin culture, combined with their widespread efforts to secure and maintain allies against elug incursions, has made their language the primary means of communication between diverse peoples.

For instance, a merchant of Cardoroth addressing a Duthenor warrior would speak Halathrin, or a simplified version of it, even though their native speeches stem from the same ancestral language.

This glossary contains a range of names and terms. Many are of Halathrin origin, and their meaning is provided. The remainder derive from native tongues and are obscure, so meanings are only given intermittently.

Often, Duthenor names and Halathrin elements are combined. This is especially so for the aristocracy. Few other tribes of men had such long-term friendship with the immortal Halathrin as the Duthenor, and though in this relationship they lost some of their natural culture, they gained nobility and knowledge in return.

List of abbreviations:

Cam. Camar

Comb. Combined

Cor. Corrupted form

Duth. Duthenor

Hal. Halathrin

Kir. Kirsch

Prn. Pronounced

Alithoras: *Hal.* "Silver land." The Halathrin name for the continent they settled after leaving their own homeland. Refers to the extensive river and lake systems they found and their wonder at the beauty of the land.

Anast Dennath: *Hal.* "Stone mountains." Mountain range in northern Alithoras. Source of the river known as the Careth Nien that forms a natural barrier between the lands of the Camar people and the Duthenor and related tribes. Also the location of the Dweorhrealm, the underground stronghold of the dwarven nation.

Aranloth: *Hal.* "Noble might." A lòhren of ancient heritage and friend to Brand.

Arlnoth: *Duth.* "White bear." Chieftain of the Norvinor tribe. Cousin to Furthgil. Intermarriage between the five tribes is common among the nobility. However, the chieftains of the Duthenor avoided it.

Arnhaten: *Kir.* "Disciples." Servants of a magician. One magician usually has many disciples, but only some of these are referred to as "inner door." Inner door disciples receive a full transmission of the master's knowledge. The remainder do not, but they continue to strive to earn the favor of their master. Until they do, they are dispensable.

Attar: *Duth.* "Long-horned ram." A Callenor lord. Related, distantly, to both Arlnoth and Furthgil.

Black Talon: The sign of Unferth's house. Appears on his banner and is his personal emblem. Legend claims the founder of the house in ancient days had the power to transform into a raven. Disguised in this form, and trusted as a magical being, he gave misinformation and ill-advice to the enemies of his people.

Brand: *Duth.* "Torch." An exiled Duthenor tribesman and adventurer. Appointed by the former king of Cardoroth to serve as regent for Prince Gilcarist. By birth, he is the rightful chieftain of the Duthenor people. However, Unferth the Usurper overthrew his father, killing both him and his wife. Brand, only a youth at the time, swore an oath of vengeance.

Breath of the dragon: An ancient saying of Letharn origin. They believed the magic of dragons was the preeminent magic in the world because dragons were creatures able to travel through time. Dragon's breath is known to mean fire, the destructive face of their nature. But the Letharn also believed dragons could breathe mist. This was the healing face of their nature. And the mist-breath of a dragon was held to be able to change destinies and bring good luck. To "ride the dragon's breath" meant that for a period a person was a focal point of time and destiny. The Kar-ahn-hetep peoples hold similar beliefs.

Brodruin: *Duth.* "Dark river." A lord of the Duthgar.

Bruidiger: *Duth.* "Blessed blade." A Norvinor warrior. Brand's father once saved his father's life during a hunting expedition.

Brunhal: *Duth.* "Hallowed woman." Former chieftainess of the Duthenor. Wife to Drunn V, former chieftain of the Duthenor. Mother to Brand. According to Duthenor custom, a chieftain and chieftainess co-ruled.

Callenor: *Duth.* One of several tribes closely related to the Duthenor. This one inhabits lands immediately west of the Duthgar.

Camar: *Cam. Prn.* Kay-mar. A race of interrelated tribes that migrated in two main stages. The first brought them to the vicinity of Halathar, homeland of the immortal Halathrin; in the second, they separated and established cities along a broad stretch of eastern Alithoras. Related to the Duthenor, though far more distantly than the Callenor.

Cardoroth: *Cor. Hal. Comb. Cam.* A Camar city, often called Red Cardoroth. Some say this alludes to the red granite commonly used in the construction of its buildings, others that it refers to a prophecy of destruction.

Careth Nien: *Hal. Prn.* Kareth ny-en. "Great river." Largest river in Alithoras. Has its source in the mountains of Anast Dennath and runs southeast across the land before emptying into the sea. It was over this river (which sometimes freezes along its northern stretches) that the Camar and other tribes migrated into the eastern lands. Much later, Brand came to the city of Cardoroth by one of these ancient migratory routes.

Cartouche: A rectangle, inscribed or engraved, around a royal name. Often referred to by the Kar-ahn-hetep as a Shenna.

Char-harash: *Kir.* "He who destroys by flame." Most exalted of the emperors of the Kirsch, and a magician of great power.

Dragon of the Duthgar: The banner of the chieftains of the Duthenor. Legend holds that an ancient forefather of the line slew a dragon and ate its heart. Dragons are seen by the Duthenor as creatures of ultimate evil, but the consuming of their heart is reputed to pass on wisdom and magic.

Druimenor: One of several tribes closely related to the Duthenor. Named after their first chieftain, Druim. Legend holds he was a brother of Drunn I, first chieftain of the Duthenor.

Drunn: *Duth.* "Man of secrets." Former chieftain of the Duthenor. Husband to Brunhal and father to Brand. Officially known as Drunn V.

Durnheld: *Duth.* "Earth defender – someone who commands a hillfort." A hunter of the Duthgar.

Duthenor: *Duth. Prn.* Dooth-en-or. "The people." A single tribe (or less commonly a group of closely related tribes melded into a larger people at times of war or disaster) who generally live a rustic and peaceful lifestyle. They are breeders of cattle and herders of sheep. However, when need demands they are bold warriors – men and women alike. Until recently, ruled by a usurper who murdered Brand's parents. Brand swore an oath to overthrow the tyrant and avenge his parents. This he has now achieved.

Duthgar: *Duth.* "People spear." The name is taken to mean "the land of the warriors who wield spears."

Elù-haraken: *Hal.* "The shadowed wars." Long ago battles in a time that is become myth to the Duthenor and Camar tribes. A great evil was defeated, though prophecy foretold it would return.

Elùgai: *Hal. Prn.* Eloo-guy. "Shadowed force." The sorcery of an elùgroth.

Erhanu: *Kir.* "The green wanderer." A star. According to ancient stories of the Kar-ahn-hetep, this star was once a god. Other stories, even older, speak of it as the original home of the gods.

Esgallien: *Hal.* "Es – rushing water, gal(en) – green, lien – to cross: place of the crossing onto the green plains." A city established in the south of Alithoras. Named after the nearby ford.

Ferstellenpund: *Duth.* "Fer – to bring, stellen – peace, pund – sacred enclosure." A sacred tarn within the Duthgar and revered by the Duthenor. Each of the five tribes conducts rituals at such a place within their lands.

Furthgil: *Duth.* "Head warrior – a commander of an armed troop." The preeminent surviving lord of the Callenor tribe. Related to some houses of Duthenor nobility, though not to Brand.

Garvengil: *Duth.* "Warrior of the woods." A lord of the Duthgar.

God-king: See Char-harash.

Gormengil: *Duth.* "Warrior of the storm." Nephew of Unferth. Rightful heir to the Callenor chieftainship, until Brand defeated him in single combat.

Halathrin: *Hal.* "People of Halath." A race named after an honored lord who led an exodus of his people to the land of Alithoras in pursuit of justice, having sworn to defeat a great evil. They are human, though of fairer form, greater skill and higher culture than ordinary men. They possess a unity of body, mind and spirit that enables insight and endurance beyond the native races of Alithoras. Said to be immortal, but killed in great numbers during their conflicts in ancient times with the evil they sought to destroy. Those conflicts are collectively known as the Shadowed Wars.

Haldring: *Duth*. "White blade – a sword that flashes in the sun." A shield-maiden. Killed in the first great battle between the forces of Brand and the usurper.

Hathulf: *Duth*. "Honey hunter – generally interpreted to mean a bear, but can also refer to a brave warrior." A lord of the Callenor.

High Way: An ancient road longer than the Duthgar, but well preserved in that land. Probably of Letharn origin and used to speed troops to battle.

Horta: *Kir*. "Speech of the acacia tree." It is believed among the Kar-ahn-hetep that the acacia tree possesses magical properties that aid discourse between the realms of men and gods. Horta is a name that recurs among families noted for producing elite magicians.

Hralfling: *Duth*. "The shower of sparks off two sword blades striking." An elderly lord of the Callenor.

Hruidgar: *Duth*. "Ashwood spear." A Duthenor hunter.

Jarch-elrah: *Kir*. "The hunter that laughs as it kills." A god of the Kar-ahn-hetep. The form he chooses is human, but jackal headed. Reputed to be mad, but the minds and intentions of gods are not easily interpreted by humans. Some ancient magicians contend his madness is a ploy to assist him in remaining neutral in the disputes of the gods and enables him to avoid aligning himself with the various factions.

Kar-ahn-hetep: *Kir*. "The children of the thousand stars." A race of people that vied for supremacy in ancient times with the Letharn. Their power was ultimately broken, their empire destroyed. But a residual population survived and defied outright annihilation by their conquerors. They believe their empire will one day rise again to rule the world. The kar-ahn element of their name means the "thousand stars" but also "the lights that never die."

Kar-fallon: *Kir.* "Death city." A great city of the Kar-ahn-hetep that served as their principal religious focus. Their magician-priests conducted the great rites of their nation in its sacred temples.

Kar-karmun: *Kir.* "Death-life – the runes of life and death." A means of divination that distills the wisdom and worldview of the Kar-ahn-hetep civilization.

Kirsch: See Kar-ahn-hetep.

Lady of the Land: The spirit of the land. It is she whom lòhrens serve, though her existence is seldom discussed. It is said she favored Drunn I, and came to him in his greatest hour of need during the elù-haraken, advising him how to defeat his enemies and lead the five tribes to the lands they now inhabit.

Letharn: *Hal.* "Stone raisers. Builders." A race of people that in antiquity conquered most of Alithoras. Now, only faint traces of their civilization endure.

Light of Kar-fallon: See Char-harash.

Lòhren: *Hal. Prn.* Ler-ren. "Knowledge giver – a counselor." Other terms used by various nations include wizard, druid and sage.

Lòhrengai: *Hal. Prn.* Ler-ren-guy. "Lòhren force." Enchantment, spell or use of mystic power. A manipulation and transformation of the natural energy inherent in all things. Each use takes something from the user. Likewise, some part of the transformed energy infuses them. Lòhrens use it sparingly, elùgroths indiscriminately.

Lord of the Ten Armies: See Char-harash.

Magic: Mystic power. See lòhrengai and elùgai.

Murlek: A star revered by the Kar-ahn-hetep. Also the sign of their healers. A star is engraved upon their doors and on their medical instruments.

Norhanu: *Kir.* "Serrated blade." A psychoactive herb.

Norvinor: *Duth.* One of several tribes closely related to the Duthenor. This one inhabits lands west of the Callenor.

Ossar the Great: Sometimes called a star, but in reality a planet. Said to be a dead god. On occasion, claimed to be the deceased father of all the gods. At least, the more ancient stories invoke this status for him.

Pennling Palace: A fortress in the Duthgar. Named after an ancient hero of the Duthenor. In truth, constructed by the Letharn and said to be haunted by the spirits of the dead. At certain nights, especially midwinter and midsummer, legend claims the spirits are visible manning the walls and fighting a great battle.

Pennling Path: Etymology obscure. Pennling was an ancient hero of the Duthenor. Some say he built the road in the Duthgar known as the High Way. This is not true, but one legend holds that he traveled all its length in one night on a milk-white steed to confront an attacking army by himself. It is said that his ghost may yet be seen racing along the road on his steed when the full moon hangs above the Duthgar.

Raithlin: *Hal.* "Range and report people." A scouting and saboteur organization. They derive from ancient contact with the Halathrin.

Rite of Resurrection: The highest magic of the magicians of the Kar-ahn-hetep. According to legend, said only to have been successfully performed once. This was during the great wars against the Letharn empire.

Ruler of the Thousand Stars: See Char-harash.

Runes of Life and Death: See Kar-karmun.

Shadowed wars: See Elù-haraken.

Shemfal: *Kir.* "Cool shadows gliding over the hot waste – dusk." One of the greater gods of the Kar-ahn-hetep. Often depicted as a mighty man, bat winged and bat headed. Ruler of the underworld. Given a wound in battle with other gods that does not heal and causes him to limp.

Shenti: A type of kilt worn by the Kar-ahn-hetep.

Shorty: A former Durlindrath (chief bodyguard of the king of Cardoroth). Friend to Brand. His proper name is Lornach.

Sighern: *Duth.* "Battle leader." A youth of the Duthgar.

Su-sarat: *Kir.* "The serpent that lures." One of the greater gods of the Kar-ahn-hetep. Her totem is the desert puff adder that lures prey by flicking either its tongue or tail. Called also the Trickster. It was she who gave the god Shemfal his limp.

Tanata: *Kir.* "Stalker of the desert at night." A disciple of Horta.

Taingern: *Cam.* "Still sea," or "calm waters." A former Durlindrath (chief bodyguard of the king of Cardoroth). Friend to Brand.

Thurlnoth: *Duth.* "Charging bear." A lord of the Norvinor. Son of Arlnoth.

Tinwellen: *Cam.* "Sun of the earth – gold." Daughter of a prosperous merchant of Cardoroth.

Unferth: *Duth.* "Hiss of arrows." The name is sometimes interpreted to mean "whispered counsels that lead to war." Usurper of the chieftainship of the Duthenor. Rightful chieftain of the Callenor. Slain by Gormengil in single combat.

Ùhrengai: *Hal. Prn.* Er-ren-guy. "Original force." The primordial force that existed before substance or time.

Uzlakah: A tree of the southern deserts of Alithoras. Valued not just for its shade, but also the long and nutritious pods it provides.

Waelenor: One of several tribes closely related to the Duthenor. Founded by their original chieftain, Wael, brother of Drunn I.

Wena: *Kir.* "The kestrel that hovers." Leader of a Kar-ahn-hetep army.

Wizard: See lòhren.

Wizard-priest: The priests of the Letharn. Possessors of mighty powers of magic. Forerunners to the order of lòhrens.

About the author

I'm a man born in the wrong era. My heart yearns for faraway places and even further afield times. Tolkien had me at the beginning of *The Hobbit* when he said, ". . . one morning long ago in the quiet of the world . . ."

Sometimes I imagine myself in a Viking mead-hall. The long winter night presses in, but the shimmering embers of a log in the hearth hold back both cold and dark. The chieftain calls for a story, and I take a sip from my drinking horn and stand up . . .

Or maybe the desert stars shine bright and clear, obscured occasionally by wisps of smoke from burning camel dung. A dry gust of wind marches sand grains across our lonely campsite, and the wayfarers about me stir restlessly. I sip cool water and begin to speak.

I'm a storyteller. A man to paint a picture by the slow music of words. I like to bring faraway places and times to life, to make hearts yearn for something they can never have, unless for a passing moment.

Sample: Prologue for The Seventh Knight

Halls of Lore: Chamber 2. Aisle 31. Item 369
General subject: Founding of the city of Faladir
Topic: Establishment of the Kingshield Knights
Author: Ancient legend Translated by Careth Tar

War straddled Alithoras like a vulture hulking over a carcass. To the south, swords flashed and blood watered the trodden earth instead of rain. To the north, armies marched, the pounding of their boots the drum of death, their banners clouding the sky with the shadow of evil. In the west, the races of humanity were smitten as metal is beaten between hammer and anvil. There, in their homeland, they possessed only ruined dreams, gnawing hunger and soul-eating poverty.

The east alone offered hope, and thither they fled. But hope burned to ash, and was blown back in their faces as a choking wind.

They found only more war, and despair clawed at their hearts. Yet humanity was a hardy race, used to brutal treatment and the ill chances of the world. They took up their swords again. Their anguish they crushed beneath wills of iron. And still they kept hope alive like a spark against the night, for a foretelling was made, a prophecy born in the darkness of ruin, that at the end of their long travails a bright future would dawn.

Hope that should have died lived on, and it gave them reason to endure. And the frail spark they nurtured flared when they met the immortal Halathrin, they who in our time are named elves.

Bright were the eyes of the elves, and their faces were fair, and the wisdom of their thought reached deeper than humanity's. Immortal and lordly as they were, wealthy in the ownership of jewels and metals that came of the earth and the crafting from them of beautiful things, still they took pity on the downtrodden newcomers and marveled at their courage.

The elves shielded humanity from the worst of the wars, allowing them to recover and grow strong again. Then humanity girded their swords, and they hefted their spears once more, and they marched to war beside the elves as allies. In time, they became the fiercest warriors in the elven armies, for they spent their blood and lives freely in service to those who had helped them. They became known as the Sword of the Halathrin, and it was a title of honor.

The *Elù-haraken*, the Shadowed Wars, those battles are named, and more is forgotten of them than is remembered. And this is well, for they were a time of darkness unsurpassed, where evil held sway over much of the land. No bird nor beast, no race of humanity nor get of monster, no elf nor dwarf nor sorcerer nor wizard, no dragon that flew the midnight skies nor crawled in the deeps of the earth was not divided to one side or the other, not locked in a death-battle against enemies.

Elùdrath, the Shadowed Lord as he was called, drew creatures of evil unto him, and he gave them power that they may smite their enemies, and he put lies on their lips, poison in their bites, fire in their breath and steel in their hands that they may conquer and rule the world under his dominion.

But against the evils of the world, Halath, Lord of the Elves, set himself. A great king he was, and his nation followed him to war. Against the dark they made light. Against despair they kindled hope. And they drew others to them who would not bow to the shadow and would rather die than suffer evil to prosper.

One race of humanity, the Camar, grew close to the counsels of the great king, and that people grew wise, and they learned lore that opened their minds to the mysteries of the world. This lore, they knew, would serve them well in the days to come.

It came to pass that the Shadowed Lord was defeated, his armies laid low, his stratagems countered, his traps sprung and his followers scattered across the land. He was killed, and yet also was Halath slain.

The land knew hope, but those who lived mourned the passing of an age. They grieved for loved ones buried in hurried graves. And they sorrowed at the passing of so many fair things that did not survive the storm and whose like will never be seen again.

The Shadowed Lord was said to be dead. Others claimed that though dead, the evil he spawned lived on and would harry the races of Alithoras for long whiles yet to come. Some few foretold that Elùdrath would rise once more in the future, though none knew when, or how.

Few cared. The troubles of their days were a greater burden than the possible troubles of the future. Only elves and lòhrens, wise men who possessed use of wizardry, set guards and wards against Elùdrath's return. And they watched and waited. And they watch and wait still.

The Camar moved further east, and they prospered, and the knowledge the elves had passed to them flourished in days of peace. This was nurtured by the lòhrens who offered sage counsels and protection against the sorcerers who still lived.

Ever east the Camar roamed, and many reached the gray sea that crashed into the farthest shores of Alithoras.

And there, those hardy people who once dwelt in rude huts or laid themselves down to sleep beneath the glittering stars, built themselves fair cities, and they established wide realms, and they raised proud kings to rule them. And there also they made bulwarks against the scattered evils of the land that yet attacked them at times.

Esgallien was one such city, and even the elves marveled at what the Camar had wrought and the uses to which their gifts of knowledge had been put. But it is not said that the elves visited further east. Few, or none, ever saw white-walled Camarelon, nor many-spired Faladir, nor red Cardoroth far to the north, yet still nigh the sea.

Many-spired Faladir shone as a gem, and its walls gleamed and the points of its spires glittered like starlight shot from a bow into the heavens. But it was one such place where the scattered evils of the world gathered, and though bereft of their master, they grew in power and came in force from surrounding hills, forests and dark places of the earth to assail the city. And sorcerers were among them, and they possessed a *Morleth* Stone.

Of old, the Shadowed Lord crafted some few of these. And they were talismans of great evil. Black they were, of diverse sizes and strengths, and their puissance was gained from the lives of sorcerers who sacrificed themselves to make them. Their sorcery and life became one with the stone.

In the Elù-haraken most were destroyed, but against Faladir the sorcerers raised one. And this was smaller than many, being able to fit into the hand of a child, but its power was the greatest.

Faladir came near to falling, and a mighty battle ensued that ran a day and a night and until noon the next. But at the end King Conduil, his retinue about him and his eyes blazing, led a charge against the enemy. With him came a lòhren, shielding him from magic, and the king reached the chief sorcerer, whose fist was held high with the Morleth Stone within to work some spell, and he hewed off the dark one's hand and slew him, and his sword hissed with steaming blood. And the enemy dispersed, fleeing into the dark places of the world, but the Camar were spent, their army dwindled, and they harried them not.

But Conduil seized the Morleth Stone from the dead hand of the sorcerer whose twisted fingers still writhed about it, and he felt the touch of its evil, and he cast it down again.

"This thing I shall destroy," he swore.

But the lòhren slowly shook his head. "I fear not, sire. That is not its fate, though we wish it. This thing, and the evil it holds, will endure so long as Faladir stands."

Conduil was not persuaded. But his oath he could not keep, for thrice he struck the stone with his sword, and no matter that it lay on rock no harm came to it. But on the third stroke, his elven-wrought blade shattered, and yet the black stone remained unharmed.

Thereafter, the king ordered all manner of attempts be made to break it. To forges it was taken for the heat of fire to melt it. It was cast from the top of a tower unto the stone below. Smiths caught it in vices and beat it with mighty hammers, and they bathed it long whiles in acid. But no attempt broke it, nor even marred its dark surface.

Conduil grew angry. And he went again to the lòhren. "Can you not destroy this thing with your power? Being made by sorcery, surely then wizardry must be able to unmake it?"

"It is not so," Aranloth answered. But seeing the anguish of the king, he bade him stand back. Then he worked his magic, and he summoned white flames hotter than any furnace, and the Morleth Stone was hemmed all around by his power. And when he was done, the stone of the floor had melted and run like mud on a slope, yet still the talisman of evil sat unharmed.

"It is as I foretold," Aranloth declared. "This stone will endure as long as Faladir stands."

"Then must my people also endure its foul sorcery that long? Shall I not rather cast it into the sea or into some bottomless crack of the earth instead?"

Then Aranloth counseled him. "Whatever is cast aside may be picked up again, and whatever is lost may be found. And there is a power in this stone that calls to creatures of the shadow. Ever they will seek it out."

The king's anger subsided. "What must be done then?"

"This only, for no other choice remains. Keep the stone, but guard it well. Evil will search it out. The covetous will try to claim it. The ambitious will lust for its power. Like moths to a flame they will come, but it will be your task, and the task of your line to protect it, to keep it out of the hands of those who would use it for harm. It will shape you, and the realm, now and hereafter."

The king looked at the stone, and there was wariness in his glance, for he understood this would be no easy duty to perform, but there was determination also.

"And in this way shall I keep my people safe?"

"It will be so. Unless you fail in your duty."

"I shall not fail."

"No, you will not. Yet the task will be difficult, and the passing of the years will make it more so. It will be a burden without end, and it will weigh you down, and those who come after."

"Even so, I shall do this thing. I swear it."

And then Aranloth drew deep of his wisdom, and of his compassion also.

"It is a great task, but you need not carry it out alone. This is what I advise."

And the wizard counseled him then, and the king heeded him.

"An order of knights I will establish. And they will be the greatest warriors in the realm. And they will occupy a tower, and there at least one at all times will guard the stone. Their number will be six, and I shall call them the Kingshield Knights, for they will fulfill my will and guard that which must be guarded."

Aranloth thought deeply. "It is not enough that they be great warriors," he said at length.

"What else must they be?"

"The lure of the stone is strong. It will tempt the knights. Therefore, they must be not only great warriors, but men of honor and kindness. Let them learn also poetry and philosophy and all the arts according to their natural talents. This will strengthen their minds so they become as sharp and true as their blades."

The king saw the wisdom of this. But he knew there would be more. The task of the knights demanded it.

"And finally," Aranloth said, "that which they protect is a thing of magic, and some of those who seek it will possess sorcery. If the knights are to fulfil their duty, let them also learn of the mysteries."

"You would make them wizards also?"

"No. One person cannot be all things. Yet still these knights will have training. They will know how to defend themselves against magic, and to accomplish that which ordinary men cannot. And I will be their teacher."

This troubled the king, for he distrusted magic. Yet also he was glad, for his burden was lightened. And he took up the stone and went away to begin the task of his life and of his line to follow after. And he was the first knight, and he chose five others after long searching.

But the lòhren was wise, and he knew the hearts of men. And when the king had gone, he prophesized again, and there was none to hear him save a manservant in the palace who later told his tale.

"Strong as you are," Aranloth muttered, his gaze lingering where the king had stood, "you will perish even as all mortal flesh. But the evil in the stone will never subside, and it will endure, and through the long years it will ever tempt its guardians. And a day will come where that order of knights who represent the best of men will succumb, and evil will enter into the realm."

"What will happen then?" the manservant asked.

Aranloth turned to him, as though unaware that he had been there. "Then evil will rise again, and the kingdom, and all the lands beyond it, will stand in peril."

"Is there no hope then? Will evil always return?"

The lòhren closed his eyes, as if in trance. "How can it not? For darkness is in the heart of humanity as well as light, and both shape all that we touch. But against the failing of the six knights, I say now a *seventh* will arise at the time that fate calls. And that knight will be the greatest of them all. In that knight, the hope of the land will reside."

Aranloth strode away then, and soon after the king raised a high tower and there established his knights. And the land knew peace and prosperity, if even at whiles strange lights were seen atop the tower.

The knights made it a habit to ride the land, they and those who succeeded them, though never all at once, and they were the best of men. They brought wisdom with them, and helped heal the sick and settle disputes. Honor and praise followed as their shadow.

But the evil of the stone did not sleep, and the lòhren's prophecy was but dimly remembered, and the stars wheeled in the sky as the years passed, and the king died. And soon both king and prophesy became legend.

The long years marched ahead after that, century after century, and legend turned to myth.
But the knights lived on.

Want to be sure of catching this new series at a discounted price of 99 cents when it's released?

Yes please! – Go to www.homeofhighfantasy.com and sign up.

No thanks – I'll take my chances.

Printed in Great Britain
by Amazon